SOLEMN

ALSO BY
KALISHA BUCKHANON

Upstate
Conception

SOLEMN

Kalisha Buckhanon

ST. MARTIN'S PRESS ≈ NEW YORK

SOLEMN. Copyright © 2016 by Kalisha Buckhanon. All rights reserved.
Printed in the United States of America. For information, address
St. Martin's Press, 175 Fifth Avenue, New York, N.Y. 10010.

Portions of the novel appear in the following publications under the following titles:
"The Pitchfork Game." University of Kentucky's *pluck!* Issue 12. (Fall 2015). Print.
"Solemn and the Hassles." *Hermeneutic Chaos Literary Journal.* Ed. Shinjini Bhattacharjee. Issue 9, Prose (July 2015). Web.
"Pearletta." *Deep South Magazine* Online. (May 2015). Web.
"Expecting." University of Arkansas at Monticello's *gravel* literary journal. (December 2014). Web.
"Singer's." *Hermeneutic Chaos Journal.* Issue 5, Prose (November 2014). Web.

www.stmartins.com

Designed by Anna Gorovoy

The Library of Congress Cataloging-in-Publication Data is available upon request.

ISBN 978-1-250-09159-8 (hardcover)
ISBN 978-1-250-09158-1 (e-book)

Our books may be purchased in bulk for promotional, educational, or business use.
Please contact your local bookseller or the Macmillan Corporate and Premium Sales Department at
1-800-221-7945, extension 5442, or by e-mail at MacmillanSpecialMarkets@macmillan.com.

First Edition: May 2016

10 9 8 7 6 5 4 3 2 1

For my grandmothers and great-grandmothers, with love:
Shirley Whitlow, Vanilla Hudson, Magnolia Whitlow, Lola Buckhanon,
and Mary Lee Luckett. And their husbands, our men: Gus Whitlow,
Tommy Hudson, Nora Whitlow, and George Buckhanon.

ACKNOWLEDGMENTS

I must first thank some special writers for reading parts of this book in its various incarnations, and particular members of the Chicago Writers Workshop who encouraged my native writing compulsion back to the surface: Tacuma Roeback, Diane Gillette, Allie Tova Hirsch, Maggie Queeney, Steven Ramirez, Dan Portincaso, Matthew Thomas, Laura Nelson, Aaron Frankel, and Susan Dickman. They read through the first avalanche of characters and scenes I created years back; I owe a huge debt to them for helping me sort through the wave and stick with it. This book would not be here now without them.

The same goes for Sisters in Crime, the best organization for women writers I know of. I am so proud to be part of them. I am appreciative to organizational leaders Martha Reed and Cari Dubiel for giving me a spotlight in between books, through appearances for SinC at conferences and on true-crime television shows. My sisters' newsletters, SinC links, programs, and events are godsends that keep me typing.

I have bounds of gratitude for my inspiring and committed literary agent, Albert Zuckerman, and his Writers House ship, Mickey Novak and Michael Miejas, in particular, for always igniting the real writer in me and blessing me with a literary haven to be proud of. I am so happy I found them. I give thanks to my publisher Sally Richardson; editor Monique Patterson; editorial assistant Alexandria Sehulster; copy editor Barbara Wild; cover designer Elsie Lyons; and the entire team at St. Martin's Press/Macmillan, for bringing my private work out to the public world once again.

Some passionate editors at global and nationwide literary journals encouraged the book through their acceptance of early and revised excerpts they published for the public and me: Bianca Spriggs at *pluck! The Journal of Affrilachian Arts and Culture* at University of Kentucky; Shinjini Bhattacharjee at *Hermeneutic Chaos Literary Journal*; Erin Bass at *Deep South Magazine*; and the beautiful editors of *gravel Literary Magazine* of the MFA program in creative writing at the University of Arkansas at Monticello.

And the cats, for everything: Nibbles, Bubbles, Ralph, Alice, Sparky, Pepper, Mona Lisa, Nittle Kitty, Red, Mr. Midnight, and Sybil.

1

BLEDSOE

think I was just past eight when it all started down in Singer's Trailer Park.

That woman down the way, past the well, was not my mama's friend or my daddy's or nobody's there. She was just somebody, movin round us like some old relative showed up at the funerals before it's time to eat: lookin like the dead, finishin all the jokes, nicknamin, pickin bones. But my daddy was a good man and a fix-it man and he got in between loose dogs chargin and picked up kids tripped in the dirt. He was that kind of man. Good-lookin too: brick color, long lashes, good hair.

When he met the younger woman down the way, Mama was at church. It was a Wednesday, Bible study. And Landon—all mysterious—was out with his friends and they was probably shoutin bout guns, power, revolution, fuckin em up, fightin em off, turnin tables, drawin lines. My mama put supper for us on the stove fore she left. I wanted pizza though. Daddy agreed: he drive me out for it, throw away the box. And then I could watch things on TV Mama normally turned off. Then I could turn on the radio until Mama get home, then set it back on them AM gospel stations where the singin and music make me think about the Saturday night scary movies.

We went out to our Malibu, sunk in the gravel near our trailer under moonrise, so the car shined more than it did in the day. With the radio on some fast song, and the smoke from my daddy's Kools working cross the dash, and the long but easy road to town in front of us, we saw the barefoot woman walkin at side of the road, heels in her hand. If the headlights hadn't been turned on bright, cause they had to be, we mighta missed her. Or we coulda struck her. She walked long in our direction near middle of the road like she ain't never carved no place on one.

Daddy slowed down. He recognized the woman. We could all recognize each other, when we wanted to. I wanted to keep goin. We had green beans and yams and fried corn and some trout on the stove, but they was there the last week. Maybe the week before. Recently. It was fishin time. We wasn't gonna go hungry, I knew. Still . . .

Daddy waved his hand out the window cross to the woman. The woman looked up out of, like, this daze. She waved back. She still didn't seem to know him. He knew her though.

"You goin back to Singer's?"

"I am," she said. She squinted through the bright lights in her eyes.

"It's dark out here to be walkin like this," my daddy told her. "I'll lift you."

"Oh no," she said. "I'm fine."

"Barefoot out here?"

And then the woman looked cross both sides of the road fore she walked to us.

"Get in the back, Solemn."

I left my door open for her. She slid in my place. I took up in the back. In time with old music, I tapped my feet at back of the woman's seat. Daddy turned us farther from pizza in town right back into the gates of home.

I couldn't hear they conversation, over the music and the speakers thumpin out bass on me. It felt good. Like my own fists workin themselves up and down Daddy's spine when he was stiff. He gave me dollar bills for my little hands to run down his back, cause now I was too heavy and my feet was too big to walk on it like I used to. But a word or two bout "that nigger" put me in grown folks' talk. I looked at my daddy's eyes in the rearview mirror and noticed a glint in em.

"He switched up on you like that?" he asked the woman. "Put you out your own car, made you walk all the way back here?"

"He's unpredictable," the woman said. She was the color of a prune. "Gets these mood swings. A simple night out can turn into a mess. Can't reason with him none."

"I've known him for a little while now."

"Who?" I asked. They didn't hear me.

"Well, you should know he got a temper," the woman confided.

"I heard a little bit of it," Daddy said. "We all pick up boys in these parts. Do what we can. I heard nobody wanted to work with him too long."

"Imagine being married to him."

Daddy passed our trailer and moved down a steep we never had to go down.

"I'm near the woods," the woman said. "Past the well. One of the last ones."

It wasn't no camp lanterns on the last ones. Mama told me to call em "compact" to be polite, cause one time she heard me call em "shacks" and said I was careless. These crows flocked and slumped at edge of the well, sleep. Just when I thought they was all too identical and might only be decoration, all they gray eyeballs shot out at once. The car stopped and the music stopped. And Daddy turned down the radio to say bye.

"I thank you," the woman said. "It's chilly in the air, and I'm just now gettin over somethin'. Makes it all worse, huh?"

"No problem," Daddy told her. "That woulda been too far to walk."

"And I'd already come so far. I got some cognac in the house, if you want."

I wondered what was cognac, cause I'm always up for a new thing.

"I gotta get my daughter some pizza . . . my wife don't cook on Wednesdays."

"Oh?"

"Bible study."

"Oh."

"Best I'm gonna do tonight is sneak a beer in with the pizza."

"Understood," the woman said. And I think she called me "pretty."

But there was somethin bout a woman punishin her own feet with a dirt road when she coulda worn shoes, namin her husband "that nigger" when her own name went unsaid, and seein my father a good man made her sound more than I think she intended it. He spinned up the path back to our trailer, and dropped me off.

"Yo mama cooked," he told me. "Lock the door."

I knew how to be by myself. Daddy was always away playin cards or talkin at the well while I fussed on my own with my balls and Barbies. In the quiet time when crickets chirp and porch lights fade out one by one,

I had a plate of cold yams and soggy fish on my lap. I snuck off half a cheese Danish cake I couldn't have no coffee with in the mornin. My cat squat with her paws at the rim of her litter box. A toad stuck to the window in front of the TV, scootin round in its film. Daddy came back 'fore the church van pulled up.

"Who was she . . . the woman?" I asked him, a sloppy grin on his face and a syrupy sweet on his breath and beads of sweat at his lip. It was a puzzle. In just that little bit of time, such a normal known face became so incorrect.

"She a neighbor of ours," Daddy told me. "You don't know her sweetheart."

"Why was she just walking down the middle of the road all by herself?"

"I don't know," my daddy said. "But don't tell your mama for me, you hear?"

And I never told. And a few more Bible study nights after that he disappeared, left me with a cold supper and a secret. But it was always too dark for me to go out at night to prove if the crows was real or not. So, I always went down there in day to see if the woman was. And even though it came to be hard to recall why that well came to be my place to be, I knew Pearletta Hassle most certainly had been real.

And maybe we wasn't happy as I had thought we was. Maybe was poor, too.

No matter how dark it got, stars and moonrise and love for the world can light it up. And little later on, that didn't mean I could really see much past the papery man swingin his baby by one arm down by the well. Not too careful at all. Not too uncareful, either. Too slow to be up to no good. Too fast to be up to nothing. And I ain't planned on runnin so fast and hard I fly past my own house cause I was confused. Cause when I flew, it felt to me like the Malibu was there behind me on that night, but I ain't so sure . . .

I wasn't sure of too much of nothin after that, except somebody round there was gonna have to make some money to set us all free from going crazy or dropping dead.

ONE

Around time Solemn Redvine was between ten and twelve, when her favorite song was Jennifer Lopez's "Waiting for Tonight," at the turn of the century, inside merciless July, in Bledsoe, Mississippi, where the Drinking Gourd never lies and the moss always grows north of the trees, where the morning glory field has no fortress, where people connect the face they miss into the stars of the night, where an outhouse is a staple and not a shame, where feet grow tough enough to steady on gravel, where the mosquitoes can be told apart, where every walk or run is déjà vu, where mourners travel as far for a funeral hat as they travel for the mourn, where Saturday night's last call is just a few tiptoes from Sunday school's start, Gilroy Hassle got mad at his wife Pearletta because he thought the baby in their trailer didn't look like him. So he tried to break her neck and knock her out. Then the baby child got lost down a Yockanookany River cobble well.

Solemn saw the last part.

That night, scent of cornmeal-coated, onion-packed salmon cakes incensed the Redvine trailer. Solemn's daddy gulped down his cakes, with canned peas and sugared Uncle Ben's. Then about town, he told the family. He had a duffel bag at his hip, on to one of the two or three bars to gather with the rest of the odd-jobbers, jacks-of-all-trades, and salesmen of random things. Solemn's brother,

Landon, marched to a ranch house or barn somewhere. He schemed with young Black Power resuscitators. They gathered to complain about having no civil rights. The cat, Dandy, was out and about, for a mouse or a mate. When she found one, she liked to meow like a cock to let the whole house know.

After supper, Solemn caught up lightning bugs in a rinsed-out Vlasic jar. A baby one wriggled through the slit Landon carved into the lid for their air. Just to catch it back inside with the others, Solemn went through a couple of stumbles. One ended with a gummy film of pink skin torn into her right knee. Its scab commemorated her birthday, every July, as the time or moment in her life gave rise to a frothy, slushy outlook on it all—*daring and sudden dark figures in the corners of yo eyes, senses lost, head upstream of the next rumor and ahead of the outcry, bored, knowin what's gone happen next without turnin the page or comin back after commercial, a whole new odor now—*

From the trailer, it was a few diagonal acres to the flatland development's only steep, upon a pond. Solemn's placement in the pattern of the mobile homes was a distinction of sorts. Supposedly, she was on the better side. Down the steep lived the few trailer park folks nobody ever saw out to barbecue, drink outside, drain their tanks, mow their lawns, or pop fireworks on the Fourth. Bledsoe summers could be spectacularly cruel or gloriously pleasurable. Those ones at that end stayed oblivious either way. Those ones either could not afford to or did not think to erect awnings, post tents, attach patios and decks. Those ones never strung Christmas lights—no snow to punctuate their parts, but still. They didn't rear tulip trees for the honeybees to flirt with. Those ones didn't bother to scrub campers to a higher value in their eyes. They kept it spare.

Gilroy and Pearletta Hassle were among the ones who stayed in. Solemn looked for Pearletta—from time to time. She sensed remembrance of a time her father had given the woman, barefoot, a ride home. Solemn remembered the way their car had gone, the direction the woman's trailer pointed. In her mind, she was a spy. She checked on the woman often. But when she snuck out in dark to go find that woman's trailer, down the steep and past the well, the all-around trees with no shadows sent her home quick.

Solemn saw Pearletta was very round at a summer's Solstice, but back slim by the following start to school. Solemn had seen plenty of pregnant ladies, but none with crow's-feet and gray roots. Pearletta was worn. Any new mothers Solemn saw were all fresh from prom formals and yearbook photos. And other pregnant ladies gave parties. They bought home soft, colorful bags. Whether she was round or not, Solemn only saw brown grocery bags and black plastic sacks in Pearletta's hands. She and the man in her trailer kept the blinds closed all the time—even in the day. The couple gave no shower or announcement or viewing invitations or birthday party for the baby. No one even knew if it was a boy or a girl. No one saw it until a *Star-Herald* obituary announced it was gone.

But let's not skip ahead.

Solemn was close to her again, once. Pearletta hung clothes on the line until the end of the pregnancy. Pearletta thought to pass Solemn her line for a jump rope. But when Solemn thought the woman saw her through fluttering sheets, she ran away. Pearletta did see Solemn. And again. More even. Once she bumped into Solemn on one of the walks she took to manage her hips. The woman smiled at the girl she called "pretty." She didn't stop to talk. After the baby came, the man started to drive Pearletta to a town Laundromat. Solemn wanted to come back and watch the sheets blow, know the woman saw her, trot away, play it. Before dark, Solemn could hear the baby cry from the trailer windows. She sat on the well to listen until it got too dark. She thought to ask Pearletta if she could babysit the baby, to hold the child and stare into its eyes. But Solemn was young. And Pearletta had never shaken hands with her mother. It was inappropriate to ask without that.

To go back, these were plain black people. They made a heaven for a time.

Even when their safest part of the world began to crumble and tumble on down, it still smelled of fresh paint, like a stretch of new city projects some decades ago instead of now. They didn't own the land. As good neighbors they had come there in spurts to hide from an untrusted ending to Vietnam, a death penalty reborn to America, a season of cicadas come down to Mississippi, and shirked offers for their hands in the tenant farms aplenty. This was cheap, so much nicer. The rest of them followed a few of them who found a distant portion of a tiny place called Bledsoe, on outskirts of the bigger place Koscuisko. There, lynchings had been possible but spared. There, none had yet erected mailboxes or signposts of ownership. There, the dejected and homeless and faithful could cover their heads. It was just there, a part of town with no townspeople. So some had come there with old rusted pickup trucks and improvised tents and donated trailers and short mobile homes HUD had just begun to regulate. But they didn't own the land.

They piled up like pioneers headed somewhere and fugitives run away. They dug multiple outhouses to share all-around including up-keep. They cleaned and reinstated a well. They made babies and families. They pooled the kids among them to a few schools they could actually go into now, so long as they could figure out a way to get there without asking a white person to come pick them up. They didn't vote.

There, every head of a household could be proud. They were all owners. In less than ten years they got so used to it they talked about it outside of it too much. When sounded as loud to strangers as eyes on potatoes once the pantry is spare their contentment and joy sheared down. They got found out. And they never owned the land. A young Eastern European immigrant turned tenant farm capitalist turned real estate developer in Vicksburg got mind to buy their sprawling prairie, install electricity and piping, cajole Bell South to bless them with phone lines, assure them: "Oh no, y'all can stay." In lieu of fenced plots ("Too expensive"), he wound rope around staves. Then he charged bit by bit for the people's rights to stay there, until their forty acres accidentally had its own spot on a Mississippi map as well as its own name: Singer's Trailer Park.

Now let's skip ahead.

The night a baby child was lost down the well there, Solemn helped her mother clear the table and straighten up after supper. Lucky tonight she was; no wash piled. She was restless and curious with no one curious enough to see it in her. With exception of Lutheran school and Baptist church, both of which scared her, Solemn lived to get out. She was afraid of a pattern or fate or inheritance demonstrated when only she and her mother alone occupied her home night after night after night. In Solemn's house, the men stayed out. Night after night after night. More troubling than their absence was Solemn's guess she was supposed to accept it but not imitate it. It was unfair.

Sometimes she found loose change in the dirt, even stuck to spilled, dried coffee or soda in the cupholders of unlocked cars. She would put it away, into her savings, she rationalized. But she didn't speak up about it when she could tell her daddy stomped off after talking about the bills or her mama smoked after looking at them.

Starting with a dollar she found under her pillow upon losing her first tooth at seven, she kept her money collection in the secretly dismantled underside of her music and jewelry box-in-one, its lid encrusted with rhinestones and a gray unicorn affixed to a top for the handle. She saw its contents as the one thing other parts of the world kept in common with her, but maybe also over her. She counted it all that night: $91.67.

"Fixin' to go out! Call out if they gonna play 'Waiting for Tonight' again . . ."

"Girl, we bought you the CD . . . I'm so sick of that song," Bev snapped, in the part of their trailer that home tripled as the study room, den, and kitchen. She put some wooden clothespins in her mouth and stepped to the laundry rack. Then, she spit the pins out and stepped away. No wash now, thank God. Actually, Bev was pinched to ask Solemn, "Can I go?" And she should have. She and Solemn could have talked. They could have hummed choir songs. They could have cracked jokes about "dem boys." Instead, Bev fished for the dishrag. Another night of scraping dinginess to sparkle, cajoling old to look new, fending off wishes, paying no mind to the girl child who sees the discrepancies . . .

The latch door of the trailer clicked and then snapped. Solemn had a wish to see the crop dusters, come by more and more over the sweet potato and cotton and tobacco fields. They were the only planes she ever saw, so she loved them.

Why would you even stay here? I won't. I'll fly away. Stay here if you want . . .

Solemn's place with a name of "Singer's" told her who she was and what she was supposed to do. She planned to save little by little, dollar by dollar, for her trip away from Bledsoe, with just a few diners and a gas station and slumpy houses and mechanic places, to return in a big car and fancy hat and high heels. On television there was a superstar named Oprah with her own show, and even a road and a billboard called after her in the big town. And, she was black just like them. So it was foreseeable. Solemn heard the bigger folks say "the Trace" rode all way to Nashville. She figured out singers lived in Nashville. She learned in school that Nashville was in Tennessee. She wanted to know if she could be allowed out of Bledsoe, near Kosciusko, Mississippi, and on to Nashville.

On this night, cotton wisps flew from the dandelions. A whole silver, lavender, and gray universe out there accompanied Solemn in her dance of freedom: a carefree half step one second, a brisk skip the next, a flip-flop high and wild to find something worth mentioning in the darkness, and, at last, a split—out a blue from nowhere, like a gymnast in her win or a prima donna in her audition. If she cartwheeled at the bottom of the steep, around the ones who stayed in, no one would see when her dress fell down. Solemn ran alongside the trees without a look in their direction. Like the rest of them, she took her trees for granted, with their grave stories locked in raspy trunks and long-winded roots. There was so much freedom, playfulness, happiness, beauty, and security around her, but Solemn was aloof. Even the well's head—stuck up like a bunion on sweltering plains—was a point to make, a goalpost in her eyes.

Her family never visited the well much. Daddy just always had the water. The well was something to look at from afar, and then up close . . . for Solemn to see that frantic stalk of a man marching toward it. And for him to see her in turn. Maybe he could show her how to pump it, or maybe he would ask for her help with something and pay her a little bit for it. Or maybe she could dive in the well and get rescued out of nothing but a wet, ruined outfit for her parents to complain of. Solemn was pissed and vinegared, bored, curious, restless, wishful, and looking for even more to be on top of it all.

She found it.

TWO

W ell, sir, I don't know how or why my husband would kidnap my child. I wasn't there. I was probably sleeping. My husband beat me up pretty bad."

Pearletta shivered under the thin shawl she snatched from a slim pine cabinet on her way out the trailer. She screamed into a magnetic blackness, with a second-guess as to which key fit the ignition of the 1995 Ford coupe her parents gave her as a wedding present—disapproval aside. They intended to give her a sure way up to Jackson, where she was born, to keep her from going down barefoot and pregnant and high. But Gilroy took over the coupe quickly, pretending and musing around. Now she had just stopped him from breaking her neck. Her elbows locked her arms too straight for him to to push it down. She was certain he had wanted to kill her. Pearletta was so beside herself at how her life turned out. She could not admit Gilroy's efforts this evening were not exactly abrupt. It had mostly been like this. No matter her age, Pearletta found and married Gilroy late. Or perhaps too early, given how it all turned out. But, way back when it seemed now, she was addicted to *that stuff*—anything at all it could be: weed, coke, booze, rock. She blamed herself. She had been the one to walk off from other comforts. The only reason she spoke the truth aloud now was because her child was involved. All that was left of the baby was a soft pea-shaped impression dug into the covers of a cot.

Gilroy wanted to upset her. He had to have the baby to do so. It was his highest card, after his cooking and his strength. They had fought before, though never quite like this. He had a problem—not so much drinking and drugs, but skeletons fiddling keys to the closet. Gilroy wasn't quite right in the head. No one he introduced her to thought to warn her about it. She came to Singer's, rebelled too far against her family, fell for too many smiles, and thought marrying a man at the wrong side of the tracks would be okay.

The little township of Bledsoe, Mississippi—parish, really—took its go-to precinct as the one in Koscuisko, the main town, less than eight thousand posed in Norman Rockwell fashion at any one time. She arrived alone. Two policemen filled a cooled room with her. White folks—with pursed, pinched lips underneath gruff red and brown moustaches and slim, sunburned noses. Pearletta smeared snot onto her wrists. The black officer, a thirtysomething tagged "Bolden," went to find her a box of tissue. The men had seen worse. Much worse on those by the Good Book, helter-skelter, Harley-ridden, Mississippi vestiges of prairie. To all of them and right now, Pearletta Hassle was lucky.

"So?" an officer tagged "Hanson" inquired. "You say your husband carried your young son out of your house—"

"My trailer."

"Your trailer. He did something with your child, but you don't know what he did? And, you ain't seen your baby or husband since early this evening?"

"Yes," Pearletta cried. "That's what I'm saying."

"And," the sergeant Nichols said, "you was apparently recovering from a fight with your husband, so you ain't see and don't know the whereabouts of your own baby, that you thought was sleeping?"

"Yes," Pearletta responded to the men, looming above her, arms folded. "I still don't . . . It took me a minute, a while, to realize my baby was gone. But when I did, I did and, well, I don't know."

A drained and stained coffeepot sat on a rack of papers and folders in the corner, tucked tightly into a baseboard full of dusty neglect, ignored and cold cases run amok. Pearletta wondered why no one had asked her if they should make more coffee. Her reporting all this was nothing like she had expected: no alarms, no big men with guns, no APBs, no FBI. She wondered why she even came. She wished she had one true friend at Singer's. The Redvine lights were off when her coupe motioned the dust onto their path.

Officer Bolden returned to the stuffy, hot interrogation room with a floral box of tissues, the hard industrial kind. Pearletta snatched and cradled a bunch. She never thought she could possibly be examined for the kidnapping of her own baby—wished for, dreamed of, and imagined but finally delivered to bask in its only-child status and sparking a huge change inside Pearletta. But, she was a black woman, immune and tolerant to higher noses on shorter heights, her inquiries and concerns with law enforcement were scrutinized for her phony character and defamations first. They would get to actual feelings and point last. Even now, the rules were entirely different.

Nichols cleared his throat once more. He wasn't in a rush. He picked up a pen to write the first things written since Pearletta arrived. "What was your husband wearing when you saw him last, Mrs. Hassle?"

"Please. Don't call me Mrs. Hassle."

"Okay, um, Pearletta, what was . . . er . . . Gilroy wearing when you last saw him?"

Pearletta squinched the skin atop her nose with the thumb and middle finger of her ring hand. She could not recall. She was coming out of an era, a fog, a time warp, a phase. She hoped. She stopped focusing on Gilroy months ago. Like a snapshot of a funny-looking baby one just smiled at, no real look to commit its features to memory and retelling. But Gilroy had worked today for somebody. For whom, Pearletta did not know. He claimed he was always working, odd-jobbing, tinkering with cars, washing them, and moving furniture. He would have worn his overalls with some sort of T-shirt underneath. Bleached white, courtesy of her dry and itchy hands. A red paisley print scarf. Wore that scarf all the time. He would have started off in thong sandals and switched to some black work boots when he arrived at any job. He would have put the thongs back on when he got home. That's what she told them.

"And the baby?" Office Hanson asked.

This she recounted perfectly: "A light blue T-shirt said 'Bad to the Bone' in black letters, and some little Levi denim shorts my mama sent, and some red socks 'cause I didn't have any white ones washed."

"And, Pearletta," Nichols said, his head down and pen pressed into a carbon copy form the department refused to discard, "what was last thing you and your husband did before this fight? Any walks around where someone may have seen you or him?"

"We played Mille Bornes Monday night," Pearletta answered. "We played that until *The Honeymooners* reruns came on after midnight. I met him at a party where we played it. Somebody I went to high school with invited me to it. Gilroy was there. He was her boyfriend's friend. Not many people there knew too much about him."

"And you ain't got relatives in town you can call, or houses you can go to, or best friends you might could stay with while he's so mad at you?" Nichols continued.

"A few folks, here in Kosciusko. But nobody in Bledsoe where we are. My relatives aren't from here."

"What about his friends, relatives, working buddies, what?" Nichols asked.

"Lot of friends. A few relatives. A cousin he go out with all the time. Drives to Jackson with for the weekends sometime. I think to go to the girly clubs, got some women there or something. Random fellas who stop by after work. But I called all them. The ones I had their numbers. Nobody heard from him. It sounded like they was telling me the truth."

Nichols squinted again. "You mean, you don't know any of your neighbors? I know Singer's. It's pretty tight. He had to have passed somebody who saw him, know what direction they went . . ."

"What was your fight about?" Bolden asked.

"I thought we had relish. I want some tuna. Where the saltines? We outta those?"

This was common.

Pearletta thought about where her Avon shampoo could be, with her legs crisscrossed on the couch and her fingernails working on her scalp. She was gonna put on her makeup after she did her hair, maybe take herself to the

*show or bring the baby up to her parents' on the Greyhound, so Gilroy
wouldn't bitch about not having the car. Daydreaming helped her manage
irritation, a side effect of not smoking and drinking and getting high like they
used to do together, like maniacs. She used the pickle relish for the potato salad
on Monday night, when they played Mille Bornes and had sex on the couch.
This was the type of thing he lured her into in the first place, on account of
having his little trailer down in this little park. He was an owner. Gilroy
was involved with a joint and a jug of Southern Comfort. He slammed a few
Formica cabinets and the door to the icebox. Pearletta cautioned him not to
be "so loud" and "wake the baby" or "tear up somethin." Pearletta heard the
can opener grind a tub of Starkist she intended for a tuna noodle casserole.
"Well Gilroy if you're gonna open up all the tuna, you should at least open
up the door and air it out in here. It stinks." Gilroy heard "stinks." But he
didn't. Their comforter did. To him, it didn't smell like him. And he didn't
think the baby looked like him, either. He been out slaving, running from
stubborn acres of white cotton with white bosses passing dollars to black
hands. He found better—a dude call him sometimes to help out with his portion of a tobacco field, for an old farmer whose sons moved to Atlanta to
work for banks. "Shit . . . ten dollars an hour to find worms and mice and
rats in tobacco bales shipped off to R.J. Reynolds to pass off as Virginia tobacco for Camel cigarettes . . . tufts of tobacco to my pockets when ain't nobody lookin. Sell it on the side. Jackpot." He was hungry. Needed protein and
maybe a little sugar too. Had already heard his wife tell him she wasn't
thawing out and cutting up and frying no chicken tonight. Not tonight.
Twice in one night was too much for him. So from arising happily from
making love to guarding tobacco to planning tuna noodle casserole to fishing for tuna fish to cornrowing hair to looking through makeup, two people
passed smart words and one slapped the other and the other was tired of
having her hair undone for it all.*

"Gilroy was complaining," Pearletta told the policemen. "I stopped
drinking, getting high. He's kept on. So, he picks fights. I think he's
jealous I'm clean . . . he said somethin 'bout he thought another man's
been around. Ain't true. Then I didn't feel like frying chicken. Too
hot for all that. And he couldn't find any pickle relish or crackers for
his tuna salad. He has funny munchies like that."

Bolden slipped toward the corner and the last bit of coffee left in the pot. He sipped without slurping. The woman shivered every couple of minutes, announced her sadness and disappointment with every syllable and gesture. Had this creature named Hassle run off to Jackson, or Magnolia, or, indignantly, stayed in Bledsoe with a baby shrieking through a soiled diaper? Who would connive to snatch a baby so a woman could worry, wait, ponder, submit, forgive, and forget? There had to be more to it.

"So, are y'all gonna call in some dogs?" Pearletta asked the police officers.

She had seen this, on the news: the hype, the hysteria, the hoopla, the results of missing person reports. A pink baby wanders off too far on the unmapped roads. A brunette or blonde or redhead goes missing after a mass or a dance. Two rumpled parents shoot onto *Mississippi News Now* in front of microphones and a tearful crowd. A determined, synchronized front line of volunteers and FBI folks and police personnel walk a straight, long, hand-to-hand, person-to-person, unbreakable human chain over forest, meadow, state park, brush, hidden ditches, ravines, corners, tree hollows, river edges, Sanchezia bushes, weeds, and any hint of a shallow grave a missing person could wind up announcing itself from. And those persons find their ways—a statewide and national movement, a rally cry, an importance. Pearletta wanted, at least, a handsome and high-eared German shepherd or a fanatic bloodhound to sniff one of her baby's undershirts or pillowcases or socks. She knew the smell. They could follow her from her trailer steps in search of the scent, and move out through the yard and trailer park and town and state and nation and continent and world. At least.

"It's been less than twenty-four hours," Bolden told Pearletta. It's what he had been trained to say, what he knew to do. Still, he knew where she came from. There should have been a band of men around her to stalk through the dust and snatch this man out of his overalls, give him something to cry about. Where were they?

"Twenty-four hours? Twenty-four hours?" Pearletta said. "We're talking about a baby here. *My child.* This isn't some big grown kid who could have run off with friends or tried to run away. This ain't somebody who can read or find a way or be mischievous for the hell of it. This is a baby. My baby. In twenty-four hours my baby could be dead. Are you crazy?"

"Mrs. Hassle . . ." The officers seemed to all echo to her at once.

"No! I drove myself all way to town for you to tell me to come back in twenty-four hours? Wait for even worse to happen than what probably already has. You think I'm joking?"

"Well, we definitely gonna look for your husband and send him home."

"That's not what I'm here for, sir. I'm here to report a kidnapping."

"Ma'am, how this department handles domestic disputes—"

"I handled my own domestic dispute. Look at me." Pearletta rolled her eyes. She shivered in her seat. Her bony collarbones jutted forward. Her prune-colored skin blushed to purple. She looked neat and presentable like a respectable mother and wife, a good daughter, a refreshing friend. She had been, before all of this, before she met Gilroy.

How could I been so stupid? Cut myself off like this? Somebody could see or know something. Figured all this out by now. Returned my son. Shot Hassle. Joined me to pin clothes on the line. Then the covers would've been washed fresh and no argument would've even started. Played tiddlywinks in the yard with me. Brought over a six-pack (or twelve). Barbecued some pork chops and sausage and fish. Sat in lawn chairs. Snapped our fingers to new music on the radio. Beyoncé. Christina. Like I'm a real young gal. Gone up to see my folks. None of that had happened. I'm just here, now.

Nichols glided the ashtray in the center of the room's folding table. He strained the back of the office's squeaky folding chair to pull the Camels out of his pocket.

"Do you mind?" he asked Mrs. Hassle, behind a web of smoke.

"No," she answered. "Do you mind if I have one?"

Nichols passed Mrs. Hassle his last, upturned lucky one. It was Pearletta's first since she had found out she was pregnant a few years ago. She enjoyed it, very much. The three men and woman were all quiet for the next few moments, before parting their unfortunately made way. It was little more to ask or say until someone else said something about it. Pearletta Hassle was definitely heard. And sympathized with. But there was so much else to do. It was just expected her story would not end well.

THREE

Tucked right in the bull's-eye of Mississippi where all once predicted King would be shot, Bev Redvine was wrist deep in well water and Palmolive and cast-iron skillets and racing thoughts. She wanted her family to squeeze onto their convertible couch to watch the Fresh Prince with her; every day she threatened to announce her enrollment in the Magnolia Bible College, twenty miles away. She thought the trailer walls heard her.

No saint she was, but a Southern belle she liked to think of herself—without the slurry talk, slavery braids, and molasses preference she saw put on the South too much.

We doing good . . . been married seventeen years now.

Once the first ten years passed, the gossip about Bev went from "She had Landon before he married her" to "Least he married her." And, she *was* a housewife. She didn't work. That alone was worth the sacrifice of a grounded house, though Bev made her trailer close. Every day, she swiped vinegar across the fingerprints on the glass end tables. She burned incense. Malcolm, Martin, and Bobby Kennedy were the core faces in her fine-art display: small copper and brass–framed family pictures. She saved the *Time* magazines with Bill Clinton and Princess Diana on the covers, to sit atop the rest of the material stayed on her coffee table, to show how she did pay attention and she could talk smart. She bought Tupperware like it would go out of style. Her ability to make anything taste good—a cup of tea, unmarinated meat, okra, cabbage, smelt—was unprecedented. She walked to the gas station with dimes to call 1-800 numbers to clerks at Mississippi State, Grambling, Bethune-Cookman, Spelman, and Morehouse. She wanted the brochures. For her children. She had two bedrooms and a living room and a yard, no outhouse or dead-end pipes or water pumps or collapsing porch. Sky-blue and beige stripes papered most walls in their 750 square feet. She had done it herself.

After Bev bought her daughter her first training bra, her son began to roam. His loose sneakers tripped them all in the middle of the nights. His jackets stuck wrinkled in the crook of the couch like old men. Solemn, of all, was home the most. She usually busied herself with one of the Barbie dolls from her last Christmas or birthday. By now, the figures in her collection were naked and screeched and scratched, with dready blond hair dark fingers once tried to braid. Hopeless. And the girl sang until the radio got too loud and mimed with the singers on television until Bev slammed the power button. And she begged for her allowance too often. This was their small life.

It had taken Bev more than forty-eight hours to deliver Solemn, at Monfort Jones. Monfort Jones Memorial Hospital was central, at least, to everybody they could know. Bev's mother came to help a few days, as she had with Landon. Everybody had a few days of patience to savor. They used them to ignore Bev's cries or to make funny smiley faces outside her room window. When the time came near, family bought her balloons and tiny flowerpots with ribbons around them. Bev got to stay admitted three days. It took almost a day for the quiet gray-white obstetrician to pin down the source of the terror and torture: Solemn was a frank breech birth—a newborn kicking out her behind first. It was almost as big as if Solemn were premature, without others' understanding the importance. Instead, the trait was only Bev's recollection and story to tell until the day she died. It was hers to use for and against Solemn, when the girl was either troublesome or unique. It underwrote the girl's tendency to be distant, then and now.

As was her name. As such an oddly positioned baby, Solemn drove Bev to painful vomit and insomnia. An interventionist ultrasound speculated Solemn was a boy. A boy was exactly what Redvine wanted. He already had a name: Solomon, the only official brown king in the Bible. And the richest, too. Landon's name had been *her* choice, after a tribute to Bev's mother's father, because he paid for their wedding at his two-story home in a good part of Kosciusko. So Redvine got the next one, when it showed up. The young couple fiddled around with extensions of his name a girl might possibly be able to live with: Earline, Earlane, Earlestine. Redvine called the child "Solomon" for its last three months unseen. He couldn't break the habit once she came. Finally, Bev took over with a word she saw in hymnals and the pastor verified how to pronounce: "solemn."

And this was why he loved her. Bev never settled to speak of problems without a postscript of solution. She never bashed anyone. One day she got a funny call and Earl drove her, his first passenger in his first Chevy, to Magnolia. In a low two-room house with a few two-stories in view, her father rolled a wheelchair on a dirt floor while he spit out snuff and explained himself. The personal-care lady who drove all that way assured them he was blessed out of losing balance in the outhouse. She kept him changed and cathetered fresh. Two more times until the drinking man died, Earl drove Bev to play catch-up over town takeout they left large containers of. They returned to Bledsoe for all sorts of card parties and yard dances and front-room get-togethers among Earl's sisters and crinkly eyed, knee-slapping parents. That was why she loved him.

Before they found Singer's Trailer Park, when Earl was infatuated with everything from the cute grrrrr of Beverly's crooked teeth to the way she dared him with misunderstanding his every joke, the brand-new Redvines had rented a clapboard house in Bledsoe proper. A stream flowed behind the yard out back. They traveled to Lake Itasca together, and paddleboated down the Mississippi River, and invited friends to the kids' birthday parties, and drove Christmas gifts to the primary relatives, and mailed holiday cards to all the rest. They were stable.

But they had problems with the supposedly gas stove. Dandy

turned up too often with mice. Cracks in the windows meant fly-traps hung from the ceilings like drapes and trumped as centerpieces of the rooms. Then Redvine hit some kind of lottery. He put down on a double-wide in middle of Singer's. It had space and quiet, and just a little bit of work to get the propane so Bev could cook. Though Beverly missed having an attic, and an AC would be nice, nobody could say a word edgewise about her or her family. Salt-of-the-earth people, and her kids were definitely going places to boot. Others could only prove the Redvines wrong if what she declared as perpetually "fine" became a grassroots news tragedy, a sudden funeral to attend, or a broke and homeless quartet for relatives to prepare the extra bedrooms for.

So Bev chain-smoked her husband's Kools for two hours on the night in Bledsoe, Mississippi, not too many acres from where a child floated in their Yockanookany River cobble well. She stayed calm. There once had been *that* story in the *Star-Herald,* of the fourth-grade girl walked straight out the church to vanish into broad daylight before the benediction. That poor girl was found in a shed amidst unmentionable circumstances. But that was yeeeeears ago. There had to be only one story like it for each person who could hear in a life-time. So, it couldn't be her story to tell, too.

Solemn is a good girl, Bev thought. *And, I have a good husband and son. Nothing wrong—no, certainly not my daughter deflowered and decapitated to decompose unsanctified in a junky, humid shed.*

Except, they were all no longer enchanted with one another. Her family was just, now routine. Any break in their routine was like a fever: duly noted, checked on, hurried for, and taken way too often for its drama more than its results.

When Solemn was not back after the sun set, Bev foraged for coins to offer a neighbor. One might let her tie up their phone, to hunt her husband back to drive around to look for Solemn. With the pockets of her housecoat weighed down by dollars in quarters, she put on sandals and marched out. The strong metal hills of the for-mer bayou oil fields granted her bearings in the dark. She looked for the first open door.

Light and laughter drew her down to where she never went, past the same old sheds and storm cellars and bikes and fire pits she saw outside her windows too many hours a day. And she didn't choose the way. The way chose her. She watched her steps on the same steep she often saw Solemn hike, to the well. Lights strung around trees, a sweet-scented wind blossom, morning glory sprung, pitchforks in the grass, the first stars. All this surrounded these other Singer's people she only knew due to scarce sightings.

"Sorry to interrupt," Bev said to who she presumed was the lady of the house: a woman sat down on chalky white patio furniture, in a yard larger than normal, adjacent to a man working up charcoal for a grill, leaning onto a Siamese-eyed daughter wearing all pink, both staring into the fat book the woman held in her hands, and both so absorbed in the story or each other or both they hardly noticed Bev approach. When they did, the woman smiled and she really meant it.

"No interruption," she said. "How you?"

"I'm fine," Bev said. Then, minding her manners: "Beverly Redvine."

"Stephanie Longwood," the woman said. She put her book down in her lap and shook Bev's hand. "Honey, you wanna introduce yourself?" she asked the child.

The little girl looked up, squirmy and grinny, and turned her face into her mother's hair.

"Oh, you know how they are."

"Don't I." Beverly sighed. "I have a daughter myself. I'm looking for her. Do you think you've had a look at a girl round here, older and taller than yours?"

"Well, hmmm . . . lemme see. My gosh. I should go ask my husband."

"Don't trouble yourself," Bev said. "I'm sure she's—"

"No, it's no trouble. We're neighbors."

The girl followed the woman. She stopped to pick up a pitchfork to dig in the dirt.

Bev eyed her new neighbor having a conversation with her man. He set down the bag of charcoal to really listen to what his wife had to say, put his hands over his eyes, looked around, and squinted his eyes like his wife. They were identical twins almost.

Cute, Bev thought. She was past that point with Redvine. The woman had set the book down upon a strong pewter patio table, webbed top and latticed sides. The woody-yellow cover picture said *The Poisonwood Bible. Good God.* Before Bev could wonder too long on what blasphemy the book might hold, the woman returned.

"That's my husband, Theodis," she said. "He wouldn't notice my new hairstyle, let alone a girl running round here. You have a car?"

"I don't drive," Bev said. "My husband do. He's out with it."

"It's gonna take him forever and a day to get the grill going. Why don't we drive round look for your daughter? By then, meat should be ready."

"Oh I couldn't," Bev said.

"Really, it's no trouble," Stephanie said. "We can't have these girls round here missing. You hear all this mess on the news these days. Nobody cares if it's one of us . . ."

"She comes back," Bev said. "But it's been a long—well, do you have a phone?"

"Most certainly," Stephanie said. "I'd be calling the police myself if—"

"No, not the police," Bev said. "I think I know where my husband is. If you don't mind, he can bring back our car and go look. I really thank you."

"Don't mention," Stephanie said. "Desiree, take our nice neighbor to the phone."

The daughter twisted herself round to the direction of the door like a figure in a snow globe, perfect pirouette it seemed. Bev realized it had been intentional, a mock performance, entertaining her mother. How playful they were. Without a word or a caution, the pinkness led her into one of the very few trailers Bev ever stepped into outside her own at Singer's. She could hypnotize herself to think of what she had as a home, large enough for sure. She recalled what her mother used to say, all the time, about how somebody cried because they had no shoes but then they saw a man with no feet.

The slim black telephone was stuck into the wall near the back screen, in a kitchen the size of ones she saw in the actual ranch house she and Redvine speculated they would buy one day. It was a cordless phone. Modern. Music came from above her, but she couldn't find speakers. Then, she noticed small patches of black dots in the white ceiling where the sound came down from—clear and abundant, smooth jazz, fancy-like.

When the pinkness left her alone with the pretty horn music, Bev almost forgot her purpose: to find a phone to call her husband, to say their daughter had gone out without coming home. Bev thought she remembered his whereabouts tonight was not a bar but a card party. At old Alice Taylor's house with Alice's new boyfriend and his friends. She called up there. One of the young boys who hung round Alice Taylor's for the free food and cigarettes and joints and beers answered quickly. "Yeah, Redvine here." Then, Bev was surprised: Red didn't sound tipsy or drunk after all this time gone, not at all.

She quickly explained. "I'm there in a minute," he told her.

Had she not feared embarrassing herself, she would have lingered in longer, to listen to the pretty horn music coming out the invisible speakers in the ceiling in a trailer that had to be at least twice the size of hers . . . wraparound sofa set, big glass pictures on walls. Outside, Stephanie Longwood and the daughter—chin on her mother's shoulder—were back wrapped in the blasphemous book.

"Things okay?" Stephanie asked.

"Yes. I reached my husband," Bev said.

"Perfect," Stephanie said. She finished the sentence she had been on before Bev came back out into the yard. Then, she minded her own manners and looked up. "I'm sure she's on her way. Feel free to stay until he gets here. You reading this book?"

"Why, no," Bev said. "I was gonna ask . . . A poison Bible?"

Stephanie laughed. "Ain't what you think. It's a novel. Bunch of white folks go to mess with a bunch of us in Africa. It's that Oprah thing. You know, the book club?"

Bev knew all about it, with everybody reading the same book for the month Oprah said they should. She had meant to get into it, perhaps try out for one of the shows where women maybe just like her sat on television with the author. But she was always worried about her English not being too good, so she never wrote in for the contests and letters like she daydreamed she would. Stephanie looked like a type who might do that.

"I been thinking about getting a little group going out here," Stephanie said. "Everybody so close, but we stay so spread out. But, well, a book club . . . maybe. Get together and talk about books. Drink some wine. Oh, and certainly a lotta food."

She leaned in close to Bev, like a high school girl behind the teacher's back.

"Best part is husbands won't know what in the world we doing." Stephanie laughed.

Bev forgot Solemn somehow. She imagined herself holding a wine-glass and laughing about a big, fat book.

"Better than slucking through all this alone," Stephanie said. "Would you come?"

"I guess so," Bev said. "I mean, I used to read so much more, but now . . ."

"We should do it," Stephanie said. "Take my telephone number." She handed *The Poisonwood Bible* to the pinkness, to pick up a tote bag slung over her chair. Inside her purse she juggled around sun-glasses, a billfold, a heavy bottle of perfume, and other things before she found a gold pen tucked into a leather pouch with a notepad attached.

"Feel free to use the phone anytime you need it," Stephanie told Bev, handing her a telephone number to force—much as Bev distrusted sensing it in herself—some trust.

Redvine had ended the game with money on the table divided equally between the men. Then, Beverly just waited. Redvine arrived home with his duffel bag on his shoulders. The food and tools he carried around for the days were still inside.

"I'm so tired of that girl running off. Red, I tell you, I'm gonna lock her in here."

"She off with Landon, at one of them meetings, learning how to complain . . ."

"But Landon was long gone when Solemn left. She didn't say nothing to me 'bout following him round nowhere. Something's wrong. I should've watched her . . ."

"You get back to the phone and I'll get to the road. I know my kids. Ain't nothin' wrong. That girl just out here getting fass. You gotta put your foot down."

"Me? And you?"

The Magnolia Bible College recruiter had said she'd graduate in a year.

In just one year, she would have not only gotten out of the house on her own. She would have also gotten a certificate to work, have her own mind, and skip out on being the only one steering kids in the proper directions. Landon agreed with her, but he agreed with everything she said. Solemn never understood what she was talking about. Redvine thought school was useless for her; they only had one car. Either he'd have to drive her to her classes or she would have to take him to work and pick him up, or they would have to buy another car for her to have all her own, or they would have to have Landon do all the driving since he had so much spare time. And who was going to watch Solemn? Would they have to pay for that, too? They couldn't leave her by herself. The idea just became too complicated before it became nonexistent. It relaxed to a wish. If the wish inched into conversation, it could not lengthen. It was a fantasy locked inside Bev's fixed stare at the television whenever she was alone. Often. And she wondered if she should run back to the neighbor's house to read the Oprah books, without telling anybody where she went off to, so they could search her out for a change. But that was the future, not real yet.

For now, Bev was worried. Bev wasn't so worried about Solemn disappearing into Singer's vortex of speckled porch lights and absolute quiet. No. Here someone would see and hear her child. Bev was more worried at the nerve. The absolute nerve. Here she was—the only one who was actually in the house, attending to the results of others' lives in that house—and every other body in that house was out in the world doing exactly what they wanted to do without even telling her where they planned to do it. Hmph. Yet had she done the same thing, the others would have had a fit.

What we supposed to eat? Mommy, where you been? Mama! Mama! Man, where she at? I need . . . Oh, well, I came by and you weren't even there . . . Yes, sure I can come back . . . Can you tell me when your mother will be home?

Bev simmered, to finish her husband's cigarettes and plan to pray the pack away next Communion. Was this her family and her life, or her prison and its guards? Was this the ceiling of regard at the end of her rainbow? If she was outside still at midnight to hunt down her own child she brought into the world, was she out of her place?

She stood outside her home and swirled dirt up between her toes, like Solemn liked to do. She flung a mental note up to the sky, hoped her daughter would catch it: *I'm sick of this shit.* She was going to be making some needed changes in her house—soon.

FOUR

As usual, before he left, Justin Bolden rejuvenated the coffeepot in corner room 106-B. Then he jotted case notes about situations or customers to tend to the next day. He returned people's telephone calls about their cases and conflicts only if necessary. For him, that meant any brown or darker face the others didn't want to see crying and carrying on. He sharpened a pencil he set down on his notes atop the desk he shared with Hanson: younger than him, white, already at the desk it had taken him a couple of years to scoot up to. His reward for all this drama was an undeniably red 1998 Buick Skylark with an arrogant hood and capable trunk, one of the last of a final production. He was proud of this detail. It impressed ladies. When he drove around to his people, he got slapped on his back about it. He was the fancy one with the good job, the legal gun, the white man's respect, the work desk, the thick wallet.

"You think the old man's gonna show back up there tonight?" Hanson asked.

"I hope so," Bolden said. He snatched up a few of his coworkers' cigarette butts from the ashtrays strewn about. "If not, lady's gonna be back in here and I'll be having nightmares about babies. Just what I need, right?"

And the babies would be black. Many of the pink, white, creamy people wouldn't even talk to him. If they did, even in this day and age, they still called him "boy."

Bolden left through the back door. He walked around to the front where he parked the Buick, unlocked, in a handicapped spot everyone knew he borrowed.

The esoteric outbacks of Kosciusko had the best bars. Their rain-pelted and toughened awnings outstretched against the plains. They begged for attention. They relied on heavens-high sweet gums and elms, postured branches in a wicked assortment of poses, to play well against a wet brain's imagination. It called more folks inside that way. Pearletta Hassle put Bledsoe back on Bolden's mind. A playful den of iniquity named "I'll Be Good" leaped to Bolden. It was somewhere obscured in the crook of Natchez Trace Parkway, encircled in or near or around Bledsoe, a little different from the rest and still the same. He would find it. First time Bolden had happened upon the spot was with a cousin visiting from Tampa. A gap-toothed smart-mouth named Tammy tended bar there. He believed she flirted with him. He emptied his pockets and stayed until 4:00 a.m. He tried to get her number. Didn't matter how long he had stuck around. She said, "No."

It was a long time since then. Little waited at Bolden's apartment but utility bills in the mailbox, a dozen tropical fish in an aquarium he always forgot to scrub, a GE clock radio with a neglected off knob, a few voice-mail messages from a gal he was trying to shake, his job, and his parents. His father wanted to be sure he would be there in the morning before work, for their fifty-push-up and thirty-minute-walk daily commitment. He was sick these days, so visits from his son were more powerful than prescriptions. He already knew his mother wanted to know if he had gotten her message . . . about getting her message. If he could have rewound it all he would have been an astronaut. It was too late.

On his way to interstate MS 12, Bolden passed the Attala courthouse on Washington Street, the joints where the high schoolers drove in circles and crazy eights, a few gas stations, the drugstore, a new Chinese buffet he thought to use for the next date when he was inspired to one, the dollar store where he once bought little cheap gifts for his daughter's mom before he grew to buy real gifts for his daughter, and a few railroad tracks with no mechanized guardrails to alert casual walkers and slow drivers. This was a part of the world somebody just had to know, or not. Bolden stopped at each railroad crossing, squinted for a light point from a distance he didn't chance to second-guess.

He had never been summoned to a railroad crossing to take care of a gnarly, twisted, unforgettable scene beyond comprehension and his own needs for bravery. He never had to rush to a far-off creek or secret basement or unbeaten path. The turbulence of their lives crashed down in the ordinary and presumably friendly places—bars, parking lots, bank accounts, park houses, picnics, barbecues, bonfires, road trips gone awry, a night somebody left the party too late, the day somebody got home too early.

He was never off. He only took breaks. As luck would have it, he graduated from the police academy in late summer and started the Central Mississippi force at the bottom of April 1992. Same day he reported, shoes polished and high-top fade fresh and badge pinned perfectly, the cops who beat Rodney King got off and L.A. got mad. The government council told his force to brace for the worst. Bolden was stuck at a job with men who originated in schools and a church and a neighborhood where every context of the blacks held such a sentiment: to brace and prepare, for they were incapable and knew not what they did, and they did not even look like real people. This included him.

So, the Adams Street sheriff's office placed Bolden on the front line of the guard that evening. He had never shot a man before. They told him not to hesitate. And they rode around the county looking like school principals ready to paddle, with adrenaline run through their haunches and excitement under their skins, to no incident. Instead, they saw subdued and stricken black faces on these streets. No riots. No bloody bacchanals. Just more people than usual out on the porch, a few less hunched over in patches of cotton to tackle what machinery left behind. He heard stirring words from somber assemblages come from under the church steeples hidden inside the backwoods swamps and glens. Into the night, stereos blasted loud, but no one made a noise complaint.

And that was when Bolden changed. He saw his job less as a purpose and more as an appointment: to daily drive on and on in a stupor, to wonder nothing at the houses or places or people or things around him, to think only of his paycheck and not the job for which he was paid, to curse his start time every day and Pearletta Hassle and her husband and her problems and all those like her. And he had seen it all get better. His uncle even joined a club in town—only way to join was for every black man to have a white friend join, too, and vice versa. The younger kids didn't seem so weary or alert. It was hard to say if that was because they were better or they were young.

By the time he arrived at MS 19, ten miles to go to I'll Be Good, he had wandered farther down the greasy radio dial. Then, he saw the roadkill.

Damn.

It would take five minutes for him to describe where he was to the nonemergency line; the freight line provided some crossroads, but the landmark itself was sketchy at best, really not one at all. The night was clear, at least. The work, itself, might be swift. It would take five minutes for that nonemergency line clerk to understand why he called. It would take ten minutes for the responder to wake the Animal Control officer out of a *Tonight Show* trance or a nap. It would take about twenty more for a truck to come with the men who would take care of it. It was a lot of work for an animal Bolden had not hunted himself. If it still had a pulse he would have to finish it off.

So with all those things considered and the nearest pay phone at least five songs back and his radio putting him right back at work should he use it, Bolden pulled over to handle the matter alone. He kept the headlights on. He remembered he had a few bottles of Guinness to rinse his hands with. He could splatter cologne to get rid of any blood smell. He imagined it would be easier to drag than sling over his shoulders. Before he stooped, he knew it was down and not worth it to check first. It didn't look like a thing that could kick his eye out or pack an interior bruise next to one of his two known ulcers. He walked alongside the grass edge dipped down from run-off of the decades; the tree roots unburied in skinny tangles looking like lady dancer's legs curled wildly around one another.

At just that time Bolden was a few feet away; there was a gentle wind across the plains and a breeze through his receding hairline. An improv of white fabric, dark pigtails, and shredded gray shoelaces danced before him. A finger, or so it appeared, circled around or near or attached to red cloth. He stopped, squinted, tiptoed closer, stopped again, took a breath, and then rushed forward when his fawn tried to get up, a firm palm in the gravel and ankle pointing up. It wasn't a fawn. It was a little girl—black—prostrate in the middle of the road, with a pickle jar of suffocated fireflies in her other palm, her panties exposed and her eyes curled back into their own thinking place. When Bolden put the tip of his black low-rise Doc Marten at the crown of her head, their eyes met.

Neither one knew what to think.

Solemn had her address, down to the nearest milepost, memorized like an Easter speech—enunciated and praiseworthy. The address was just a couple miles away from where Bolden himself had stormed out of, until he ran into the police academy. Down the road, matter of fact. In Bledsoe. Solemn bit down on the temptation to tell the policeman what gripped her to the ground. Or who. Anyway, she was unsure. The quivery but calm cop—beer on his breath—brought her back to her trailer, plastic and drained and silent.

Wrapped up in thanking God, Bev misheard the cop's part about finding her daughter in the middle of the road, waiting to be roadkill.

Redvine ripped open their flimsy door ten minutes later, frenzied, on edge, tense.

Solemn was home.

And a police officer was in the living room. No. Nothing happened. Solemn just wandered too far and lost her way.

When the men first came face-to-face, there was a reflection of each other. So small the area was, they could have been related. Somehow. Redvine shook the officer's hand to start small talk.

"I live in Kosciusko, not too far from the courthouse," Bolden told Mr. Redvine. "I like to sleep in when I get off from all this, so it makes things easier."

Bolden leaned back on their convertible couch-bed. Mr. Redvine extended an Old Milwaukee can, top already pressed in. Bolden shook his head no. Technically, two hours after his salary and shift had ended he was still on the job. Mr. Redvine took a strong slurp from the can instead.

"It's definitely easier to get to work when you ain't going that far," he said. "I can say the same. I take the work I want to take when it's convenient for me. Mostly I'm called in to the electronics plant, if they need me."

The two men were unusually tired. Finally: "Where you find my little girl?"

"Not too far off from here, at the train tracks headed to the Trace."

"That's far, for her. For us. I didn't know she ever walked out that far."

"Well," Bolden said, "she did. If I hadn't been fearing for a freight turning my Buick into a tin can I might have run her over. She was in the middle of the road, just . . . layin' there. I keep my pistol loaded. I ain't scared of no animal in the middle of the night. I thought that's what she was. But she wasn't."

"Well, Officer," Mr. Redvine said, "I'm glad she wasn't that. We take good care of our kids. They don't run off like that. We love 'em."

"I can see," Bolden answered. "Took her awhile to talk to me. But she knew where she was coming from and where I needed to take her. She wanted to get home."

Bolden wondered where Pearletta Hassle lived throughout here, if she was even back. It had looked like she could use a few stiff drinks last time he saw her. He could have asked Redvine about the woman, the man, the baby. But he would be back at work. And probably for nothing. Most didn't even call back to say *Oh, it all worked out fine.*

Solemn was in the one-person bathroom with Bev, getting yanked out of her dress, scrubbed with a cloth, and oiled up with Vaseline. Bev was cautious to enter a room where men talked. Solemn intuited she should feel the same. Solemn thought she had just a little slit in her knee, from her fall, starting to chase a lightning bug and ending with what, she was unsure. It was really a gash. A quarter bottle of peroxide, a singe of alcohol, and two cotton patches later, it felt like hope. Bev extended the cleanup until she heard a slight tap of the front screen door and the howl of a Buick.

Our part of the world was less than quiet that night. Without tellin what The Man at the Well did or how he darted to me after he did it or how I heard the splash but knew I cain't swim or how I ran from the man after, I just went to my room, off the kitchen with a shelf fit for my dolls. I woke up in middle of the night. The slit in my knee, from my fall early with the firefly, itched me into scratchin away the scab. I cleaned the blood off my fingers with my tongue. When I turned round in the bed it was three men standin shoulder to shoulder in my little room.

A snake or a bullfrog hissed underneath the trailer. Dandy shuffled from the closet and flashed her eyes at me. Branches clanked and clacked against the roof. A leaky faucet was in the kitchen. I sweated. I looked, buck-eyed and wondrous, at what men could have entered to find out something I ain't know nobody needed to find out. I crisscrossed my mind for my secrets and got ready to offer one. A breeze whished through the window and nudged my rhinestone music box of money from the windowsill down to the floor. If not for fact my room had carpet, I bet it woulda broke. The unicorn horn chipped though.

But my coins and bills flew out the underside down to the floor. Seem like money always supposed to be stolen or gone. I figured it was time for a robbery. But no. I forced myself to look again. Them men was just one of my dresses hung on a coatrack turned into my dress rack. What I thought was one of them men's long lyin nose was just a hook of the rack. Hah. It poked through the sleeve of my white dress I wear when we got to go to a special supper or church service. What I thought was the man's beret was one of my starched collars, pointed up high. How silly, Solemn, feel like my mama say. All that jerkin and freezin for nothing but a trick.

"Get on out from inside me," I told the secret. "Go on now."

She knew she wasn't so special. Had to have been the secrets somebody chased, and not herself in her own body. Until now, with this night when figures in the distance turned round and round before her very eyes, trying to gouge out what was inside, no one cared to know her. She heard the toilet flush, but couldn't tell who did it. They all had a different way. Bev held it down, to make sure. Redvine just slapped it a bit. Half the time, Landon forgot. She herself did it twice, to pass time. She wasn't at wits. Now there was a rim of dark under the bottom edge of the door, blacked out, slit in two parts. She hadn't heard anybody walk to it, nor did the trailer shake close to her way. She dreamed the knob turning. Solemn awoke the next morning to a bowl, Cheerios, and a glass of milk on a small stand next to her small bed. A belt hung on the doorknob: a reminder she shouldn't leave the house again with no notice and she definitely shouldn't return in a dirty dress.

Beyond any man Solemn saw suited up in pretend good use, or spaced out in the pews of Battle of the Cross Pentecostal Church, or flung out a passenger side, her brother was actually okay and forgivable. Solemn always discovered his better uses. She used to tag along with him whenever she asked, to catch the ball for his new beard and lank-armed friends. Lately, his boys drove up in haggard cars and trucks to carry him where she could not go. She speculated she could be just as self-absorbed and clandestine when she was many years taller like Landon. He was a D/C student at the high school in Kosciusko, but nobody minded or pressured more. When he got the diploma, he would do better than Redvine had with a GED. The dining room, a harried nook of a round maple table between two partitions with built-in shelves for records and books, smelled sharp like lemons and menthol. Landon's eyes were a rheumy pink. Solemn saw a spray of pink ovals around his mouth, more along the boat rim of his T-shirt.

But the cicadas ain't here yet . . . she wondered.

"What's that smell?" she said.

"I stopped at the drugstore and messed around the cologne samples . . . Police was here last night?" Landon poured himself corn-flakes with last of the milk. Then, he slurped last of a beer his father left undone. Solemn leaned her elbows on his thigh and rested her chin in her hands. She rocked back and forth.

"How you know 'bout that? You wasn't even here," she said.

"Daddy told me be nice to your mama today 'cause Solemn and a cop done set her off." Landon grinned. "Worried about what the neighbors was gonna say and think, if they knew. What you do to get police coming round here?"

"Nothing," Solemn said. "I lost my way home. A policeman brung me. Just one."

At back of her brother's shoulder, jagged and silent, came The Man at the Well, with unspoken malice and charm. It was a puzzle. But with Landon there, he didn't move Solemn. She closed her eyes and blinked, and it all went back correct.

Landon rose and took Solemn's hand, to the window to see the three-planked fence horizoned against the dawn. Their neighborhood's signpost and mark, like a brand, was prominent to double take and second glance: *Singer's Trailers . . . Park With Us.*

"See that fence?" he asked Solemn. Their faces pressed to each other in the four-by-four kitchen window. He pointed to the slate-gray weathered logs erected decades before, logs creased softly like smokers' faces. Solemn nodded. "Ain't no black man's blood ever drop from inside this fence and ain't no cotton come up from the ground inside it, either. Some Freemasons marked it off, before we got here on this earth. They shot up any white man who come past. Blew his head off. Popped it like a balloon."

"Ugh, Landon . . ."

"Well, they did."

"How you know? You wasn't here."

"I know. Trust me. I know. I told Daddy to move here. Well, not directly. I just hinted. We came out here together. First. I could feel it was something clean about it. No haunts here."

This was reassuring to her. The tricks would go away. Landon went on.

"You know, I been meeting and planning. Every day. Shooting my guns . . ."

"You gotta gun, Landon?" Solemn relaxed, fascinated and absorbed.

It was better than TV and a singer singing. It made more sense than her little eight-room school.

"What you talking about? Got a lot of 'em. Rifles, pistols, shotguns, revolvers. My man said he got a few Uzis he gon' bring by the meetinghouse. But, yeah, me and my partners, my brothers . . . we got 'em. Can't tell nobody though. So, you gotta stay away from them cops. They ain't your friends. You see 'em coming, you run. Fast. But not too fast, 'less they think you stole something. And you stay inside this fence. It's here for a reason. The Masons knew. Don't go out it without one of us."

"What if the cat run to the road?"

"Then let her run. She'll come back."

"Okay."

The predictability of Bev's shuffling and stirring interrupted them. Landon went along to put on a shirt with a proper neckline. Solemn slept all day. Meanwhile, Bev's reaffirmation of their life and daily reconstruction of its peaceful iconography included a red paisley print scarf not normally a part of it. It was tucked into the corner of the creamy faux velvet couch behind one of the matching faux velvet pillows. She had told Landon (too many times) to stop perching his greasy new Afro on it. And Solemn, *that girl,* she never put the pillows back uncrooked or right side up. Ever. Bev chalked the unplaced and unfamiliar item up to her son, unapproached for the new morning curfew he apparently decided on for himself but punished for it nonetheless. She threw it away.

FIVE

It took a few days before a teenage girl complained the pump in the main well was too jammed for her to get the water her family did not want to drain their own gray water tanks to run again, to risk overflow. It took a couple of well-side consultations and politicking sessions for that girl's father and the men who talked often to come up with a solution to unjam it—namely, force. It would take one of those men's woman, an unmarried girl shacking up until she could do better, to let the drunk she lived off know to stop the guessing: "Just stick a flashlight down there." It took one more day and one more lost bout with sobriety for that man to follow her advice. It took a half hour for the new white officer to figure to take the unmarried girl's sickened call seriously. It took two hours for the brown officer to volunteer to walk up to Pearletta Hassle's shell in the world—with Gilroy thinking the blue suits were the devil catchers and they should have caught up with the brute in him long ago. It took that brown officer a moment to tell Pearletta he saw what could be her baby floating in that well: bobbing, like a determined apple, begging a little blindfolded party guest to bite into it. It took less than an hour for a drunk and high Gilroy Hassle to remember he "dropped" the baby down there.

"Stay here" meant a correct way to keep on seeing things. Solemn stayed.

Bev and Redvine went to see what the fuss was about. So did as many who were home in Singer's. From the steps of the trailer, Solemn saw a group of folks looking and talking and stretching and pointing, with morning glory crushed under an uncharacteristic pile of people. Solemn strained to see through the crowd and thought her Man at the Well was just a man, bossy and controlling with children at his hands but crumbled and obedient with handcuffs on his. He spit at the other men or whomever along the path to the patrol car sending firework lights across the field. He missed Redvine because, at Bev's caution, Redvine stood back far from the circle. The couple walked back to Solemn with their faces incorrect. They left her on her own to find something for supper, put the puzzle together, and believe she saw what she saw for real, with all she saw proving Landon wrong about there being no hauntings at Singer's.

Taken aback, Officer Justin Bolden thought of the discovery of two black children in the wild twice in one week, one in earth and one in water. He did not want to seem too pesky or accountable, but it all had the itch of connection to him. He said nothing.

The first problem was Officer Hanson forgot to give Gilroy Hassle his Miranda warning before his hazy admittance. Town authorities could shield Hanson, make no mention of this fact—but a hoarse-toned female state attorney did. The second problem was lack of credible witnesses, no one to unpack Gilroy's euphemisms: "too much to drink," "can't recall," "just playin'," "can't recall," "slipped," and "can't recall." The final problem was a black baby with no dependents or friends or societal responsibilities was not worth the risk of a fight with the NAACP, or a tiny-boned black attorney driving in from Jackson for a bereaved hardworking victim of "discrimination." So Mississippi State gave Gilroy Hassle rehab, a grief counselor, and a regular psychiatric check-in package as a sentence, for the disappearance and killing of a black child. And that was that.

The Bledsoe blacks who heard about the accident or slaying or excuse or tall tale were incensed and mourned. They felt forgotten.

They shouted out their versions of hostility: "Ain't shit changed . . . We always got a white judge, all-white juries, a still-Jim Crow town, white prosecutor, white public defender, black accused, black victim." This time a black baby just happened to be cut up for the soup. The outraged who knew not to crave justice had to get to work, pay bills, eat, survive. So, nothing about what happened at Singer's Trailer Park well got a second look. The police were advised to stay quiet at the stations and ignore any telephone calls about "that baby." Procedurally, it was finished. Otherwise, it was just getting started.

The most decent of them dreamed about it and the most callous of them stayed silently turned on by it. The well was a crime scene with a question mark around it—not a spot of blood but a death. Most stopped using it for even an emergency. It took a senior couple no one ever saw, who had their young nephews come out sometimes to mow their lawn and drain their tanks, to pump it again. They did not know or understand what had gone on. No news trucks showed up for the story. Just one spectacled reporter, in hopes of a statement or exclusive, parked his Volkswagen outside the Hassle trailer. He waited awhile, approached some of the park's residents standing near, got little to no answer, went to the door, knocked, waited, walked round the other side, ran up on two lop rabbits humping, then got back in his car and left. Hall Carter got in touch with Hinckley Springs Water. He convinced all of Singer's it was time to update—payment plans even, for those who couldn't pay for a month at one time. In many ways, the well's neglect signaled the leveling of their neighborhood, a satiation of a wonder that would come back in their lives soon and often. Even with an embarrassment like Gilroy Hassle removed, the fact nothing was done about one of theirs let them know, all in all, time after time, then and now, front and back again, they were always going to be niggers.

Solemn despised she had no telephone inside or nearby or somewhere, to make a call. She would speak properly and importantly to the brown police officer who carried her up from the road. She would testify. She would tell the whole story up and down, in the middle, side to side. But she bit down on that secret, too.

———

"How you feelin' now?" Bev asked Redvine, pushing a pill into his mouth.

Redvine wasn't right at the moment. For the last couple of days actually, since the shacked-up girl reported the baby in the well. He lay coiled up in a damp white sheet with a cup of tea steam swirling around his head. He had a thumb in his mouth, not sucking it but just jabbing into his jaw. He thought it was a baby's foot, pulled up by his rough hand to tickle and play. But the crib was empty. Landon plopped a shot of whiskey at the teacup, took a slurp from the jug, and went back out into the yard to talk to one of the old church boys turned grown Army man. The man had brought him pamphlets. Solemn sat in the kitchen with a box of crayons and a notebook on the table. She stared out of the window at the man whose face used to be plumper. Now it looked square and stern, like his big light boots come up to his calf. She pulled out mint-green and beige crayons to try to put him down on paper in an outfit she was seeing more and more of these days, but it wasn't working out.

"You never had bad dreams before," Bev told Redvine. He stared at her like she was a stranger. She scooted to the edge of the couch. She removed his socks, squeezed the toes of one of his feet in both hands. He relaxed and drifted on back: "It's so much commotion around here now, my head is banging and banging . . . The crib is empty."

With the police having set foot on Singer's and neighbors standing outside in summer air to speculate and complain, it had been busy. They were all hot and prickly, on edge. Of course they were disturbed by a child—*an innocent child, have mercy*—so neglected and carelessly handled. Drowned. And not one of them heard the scream or did a thing about it. What did that make them? Heathens or monsters or a combination? Well, least they knew who did it. Wasn't nobody on the loose ready to snatch up one of theirs, kicking and screaming with bloodied fingernails at the tip of that there well.

So Solemn heard her parents say.

A white man's feet crunched gravel at their door. Bev and Redvine looked back and forth at each other. She started up, but he shook off his distraction and struggled off from the couch to go see who it was. Solemn put down her crayons and followed him.

"Good day," the white man said. He gave his hand. Redvine straightened his back and did the same, wondering how much a blue Jeep like this one here now cost a man.

"I'm Brett Singer," the man said. He was stout, wild hair and cat-green eyes.

"Yes?" Redvine said.

"From Singer's," the man continued. When Redvine was blank, he said, "You know, the owners of this here land?"

"Oh," Redvine said. His mind raced. He paid his plot dues that month.

"Yeah, I ain't been around too much. So, you probably know the others more than me. I'm back on with the family business, so might be seeing me from time to time . . ."

Redvine thought he must be late on his dues, to have a white man come this far out for him. But Bev never missed a beat insofar as bills were concerned. But the crib was empty . . . Maybe the mail was late, too.

"You get our dues?" Redvine asked.

The young man wiped a stream of sweat from around his temples.

"Oh, well, the office would know about that," he told Redvine. "I wouldn't know."

"Well, what can I do for you, sir?"

"I'm just coming along to check on y'all folks out here," the man told him. "Considering all that's gone on and everything."

Bev went to the kitchen to listen in. She nodded at the man.

"What's gone on?" Redvine asked him, Solemn watching behind.

Mr. Singer looked shocked.

"Least so far as we're concerned," Redvine said.

"W-w-ell," the man stammered, "with the baby and the well and the news, we just checking in with all you folks. Making sure everything's all right."

In all the six years or so since the Redvines had been out there on those fields, just one of about five dozen trailers or mobile homes or manufactured digs or vans with no hard addresses (and even a few tents once in a while), no one from town or Singer's or anywhere really had ever checked on them before.

"We're fine," Redvine said. "But we thank you kindly for your concerns."

"You know the family, the parents?" the man wanted to know.

"We don't know anybody out here," Redvine answered. "We keep to ourselves."

The man stood still.

"I don't know what you want me to say," Redvine said.

"You've said enough," the man told him. "Glad to hear everything's okay with you." And the two men braced in a silence Bev's pots and pans broke.

"Take good care." The man waved at them. Redvine watched the Jeep drive away. Hall Carter pulled up right behind it, with Hinckley water coolers in back of his car.

At the weekend, one week after her daddy got sick and mumbled out of leaving home (even to do the right thing, be good), at this type of event Solemn had never attended and would never again, she noticed her mother did not speak at all to the woman from Singer's, stuck to a front pew with her hair tied up. The women near her looked like witches, dressed in all black with wide hats. Just no brooms and cats roaming the yard.

"Can I go see?"

Bev thought about it and then nodded yes. For her, as a mother, it was too much.

In Solemn's walk up close after the singing and the humming and long talking, the baby's lips looked as if it had just sucked on blueberries or grape freeze pops. It had no rise or fall under a white gown, just a line of buttons in a stretch of fabric as still as the well's surface now. Its eyes were two crusted slits in a head. A line of people stood behind Solemn, connected like one—all leaned on someone, touched somebody's back, held someone's hand, linked another's arm.

Solemn knew in her own way what this was. And more important, no one could change it back to what it had been.

A woman with perfume powder spilling out of her dress nudged Solemn forward. The woman had never seen the baby before, but she wanted to keep the line going—maintain the sense of decorum, stave off the breakdowns that would inevitably flow if the show went on for too long. The relatives had driven or bussed in that morning. The fried chicken and pork chop and sweet potato pie smell crept from the basement into the pews. Bev had already said they would not eat there. Just pay respects. Hand fans flicked faster in the attendees' hands. Solemn looked up to see her mama wave her back.

Then the baby said, *What you say?*

I gotta hurry up . . . My mama want me. And this lady behind making it hard for me.

Oh. I don't even know her. They don't know me.

I know you.

I know you, too.

And I saw your daddy, too. I saw him.

You see your own?

What you say?

Solemn rubbed velvet inside the strong bed the baby rested in. The impatient lady behind her was so outwardly so, rude even, eager to see what she had never known the child looked like anyway. So Solemn tapped the baby's claylike hand and moved along.

I said, meet me at the well, okay?

Before, during, and immediately after the baby's funeral, Pearletta exhausted the attention and strength of her family and friends. They couldn't get through to her. Nor could they convince her to leave those six-hundred square feet behind, not even after she paid a few empathizing boys to accordion the baby's side out back into the whole of the trailer—like a second-degree burn healed flat in no time. It was over now. Nothing worked. Not music, church, prayer, money, flowers, baptism offers, covered dishes left at the step, and, most of all, not vacations. Not even to Louisiana, her brother offered her.

Oakland, her sister said. Pearletta turned down these offers to come "stay awhile." Even from her parents—her same childhood bedroom cleaned, cooled, crisped down to lint off the floor. She felt she couldn't be away from where her child spit and played and breathed and learned to walk. She was unsure how to visualize her baby and herself outside the trailer.

So she stayed clenched to their old nest like a leech, her ruminations dug in like tentacles. Least she wasn't the only one being talked about in all of it. There was a God. A courthouse janitor told his nephew (who parked a van in Singer's in lieu of rent) to spread this: "Gilroy came to the courthouse in handcuffs but he walked out in a silk tie." So least everybody could say they never saw any sad daddy put a good tie on that quick.

All the talk fluttered around her. Nothing worse than losing a child but being blamed for the loss. Other women were the worst. Throughout Bledsoe, the story of "that woman" was spread. Underneath their own maternal crowns, they doubted her.

"You never put no man before your child."

"She shouldn'a moved all the way out there where cotton used to grow anyway."

"I wonder if she even loved the poor thang . . . she never showed it off."

There were none among them to remove the apprehension shown to any black person who attracted controversy, whites, or public interest. And Pearletta had attracted it all. The smartest thing to do, in their eyes, was to treat Pearletta with the cordial manners they all grew up on. It went quicker that way. Their antidote to mourning, hunger, heartache, dispossession, repossession, a white: it was the same. Treat it like it isn't there.

SIX

Just in time for the holidays, the Route 17 gas station achieved a liquor license. Rumor had it there was to be a renaissance of Tudors on the nearby scrapyard's and oil field's abandoned acres, for corporate executives of Jackson to upgrade upon and Southern natives to flock into. The building was to take a few years. The journeymen would like to drink on the job before drinks after work. Pearletta took advantage and started with six-packs of beer. She figured the walk to the gas station to get it and back home would help manage the pouting belly it soon produced. The little girls on pink and yellow bikes with tassels on the handlebars did not bother her. Nor did little boys racetracking twigs and rocks and cat's-eye marbles. Nor did the growing boys who hinted she could buy them beer. It was grown men's pickup trucks careened in and out of the entrance with ample slowdown for her, and women with brown bundles balanced in their arms, and packs of teenagers with phony, immature whispers.

"Hello, Mrs. Hassle . . . How you doin' out here in this heat?"

None of them ever knew her first name. Only his last one.

"I'm fine . . . how you?"

"Good. Have a nice day, Mrs. Hassle."

At home, the Sydney Olympics occupied her—least the part including a muscular Marion Jones, a cornrowed black gal to root for. When the games ended, Pearletta fell in love with Bruce Lee, on DVDs the gas station rented now. She loved to see the young man from Hong Kong drop-kick his assailants and sneak out of hidden corners by early dawn, grunting and shouting and intimidating. Sometimes, with the blinds drawn, she followed him and replicated his moves, like he was an aerobics instructor at a YWCA her mother was devoted to. At the ends of her unpolished toenails were the faces of Gilroy, cops who looked past her when she talked, best friends who forgot her, old flames who burnt out, neighbors who did not hear the spitting and the choking and the gurgling. Sometimes, there was the little family up at top of the heap with a trailer much bigger than hers, daddy and mama and son and pretty girl inside. She drop-kicked all of them and chopped their heads off with her bare hands.

One day, near Thanksgiving, the man called Redvine pulled in with his family. Pearletta was about to cross into the bend of their shared acres long after he would have cut a soft left to head home. His beige Malibu appeared against the dusk sky and gravel road undulated to firmament. The car seemed to be waiting for her, only no one called out to tell her. This was the difference now. People stopped, stared, hesitated, and seemed to have something important to say. But it all wound around the same topic, so there was nothing. She was on Singer's grounds and she was not barefoot with heels hanging from her hands. She was near home. She knew her place.

There car trouble? Pearletta wondered. She slowed down with the sweaty plastic bag of beer pinching into her wrist. She sped up, wished to offer her help if there was any to offer. To be useful, preoccupied and snatched into sorts.

But as she got closer to the one opening of Singer's, the husband's and wife's smiles caricatured against leafy shadows upon their windshield. Pearletta stood still. Then, the wife nodded at Pearletta. To pass. The back of the teenage boy's head beed and bopped to the side. Rap music in the waxed Malibu. The little girl gripped the half-down window on her side, without moving her head, watching Pearletta walk through the gate. The husband and wife waved. The girl stayed propped, unmoving when the sedan's front wheel sank into a pothole they all usually remembered to drive around. Since the family hadn't asked her for a ride, Pearletta didn't know what to do with their courtesy. She was a grown woman. She knew there were questions in the air and connections she had made, which she accepted. He didn't look like a man who beat his wife or kids. They always looked up to him when they talked. The family drove away. She could have run into the pond and whisped down under the connection of lily pads, without them even swimming after her, like nobody swam after her baby. Then, for the first time but not the last, Pearletta splashed warm beer on an empty stomach before she got home.

She rejected the sisters from church who claimed they were praying for her but wound up speaking in tongues about hobbled parents finally succumbed. The social worker misplaced her with women whose teenage babies were gunned down in spaces between the tin-roofed houses. It wasn't that her relatives did not know or care. They just hadn't known the child. They barely knew her. Her name once switched from Pearletta to "On that stuff." She and her child were as good as apparitions to her sparse schoolgirl friends she neglected to invite to the civil ceremony, her parents who stopped mentioning her, her nephew who forgot her voice, her sister who couldn't stand the man. She had been on her own with her household and was on her own, now, without it.

Proximity to the only phone cable line within miles had been one reason Gilroy sold her on her life savings required to pay off his trailer and rent the plot. Had it not been for Gilroy and his popularity, which initially intrigued her but soon subordinated her, the clunky beige phone at the head of their bed would have remained dormant. Now that all the calls of concern and necessities ceased, it barely rang. Pearletta found a purpose for it, however. She would coordinate her new life. After a while, cops were the only folks she talked to. No one else was obligated to hear.

"Well, I could use some help packing up and moving out the trailer," she told Bolden. He took the call for her latest "emergency." It was her fourth in a week. The first two times, she thought a

masked man was in her trailer past the panel over the bedroom.
The third time she wanted to get information about her "case": the
State Attorney's name, the judge's visiting hours, whereabouts of a
death certificate.

"Mrs. Hassle—"

"Pearletta. I'll be soon divorced."

"Yes, um, Pearletta." Pearletta heard papers shuffle back and forth.
"Have you talked to any of your friends and family about helping
you relocate?"

"I can't find too many numbers. I used to know them by heart,
but . . . well, lot on my mind these days. My address book is gone . . .
think somewhere in a cabinet. There's the guest registry . . . I don't
think the funeral home ever gave it to me tell you the truth."

"Start with getting the registry from the funeral home. People
give their names and numbers for very reason to be called on," Bolden
said. He scribbled away departmental ink. Downturned hearts fashioned into faces, dollar signs next to them. "I can definitely understand why you wouldn't want to stick around there. Might be nice
to make a fresh start, you know? I know you and Mr. Hassle ain't
on best of terms, but he gotta have some pals with vans or flatbeds
to help you out of there. What about the people you gonna stay with?
Or you staying with anybody? You gotta place of your own? Any
landlord got plenty of fellas wanna get a day's work helping a nice
lady move. Maybe even for free, considering you been through so
much and all. There's the Red Cross, too. Catholic Charities. Social
service office, on Fairground Road, I think. We can definitely point
you in some directions, but I'm not sure the department would allow its officers to . . . Well, you know, we on call at all times, Pearletta. Pearletta? Pearl—"

It was dull behind four round-edged windows with the blinds yanked
down months before, a sliver of indoor parts viewable between the
slats. Smith & Wesson cocked, Bolden gave Hanson the signal to
pound the panel door. They called Pearletta. They got no call back.
Both men lunged against the door. A few porch lights came on from

the racket. One resident some feet away appeared on his slash pine deck, a sawed-off shotgun in one hand and a Hohner harmonica in the other. He saw a cop car and a white man, so he excused himself back inside—but not before he buzzed through the instrument's reed. Just as the mosquitoes and moths around Pearletta's porch light began to take their distracting toll on the cops, the latch clicked. She opened.

"Well, I'm not ready to move yet," she said. "I haven't packed a thing."

She slurped the remainder of a bottle of cognac.

"Mrs. . . . uh, Pearletta," Bolden said, "you disappeared from your call to us."

The men peeked inside. They heard a blues on a radio, smelled a spiced and citrusy sweet. There was no danger, threat, or hostility here. Only a hollowness.

"I was gonna call back," Pearletta answered. She fussed with the ties of a burgundy terry cloth robe . . . Bill Blass, her father's it had been. She swept aside her bangs, pressed and curled, for nowhere to go.

"Mrs. Hassle . . ." Hanson started.

Bolden put up his hand. "Pearletta," Bolden said, "when you call nine-one-one to be connected to your local police station and we answer, but you jump from the line, it's an emergency. By law, we gotta come on out here. Now, I'm glad you all right. But we gon' have to come in or you gon' have to come out so we can do a report."

"It's something mean about your eyes, like you was spoiled." Pearletta glared. "I bet you gave your mama a lot of trouble. Hope you paying back your allowance now."

"Hanson," Bolden directed, "I'm gonna need an incident report."

"Be right back."

"Pearletta," Bolden said. "I'm sorry we won't be able to be your movers. But I really want to encourage you to move with people you're close to."

"If I had people I was close to, I wouldn't have to move," Pearletta answered.

"Well, I'll ask around and see if any of the guys have some friends or relatives who wanna make some extra cash, or help a woman out."

"I have money," Pearletta said. "It's in Junior's cookie jar. He couldn't reach it"—she laughed—"and that's just how I liked it. His tantrums about it was something to witness, I tell you. I got one thousand, two hundred, and sixty-two dollars, cash, checks, money orders, after the burial. I think Humbert sneaked out a few dollars himself, but what you gonna do? He's the only one who'll bury us round these parts, so he gets away with it. I could've asked my folks. But, they can be snooty. I got too much on my mind to deal with the wrath. Don't think one thousand, two hundred, and sixty-two dollars is quite enough to get me one of them new Tudors. Or is it? Down payment maybe? I'm sure my folks'd chip in, if I promise to wear white and stay in church . . ."

"Pearletta, you had any medicine or pills with your cognac tonight?"

"Baby, I am fine. I'm a grown woman."

Hanson marched back with carbon copies in his hand. Pearletta noted her name and address. She provided her Mississippi State driver's license for identification. It still had her parents' address on it, in Jackson. She confirmed she was alone and unhurt. She declined medical treatment. She took her copy.

Finally, she felt like she needed another time of at least one time her breastbone unhinged so she could breathe right. The Singer boy was kind, to come on out to see about her. She knew he was just trying to find out how many more Gilroys there could be, even if it was just the one she congratulated herself for not letting back through the door of his own trailer. The Singer boy understood her grief, why she had to break into the bottom of an unsmooth Mississippi mud pottery vase where Gilroy kept stuff. But the white man didn't cringe when he caught her. He shared. More important, he listened.

That night, Pearletta Hassle showed off the vase to Brett Singer.

Made it myself, she claimed.

Get outta here, he said.

She assured him she had parents, had a big house in Jackson and they bought her things, schooled her well. He agreed that was the case for him, too. This, after a baby on her back with all others, started the laughter between them. She put her creativity to good use. She made a pipe out of foil and an empty root beer can, two slits in the side to finger air to the flame and one to suck out the smoke. They laughed. He told her about the cabin at the lodge his family owned and they could catch their own shrimp, boil and butter it. She gave him beer and cheese grits. That level of it all was the only kind of treatment she could stand now. Bolden or any other cop never heard from Pearletta again.

Prior to all this, when I could get the frequency clear, I was practicin the radio. With more time and practice, maybe some prize money in a contest, I figured I'd be closer on my way out of Bledsoe in general and Singer's trailer in particular. The North, hah, like the slaves had to run to. Harriet Tubman. You turn back you die. Funny. My microphone was a hard brush Landon left behind for his Afro pick. I looked at myself anywhere I could find: car windows, my shadow in a camper window, the rain puddles, and on back of spoons. Mama wouldn't let me watch Soul Train *or* Showtime at the Apollo *or* Video Soul. *It was contaminating, and women shouldn't move like that.*

TV show me more. The commercials explain magic liquids and gels we could buy to get past scrubbin the laundry until our elbows ached. The jingles kids sung showed white teeth couldn't have got that way with the baking soda and rag and Listerine I got. Brady Bunch *girls never sewed a tear in they dresses and nightgowns. They never cut the feet out they onesie pajamas to fit in a couple new inches. And if people worked, the TV didn't show it. What I wanted spritzed onto me from the heavy floor model Mama seemed hypnotized by but then kept me from, like a hypocrite.*

But my teachers at Miller's Lutheran Day don't see me like I'm a star. They just think I'm intendin to get shit started, always pickin on me out of the eighty or so we got in the whole school. Starin into space, losin my place in the passages, answerin, "Huh?" when they say "Solemn, I'm talkin to you." Truth is, I could barely see the boards. I wasn't gonna make a fuss about it though. We ain't have no money and glasses expensive, Mama said. I had mine inside my jewelry and music box, my unicorn on top, the bottom only I knew how to rip and put back. I had to have had more than anybody

I knew my age, at school or runnin round Singer's. This was part to a solu-
tion, maybe not the whole. But part. I even mistook buttons for coins and
wrinkly gray socks for dollar bills. If it was money it could take us some-
where, like a thin but sturdy raft.

Even if she had been asked (and she never was), she couldn't explain
it: the moment "the funny places" started. In the funny places, new
things looked deformed, smelled too strong, appeared too large, focused too clear (or not), sat before her in three dimensions with a
flat backstory she sensed. Whatever it was, specialists, education, experience, and wisdom were uncertain in its naming. There was no
social worker or nurse full-time at the school. The preachers, though
loved, were not trusted to talk alone with girls her age. Solemn got
accustomed to it, these pop-ups in her world. She even named two.
    Her hauntings from The Man at the Well and That Baby caused
her to submit to where they had all collided. The well pulled her,
tugged at her heartstrings, pointed her feet, preoccupied her mind
and thoughts. It was the compass for her longings. It excused her
disappearances. It turned her mind away from saving money for
her great escape out of Bledsoe, and onto a reason to just stay right
on there, to investigate the mystery of why she had been destined to
such bad luck. If she turned around in bed in middle of the night to
be struck by a form not there, but that she was certain of in its
broad chest and stringy hair, then she visited the well the next day.
If sight of great northern beans tumbling around one another and
over ham hocks challenged her, because they all seemed too alive,
she left her plate on the table and darted off to the well. When she
mistook a jumble of extension cords for a woman's wig with nobody's head underneath, she ran outside to the well. If she heard an
echo to her words but she had not spoken, she flew out the door
there, too. It came to be she could arrive there much faster and in
no time, due to familiarity and purpose, like the same walk to work
after decades. She was automatic and brisk. Sometimes she counted
the crows flocked at its rim, more as the winter set in.
    As one of her mother's straightforward kin may have summed it,

Solemn was "messed up." *Was there one man or two? Was there one baby or many? Did it cry? Was there a face in the window of this one or that one or not? Did the well crack earth and make it go quicker, snatch the child? Was I there? Am I here now?*

With no one using it, the well water grew stagnant and the steel bucket reeled to the pump began to rust. Like an old cow or a mare with a weaned foal, it dried up to grout. Men once came to the well with lunch bags full of fried smelts, hogshead cheese in rolls, or liverwurst fit between crackers. Now, no bones or crumbs fell. Groups of owners stopped talking for miles and miles of time while they dug into oily plastic bags of a whole fried chicken, spitting snuff and shooting shit. With its benevolence quenched, the wonderland around the well screeched to a halt, too. Insects crusted onto its screen. The squirrels and swamp rabbits that once floundered around it no longer darted near. When the leaves of the overhead beeches and cottonwoods slenderized or plumped depending on the rainfall, the disposition of sunrays struck through to the well's cobble casing appeared fierce one day. Lonely the next. When a fall heat wave hit, the dried leaves hung like witches' faces with long noses and scraggly hair. Next they fell. Both the scavengers and daintier birds ignored the well's perimeter, too. The rare eagle that pierced his talons around the well's mouth every once in a while eventually found new preferences. With it so abandoned by human and beast alike, only newborn toads remained, flipping and flapping on top of the distribution line, in the well's bottom where Solemn loved to stare.

Did you play with him? she asked.

The police car snuck behind her like a switch. Solemn didn't recognize the cop in his unusual look, white Impala with blue trim. He had a new white man with him now.

"Hey, I remember you," Bolden said to her. It had been dark, and puzzling, for them both. The night after he dropped her off, he dreamed of red nooses around unattached throats. And he wasn't even drunk. The next morning, he pulled up Redvine's name and met a grinning young boy once framed over obstruction of justice. Then, he went to a stack of files in the corner of Sergeant Nichols's desk. Pearletta Hassle's had sunk to fourth or fifth in the "TO DO" ladder.

Bolden flicked through it to the intake report. He affirmed his recollection that her husband had possibly worn a red paisley print scarf when she said she saw him last. That night, a red cloth hung from this girl's hand, like a rag doll or security blanket. He honestly didn't even know what he was doing at the well now. For now, he reminded Solemn, "I brought you home one night, 'member? How you getting along?"

"Fine."

"How your folks?"

"Fine."

"You ain't been running round in the dark in the road no more, have you?"

"No."

"Good. What you doing round this well?"

Solemn stared.

"Probably should go on home. You don't want to fall in or nothing, you know? Lemme ride you on up."

"I'm gonna get in trouble."

"No, not if I take you."

"'Specially if you take me."

"You won't."

Hanson stayed in the car. After that baby in the well, he took no chances here.

Landon answered the Redvine door with a trained grid of confusion and exoneration at the sight of an officer of the law. It didn't matter this was another black man. All were caution. Bev had nylons tied around her head for a bonnet, and forgot this.

"Again?"

"Mrs. Redvine," Bolden told her, "Solemn sure has a wandering nature. I know you love your daughter. I can see that. But, you know, law say kids her age are minors. She really shouldn't be out here all by herself."

"She out here with her own people. We don't hurt our own," Landon said.

"Might not be as peaceful as you think," Bolden said. "The garter snakes out. Can make you sick. There's a well round here where a baby got drowned. Dropped in. You gotta wonder, all the time, who your neighbors are."

"Well," Bev said, "thank you so much for seeing Solemn home again, Officer . . . ?"

"Bolden." Bolden extended his hand. Bev shook it. The camper shook, faint footsteps, then a face behind Landon's. A girl with slit eyes and a nose wide enough to make up for it. Afro around her fudge-colored face. She wore a T-shirt silk-screened with "Free Mumia" on it. She balanced a cup of chicken noodle soup on her belly. Her eyes steadied on Bolden's badge and outstanding billy club.

"Mrs. Redvine, we in trouble?"

"Oh no, Akila," Bev said. "We know him."

"Mama, we don't know this man," Landon said.

"I'm going along," Bolden said. Then: "Solemn, mind your mother."

Solemn was already in the house, past the others, on to ennui. Before Landon bolted the door, Bolden came back to Bev. She tamed Landon's puffed chest with one look. Her son stomped back in behind the young woman, her arm on his shoulder.

"You know," Bolden whispered above the crickets, "there's that woman over yonder . . . Pearletta?"

"Yeah," Bev answered. Her chin flinched up at the name and the story. She always thought she should invite the woman over, or maybe to the church. But, the few times she had mentioned it to Redvine, he told her they had enough to worry about.

"Well, she's decided to go on and move outta here."

Bev shook her head. Knew that was coming.

"I came out here 'cause she's been calling the station asking for help, and we ain't really authorized to go into people's homes for that purpose," Bolden said.

Bev stood barefoot in a patch of grass before her home with two children inside and a grandchild on the way, without the modesty or mind now to remember the stocking cap atop her head before she greeted a knock. She totally understood. And she laughed.

"I'm sorry . . . did I insult you?"

"Oh no," Bev told him. "It's just, well, Solemn's been buggin' me about that woman ever since a day we ran into her at the road, coming from dinner in town, and me and her daddy got on the subject. Told us we should be her friends. *Help* her. So, I'm just laughing you say this now. I don't know. Solemn kind of just has her funny ways."

"I can tell," Bolden agreed.

And that's how Bev, Solemn, Landon, and a few partners from his makeshift "movement" wound up moving Pearletta Hassle out of Singer's with fresh lemonade Akila pressed.

SEVEN

Redvine mumbled something about double overtime somewhere, so he couldn't help move Pearletta. Bev was so pleased to help and get noticed for a good deed. Landon was eager, unaware of what all had exactly happened, and convinced (no, certain) the "White Man" tried to persecute another brother for having a few too many beers and playing with his baby and being careless—not criminal. He corralled two other strong backs to skip school and join him, hoping for some money out of the deal. They all stood in a circle and said a prayer for God's good mercy and healing to Pearletta Hassle. Then, it was time to run along and get the work started. Solemn lagged.

"We ain't got all day," Bev told her, suspecting Solemn just wanted to get lost.

"I'll be 'long," Solemn assured. Bev sashayed down the way, on to good deeds.

Solemn had something to return, to this woman she once met barefoot on a road. She did not remember what, in the senses of things. She only remembered covering a man come down out of the trees, from dark air, against her heavy breath and her strong will, a foe to her questioning eyes and witnessing mouth. She recalled the anchor of cotton or linen or soft and sticky cloth in her hands, come down from The Man at the Well. The red of it.

Her home was placed in its usual order, where even tiny eyes in brass-framed photos pointed to the same direction. Her socks and underwear were folded inside her one dresser bureau, color coordinated from light to pastel to browns and darks. Her music jewelry box was on the windowsill and its safekept contents (about one hundred dollars now) remained. And the couch, bolted to the floor as part of manufacture, had no underneath she could pinch her hands into. Hardness alone filled the cabinets—plastic, tin, porcelain, stoneware, ceramic. Pumpkin-colored linen napkins (for Thanksgiving) and small hand towels (for other days with guests) were the only softnesses Solemn uncovered in the kitchen. Not a hat, not a cap, not a hood, not a scarf she knew did not belong to her family. But to another's, now cut down to one woman whose coffee tables and box springs were set against her trailer days before the one the Redvines promised to help her move on. Solemn finally went on, to meet them there.

She saw Landon in the yard with a few boxes on his back, steadied by his friend. They were going to drive the U-Haul truck for Pearletta. They did not know where to, yet. Solemn ran to her brother. She saw the woman from the road sat down on a stool in her soon-to-be-past yard, no words and no baby now, a hand on her cheek. And Bev was talking on and on and on to the quiet woman.

"And this my daughter, Solemn," Bev said, looking more excited than usual to see Solemn. Pearletta looked up. Solemn looked down at her.

"Hello," Solemn said, giving her hand.

"Don't she look just like you," Pearletta managed, a knot in her speaking.

"Oh." Beverly laughed, as she watched Landon falter with an even bigger box. "I always thought she looked just like her daddy. Excuse me . . . Landon!"

One of the boys had beer, Bev saw. "No drinking out here now!" Bev shouted.

"Ma'am, what should I do?" Solemn asked that poor woman. She did not answer. So, Solemn walked in through the trailer's open door, to find her own way into something to do.

Solemn packed newspaper around dishes and glasses in hatboxes, folded rayon skirts in tissue paper, and tied up ten records at a time in twine. That poor woman liked strange music: white men with girly hair, makeup on, white women wearing black pants and holding guitars. Then, that poor woman came to rest with Solemn in the kitchen, with no overbearing or fussing as to how her things were handled. She gave Solemn a tuna sandwich and pop. Solemn kept a grin on her face, to let "that poor woman" know she knew but she did not know and even if she did, she did not care or judge or gossip.

Pearletta Hassle stared often at Solemn, then looked away. Unlike the girl's mother, she had arrived at Singer's as a newlywed and left as an open space in the world. But she would forever recall the last face waving good-bye from the edge of that goddamned fence at the oddly exclusive road being a little girl she wished she had spoken to and invited over once. At least once.

With Pearletta gone, even her trailer pulled away by men who did not introduce themselves to anyone but appeared to have permission, only a straw yellow rectangle of trampled grass left to mark the stubborn Hassle plot no one bought again. The rest of the families aspired to shoo away the spell of misfortune cast by such a nightmare in their midst. Soon, they could enjoy Christmas and the holidays with no stress or question or reporters or strange news mentioning their whereabouts. Singer's Trailer Park in Bledsoe. The events of the summer, and the intrusion of strangers (white ones at that) dipping in and out of their makeshift blocks, called for a laid-back tone to the holidays.

Come first of the year, they would marvel at how a dozen or more people could jigsaw their ways into the buffet dinners everyone gave at Christmas. People lumbered home with showy shopping bags dangled at their hips like toddler ghosts. The insides were secrets causing riddles to go on well into middle of the night, no robberies though. Shiny paper mixed in with large trash bags dropped into the bins at the front of the gate, gift-wrapped trash for the garbagemen to collect. More and more yells of "What you cooking today?" sailed through the air, along with the smells of their answers. The outside air cooled off to sixty. The breeze turned to chill, lifting up handfuls of dust, which would have been snow just one state north. The families retreated in to more cheerful televisions now: holiday jingles, soap opera and sitcom sets beaming with little lights, news shows and movies carrying the themes of God, giving, and, most important, buying.

"What is it?" Solemn asked of the heavy silver box Redvine presented on Christmas morning. It had not been part of the rest of the packages Bev wrapped behind closed doors in her bedroom during December. Usual and unusual stuff: Connect Four, a new Barbie doll Solemn did not quickly unpackage by now, a basketball for Landon, a collapsible air hockey set for them both, a few shirts for them all, the more dainty earrings and jangling watches the parents whispered into each other's hands, heavy dish sets and fruit baskets brought by old friends and relatives, tree ornaments and booze from running buddies like Alice Taylor. But the electronics plant had had surplus. They already had a floor-model TV, radios, and a VCR. So Redvine decided to atone for his shortcomings, to spoil his daughter and his wife. He kept the surprise locked in the Malibu's trunk. The silver box had a tiny slit of a mouth with many small steel buttons dotting its face like pimples. It was a DVD player.

Landon and Redvine got to men's work with the cords and pinholes in back of the new machine and television. Bev was skeptical and scared. If they messed something up, then there went the shows she set her rhythm to for the day and its tasks. And how much all these DVDs gonna cost? The TV screen whisked to silver dots. Its blistering static scratched the peace out of Christmas morning. Bev fled to the kitchen, to fix up coffee, eggs, bacon, French toast, fried potatoes, and orange juice from concentrate.

Solemn tucked into the underside of her makeshift safe a twenty-dollar bill she found at bottom of her stocking, under peppermint chips and walnut crumbs. Then, she ripped beef summer sausage and Monterey Jack cheese out of a gift basket. She took the snack out so she could spy on what more others had received. Most doors were open and music coming out of them clashed. Not just because it was Christmas but because it was custom, strangers waved to her when she walked past. Looking down the steep, she saw a girl fly around a larger trailer east of her eyeshot, around peach and fig trees towered like rooks around two plots. The girl rode a pink bike with white-and-silver tassels, a red bow tied to its frame. A woman stood at the door of one of the larger homes, with her pink duster barely tied in place and somewhat open to her freckle-specked chest. She cradled a cup of something steamy and waved to the riding girl. She seemed to wave at Solemn. Solemn did a double take. Yes, she was waving.

"Come, come!" she said.

Just as Solemn was about to come on, Bev shouted to her, "Come help me set the table!" She was too far to hear, but she heard anyway. Like right there. So Solemn came back and did as her mother asked before she was asked, to please Bev immensely.

"Let's bring our plates in the living room," Redvine said. They never ate in the living room. They always ate their meals together at the family table.

"What about the furniture?" Bev wondered.

Redvine grabbed her shoulders. "It's all good," he said. The family shuffled around the kitchen to fix a heavy Christmas brunch on special plates. Redvine plopped a few splashes of rum into mugs of eggnog for his son and himself. Then, they ran to test out their work on a movie Redvine bought with the box: *It's a Wonderful Life*. Landon prepared to do the honors with the remote, but Redvine grabbed his hand to stop him.

"I got something to tell y'all," he said.

Now what? Solemn thought. Bev too. Landon was too tipsy to think.

"We been driving on past the new development out there on seventeen all this time and I ain't said nothing 'bout it yet," Redvine started, "but we gonna be moving."

Landon was halfway out the door as it was. Solemn was too tickled to move.

"When all this come about?" Bev said.

"Last week. I stopped by the lil' trailer office on the grounds to get the paperwork to get it all started . . . I'm fixing to put a bid on real soon."

"Red, them houses cost a lost of money. How—?" Bev didn't want to laugh at him.

"Look, don't fret," Redvine said. "It's not as much as you think. It's many different sizes they building. I talked to the folks even, 'bout picking up a little bit of work. So long as I get a license, they tell me. We just gotta get a down payment. Okay?"

"Shole be nice to have my attic back. Oh Red, you stop now." Bev chuckled.

"Man Daddy it wouldn't even be our house that's all a facade modern day slavery the white man own the bank and gone raise the—"

"How big the house?" Solemn asked.

"Biggest kind they building," Redvine said.

"When can we go look at it?" Solemn asked.

"Let 'em get built first, Solemn, and then—" Bev told her.

"Soon," Redvine told them all.

Somehow, all four knew one was lying or fantasizing or dreaming or all three. But it was Christmas, and so they just laughed about the new goals and waved to some folks walking by. Bev was satisfied this Christmas morning, to have more than energized feet run out the house in response to a meal she cooked. They ate their meal in silence and let the pictures do the talking for them. The surprise alone, not to mention its revelation—a machine they could remotely stop and start and pause the pictures on, unlike how the television stopped and started and paused them—was enough for them to resolve the movie's title as correct, as their mandate and approach to the next year.

EIGHT

Stephanie Longwood was the only one within Singer's gates with a fruit tree. Three, actually. Wasn't nobody else going to pay extra for adjoining plots. But the Longwoods thought one peach and two fig trees were well worth it. Figs always came first, peaches later. If the subject of a house somewhere else came up, Stephanie put her foot down: "Hell no." She would miss her trees. Because of her husband, Theodis, Stephanie was one of few women she knew who could say she had looked down on the trees—not up to them. He was a security guard in Kosciusko, shifting around downtown depending. She surprised him sometimes, in bank buildings and such. Not too many black folks could say they pulled a full-amenity twelve-hundred-square manufactured home atop three plots of property—with fruit trees alongside to match. With money in the bank to boot. They were lucky.

Stephanie knew it wasn't no accident Gilroy Hassle dropped that baby down the well. She did remember, well, seeing the child a few times, on account of living closer to the Hassles farther down the steep. The baby hadn't looked all that healthy, like it should have nibbled the tit a little longer. Took all them and all that to figure out something was wrong with Gilroy? So, when police officers and reporters and property owners started to appear to ask her if she knew him and her and them and "it," she did not. Stephanie always spoke but knew how to hold her tongue.

Her birthplace was situated in Sunflower County, Indianola, where Mississippi greased up a death chamber. To make a better than good life, her maiden name people capitalized on purchase of multiple left-over stops from the Underground Railroad, sweeping out and up-keeping the once-secret "barn in the back" and "cabin 'long the creek" and even a "big ole church on a hill" with a bathroom trapdoor for tunnel to a conductor's safe house, chamber pot on top of the latch. Unlike most could not, her father's father learned not to pay no mind to the fret horses and cows and his own goose bumps when the captured slave souls awoke. Eventually came a small ranch with pasture to land the little planes he shared with a league, some being carryover from Tulsa's Black Wall Street who lived to tell. Stephanie's mother married into circumstances to self-employ as a driver of gift and food donations. She had even watched her mother give free pony rides to the most abject kids' birthday parties. And free horses to the parades. Soon as Stephanie came of age, one of her mother's friend's sons took her to the Ebony Club. They snuck in underage to drink, and he proposed. Uninterested in her gritty measure of prestige, they left Indianola when Theo's job asked. Stephanie returned for her dad's homegoing and very often to make sure her mama's help minded.

But Stephanie didn't bother to tell all that. Where she came from put her at risk to be overrun with favors, unpaid tabs, and unclaimed baggage. When it came time to divvy out a couple Cessnas her heart-attacked father left, she passed. She took his silk pajamas instead. Even the Cadillac and Harley were too telling. She traded them in for her Imperial and remainder checks. For even more affect, she sent her only child out to collect bottles and cans for full display in clear plastic bags outside the trailer. Her luck was never going to be a gossiper's mantelpiece. She made it easy on herself. That way, she could say no to any hint without backlash. Or she could say yes (like she would today), with the faith that one word would be appreciated like it was all she had.

Right after she met her mama looking for her, Stephanie started to always see that little girl—Solemn she now knew her name as. Matter fact, she had been seeing her all along. Matter more fact, the girl's daddy skipped out the Hassles' a few times. Then, the girl's mama helped that poor woman move out. Much more attention than anyone else paid the Hassles. The little girl pussyfooted around a lot, lugubrious, usually by herself. Sometimes with a cat behind. Stephanie could never really figure out where she had come from or where she was going. She just knew she belonged. They had few places where they could feel like they belonged totally. Solemn was included by default.

Stephanie set deviled eggs on the patio table. Bev Redvine was supposed to get there around four. Wound up being about five. So, the eggs were warmer than Stephanie would have wanted. But that was just her. Bev wore a nice teddy dress and some shining black flats with a curve. The girl was barefoot. They brought a mud cake (store-bought).

"So, Stephanie," Bev started, "thanks for having me by. I was getting worried when no one came by after my note, about what I was going to do."

Stephanie pulled out their chairs. She balanced her new Tupperware tumblers and a few linen napkins for them. She pulled her ribboned and straw sun hat down further.

"No problem at all," Stephanie said. They sat down with the sun behind the trailer. The Longwoods' awning had gotten rusted and ornery over the hand-dug patio. The well seemed just a sideways glance away, keeping them from enjoying things.

Bev elbowed the girl as unexpectedly as a booster shot. "Say hello, Solemn."

"Hi," Stephanie heard. She scooped some deviled eggs on napkins and waited.

"Well, Stephanie," Bev said, "I'm thinking 'bout going to Magnolia Bible College. It's gonna start soon this fall. And my oldest . . . well, his grades wasn't good for college."

"That's okay," Stephanie told her. "I think I've seen him with your daughter."

"He liked talking more than school and sports, running off Klan, so he thought . . ."

"I could've told him they're here to stay."

"He realized that wouldn't work when nobody gave a damn 'bout that baby throwed down this here well like that."

Bev pointed in the direction Stephanie never looked anymore.

"Such a shame it was," Stephanie said. *They couldn't have been related, then . . .*

"And he just had a son gonna need some taking care of," Bev went on. "And his daddy took care of him, so he should take care of his. He's off to the Army."

"Oh my."

They had bumbled back from the Gulf War by now, all around them, even now searching for a footing and reminding anyone who would listen that they were "Desert Storm"—looking for work, for homes, for new ears to put war stories into, for new women to love or the old ones they left behind. Supposedly they had a syndrome: depression, lethargy, listlessness, even rage. With no plans to upgrade to a bigger house anywhere and Landon not finding a full-time job at a store or the electronics plant, Bev put on a good barbecue for him—family mostly. He was set back home filling up on her suppers and Solemn's company before basic training started.

"Well, it is all over, isn't it?" Bev asked. Bev saw Stephanie's confidence and liked it, assumed it as her own, took its nice effect on her.

"It is all over," she repeated. "Good times just beginning. Cicadas on the way, next summer. Good luck."

"I suppose." Stephanie smiled.

She wondered how much the woman would offer to pay, or if she would even offer. Offer was payment enough. Although she planned to address her husband, in some way, on bleeding too much cash in Nashville. It started off as Percy Priest Lake catfishing trips, then derailed into feeding mechanical bulls and tan-going slots. The strait was far from dire. But still, Stephanie preferred surplus. The women skated around the subject of pay until the unspoken agreement became there would be none.

Summer was ending. The lightning bugs came and left earlier by this time. Solemn walked on away from the table without asking or telling. Stephanie saw Solemn spot a lightning bug to run after. It hadn't even lit up yet. Stephanie only saw what it was once Solemn caught it into her hands.

"No one home anymore around time Solemn get off of school," Bev continued. "And I might have to go to town with my husband some days to catch the right bus to the college. My husband sell stuff. He gotta drive our car into Kosciusko every day to see if the electronics plant need him. Gotta be there early. It's been going all right these past few years. Guess more people needing TVs and radios and stereos and DVDs these days. World's changing so fast . . ."

"Sure is," Stephanie said. "And yes, you wanna know if I could carry Solemn on to school when I go into town with my daughter and keep her after?"

"That would be so helpful," Bev said. "I would pay you."

Bev stared at Stephanie's deviled eggs for quite some time. She chose one to try. She popped it into her mouth for one whole bite and swallow. She squished her eyes together and grabbed another. They were impressive.

"Oh my goodness, these are so good. Taste different from ones I know."

"I put a little sugar and dill in mine," Stephanie said.

"Well, I'll have to try that for myself," Bev promised. She liked sitting next to the side of a trailer nearly half glass, a special door to special drapes to see how especially wide it was all inside. The new wood cabinets, not Formica or aluminum or tin even, in some she had heard. A few air conditioners. The sinks and faucets looked bright silver, not screeched and water-stained pink. The soft parquet floors had a grand design, like from a museum she had seen pictures of in school. She poured them some sassy water. Her fingers tipped a fair amount of lemon and lime bits and mint in both their glasses.

"It's no problem for me to take Solemn along, Mrs. Redvine," Stephanie told her. "I'm going that way anyway. I just don't know exactly where y'all are around here. Sometimes, you know, the mornings can be a bit rushed, and my daughter don't want to go, and I'm trying to wash the breakfast dishes and it gets kinda busy, so . . ."

"Oh no, no, no," Bev said. "Call me Bev. And Solemn'd walk on over here, every day. Or me or her daddy drop her off. Solemn know her way around here better than I do. I'd be sure she got on out in time."

"Oh, okay. Uh, where is she, by the way?" And that would pretty much be the story with the girl from the time the arrangement started until it ended.

Dear, dear Solemn, Solemn . . . It was a child and name and name and child the mama would never in her whole life be able to forget.

As eager as she was for her first day of classes at Magnolia Bible College, a real student she was now, Bev just dropped Solemn off at the Longwoods' door. She only had to knock once. Stephanie was waiting, minutes early, tapping fingerprints in a tin of rosebud salve. Prompt and dressed. So was Stephanie's daughter, ready, with just one of the many new stiff dresses she had for the year. Solemn had grown a bit, but the school clothes from last year still fit her, so she could wait until she grew out of her closet.

"This is Solemn, Desiree."

The smaller girl seemed gobbled up by what looked like twice as much space—and almost was—as her own home. Stephanie's knack for scrutizining and mastering light colors worked out this way. The girl sat cross-legged on a wraparound leather couch with her dress open and the thicker crotch of her white cotton tights in plain view. *Hmph.* Solemn could never sit like that, legs all opened. Especially not for company. But she didn't know what to call herself here with these people. She wasn't company. She heard she would be shuffled to them every day. No one even came to their home every day but Akila maybe. Now, and with her belly growing.

"Hello," the girl said.

"Hi," Solemn said back.

"You the one gonna be staying with us?"

"She's not staying with us," Stephanie said. "And sit properly, would you please?"

Desiree giggled, but she didn't change. Solemn didn't know why she was dropped off so early. It was only seven thirty. The ride to the school for eight thirty was only about twenty minutes at most.

"She's riding to school with you. From now on."

"I seen you before," Desiree said.

Solemn couldn't recall her. But Desiree was a bit younger. The older kids didn't look down much.

"You got B lunch," Desiree said, correctly. She had seen Solemn before.

"You *have* B lunch," Stephanie corrected. "You hear me? Desiree? Desiree?"

The girl continued to stare at Solemn, entranced. Solemn sat on the couch right beside her, with her legs crossed Indian-style, too. Only there was a quarter-size hole in the tights. Between her thighs. Desiree paid this no mind. Solemn smelled toast, and the Nutella she saw Stephanie wipe across it. Then she smelled a banana, cut wide open, a swoosh of sweet green vines with them now. And the caramel goddess woman was before her and the girl with two light-green saucers and full, very full, glasses of juice.

Over at Stephanie's house, where Solemn could sing. Or sang. Loud as she wanted to. She could even jump around and dance. Stephanie never yelled. Solemn had swing in her hips and Desiree had born rhythm in her arms. When they were famous, they would call themselves "Desi's Child." At her home, Desiree had control of the remote. Solemn had control of Desiree. If it wasn't Beyoncé it was Mary J. Blige and Angie Stone. Michael Jackson and 'N Sync. Nelly and Juvenile. One night, Solemn got to stay over and up to watch the late movie. It was *Boyz n the Hood*. Solemn didn't have to turn her head when the boys got the holes blowed through them in the alleys, or when the boys and girls did nasty stuff in the beds. Desiree, just nine, did not know it was nasty stuff yet. Solemn let Desiree in on the secret of Nashville, where the singers were. Along with the well, it was a new shared destination for them both.

And we can make a routine to show everybody and maybe take it around town . . .

When Landon disappeared for the Army, right after there were big explosions in America where she lived (so Solemn heard Oprah and others on the television say), in the place called New York, where Dick Clark did the American Bandstand on New Year's Eve every year, while her parents drank frosted Corona beers with limes put in, as she watched her favorite stars sing in a place called Times Square, until a big ball dropped for a whole new year to change all the numbers. The explosions there sent women crying on television with firemen and policemen cradling the whole tragedy, and the white man President Bush on television having the gall to interrupt Oprah's show.

But Landon had already promised to be gone to fight, to be a black man with a legal gun and show to the whole world black men were brave—maybe in a place called "Afghanistan." Solemn tried to pronounce it still. She heard talk about it. The Redvines were not sure. They just knew he was gone, it wasn't good, life was fraught, it was war. In their America. They prayed for them in the trailer every night. They all emptied out from Landon's unavailability with only the assurance he might send letters to fill them.

Solemn watched her parents sulk, worry, fret, wonder, and frantically archive his belongings in storage compartments under the camper. Landon was eldest, the firstborn, the cement to them, the inconvenience who had prevented a turn-back. The Redvines' readjustment included more attention to the child who was not there than the one who was. Solemn hung the five-by-seven uniform photograph of her brother on the door of her closet.

Bev had something else to talk about and it impressed the church. Her first class was Religious Fundamentals.

"But hell, I already know the Bible so good the professor like me," she told Redvine and Solemn. She wrote it in her notes to Landon: "I'm a real good student . . ."

Solemn thought it was funny to see her mother with homework. Still, it was better than hearing Bev tell her to do her own. She and Bev did it together. Redvine sometimes offered to cook, so Bev could look in her books stationed at the kitchen table from now on. On some secret times, she rode down the Oprah Winfrey Road in town with a white woman named Ruby—"for my head of hair Ma named me." Ruby loved to have chocolate classmates around now to talk about how much she was never a bigot and she always had black friends—even when her ma and pa said they'd whip her for it. Ruby had three grown children in college. Plus, in the summer, she went twenty hours on Illinois Central Amtrak to Chicago for *The Oprah Winfrey Show*.

"I told everybody in line, Bev, I was from here and they liked me so much," Ruby repeated to Bev every time she gave her a lift home if Redvine forgot to show. Bev wrote it off. She had a good husband. And Ruby loved to help. Ruby told Bev Chicago was very, very integrated with everybody running the same streets to no division. Bev wondered what it would be like to see Chicago. Maybe take Solemn along, for a treat.

The arrangements even provided a boost in the love lives, with Bev seeing Stephanie wouldn't complain if she was a bit late. If both the girls went on Stephanie's orders to scavenge for bottles and cans they came back with less than Desi would have on her own, but they stayed gone longer than she would have. The relief of their daughter having a partner in a lengthened venture gave the couple permission for foreplay.

"The door locked," Solemn would say.

"No, you just ain't doin' it right," Desi corrected.

"Okay, you do better," Solemn challenged. They wound up still outside and turning the key the Longwoods just kept in the car. The girls flopped about to the radio until Stephanie came out, fresh faced and claiming a nap. Solemn was quite eager for the job, since she kept most of the profits. According to herself, she was saving for a long trip out of town and would never come back. She was up to over $182 now, she could say.

"How nice." Stephanie smiled down at the eager, honey-colored gal. Then, she offered her chance to make more with more cans. Desiree came back one time hollering: a knot on her forehead and in her hands a tattered slingshot, a present from Solemn, she said. Stephanie made her bangs. Another time Desiree had a little tack stuck in her foot. She was inoculated, so it wasn't much but a pain. Solemn always had a good story for it.

Desiree was friendly, so Solemn took over her bike, standing up to push the pedals while Desiree rocked on the seat behind. They rode around the circle of Singer's until they returned hungry and sweating. They shot stones at cans perched on four-by-fours they stuck in the dirt. One girl had to always ask to stay or go home with the other. Long dinners and visits through weekend errands were the best the parents could do with the little girls who pulled at their skirts or pants waists to ask favors. Stephanie drove them all in her Imperial on a voyage to Dillard's in Jackson and then Boston Store in Biloxi. Less than a semester after Solemn first rode in the backseat of the van on to Bledsoe and Miller's middle school, where just twenty whites were actually the minority, so it was fun, Stephanie had had to start cooking enough for five plates; Solemn ate enough for two.

The girl had her advantages, but Stephanie soon tired of all the ongoing tall tales. And, she was kind enough to find and hide a note the principal sent home with Solemn about her behavior. To her, it was just like lying, so she said she wasn't doing it again.

"She told you *what?*" Stephanie said to the latest Solemn story: a giant man around Singer's was looking for babies to chew up and spit out. "Girl, quit lying . . ."

"She did!" Desiree insisted.

A stray mix galloped toward the door. Where there was laughter, there might be scraps. But there was never anything near that one's door. Stephanie never accumulated leftovers. Her strong point wasn't reminders. Who wanted to unthaw or retaste a meal an argument or bad news had hovered over? She never knew which one of those would come around again; she only made enough for three and for one day. Then, Solemn just happened to start riding with them to Miller's and coming along after school. Stephanie only started to make extra food for Solemn's lingering. She threw the rest out for scraps the mutts could tussle over. Had it not been for Solemn being part of the house now, the strays would have never come near. Just another consequence of the new child.

Stephanie piled a few aluminum pans atop her breasts and toppled reminders out of the pans one by one. The dog outside groveled and bayed at the spilled potatoes, stringy pot roast, greasy carrots, and cabbage. Stephanie winced at the wretched slopping.

"So, this man at the well walks around Singer's in the middle of the night, and sleeps in Redvine's trailer? That's what Miss Solemn told you?"

"Yes, ma'am." Desi smiled.

"And you saw him at the tent, and heard him in her trailer?"

"Uh-huh."

"And he looks like Solemn's daddy, who I hope you're calling Mr. Redvine?"

Desiree was not.

"Desi," Stephanie said, "I really don't think there's any men hiding in trailers or hanging round at night." She knew Gilroy's ass had thrown them off, all of them.

She went on: "Doesn't matter. You got no reason to go 'round there. Everybody gets our own water these days, from the faucet or the store. You see your daddy lugging the water coolers in this house every week. Appreciate it. It's about time folks got less dependent on that well, even though we got the best drinking water in Mississippi. Somebody need to cover it. Out of respect. But there's no one out there, sweetheart."

It's not what Solemn convinced Desiree inside the tent, before the very first time they hugged each other. Theo Longwood spent all night fashioning old lace window panels and the old sheets around his fishing nets. The mosquitoes gave up but the chiggers hung on. So the calamine lotion scuffed up their skin. Stephanie had already spread it down their arms and legs, but the girls wanted to do each other again on the feet, middle of the backs, and arms. The favor of the owls who paid them a visit was welcome. When the sun went down, the owls began to chatter and so did the girls.

"You have to go down in the well with me, if you wanna see him," Solemn told her.

They clenched a scratchy throw tucked up to their chins. They moved in close. Desiree's eyes widened into wonder and trust. For everything in the Longwoods' house was structured, ornate, comprehensible. Their telephone chirped with the volume low, the school clothes ironed in advance, her shoelaces replaced regularly. She did not grow into high waters. She accompanied her mother to the Salvation Army, to take a fast ticket to inventory all their donated clothes rather than a patient browse through the Goodwill aisles. And figs drained the stigma from their daily oatmeal. Their own peaches sweetened their ice cream. Pretending shook things up a bit.

Solemn dictated Desiree pretend to be Oprah Winfrey and she would be the star onstage, with the audience on their feet and maybe even fainting when they saw her.

"What he look like?" Desiree asked her guest, entered through the tent slit.

"Like a man," Solemn thought back. "Nothing different or bad. But tall. Really tall, and walking kind of crooked. But but he ain't got no face."

"No face? Then, Miss Solemn, tell me how come he don't look different?"

"'Cause he don't look like nothing," Solemn said. "We all look like something, but not him. Or he look like whatever you want him to. If you want him to look nice, he looks nice, but don't believe it. And you can't tell nobody about him. If you talk about him, he'll just follow you. He'll start asking you questions. Or telling you lies. 'Cause he said he ain't through. It's gonna be more of us. Could be me. It could even be you."

Desiree screamed. They jerked around to see if a door yanked open, the flimsy covers of their tent torn back, a roar to "get yas asses back in here right now!"

But there was no one. No one but the owls.

"I'ma take you there, one day, soon. Down far . . . And if we just keep on collecting the bottles and cans, doing what we can, working . . ."

"Hey, Oprah don't work," Desiree said. "So I'm not supposed to—"

"But you got money," Solemn said. "So, we make enough money one day soon to go on to the rest of the world to meet new people. And nobody gon' tell us what to do again. If you get on the shows or I get on the shows, we make sure to pick each other too."

So Desiree became the second, after the good brown cop; Solemn gave a peek. She would wait until maybe she got to the place called Chicago and talked to Oprah Winfrey, to tell it all there because everybody would listen and nobody would laugh.

Them girls started a game of tickling, mostly barely touching. Desiree remained an accomplice to Solemn's sanity, to dwarf her imaginings down to mere stories and twist bad memories into tolerance. Nothing more. Just stories and living dreams. Just to be able to tell somebody was a revelation, enough to ease the confusion and wonder. Solemn's visions became no more than fables to share word for word and bit by bit on an occasional morning she remembered them. The secrets became harmless. Even invited. Through a semblance of a yard accentuated by the few fruit trees Singer's Trailer Park could show off, on a fine dust grain dot of the Earth appearing to be the only world to them, with a sheet of haughty mist coordinating its fine shadows, and the graciousness of garter snakes held at bay, those two girls saw and imagined together.

NINE

Even the cicadas, brood buried for thirteen years, weren't so sneaky as the weather proved to be in 2002. Some didn't have televisions or good reception to watch the news. The radios went to music. The newspapers got pored over for the obituaries and coupons. If a telephone happened to be in reach, weather was never the message. They were used to heat. The rain was always welcome. The tornadoes happened to *"those"* people, their curse for being able to stretch front and backyards across acres. The sewage water, from the slaughterhouses dumping the hog and cow shit, only ran up on the neighborhoods fortunate enough to stand tall near the rivers and ravines. God didn't bother blacks. White people did.

The Bledsoe Festival was nothing newsworthy or even well-known outside of where it took place. It was the brainchild of a few retired teachers and set councilmen who used it to pull Bledsoe folks into Kosciusko to vote. It was the demarcation between winter and not, in a place where there was rarely a chill or snowflake to remind them of earth's balancing acts. It was embedded in the people's circadian time lines and holiday schedules. Toddlers could sense its remembrances in adulthood. Some dying noted it as their last good time. Families buried the hatchets under its ground. Newbie reporters noted it, affectionately, as their first byline. Its talent show contestants hoped it would launch stardom. The day came and went, with indigestion and gossip come along. The hatchets always resurfaced the next mornings, sharpened. The makers were still met. The babies grew up and no longer spent the whole days there but saw it as their chance to run away while the parents were occupied. Its reporters promoted to the obituaries and honor-roll lists. Rumor had it one studious girl, Muscogee tribed, went on to *Time* or *Life*.

The Festival, Easter Holiday, and Tax Day fell almost two weeks to the days apart in 2002, in the new war, when they all waited with bated breath for a variety of cinematic definitions of it to appear in their lives and worlds and homes. *Platoon. Saving Private Ryan. The Deer Hunter. Red Dawn. Glory.* They discovered their war would be a duller testimony for them. Instead, their war only spiked up conversations from the elders voicing over their own Desert Storms and Vietnams and Koreas and Second World Wars, even a few holding on to mumble about the first one. Because of the unrest, Hall Carter used the coincidences to scare up more money. He appeared earlier on the courier bike he rode for Kosciusko businessmen—his briefcase stuffed with forms, stamps and pens strapped to a rear rack. He left many in Bledsoe hungering for refunds in the mail by Easter, on or before the very end of the month. What they might wear on Easter became the point of going to work, the balm on hands dried out from laundry, the motivation for the organist to try a different key with the same songs, the pedal behind the sopranos' stretch to one octave higher, the promise blown on hot classrooms in spring fever, the empathy to coach more fish out of water. This year, the talent-show prize was up to $250, more than most of them made for forty hours of work a week. And that was before taxes and rent and utility bills and baby formula and gas and daily bread money.

Bev invited Ruby.

"Oh, Bev, now Easter for the family," Ruby replied, like she spoke to a student.

Bev didn't push it. Sounded like the same response the so-called friend gave when invited for supper. The sting didn't last long. Bev had Stephanie now, an ally against whites. They had shit to do. So Bev started talking to Stephanie about their custom orders and dress efforts long before the Festival, just for them and separate from parades and street festivals in town. It wasn't that there was anything remarkably wrong, now, between whites and blacks. That part was better. No choice. It couldn't have gotten worse. There were just, still, different ways and tastes the blacks always had to put down until white folks got through acting up. If they kept it separate, this wasn't necessary.

Bev planned a partly chiffon red frock she saw in the *Jet* Photos of the Week on somebody, amending a similar one she spotted at Sears.

Stephanie ordered her yellow-and-blue-floral sundress way in advance from Marshall Field's in Chicago, out of the new spring catalog. It was hanging in her closet by March.

Solemn and Desi wanted to match. They chose cutoff jean shorts and hot-pink baby-doll shirts.

Redvine was out either trying to think of or looking for something to sell there.

Theo Longwood, banking on a fortune, planned to import pony rides off connections his wife's father left.

Landon wrote Easter would be his selected first break. He wouldn't kill anyone, he promised.

As Bev liked for it to all appear, they all were very "fine."

Desi now oddly complained of fevers, often. Solemn followed along. If Desiree was sick, she wanted to be sick too. Usually, the palm test conducted by the two mothers came up unconcerned if not conclusive. The girls gulped baby aspirins, castor oil the chaser. They sat still while their mothers rubbed their throats with goose grease and checked their temperatures with mercury thermometers, like the babies got.

"Told y'all not to be running around with no shoes on," Mrs. Redvine reminded them. She wiped the drizzle from Solemn's mouth, so less neat than the other girl.

"Right after wasting my good polish to paint your toes," Mrs. Longwood added, satisfied she had confiscated the pitchforks. She told her husband to say he needed them.

The girls' toenails were smudged and overlined with a usual ridge of soot.

The women always thought the girls either weren't listening or didn't know what they were talking about if they were. Truth was, the girls grew out of "One Two, Buckle My Shoe" and moved on to the pitchfork game. Stephanie couldn't understand it. Tonight, she couldn't get the girls presentable for the PG-13 movie she promised them for later. They just weren't interested. Bev called. Would be late to pick her daughter up from the free babysitting Stephanie provided. Again. It seemed she was making new friends now, at the Bible college. Fine. But . . .

The girls spread their Hula-Hooping and flopping around to include all their trailer park's acres. Stephanie didn't like them running too far off to that other section and part, where some of the mobile home owners just never emerged or, when they did, it looked like they shouldn't have. The girls often chose the far-off, misty shroud of weeping willows fringed by witch hazel and spurwort. Beyond a few peeks inside, the woods held too many bugs and thickets and unexpected pitfalls to dig a trailer into, or to even bother with going for the petunias and pink ladies clustered inside. Though the area was virtual steel wool on acres, some fed-up undesirables cut through from time to time. If and when they crawled out, they could always find three squares somewhere. But as narrow as both girls were—not yet filled out, getting to it—they could boogie slowly into the nooks and crannies. It was a form of being lost, and missing, with only so much space to be found.

To count up high and start walking in different directions without looking back, until one of them shouted about it, was Solemn's idea the moment she set eyes on the pitchforks. Stephanie's father had once used them to mince hay for his horses. Solemn took to them, three—one for her, one for Desiree, and one to dare any man to come after them with. Now, Stephanie didn't so much mind the pitchforks' reincarnation. Had she not expected it, she would have kept them in her mother's care in Indianola. But the pitchforks had more use than the designer cuff links she went ahead to give to her father's greedy brothers. They were much sharper. When summer waned and it darkened earlier, Solemn's push for Desiree to investi-gate the spookiness of the woods, with only the tips of pitchforks to help them find each other again, just didn't seem safe. Not at all. But they always marched back: pitchforks in one hand, the other fixing their hair or holding their sandals. Hungry, leaving the pitch-forks crossed in the yellow grass to pressure Stephanie's beds of struggling dogwood and evening primrose.

Since a little blue was turning into nothing but black within the hour, not to mention they had missed time to get pretty for the movie, Stephanie took the flashlight. This was something she ex-pected her husband should have done. But he was not at home. Again. Along with Bev's delays to pick up her child, her husband delayed coming home to his own. Folks had noticed this: "big old trees, nice Imperial, daughter dressed to the nines, but that man . . . hmmm . . ." The last thing Stephanie needed people talking about now was her girl coming from the woods none of them bothered with, looking like she had been raised by wolves. Enough was enough.

Stephanie was a pragmatist. Never had her imagination coiled into intimidation: silly faces hidden in dried bushes or the nagging bite of thin branches. Now, she was unclear. That cobblestone well simply bothered her. She hated it. The number of accidents floating inside of it just did not seem to be a coincidence. Nobody drank its water anymore. When burnt apartment buildings in the cities showed up on the news, it was only a matter of time before they were torn down, to keep anyone else from dying just by looking at them. Steph-anie thought it should be so for the well. Desensitized, she crept on past it the way a grown woman should. Finally, she heard the girls' laughter and called their names. They did not call back.

For a while now, this had gone on. Shady disappearances Steph-anie chalked up to the defiance collectivity encouraged. It was part reason she preferred an only child. It seemed she had two now. Out the kindness of her heart she had agreed to babysit the girl, for no pay. Yes, she knew this was her say. Now it was turning into a chore.

She hadn't even bothered to change her white capris and sandals into something more suited to hunting through thickets. She was dusty and soot footed suddenly, a running theme in her daughter since this Solemn had shown up. Along with the extra food gone. She crossed a thin line of clay to another portion of the woods where it seemed she had heard them. Despite the Diet Coke and Dexatrim, her bosom and behind were just too meaty now to make it through like the girls obviously had been able to. She gave thanks for trees grown sideways to step over them, rather than try to work herself in between, her ear out for hornet's nests and nose out for skunks. But behind a shifty fence of Solomon's plume, Stephanie saw the girls. She stopped breathing for a moment.

For atop a significant dirt mound with pitchforks laid down at its bottom, Solemn and Desiree sat with their arms around each other and their tongues in their mouths. And they pressed their chests into each other's with their hands on each other's behinds. Stephanie blinked, but she saw what she saw. She would have yelled out to them so loud they went deaf, but just her mouth open startled a coven of bats into screaming forth, straight to her. Even so, the girls did not mind the bats. They kept on.

Solemn and Desiree appeared at the trailer after dark and sandals in their hands. Bev and Stephanie weren't talking to each other like they normally did. Bev tried, but finally gave good parting. Stephanie just didn't know what to say to anyone. She left it to Bev to collect Solemn, and she prepared a quiz-slash-speech for her daughter Desiree. She never gave it. Instead, she lay on her convertible couch-bed inside her double-wide trailer, without her man home on time and with her satellite TV turned to the higher channels: committed to showing Mississippians the running, guns, burning lands, and foreign tongues narrating in places not America. And all night, with the cognac set down on the carpet at the edge of the couch, this was so much easier to think about than the alternatives . . .

. . . *And the alternative keep me up at night thinkin 'bout my friend and what on earth she doin 'cross the way without me. So I got somethin more than a chore, better than a good grade. I got my own curtain yank it shut to cancel out the world's surprises: rememberin, liars, baby harmers, sad women, and crazy men. It ain't just Desiree give me the feelins, but pink too: Desi's favorite. For now, so long as feelins keep the world lookin correct and my nights full of longer sleep and Desiree fillin the days, I can pretend I don't want for nothing . . .*

Next time she and Bev hung out, Stephanie was unsure what to say about the alternative so she came up with something else, or something else came up with her.

"He's cheating on me, the son of a bitch." The breeze blew some napkins away, but Stephanie didn't boss herself to keep it neat. Bev was trustworthy, less a talker and more a listener. She didn't know what to say about Stephanie's ideas on her marriage, how to get in the middle of it, plus stay out of it. She liked both the Longwoods, all of them really. But it was Stephanie she owed. Affairs were certainly possible, sure. It took commitment to mundanity more than a marriage to just never think about it. There could be joy there . . .

Solemn and Desiree rushed outside. They played "One, Two, Buckle My Shoe" in circles, hands held and jumps in unison and in sight.

"Mind's playing tricks on you," Bev told Stephanie, not as attentive as normal and without a bra under her day-old T-shirt. Last thing she expected was for somebody like a Stephanie to be wading in alcohol over a man.

"Money's missing, gone three nights last month to Jackson. Oh, I know . . ."

The treat this afternoon was pralines, peaches, ice cream, bourboned coffee.

"See," Stephanie went on, "I just never been the type to snoop. But I know."

A disadvantage of Singer's was its intimacy guaranteed all would know why your bed was loud or your kitchen table was silent. Folks had to travel to do a lot of fussing or a little dirt. More than a couple of times were some yards embroidered with scenes of a busted romance and carrying on, to draw snickers and views from indeterminable points; everybody at Singer's saw it, yet nobody was around. Quarrelers could never live it down. Stephanie wouldn't do it that way. She had a different take.

"Well, what would you do? You out here somewhere, class or

church, trying to pull your weight and do your part. he's carrying himself off yonder for some tail?"

Bev thought. "Just concentrate on the Festival," she said.

"At end of the day all I got is my daughter. I'm not thinking about anybody else."

"And I got mine," Bev said, thinking back to ones in wells and sheds and the TV news and *Unsolved Mysteries*. "We lucky."

"I'm a good woman," Stephanie said. "You too. So, really, what would you do if you were in my position? Your man got another woman in the car and bed and whatnot, and you ain't none the wiser? Or they think you aren't. Honestly, that's the killing part. I'm not dumb. What would you do?"

Bev but could come up with no answer better than, "I'd kill him."

Solemn came from behind for another praline, prepared to beg if she had to. The eavesdropping made her think: *man supposed to oochie coochie with the girl everybody knew they got and see him with all the time that's it . . . if not, hell.*

"If I wasn't raised so right I'd get him on one of those talk shows and make him take a lie detector test," Stephanie continued.

"Aw, that's embarrassing . . . You'll never live it down," Bev offered.

"What we need is Oprah," Stephanie said. "We need Oprah to just come on down and let us vent on her stage, what we put up with every day. We need to come together . . ."

"How 'bout we start with the book club idea you talk about first? That'd be the easiest wish. Might be nice for everybody to do the book club, like we said."

"It's not about everybody. It's about me. I could've gone to college, been a professional, made something of myself. To give it up for a man, just to realize your trust in him weighs more when you're half full . . ." Stephanie hiccupped.

"I never realized you wasn't happy, Stephanie," Bev said. "That makes me unhappy. 'Cause I gotta say, you one lady I really thought was really happy."

"Well, you be happy for me and for yourself then . . . Earl adores you," Stephanie said. "Y'all good eggs."

"Thank you. Likewise."

"None of us, none of us, gave two cents 'bout them crazy-ass Hassles. Never even went over there. I don't know. They just acted weird. But you and your husband . . . Y'all be blessed. Nice of y'all to at least go over there so much, help her move."

"Redvine ain't help none to move her," Bev said. "He had to take some work on that day. Shole coulda used him though. Good God, that woman had so much stuff . . ."

"Well, he had to do what he had to do. He was good to them before then—"

"Redvine ain't even know the Hassles. Never met 'em at all."

Stephanie looked. She thought about it.

Nobody knows how to love anybody anymore, she better left unsaid. One tear.

TEN

They met in spring at a secret rally in a ghosted, sand-floored, hijacked barn. He had sat near her, pretending to explain everything and everyone being discussed: Mumia, Assata, Diallo, many many more than two Kings and one X. Roaring about the big-city troubles lifted them above Mississippi and their lives. She was drawn to well enough about him, felt in her mouth the smell of his breath at her earlobe. They stayed behind drinking cans of no-name beer, and she had never had a drink before. Once everybody else went off to bed or the same, the two of them tumbled into groping each other amidst the bottle caps, cigarette butts, and protest notes. They did it atop a bale of hay raked to the back of the barn, a remnant of the fled sweet potato farm's past vitality. They slept there. A rotted rafter gave in. It clashed down before the sun came up, and they were both embarrassed to wake up that way. Then, he walked her four miles home to Bledsoe proper in the morning and apparently doubled back to his own home on the outskirts.

Since the Redvines were stuck in a trailer park with no phone, Akila had to wait for days to know if Landon would call her. Even when he did, her mama was stingy with his message. When he called back, her mama warned her not to tie up the phone. Their touch-and-go continued with rushed sightings and fooling around in an eccentric variety of locations. Finally, she learned where he lived, planted herself there in innocent dates in his kitchen and living room; Mrs. Redvine seemed to enjoy their dates more than Akila or Landon did. And his little sister was chatty with her, eager and clingy, as if she were a long-lost relative and not a stranger. Then Akila discovered all the antics before got her pregnant. She was recommended to wait for Landon if he had to go off to work, for all his effort to do better so he could do right by them all. He ran off to the Army, his "movement" friends who had no jobs doing the same. It was outrageous.

To prime her own self for her own long haul, Mrs. Redvine gave rosy lectures to the girl Landon made a mother before a wife, unlike she had taught him. She wanted Akila near. Akila held the baby who was Landon and therefore she was Landon, too. The canning and pickling and preserving was just the excuse used to get Akila there.

When the baby came, Akila included Mrs. Redvine generously in the resulting child's life. She preferred Mrs. Redvine actually. Her own mama was too contorted into outrage with her, in premonition her grandson would wind up just as fatherless as her own children had. But Mrs. Redvine would have never had that. With her own young daughter so strange and Landon so far, Mrs. Redvine poured her vessels of knowledge and expertise upon her grandson's mama and maybe daughter-in-law: how to avoid lumpy gravy, how to dart thread through a needle's eye without spit, how to reverse a scorched pot or pan, how to hotwire a car, how to recognize the situation where this was necessary, how to pin clothes on the line without wrinkles, how to respect the black man with no carrying on necessary. And, according to Mrs. Redvine, Akila was more than welcome to join the new book club, soon as she and Stephanie got time to get it started.

"With all that mess over here, over there, everywhere, we have to be light and fluffy for our men, not so muscular and knowing," Mrs. Redvine counseled.

This encouragement worked. It sent Akila to work at Home-Away-from-Home Motel, right on the Trace headed out of town: fluffing towels, cleaning toilets, scrubbing cracked bathtubs, making firm and skinny beds, leaving flat shreds of soap for the next guests, greeting the few tenants who enjoyed a tab instead of a lease.

And just a few months after Landon sent his first letter to describe his uniform, Akila and her mama crowded around the television to hear the president tell them the United States was in a war. She was sick for the rest of the week: couldn't draw milk or even eat anything herself. "War" meant there would be dusty yellow explosions at the roads, men with black boots and huge guns outside the stores, screaming people fighting at the Greyhound station, chaos and fear, bottleneck traffic, pickup truck and motorcycle gridlocks on Natchez Trace Parkway, an exploding volcano on top of a lottery-filled tunnel in the unreachable distance, white people at the door to say her baby's father was dead. But nothing changed.

"You fine?" Akila asked Landon, when he suddenly appeared in the spring, peeking behind her and into the house where his son cried, wearing his uniform and a smile. He was still tall. Nothing at all about him was blasted off—no holes in his face, or tears in his legs, or torn arms, or gouges in his torso. If anything, he looked entirely better than he had when he left Mississippi. He looked slimmer, rested, no longer so angry about something, less confused and more patriotic.

It was an illusion they made love past.

On Good Friday, Akila finished her shift. She walked past Louise, the white narcoleptic front desk attendant who always told the night manager how tardy Akila Montgomery was. Every single day. She got warned but not fired. Akila heard Louise snoring and then she glanced through the open guest registry to spot a blank space at 28. She fingered the master key in her apron pocket and latched the cubicle door shut just as Louise fluttered awake, mumbling something about spilling Melissa tea and pulling up the nightshades. Akila puttered to the side of the motel to stand under the building's side light and in its glow, where Landon would find her. He pulled in shortly with the aid of her mama's peachy Mustang. Akila walked to the car. They hugged. She was hungry for more than the silent emotions Landon's short and tardy letters conjured. Once alone with him, she settled their baby on the side of the bed lest he wake up.

Landon Junior would just have to cry it out. She pulled Landon and felt herself pushed toward the dresser top, where they stayed for two hours or more.

When Akila was spent and sleeping, the creaky ceiling fan above him cooled Landon's chest. The baby slept between him and Akila, his woman. Honky-tonk twitched from the clock radio in the room. There was a fly inside, near the barbecue he planned for them to spread out into breakfast. Then a flashlight was into the room, gliding across the opposite walls, robotic speech and beeps, from a walkie-talkie. Landon shot up and Akila, too. The baby remained still, ambivalent and at peace, sleeping alongside a man for the first time.

"Landon?"

Landon motioned for Akila to stay silent. Then, he turned so his body covered her and the baby. The light and voices strolled down the sidewalk encircling the motel. Landon rolled himself around and slid from under the covers onto the floor. He crawled to his bag rested on the chair in the room. He pulled out a Swiss Army knife. There must have been others beyond those with the lights. When someone pounded on the door, Landon nearly jumped straight off his feet. The pounding continued. Landon reached behind him and placed the blade in the back of his pants.

"Take the baby in the bathroom," he told Akila. She did.

The door had no peephole. Landon peeked behind the only curtain to see a police officer standing against a backdrop of a squad car in the parking lot. He saw the officer in front of his door motion to another to join him. Knowing law and its realities, Landon pulled the knife out of his pants. He felt the blade graze his back. But it was no longer concealed. It rested on the window's ledge in plain sight for all. The pounding got harder.

"I gotta put on some pants!" he shouted. "I hear you. Lemme put on some pants."

He tripped while he placed his legs in his pants. He had a United States Army uniform in credentials. He had an address in town, two parents in it. He was with a woman and child, both unharmed. He could, though he didn't, forget the address of the barn and church where he met men and they plotted to take down the blue suits. But he wasn't supposed to be in the room. He could pay. Akila could explain. She knew the manager's home number, accessed often when the baby was too colicky for her to come in or she had no ride. She could call him if there were questions. Sunglasses at night were never a good sign, and a white officer wore them. Landon cracked the door.

"Can I help you officers?" he asked.

One cop, black, stretched his neck to try to see inside. Landon widened the door only a bit more, so there would be no request.

"I'm Sergeant Nichols," said the white one, sunglassed. "You got ID?"

The flimsy construction meant the door rested open without Landon having to do much for it. He walked to the dresser and retrieved his shirt. His name, Private Redvine, was marked on the insignia near what was his breastbone when he was dressed. The police officers shifted slightly back and nodded their heads.

"We checking in about a woman who was in room eleven," the black cop explained. He seemed benign, familiar even.

"What happened?" Landon asked.

"Well, it could be a variety of things from what we found over there. We still have to investigate the whole place and situation."

"I didn't do it," Landon said.

"We hope if you had, you would have left by now," Sergeant Nichols said.

"Maybe she just checked out," Landon offered.

"It's a little more than that," the unidentified officer explained. "She was supposed to have checked out. Guess that happens all the time here. But the front desk clerk checked the room tonight to remind her of the bill. It wasn't a good scene."

"When you arrive here, Private Redvine?" Nichols asked.

"Maybe about eight, nine o'clock?" Landon answered.

"Did you see anything looked strange, worth telling?" the black cop asked him.

"No I didn't, Officer . . . ?"

"Oh, forgive me. Bolden."

"Pleased to meet you Officer Bolden," Landon answered. "Have we met?"

Bolden peered at Landon as well. They saw so many faces in and out of their minds, all day long in that job. It was impossible to pinpoint anyone for sure. He could have been staring at a pickpocket picked out of a lineup or an FBI's Most Wanted List inductee and he would not have jumped to conclusions. The worst place he saw familiar faces—dead and alive—was in his dreams. It was why cops dropped like flies. Hanson had by now, unreplaced. Commissioner had a talk with Bolden about picking up the slack.

"Maybe you seen me 'round," Bolden said.

"Well, now that we're all properly acquainted, I can honestly say I'm just home from the service. I came straight into the room without looking around too much at all. I didn't see nothing."

"Well, according to the register, you didn't even see the front desk to pay," Nichols informed him. "Your name or occupancy is not listed."

Landon bristled.

"How you get a key to get in the room, my man?" Bolden asked.

"Must be some kind of misunderstanding," Landon told them. "I can't be responsible for how the employees do their jobs. Obviously, I didn't break in here."

"No, you didn't," Sergeant Nichols said. "But, of course, as customary we need to know everybody on the grounds. So far, names match up to the rooms where everybody supposed to be and this one 'sposed to be empty. May we come in and look around?"

"There's nothing in here," Landon said. "And I haven't done anything."

"That's what we planning to confirm," Sergeant Nichols said, with his hand on the door to let Landon know he had no choice.

Akila's light-pink work dress spilled over the ledge of the bed's headboard. Her sandals pointed in opposite directions, one back and one front. Bolden slipped on the baby's bottle. Sergeant Nichols started for the closed bathroom door. Something about Landon's swiftness behind him caused Nichols to grab his arm. Akila had wrapped a towel around herself. She sat on the toilet with the baby cradled near her breasts. Akila stood up. There was no way to catch her towel and hold on to the baby, too. The men turned away while she covered herself, stretch marks leading to bright indigo nipples.

"Officers," Landon said. "We weren't even here that early or near this room. I'm here legitimately with my fiancée and my son and we're being disrespected."

"We mean no disrespect," Sergeant Nichols said. "We're just trying to get to the bottom of what happened in this other room."

"Shouldn't you be out in the backwood somewhere, looking for killers?"

"Prolly," Bolden remarked.

He was seasoned in the job, against his heart and will. He wondered if it was time for him to tend bar alongside his dream girl Tammy, who had him coming back to I'll Be Good for nearly a year now. She was a break in the headaches he got, like after the senior he found decomposing facedown in her greenhouse or the few farm-accidental limbs mauled to stumps turned lifelong conversation pieces. And the woman missing from room eleven made him think of his new girlfriend: dark skinned, bartending, wild haired, narrow hipped, an exuberant face, an eager smile. And now he had privilege of making accusations in a young couple's chosen den of iniquity, possibly interrupting their pleasure and shaming the woman in the process. One of his friends from high school—who got expelled—had found good money in running bulls crazy so he could catch the sperm and sell it to farmers near and far, to keep the cattle giving. Almost as much for one splash as Bolden made in two or three days. But, how many times could . . . ?

"Thank you for your time," he told Landon.

"You're welcome," Landon said. His son began to stir awake. "We'll be sure to visit the front desk and straighten out this mistake come early in the morning. For now, we just want to get back to sleep."

"Understood," Bolden said. Landon's looked like a face he could trust.

The next morning, Akila was too petrified to go to the office and try to return the master key without Louise or her boss noticing. Landon had no appetite, not even for the delights between her legs. They showered only out of good manners, to leave quick. Akila could explain the missing key as a mind harried by motherhood, the back-bone currency she learned she could pay off her humanity with. In the shower she most surely had been the last to clean, Akila determined: the keeper of this place would have to copy a new master key, she wasn't coming back, and Landon would have to marry her to make up for all this drama put on her. Given the controversy, they went through no great pains to obscure themselves on the way out. They had no comment on a strap of yellow tape around the corner of the motel where a woman guest had once been. Many people would hear her name again the next week, when the story was printed. And now was not the time for Akila to displease Landon, as she saw any words about the controversy would. "Baby, this shit ain't none of our damned business," he told her.

And so she did the best she knew how to do for who and where she was at the time. She heard, but she didn't listen. Nonetheless, she obeyed.

ELEVEN

Her maiden name was Weathers and that's how she signed everything now. She was the daughter of a Jackson banker and homemaker who did not see her for several months before the last time. They made reports. Several. Pearletta Weathers once bounced around adjoining counties with other college dropouts. The marijuana use marched to acid and mushrooms before it landed on the heroin they had no prior context for. Before Gilroy, she favored white boys. So she flip-flopped. She idolized rock music to draw even more of the white. She met them in their parts of the world. Her dressed-up and impressive parents traveled to the junctions, visited local motels, tore up the seedy parties in the park where those types collected. They paid off the outstanding tuition. The only benefit they could see in Gilroy Hassle, untalkative but mannerable, was that they could keep a tab on Pearletta then. Maybe. Since she had never brought the baby to visit—and it was so far from Jackson and the trailer couldn't really keep nobody for too long without an outworn welcome—to them the biggest disadvantage of the death was Pearletta again unleashed. Most recently, they waited on her call for two months. Pearletta had checked into Home-Away-from-Home last week.

"I'm sorry."

Akila entered room eleven under assumption of no guest. No one was paid to be on the register. She did not have to use the master key. The door was unlocked. Pearletta didn't understand Akila's nice, albeit surprised, greeting. No connection whatsoever to the "Hey, how you?" and "'Member me?" and "Mrs. Hassle, right?"

"No bother," Pearletta said. "I need new shampoo and towels." Then she wrapped the cream motel cover around her. She smiled. Akila pushed the cart inside. She headed for the garbage can under the dresser. She avoided taking inventory of its contents. She dumped whatever was up there into the trash can she rolled with the cart.

"You been working here long?" Pearletta asked. Akila pulled back the blue curtain shielding a shelf stacked with linen.

"No," Akila answered, even more puzzled by the calm and cognitive dissonance.

"You like it?" Pearletta asked her.

Akila had never had time to even worry about all that. She and the baby needed money, and one of her aunts knew somebody who knew somebody who knew somebody who knew the manager. She drove over to the motel she'd driven by, talked to him, and started to work. In general, despite the budget pricing and the element one star could attract, the guests were okay and even funny sometimes. As if just by having to reside in such a place, for a night or a while, gave them the need to at least dignify how they left a room behind. Most attempted a taut bed, flushed toilets, trash out in one section of the room, nothing too terrible about them left behind for another to confront.

"Yes," she said.

"Sit down," Pearletta told Akila.

"I have a lot to do," Akila told Pearletta.

Akila remembered a few fellas come out of the room in the last week with a complaint from a nearby lodger about old helter-skelter disco music rattling walls.

"I would love a job," Pearletta continued.

A few cardboard fast-food trays, napkins, and socks littered the bed. Akila brushed off the corner of the tousled linens to sit.

"Why don't you get one?" Akila asked her. Pearletta rested her hands atop the covers. Akila winced at her forearms—crisscrossed with hysterical marks a child could have easily drawn in pencil as a prank. Beads of dried brown blood, scabs like stitches.

"If I did get one, I'd want to cook, like Julia Child." Pearletta laughed.

Akila was shaken just from the first time someone passed her a joint. She never cared for it.

"You wanna hear about a fucked-up person?" Pearletta asked.

"I guess so."

"I like white boys, sorry to tell you. Tried 'em all, I'm 'shamed to say. I like how they smell, like sawdust or new dolls. White boys love them some stuff. Can't get enough of it. They been coming 'round 'cause they know I got money my daddy wired, and the stuff the money Daddy wires can buy. White people never miss an opportunity."

"No, they don't," Akila agreed.

"You gotta man?" Pearletta asked her.

"Huh?'

"Tell me."

"Well, yeah." She said nothing of her son. She didn't see it as good reason to make Pearletta recall. "You met him one time. He helped you . . ."

"Nobody never helped me. Where your man, honey?"

"In the Army."

"Oh, you got you a fine man . . . soldier boy! Well, ain't we lucky?"

"He came home last night for Easter. I'm supposed to see him later."

"Easter's here," Pearletta told Akila. "I used to skip church every Saturday."

"Saturday?"

"We Seventh-Day Adventists."

"We?"

"My family," the woman said. "You believe I grew up in one of those crazy church houses? We had to go to church on Saturdays, 'cause that's really the seventh day. And on Friday nights, we couldn't watch TV or go to movies or read the paper or anything. It was the Sabbath. We were supposed to pray, but went to bed early."

"That's odd."

"No, it was fun. Even now, I fall asleep early on Fridays. Pump me up to party on the weekends."

"That's one way to look at it."

"Go to the dresser. I gotta picture over there."

The top of the dresser shed more light than her trailer had. Pearletta loved nylons. A few pair were balled up and worn already. Another pair in a package. Pearletta hadn't seemed the type before to love makeup: willowy brushes, turquoise and emerald eye shadows with flecks of glitter, tubes of lip gloss. Disco looks. Two plumed perfume bottles announced themselves in a heady scent beyond them. A makeup mirror sat with a razor set upon it and a fine powder Akila guessed was not for any baby's bottom. A picture was right next to it. In it, Pearletta flashed a big Afro waved down with a texturizer. She was reinvented, now. A redhead white loomed behind. A look so serious on his face it was silly. He had on a Tupac T-shirt. His forearm gripped Pearletta's neck. There was a joint in his mouth, a chimney; smoke billowed all over his image.

"Is he . . . your boyfriend?" Akila asked.

"Oh no." The woman grinned. "I'm just having me some fun. I'm waiting on him."

"Well, I won't be long."

"No. Stay. I sent him off for it," Pearletta said.

"For . . . what?"

"Our stuff," Pearletta said, just like she was talking about number one on the Top 40, but Akila had yet to hear it. "He's worse than me. Come 'round to see about me where I used to live. Trailer park out yonder. His family own the whole thing. My husband used to pay them for our plot there. Long time ago, that was. We been friends ever since."

"You both look like two very intelligent people," Akila said. "I'm sure if you-all stopped some things you could start a family. Make a good life."

Pearletta rose up in the bed.

"Family? Family? That ain't shit," she said. "Oh, I'm smart all right. I almost got a business degree. Went to school in Huntsville. Oakwood Academy. Religious school for black kids. Hah!" Pearletta stared at the ceiling as she reminisced.

"And today, you know, it's Good Friday. I do still pay attention. But anyway. So I skipped church one day, trying to remember my way to the theater. It was farther than I had thought. Well, I come to one of the only stoplights in this goddamned town. This car waiting to turn left. But the guy driving saw me. And there were other cars behind him, so he kept on going, straining to look at me. He almost hit the car in front of him. I get to the end of the block, by this fabric store I used to go to with my mama for things she likes to do. And the car pulled up again next to me. Out the blue."

"Did you holler for police? Was he trying to kidnap you?"

"Oh honey, no. Over and over he kept on asking for my number."

"Seem like he was desperate." Akila chuckled.

"I thought the same," the woman said. "But still. He had these really gray eyes, five o'clock shadow, big cheeks, dreadlocks . . . all the way up to the roof of the car. He called me, over and over all day every day, until we were talking all night. Every night."

Akila would never have such a story to share about Landon. That era of her life—of giggles under the covers on the telephone with boys, or even sneaking out of dorm rooms to meet them—ended before it began. She found Pearletta's nostalgia remarkable and immature, so different from how she saw she had framed her. She enjoyed it.

"I was supposed to meet up with the guy," Pearletta kept on. "It was a few weeks. I didn't know what was going to happen. So, I showed up where he told me to meet him."

"Was he there?"

"Yes, he was there. But not like I had imagined him."

And Pearletta laughed until she cried, but she was still too high to move much.

"He didn't have no legs. Scared me half to death. I was walking over. He opened the car door and was just sitting there with his arms out, like a tree trunk."

"But-b-b," Akila stammered. "He was driving . . ."

"That's what I thought, too. They drive past you, look, stop. Honey, I wouldn't even come close to the car. It was too . . . weird. I had been imagining he was tall. But I saw two things in his lap looked like canes. I guess they're what he used to drive. You know they come up with everything these days. But this sucker started yelling some shit about Desert Storm. 'I'm a soldier, doll . . . I swear 'fore God, I'm a soldier!' Hmph."

"What you do? You keep on talking to him?"

"Hell no, I didn't keep on talking to him. I laughed at his ass. I laughed and laughed until I just couldn't no more. Next day my friend asked me to go to a party. So I did. And I met my husband. Thought I wouldn't never be scared of a man again."

"You still married?" Akila asked, recalling a little of it. Not much. Just enough.

"Sometimes I wonder what might've happened if I hadn't laughed at him. If I gave him a chance. Like now, I think about it all the time. If he wasn't such a bad guy. If, due to his disability and all, he would have been good to me. Better than the rest."

"Don't matter sometimes. A dog is a dog, hind legs or not," Akila said.

"Well," Pearletta said, "he could've told me. You know?"

"I know," Akila said, wondering of the time.

"Like it was this other man in a car one night, with his little girl. Out at the trailer park I used to live in. We liked each other, for a little while. They call him Red. Hah!"

Akila missed it, but it would catch her later.

"Now, he told me he had a woman," Pearletta continued. "Almost twenty years married. He told me. He did. Daughter and son too. He gave me money. Sometimes."

It caught Akila and let her loose. Then, caught again. Finally, it slipped away . . .

"Honesty the best policy," was all Akila said, rising from the bed to go now.

"Do me a favor."

"What?"

"Don't tell nobody you saw me here, okay?"

Soon as Akila said, "I won't," Pearletta snuggled under the covers and closed her eyes, hummed to herself. Akila felt like she was getting away with something, goofing off with a guest. She wondered if Pearletta would have liked to sit up with her and Bev, talking and cooking and watching Oprah Winfrey and pinning clothes and playing with the baby. Akila saw the television was on *All My Children*. That poor woman must have forgotten she turned it on this Good Friday. Akila watched the television for a few moments. She rested. She had wanted to remind Pearletta, there was always home, somewhere she could go. But the guest had already drifted off into a sleep. Akila grabbed a generous handful of soap and shampoo to place on top of the even more generous pile of towels she left. Then, she turned off the television and lights and locked the motel room door. She had just met Pearletta Hassle, and the Redvines, for the first time, it seemed to her.

TWELVE

I t was a rare occasion Bev practiced her actually pretty nice voice. This was it.

The friendly families reclined off excess of barbecued corn on the cob and fried chicken, two sweet potato pies Solemn and Desi consumed most of, and just enough watermelon so to wet their tongues without having to run to the few outhouses too often. Solemn and Desi wolfed down several ears of corn. Then, they ran off to find some of their more interesting classmates from school. To practice their routine. The rest thought Akila took the moment to run off to find the other girls she hadn't seen in all the time she was in the house taking care of a baby alone. Truth was, something was strange now in looking at Mr. Redvine, fogged up in riddles and crooked talk. Soon, Landon passed the newborn on to give speeches his work, for Uncle Sam had yet to interrupt.

"... I wouldn't lie. They want us to shut up ... make everybody think it's all right. They just put that death penalty back on to kill the black man legally ..."

"They're playing my jams, too, Bev," Stephanie said. Then, "Landon, I find what you're saying to be very interesting, and certainly true."

Landon confounded Redvine. Here he had a healthy son about to travel and get into shit he himself had never been able to, but still unsatisfied and hotheaded.

"The whole barracks filled up with white boys get a good job while we slop shit. We ask to know how the communications and mechanics and surveillance work and get told not to worry about it. But when it's time to figure out how to whip up some biscuits, we gotta be all ears. And the honkies sitting down eating and reading books . . ."

"Landon, you working now," Redvine reminded his son. "Got yourself a good, fine military position, boy. You gonna mess around and—"

"Yeah, but only 'cause a white boy started having seizures and had to go home. It was a handout spot, not a first-choice pick. Now I come back here and see they got a whole scrapyard and refinery tore down to give white folks new mansions. What about a college or a school in walking distance for the folks round who need it?"

"What about you change this child's diaper?" Bev asked.

"Mama, you ain't never listened to nothing I'm telling you about all this."

Landon grabbed the baby. Redvine leaned back in a webbed lawn chair, satisfied. The infant was not used to his daddy's arms, and the daddy was only used to letters about the baby or rare photos of him. The diaper change did not go well.

Bev shooed him. "So you wanna shoot guns but can't change a diaper? I tell you, men are something else . . ."

"Man ain't supposed to change no diapers anyway," Redvine said.

"Aw, now here you go . . . out here in front of people trying to front. You know you did this with your own and you do it with this one here."

"Not s'posed to."

"Would you like a cookie, or how 'bout a night with me at the Ritz-Carlton?"

"Cookie taste better."

A gang of unsavory characters strolled along past their posts, dense with the budget whores and well-fed pimps everyone recognized. Behind them were strung-out salesmen who, in the high-eighties temperature, wore shark suits with wing-collared jackets fanned out into racks of gold chains and bell-bottoms, weighted down with other stolen tokens. One of Landon's coconspirators showed up where Landon had said to meet him, with an armload of picketing signs and a handful of flyers.

"You ready man? 'Bout as many people here as ever," the spectacled boy said, too tense and stern to be so young. Landon nodded. The young man gave the greeting he was trained to give: "Howdy, good peoples. Sir. Ma'ams . . ."

They all responded, but Bev had a thought. Solemn and Desi were nowhere in sight.

"I should go look for the girls," Bev said. "Plus, it's gonna be time for him to eat soon and I ain't got nothing for him. Gotta find Akila, too."

"Girls all right, Mama," Landon said, poring over the flyers his friend had prepared. "Sit down and enjoy yourself for a change."

"And just what you fellas planning on doing with those?" Redvine asked. He motioned his son's friend to put a flyer in his hand.

"Elevate and enlighten the people, sir," the friend answered.

"Hmmm . . . I see: '*death penalty and the black man, incarceration and the black man, front lines and the black man . . . Rodney King and the black man . . .*'"

"Ain't nobody gonna be interested in all that today, hate to tell you boys." Bev sighed.

Stephanie tried to change the subject: "You know what Beverly, we should create us some flyers to pass out for our new book club . . ."

"What book club?" Redvine asked.

Bev creased a shawl to create a nest for the child, smiled at him. She turned his head to the side to put a bottle of water in it. She told them all she would be back.

"I'll go with you," Stephanie concurred. "Not used to all this sitting. They're probably at the pony rides. Theo's been talking about those ponies all damned year."

"How far is it?" Bev capped her eyes from the horizon with the straight line of her free hand. Her modest engagement stone glistened with a sunbeam's strike.

"Not far. 'Cross the field," Stephanie remembered. "Near the bingo tent."

Bolden's uncles invited him out here. Some missed him. Most just had to check to see if he didn't think he was too good to come. But, with the address on Pearletta Hassle's DMV report turned up to a well-off Jackson, Mississippi, avenue and her mother's call passed on to him, she was in his hands whether he liked it or not. He drove past the gate of Singer's and cursed its recent dystopia. Everything black folks have gotta get messed up? He was one of the ones who dreamed of that baby. At the park, supposedly involved in talk and cards with family, he couldn't help himself: when young women walked past he looked; when couples strode by he inspected; when he saw familiars he asked. And the young mother whose nipples he saw just the night before looked carefree today. So rather than remind her he let her be. Same went for those Redvines, good people, he thought. And it wasn't nothing too much. Folks should understand a woman been through all that needing to self-medicate, hide from whispers, start all over, find herself again. But while he entertained the distant cousins who always wanted to know where his gun was, Earl Redvine came up behind him.

"Where's your uniform, sir?" Redvine said.

"Should be a church suit. Sun won't allow it."

"We all need to relieve stress."

"Gotta thank y'all for what you did for the Hassle gal," Bolden said.

Redvine's face stretched. "I . . . I beg your pardon?" he asked Bolden.

"Helping Pearletta Hassle move," Bolden said. "That was nice of y'all."

"Oh." Redvine came to. Then, "My wife and son did that. I had to work. I mean, I would have if I could have."

"We'd all like to do more than we could. You seen her around, lately?"

"No sir, I haven't," Redvine said. Then, he excused himself back to his family.

In Redvine, Bolden's bother by the Singer folks' indifference to Pearletta and her predicament crept up to him again. He seemed such the opposite of his wife, Bev: caring and concerned and proactive. Bolden couldn't judge. What he wouldn't give to have his daughter and her mother under one roof with him. It was the right way, he had finally determined. Chances are he wouldn't care too much about nobody else, either, if he was a family man like Redvine, lives and interests to shelter, mouths to feed, fantasies to tame.

The wives walked along a makeshift path intended for sales but mostly replete with women who chased kids and boys who chased girls. Scant customers counted out change and wrinkled bills in back of the tables. It was a shame to approach tables without intent to buy. The blacksmiths and librarians and homemade ware makers depended on the shame, beckoning anybody over who lay a foot in front of their tables. Up ahead, a bright constellation of helium-filled balloons flew stark against the horizon. Pink, yellow, turquoise, red, blue, and white. A crowd of kids gathered in front of the table, for ice cream filled to the tops of pointy paper cups. A jolly voice drew them close: "Ice cream and balloons, one dollar . . . Ice cream and balloons, just a dollar. Enough for us all."

"The girls might like a balloon," Bev said.

"And I'd like the ice cream," Stephanie answered. "My treat?"

"Oh no . . ."

"You can pay me back if I lose my mind at bingo," Stephanie told her.

She fished in a leather coin purse for change. Bev untangled a few balloons from the knot of yarned strings. Stephanie got their ice cream. Bev held a red and a white balloon, with mind that the girls could carry them once they were found so they would not be too far out of sight again. Already above them, legions of balloons drifted and strutted around in the sky—a consequence of lost marbles the string tied around. Ahead, they saw the part of the clearing where Theo showcased two dark-maroon ponies and one ivory one. The plaid-shirted cowboys who brought them collected ten dollars a ride from kids and grown folks alike. Stephanie saw her husband and quickened her pace.

On the way up to him, she explained her replenished mood to Bev: "False alarm." She laughed. So did Bev. "I told you, girl," she said—glad it was all all right indeed.

Theo showed a group of parents just how to hoist the kids up on firm, slippery saddles. The proud parents laughed while their kids waited in line. Some had the newer digital cameras ready, waiting for just the right time. The kids shook at the knees. Two stout cowboys counted cash, happy to be in one of the more popular parts of the Festival. Another demonstrated how tight he could draw his spurs. He teased a few teenagers with his Winchester rifle. After a while all three business partners would dismount the kids and ride themselves in the parade, pied pipers: one man at the front alongside the American flag, another man in the middle, and the last man at the back to wave at the crowd lined up in a dusty field like they owned every single road they would travel back home on.

"I was hoping y'all might come along," Theo told his wife. "I'm smelling nothing but food 'round here, but I ain't got none in my belly. 'Bout another hour why don't y'all bring me some back?"

"Not sure, Theo," Stephanie told him. "We gonna be busy winning bingo games."

He rolled his eyes. "Now, there you go . . . gambling all my money away."

"It's about time I got a turn."

"No gamble this year," Bev told him. "Festival raised money beforehand. They got tired of folks complaining about pay to play."

"Shouldn't have to pay to play," Theo said. "Only to win."

A younger woman handed out sparklers to her young brood. She couldn't light them fast enough. "Hurry on up y'all," she cautioned. "We getting out of here and going on home right after y'all get ya rides. I ain't goin' home soaking wet."

The downcast danced around. There had never been a thought, reason, or idea to plan for rain. With it, nobody knew what to do.

"S'posed to rain?" Stephanie asked the woman, but the flustering kids tugged at her to rush matches to the tips of their sparklers. She didn't answer Stephanie.

Theo hurried the children off after just ten minutes and not twenty for more profit, with thanks to fond friends of his deceased father-in-law. He owed nothing for the stock rentals. The young ponies were to be sold and institutionalized into family pets, as it were, not for sport riding or prize showing. Just status. The early conditioning to children's tinier hands and gentler commands was good for the cowboys as well. The new customers wriggled atop the ponies with legs spread and bladders running full. The adults were the worst. They pulled at the reins for balance as the cowboys had instructed them to. The youngest pony parted and the children sat cross-legged at side of him to watch the outcome. It was almost four. Parade started at five.

Bev surveyed the crowd for their wayward daughters. She spotted their matching jeans near the bingo tent, in a cluster of girls waiting for a chance to turn or jump double Dutch. She tapped Stephanie on the shoulder and pointed in their daughters' direction.

Solemn and Desiree held hands and skipped to the back of the crowd as one of their mamas drew near. The balloons behind Mrs. Redvine jerked back. The double Dutchers paid her no mind, especially since a tiff broke out when one of the turners leaned a little bit too far to the left. So, a grass patch interfered, to trip one of the jumpers. Wasn't fair. Solemn and Desiree chose their balloons. Bev quickly snatched the balloons from their fingers. She had something else in mind.

"I didn't buy these for y'all to play with," she revealed. "I'm tying 'em 'round your wrists to keep up with you."

Bev removed the marble at the end of the yarn and made their security bracelet.

"Don't get lost," Bev told them. "Matter of fact, go back to where we were."

Solemn groaned. "Don't sass me, gal," Bev said.

Eventually, new pep in her step, Stephanie jogged in their direction. She patted down Desi's hair, frizzy at the ends now. She turned her nose up: she might have a tomboy on her hands. Wondered what a little brother or sister might look like. Kissed her daughter.

"Go on back now," Stephanie told Desi.

Solemn had better things in mind: "We can get in the parade if we try."

She saw the stage: lights and sound system. She flicked her red balloon up while Desiree looked up at her white one. Neither of the girls had ever been in the parade. They were too young to follow the crowd and directions in prior years. But, just like on *Soul Train* or *Showtime at the Apollo,* she would be seen. Two hundred and fifty dollars was at stake; so she heard.

"You have to sign up for that at school. The teachers told us, Solemn," Desiree insisted. It hadn't really been her dream to begin with.

"No, anybody can do it . . . all we gotta do is walk over there to see."

It had gotten tiresome, these opinionated battles with Solemn, the ever know-it-all, the show-off, conjuring much but showing little. Still, the Man at the Well had not appeared. Neither had their "sexy" boyfriends or magic carpets. Even the kisses were the same. Their rides home from school had become characterized by Mrs. Longwood's unanswered questions to the girl of: "What happened *today*?" Many incidents sent Solemn into the car cross-armed after yet another teacher's stern look or coarse words. The bad attitude Solemn often displayed was just as funky as the newborn odor under her arms. Infatuation with her friend had waned, replaced by a given code-pendency and familiarity no more exciting than breakfast.

And Desiree never perceived the things Solemn tried to get her to. The chicken wire rolled and ready to keep snakes from the root-vegetable plots was only that—chicken wire. Not the remains of the monstrously giant spider after God tore it out of the sky and balled up his web, as Solemn told her. The thick garden hose coiled in and around itself on a hook at the side of somebody's trailer home was just an innocent tube, not a bodiless visitor with its shredded, sagging face. The only outcome that ever came out of all Solemn's nonsense was a nightmare. Now, as they debated the reflex of obedience, there was another: time wasted.

"I don't think they're gonna let us in the parade," Desiree told Solemn. "And I think we should go back to where my daddy is or your daddy is or either go to the bingo tent. I'm tired." She started in that direction, just four footsteps to cement her point.

Solemn glared at her, unaccustomed to this odd disagreement Desiree displayed.

"I'm just trying to have some fun."

The only answer was the flap of Desiree's thin leather sandals.

I stopped. I heard the plop of geese-web feet hittin water. And my feet felt heavy, like a crop duster want to take me but I can't go. I wanted to tell my friend to wait, keep up, stay with me, forget it, move on. For once I could agree. Well, lately I ain't have no choice. Our nights touchin went strange and interrupted and old news, too. And she left me, paid no mind to if I was behind. So I fumed behind, in a hurry, and silent, and slow. And Desiree blurred in the crowd, threaten to be lost from me. And this knockin at inside of my chest and my temples got tight, but it was too late to act like I never met her. I had already told her everythin and showed her a lot. So all I could do was think to make sure Desiree met the Man at the Well, soon as we was allowed together again.

THIRTEEN

A church ran the bingo games under a tent it normally reserved for the revival. It asked for five-dollar donations at the door, to be handed to the laundry hamper reserved for the baptism towels. A typed note affixed to the hamper announced anything in it was for the Building Fund, going on for about as long as the church was built. Stephanie walked past it. Bev dropped in ten dollars for both of them. Women dressed in white, down to gloves and orthopedic shoes, handed out the cards and called the numbers. Only two cards allowed for any one person. No limit to the games. Some had been there all day and won nothing. Some stayed half an hour to leave with a forty-dollar prize and the way home, lest they lose it. Mostly women, mostly senior, and mostly grinning over friendly competition rarely encountered between them. The humble stones their husbands had given them shone under the church spotlights as they tinkered with the red tokens to pat down onto their cards. A few impatients who really needed money pushed glasses up and down their noses. A bullhorn shouted above the winding-down performers and all the radios outside.

Bev and Stephanie settled next to women who greeted, "Howdy." They placed red dots into free center spaces and waited for the calls. One renegade at the table played with beer bottle caps. She was drunk;

judging from the sweaty forty ounce of Coors in front of her, she didn't know it yet. A few of Landon's flyers, crumpled into impromptu napkins after cursory glances, sat in middle of the table amidst tossed bottle caps. They warned them all of forced unemployment, poverty, and welfare monitoring—too much to make sense of on what was meant to be an easier day.

Letters and numbers droned on and on, while the women stared at pots of gold on paper. It was all in fun, but they wanted to win. They exchanged shoulder hunches and frowns as the game went on. A woman shouted, "Bingo!" The few ladies around her had to settle the table and jiggle her card so the dots would fall back into place. An officiant made her way to the back of the room to check the card. The proclaimed winner's card was quickly certified as valid. She jigged up and headed to collect her prize.

"The Lord giveth and the Lord taketh away," one officiant said from her microphone, while she adjusted her wig. "Remember your tithes, good people."

"Tithe to your own church, nobody else's," Stephanie mumbled.

"Better yet, your own house," Bev told her.

Stephanie pointed as a few of their playmates heard her: "Even better."

"Folks always tryin' to get in ya pockets these days," said a player across from them. "Lord, I done spent so much money out here today . . ."

"You, too?" said another. "'Bout time to get some of it back."

A sudden drone of thunder came down, unwelcome. The bingo tent seemed the best place for them to be. Not many thought too much of it. The bleaker packed their blankets and reasoned they could settle into their cars and trucks nearby until any rain passed. The main stage had an awning to protect the sound system, wires, cords, and lights. The vendors prayed the weather would cooperate just a little longer for them to get more comfortably past profit. The children planning for their part in a parade started to look worried of their chances, if not teary eyed in prediction. And the sought-after cowboys reasoned it might be time to set the ponies back into the hauls.

Bev and Stephanie had just gotten to the tent, hadn't played one full game, wouldn't get out again possibly for far too long.

"Walked all this way here," Stephanie said. "Gotta play one more game."

"At least one," Bev said.

The bullhorn called out, "I twenty-two," to distract the players from the weather, maybe draw a few more folks concerned about hairdos and outfits into the tent with their dollars dropped down for the shelter. By the time the call was finished, it was fifteen minutes later. One brazen grandmama came up to the front with her card in hand and her victory walk. They all heard another crackle of thunder, followed by footsteps of more thunder pounding down. The winner was paid as the caller began a new game. By then there was a sprinkle. It started an exodus both out of and into the tent. Stephanie and Bev had only to look for red and white balloons.

"Red and white ones," Bev reminded Stephanie.

A prickle of lighting in the distance ended the tumbling team's show onstage and the vendors' hope. Bev and Stephanie passed Mr. Longwood. He had already turned down the last few customers and started to shake hands with his business partners for the day. The ponies stomped and spit inside the hauls behind the cowboys' pickup trucks. They swung tails and snorted out a prediction they had tried to offer in impatience with the last hour of riders. Solemn and Desi were nowhere in sight when the first raindrops glided down, softly as cats' tongues, tender and dry.

Stephanie shouted to her husband: "I'm gonna go find Desi! . . ."

Bev caught the full fabric of red dress up at her hips or else it would have tripped her down to the soon mud. She then caught her flip-flops at the edge of a pile of manure for trying to keep up with Stephanie. The blankets once served as resting spots now played as covers. Cars began to rush out into makeshift lanes. The tables once filled with things to sell now weighted down with boxes of items hastily thrown in.

Without seeing the balloons, there was no way for the women to get a real handle on where their daughters were. So many children still had them. Bev came up upon sight of a red one waving in the sky, just inside the thickness of a group of girls showing off the latest gyrations. The mothers stopped running. They pushed many girls aside. But they only met a toddler with a balloon in one hand. A leash in the other. At the end of the leash, a greyhound with a red bandana tied around his throat and his right hind leg missing. The girl spun in a circle and forced the dog dizzy until they both toppled down.

"I think they went back to where we were," Bev reasoned.

"I think you're right," Stephanie agreed.

Then another string of lightning, more running from the people who didn't want to be caught up in it, and more thickness in the crowd. The numbers who seemed dwindled when sitting or dancing now seemed unbearable when all standing. A man with his pants unzipped flung out of a rattled outhouse. Any reprieve kids gathered from the adults' good moods was gone. They were pulled by one arm and slapped 'cross back of their heads and shoved into compliance to hold the loads of things families either had to walk away with or share rides to get home. Little babies cried and toddlers whined. Teenagers got in their last laughs. The last few acts who waited to perform stomped away. The backs of swerving pickups slumped down with riders shouting out their telephone numbers, addresses, or plans to meet up again. The wind blew blankets, paper plates and cups, paper signs, plastic bags, gentlemen's hats down, ladies' skirts up.

No problems or fights erupted, only the undercurrent of sadness that the day had been cut short. The rushed exits mocked the deranged mayhem in the skies. In a cluster of swamp maples at the head of it all, many boughs dueled at once. Their leaves followed in waltz. Crows soared along for refuge should the clouds break. Or maybe they were bats. A network of pigeons outflew the falcons behind. Kids pointed to the sky and so did adults. They waited with bated breath for a storm to remember to happen, to become something they would grumble about. Most of them were already planning to reminisce on just how much their hairstyles and outfits and perfect dates got ruined.

With heads twisted to and fro and their daughters' names yelled by voices that would soon grow hoarse, Beverly Redvine and Stephanie Longwood skipped along.

And there was no noteworthy thunderstorm, that day . . . but that night, much later it waited for, to appear and magnify into tiny cuplets of rain in the newly budding leaves and early quench for set garden plots. First time that happened, ever, the day of a Festival. Easter Sunday, too? But that day, that time, that moment, when two mothers ran and one girl followed the other one who led, there was an incident the newspaper reporter was long gone to report first-hand, and only a scattered few would recount being close enough to, so as to gain the glorified retelling of it for the rest of their lives. All the few told the story the same, wispier than a news story but more concrete than a rumor . . .

That sad incident of one girl in her little jeans, running in the direction of the part of the clearing where she knew she had come from, another little girl behind . . . And both of them with their hands out straight but balloons hanging from 'em. On Easter. After church. When folks normally would have been eating supper and going to the nursing homes to show face to the ones who, even if they don't show it, know who they are. And nothing was wrong. No, nothing. We all was running. Nobody was fallen, stomped, or crushed. No, just peace. Order. But they shouldn't been out there by themselves. Somebody older shoulda had 'em. Now nobody ever out there on malice, everybody good. And it was Easter Sunday. No blues on the radio. But still, you gotta wonder . . . Anyway. That little girl in her little jeans marched, surely and okay, big pretty eyes up to the sky for a few seconds she did stop and look up like it was a message in the clouds just for her. Just her. And the girl in behind this one, same little short blue jeans, matching, trying to keep up, arms crossed, just a few steps behind, but thank God not right alongside or holding hands or nothing would have connected the two. Only difference between the two is one had wild hair flying all around and the other one had French braids damn near stitched to her scalp. Other than that, they could have been sisters. And we was all running. Coulda been any one of us, praise Jesus. The one in the back was taller and seemed a little older for some reason. So I think that's the one everybody was looking at the whole time this thing happened. Or maybe it was the pigeons in the sky, all wild and fanned out, outrunning them falcons furious they couldn't catch 'em. We was all looking at something, every one of us, even her. 'Cause then this little girl in front of another one was jerked up like a jack-in-the-box with the lid tapped. Then she flopped to the ground with her arms and legs long and stiff. And we kept on running. Nobody stopped for a while. And that balloon was low, just sitting there first, then batting at the wind. But it could only go so far, 'cause the girl who had it tied to her wrist wasn't getting up. And some of us saw it. Some of us thought we did. I don't know what she saw 'fore she fell. Never saw anything like it in my life.

A bolt of lightning put Desiree Longwood down on the spot.

There was no one in the field but her and Desiree, now. All were gone, spinning in a fast wave of pictures around Solemn's head. Like the DVD player put on fast forward. Solemn fell with Desiree's hand around hers, to a sprained ankle in her left foot. It would turn into a permanent ache, but no real pain behind it until it was all over. A local bishop's truck passed. The bishop looked just in time to see balloons come at his windshield and girls under it on the ground. Then, startled passengers inside saw the folks running up behind to tend to the girl. The sprinkles stopped. Unsure of whether to run past or run near, a few men who did not comprehend recalled lightning never struck the same place twice. One of those retrieved the girl in his arms. A cripple threw himself to the dirt and offered his chair to wheel the girl. But the holder was strong. With the attention on the girl, the cripple and his chair remained there until he started to holler about it. Solemn thumped behind to pat her friend back awake. She led the crowd in back of the man who carried her friend to a patch where the parade was supposed to pass. There, two parents thought the girl could be revived with their expensive medical cards. They were calm. It was Solemn's family who were frenzied. The Festival parade became Missy and Nelly music on the tail of the Longwoods' Imperial as it raced to Montfort Jones.

Landon and Akila went on their own, with his friends, and the baby. Justin Bolden took license to speed past all others in the Buick, unsure of what had gone on and ready to investigate whatever it was. Solemn scrambled into the Malibu's backseat, turning from side to side to glance at all the cars piled near on top of one another, honking horns, flashing lights. It was better than the parade. The folks who didn't even know what was going on acted like they did. After six miles, the EMTs ran to meet the trail of black people at the emergency room entrance: "What happened?" The bishop answered, "Lightning." A few minutes after the match-scented child flew back through winged doors on a rolling bed, the only black nurse working Easter at Montfort Jones came out to tell the crowd they had started to work. She identified the mama herself, as the woman fallen to the floor just as suddenly as her child had met the ground moments before.

That Monday, a nice photo of a few luckily chosen revelers graced the front of the news. They hid the beer bottles and cigarettes behind their backs. They clutched fingertips of their children and grabbed their lovers' shoulders. One couple even kissed for the camera. There was something said about a woman missing from a motel room, any leads welcome and appreciated. However, most discussed was the story of a little girl who was swooped from the obituaries by good doctors very few of them could afford.

Stephanie and Theodis Longwood always thought they should have more than one child. Most thought it was unnatural she didn't have a few more to show for it. They had been considering it, though doing so would most certainly mean they had to upgrade. But Stephanie was too vain. It took nine more months of near starvation to get her figure back. And since Desiree was such a greedy nurser, Stephanie's firm bosom fell into a flat canvas only custom-ordered underwires could raise. She was young enough to change her mind but old enough to know it was a risk. They could have a bigger family. Move from Singer's. Pay a mortgage or, God forbid, rent. Sometimes, Stephanie longed for a bayou view, maybe the jingle of a brook at night, the comfort of a grove in her backyard, a ceiling of Christmas senna to draw the butterflies, the strut of horses and cows across the meadows. Rather than a view from her window, which could look like the path through a dump on the wrong night with the right light.

There was comfort in the density of people around them at Singer's. Mothers stayed at home. There were rarely fights, which made the story Gilroy was in there beating Pearletta so harsh on most of their ears. Families paid for kids to go to religious school, and even the public schools would have been okay. But these kids *did* graduate, came back, and said "Hi" even, in starched military get-up or boxy suits with pumps. Some even stayed around and grabbed certificates from the community colleges. Once in a while, a heretic hobbled through with a song about Jesus. The quarters were crowded, but still felt distanced. No one felt it was too much of a bother when a muffler went out or a junk car sounded like a motorcyle. Nobody complained. If anything, somebody would recommend a shade tree mechanic who could use the work.

Then, kids dropped into wells. Change. A ho here and there staggered from a trailer in the morning. Change. Idiots got careless with the reefer, let it float on out the screens and entice the oblivious. Change. Squished-up generic beer cans peeked between patches of once-tended but now-tacky lawns. Change. Then, her own daughter talked of black boogiemen and left her black dolls gathering dust under the bed. Change . . .

She and her husband had decided to wait.

FOURTEEN

Bledsoe had changed. Just changed. They were bewitched. People half-expected furies to walk around and look for them, emboldened and enabled now. Between the sad demise of the Hassle baby, then Pearletta Hassle with her confusing departures, and now Desiree Longwood with her unexpected and inexplicable accident, the community was no longer so sequestered in a blank stare toward God.

At first, there was nothing on the news about the chaos. It was only chatter among them. *If you have any information leading to our finding of our Pearletta Hassle...* glared back from the windows and doors of the gas station, dollar store, diner, and hop bars. Where there had been none or few were now "stories"—things for the kids to grow up and retell, and memories for the adults who survived and escaped them. A cabin fever, a stirred crazy. The stories wore like days-old hospital robes, to humble and unite them all. And of course, there was heightened viciousness no one wanted to admit to. Menace came in between them, with an ensemble of altered lives to make it complete. Any child who acted up now had a capable threat: "You gon' get yo' little bad ass throwed in the well . . ." Any woman who didn't behave had an incentive: "You know what, bitch, you gonna wind up missing just like that bitch in that motel down the road." Any man who insisted on wandering got a second thought: "Motherfucka I hope the lightning strike you just like it did that little girl!" They made themselves part of the tragedies after the facts, just to feel pathologically unsettled with the rest.

One would think, over time, these things would go away and no one would remember them. But they would be wrong. Their version of activism—sharing the story and praying for its characters—compounded the apathy extended to the victims. Worse, the changes reeked of hillbilly status, though they'd come so far.

Once Landon said good-bye in those days after Easter, Solemn limped to the well and fell asleep against its cool stone side. Normally, she would have had her friend. Her ankle was sprained, but she never cried. No one noticed her new gait but the cat, who followed her and licked the spot she pressed often. She dreamed of scarred hands who plopped dollhouse babies in a cauldron along with chicken wings in crackling lard. She tried to form where drowned babies and burned little girls went, all on her watch—as if she was cursed. She wondered. She needed to know what she felt and imagined before others knew. She talked to the cat about it. The cat didn't answer. Her parents often mumbled in her direction for seconds. Then they were silent for minutes. They gave her Lipton's and chicken broth and cod-liver oil and oranges. She wasn't sick.

By middle of the week, Pearletta Hassle's mother shot onto their televisions.

Bev, glued to the thing, saw it first. Solemn next. Redvine didn't notice.

Soon they all came to recognize Viola Weathers by her rounded-up dreadlocks and the gigantic stone on her left ring finger—a dame who wore anger, off-red nail polish, houndstooth jackets, pearl earrings, starched collars, and a crucifix atop her broken heart. As soon as the trumpets blared to signal the newscasts, Viola Weathers stormed into view, whether folks liked it or not. She spoke in flaming tongue to rival the newscasters' belabored diction. She shut down reporters who offered condolences. If there was mention of her daughter's history as a runaway and druggie and negligent mother, she glared at the speaker, pushed him into a lingering stutter other would-be controversialists learned from. She dared the bastard who stole her child to come speak to her directly at the cemetery, should she have to bury her own child. She bookended many newscasts with a demand: "Where the hell is my child?"

For once, the Redvines had no wonder of where Solemn was because she was at home, pattering about from room to room and opening the cabinet doors to look but eventually select nothing. She hadn't taken off her new outfit yet, only changed her panties and shoes once. Akila came by soon after with the baby and rebraided her hair—pulled out dry grass and tiny twigs caught in the loops. She got to sleep late and avoid school. She had no ride, she somehow knew. She didn't have to say, *Hello, how you do?* or anything to her parents' friends. So many kept stopping for coffee and conversation. Prayer. Once, she went to make coffee when she saw two of her mama's friends from church step onto the front mat.

Inside the bottom of a pot missing its lid and boasting an age older than Solemn's, Solemn dropped four heaping tablespoons of instant coffee the way she had seen her mama do. She grabbed one of the four mismatched mugs they had room for, filled it with water, and trickled drops into the pot of coffee grounds until they were moist. The playful grounds softened, nervously and hesitant to dreg. Their soft, round forms relaxed, slipped down one by one into a muddy bottom until there was no separation. Just one thing, from many, like a graveyard with no headstones or bouquets to smooth it over. Solemn left it until Bev entered the kitchen for the same project. Solemn knew the adults were talking about her but not talking to her. She was used to this. After the people walked off from the yard, Solemn approached her parents with some things in mind.

"There something wrong?" She looked to her daddy, who seemed to have a secret ready in his pocket. Bev glanced at Redvine. He bent forward to switch off the television.

"You know how we always tell you to come in when thunder and lightning start, less it come down and get you?" Redvine asked.

"That's what happened to Desi?" Solemn asked.

"Yeah," Bev told her. "You really did a good thing letting everybody know."

Before they planned to carry Desiree back into Singer's with cold compresses and topical antibiotics and tiny tan tranquilizers, Stephanie told her husband to go to the Redvines' door and sugarcoat it under "tired" and "busy" and "time" and "soon." Were it not for Solemn, they knew, their daughter would have been with one of them that day. This would have never happened. Plus it got them getting talked about for neglect . . .

"It's nothing to worry about anymore," Redvine said. "Lightning is the Devil winking. Sometimes it's okay; the person just gets a little sick or faints or don't remember. Desiree was lucky."

"Can I go visit her?"

"Soon," Redvine said.

Solemn sat down on the table atop the pile of *Ebony* magazines her mama set there. An energy drained from inside of her, energy that had commanded her to move move move like the ladies on the television and fight to harness her tone deafness.

"Is it 'cause we skipped church on Easter?"

"Honey, that's ridiculous," Redvine said. Bev had thought about it.

"But," Bev said, "I'm gonna be here from now on with you. We gonna save us some money. I ain't takin' my classes no time soon. I'll be around."

Solemn trusted this.

Me and her was supposed to dance in the parade, twirl batons, and wave to our mamas. We was gonna peel boiled eggs and crunch salt after we left the Festival. We was gonna suck jellybeans to gum. Desi would have followed along, eventually. She was just fussy. And her monthly was totally brand-new. I just needed to think I took another nap. I later heard all these voices behind the thin accordion door to my room. A chorus almost, and somebody say somethin bout "Solemn's lil' friend." I never known that many people noticed or paid attention to details associated with me.

I stretched and got out my sleep. I drunk the orange juice somebody set on my windowsill. Then I came out. Daddy was gone. My mama's back was turned to the stove. The front room and kitchen looked like a carnival: Easter-color hats all over. Many ladies from Singer's, or church, or around—Alice

Taylor, Akila, Mrs. Longwood, the aunts and cousins who smiled around on the holidays. It was a feast laid out on the kitchen counters, table, and stove, from Easter and the Festival's leftovers. I tried to count this number of people twistin around in my home. I had never seen a crowd like it. It was like a payday party. The women turned back their paper plates, to fan themselves and one another while they talked and laughed. Even some of the ones they called "stankhoe" was there, the ones who hobbled in miniskirts that the married women squinched eyes on till they dropped off the horizon. One was pregnant, no weddin ring. The partyers inside peeked out our curtains a lot, fussin and lookin. But I was standin right there. Seem like it was a party, help me feel better. Then, somebody peeled back the screen door. They was all clappin. I felt pushed. I froze up. Cause I had never, ever seen a person from television. And it was the Viola Weathers, one started askin for Pearletta on the news.

"Clap!" they told me. And so I did. Even if it wasn't my party, after all.

Viola Weathers shook her head and smiled, put both her hands up to fan everybody back to they plates and seats. But they kept on clappin, even Mama and Mrs. Longwood tremblin on they tippy toes at sight of her.

"You're too kind, too kind, to let me stop by here on my tour," Mrs. Weathers told them all. This silver broach on her lapel struck back a ray of light cast by the sunshine in the back window of the trailer. "Oh please, sit, sit."

She fanned her hands at us. Finally, we all sat. Then Mama got up to give her a sampler plate from everything there. Mrs. Longwood brought her the hummingbird cake, perfect triangle on a circle dish. The ladies stuck their pinky fingers out while they nibbled on their crackers and desserts. Outside the television and right in front of us, the woman looked so much smaller and weaker and softer. She spoke in between chewin, whiskeyed sweet tea to wash it down. President Bush came on the television to address the nation. Mrs. Longwood turned the television off. Then, we all started to listen to Mrs. Weathers. We liked her face right here with us now.

"We must be grateful for everything we have," Mrs. Weathers told the intent women. "And, no matter how useless it might seem to challenge our challengers, stand up—always. Never, ever lie down. Always, no matter how tired or weak or sick you get, how pushed aside you are, stand up. You'll be happier that way. From any one situation you can look at it from too many sides and angles to ever be mad about one. Some folks good at spreading the frosting. Others need to lick the bowl clean. We all have a place."

She put her eyes on me without even movin em, seem like: "Come here, girl."

I moved through the big bottoms and flared skirts to stand before the woman. Mrs. Weathers grabbed my arms tight at the wrists. I kept contact with the lady's eyes, pink-rimmed and speckled with bronze spots at the corners like pennies in a well.

"Do you understand, and know who you are? What makes you special?" the Mrs. Weathers from the television asked me. Everybody else paused and waited for me. And I really tried to answer, but nothin came. Mrs. Weathers shook and shook on our weak kitchen chair. Then she pushed back to laugh at me and I just stood there. Mrs. Longwood just put her hands on her hips and tilted her head, to shake and shuffle her auburn hair more let loose than it was anyway. Mama looked happy next to her friend.

"You think it's some oasis somewhere waiting on you out there?"

I had heard of a oasis, but couldn't recall what it was. I was too shamed to ask.

"No ma'am," sounded safe.

"You don't know?" Mrs. Weathers teased. "Haven't figured it out? Y'all ain't tell the girl yet?"

"Tell me what?" I wanted to know. "What?"

And then Mama woke me up for supper.

FIFTEEN

hat the hell we need to make statements about?" Redvine
asked his wife.

"How should I know?" Bev told him. "Stephanie ain't talking yet. It was Theo came by . . . said there was mess said 'bout Desiree being underage and unattended to, that's all. Mississippi Children's Home Services gotta investigate, I guess."

"We under investigation too, then?"

"No, Red. Solemn ain't get hurt."

"What the State gonna do, take the rest of they kids? The poor folks ain't got none other. Shit happens."

"Well that's what we gotta let 'em know, Redvine . . ."

"I ain't cool with taking Solemn to deal with no police," Redvine said. "I'm all for respecting the law. But I gotta side with Landon on this one."

"We don't have a choice."

"Lemme least get a beer or two in me 'fore we talk about it any further. Shit . . ."

Two six-packs and one dawn and a quick car wash at a two-dollar do-it-yourself station later, the gas in the Malibu stretched to the police station. Back remained to be seen. Solemn still hadn't changed her clothes. To make matters worse, she started her period. Except for a few times Redvine fussed with the wannabe wrong crowd and jumped too bad with a white person for it, none of them had ever been in the station. Once the trio broke past the gristle of a half-dozen homeless staked out at side of the building in silent protest, the station was at least air-conditioned inside. Bev sat down in a chair alongside a wall. Solemn sat beside her. Redvine went to the front counter, spoke with a blond female officer. There was a vending machine. Vents rattled out cool air. Office doors opened to clean rooms. White tile floors shone. Redvine put one elbow against the counter and a hand in the pocket of a sports jacket he threw on over blue jeans. He chilled like he did when he made bets at the greyhound track he took the family to, on motel trips to Arkansas back in better days, serious and more distinguished with each wage.

"Where are the cells?" Solemn asked her mama.

"The what?"

"The cells . . . for all the people got to get put in jail?"

"Oh, they got 'em all right."

"This look way too nice to be a jail."

"This ain't the main one. This just the first stop. Nothing nice 'bout that last one at all . . ."

Redvine came over to his family.

"We gotta wait to talk to that cop, you know, the black fella. Make statements."

"How long we gotta sit in jail?" Solemn asked her daddy.

"Long enough."

"Can I get something from the vending machine?"

Redvine went into his pocket to pull out four dull quarters. Solemn stepped away from them, closer to the area of the station where a few interrogation rooms and the cubicles were. Her mouth watered: Doritos, Flamin' Hot Cheetos, Pepsi, Coke, Sprite. She had trouble figuring out what to do with her coins. Around the bend, near where the restrooms were, she sensed something to look at. She glanced back at Bev and Redvine, talking among themselves, the automatic habit of grown-ups. The bathrooms were within eyeshot. She could say she had gone there. Her mama knew she had her time now. The officers who had rumbled with laughter in the corner vanished to work now. The blond officer sat on the phone at the front counter. Solemn slipped away.

Down a hall, stock gray square desks with heavy telephones and many papers—so many papers in their belligerent and grumpy piles—were vacant of busy cops sitting at them. This was nothing like the police stations Solemn imagined and saw and fantasized about from scarce episodes of *Law & Order* or *21 Jump Street* she caught. The clocks seemed to be off, dusty and cross-eyed. A radio played honky-tonk, bluesy and throaty and raw. The facilities smelled clinical and clear, not nearly as beguiling as the hospital halls. Its blandness was inviting but disappointing. Solemn wavered a bit, but then she continued on. She was unnoticed, in her same clothes from Easter still—a new outfit nonetheless, so as better to discount any grime collected over the days. How no one could see a thick-haired black gal in days-old clothes wander through the main police precinct with her parents nowhere in sight confirmed the forced anonymity Solemn resented. She went on anyway. She happened upon a room where four persons sat slumped over in deep conversation behind a window.

And who and what she saw stirred the innermost arousal inside of her, pleasure so strong it grew into a light head and dizziness not even her recent event in question had overcome her with: inside the room, with an older man and two officers in a uniform, was the woman from the television . . . Viola Weathers. The "poor woman's" mother, no mirage. Solemn stopped dead.

She was much smaller and softer than she always appeared on the television. It *was* the woman from the television, alive and real. A celebrity—like Oprah or J. Lo. Had Solemn not been frozen into place she could have touched her with her own two hands and felt what it was like to have a real famous person at her fingertips, in all the imagined glory it was. Only now, the woman appeared just like her—decipherable and pat. She wore no makeup on her face.

"There must be something, something to do," she cried, naked of her chunky earrings and pearls. The white officer stood up, stepped back, lost his place.

And the brown officer Solemn recognized listened. The older man from the television as well sat stiff and somber. The brown officer met eyes with Solemn—stiffened at sight and sudden remembrance of her.

"I won't rest . . . I can't!" Viola Weathers shouted to them all.

The brown cop came to the woman from the television, told her to calm down.

"Now, Mrs. Weathers, we doing our best, but your daughter done this before and we gotta . . ." the white man tried to say.

Viola stopped him. "You will *not* slander my little girl. If she was a white gal with even more you could say, then the more'd be an unmentionable. Pearly's a good girl."

She was nowhere near calm but not close to hysterical. She had no cameras, and still she had a mission: a voice heard. Viola Weathers looked up at the side window in the room. She locked eyes with Solemn—

"Not too much different than my girl was at your age," she say to me . . . "Go back to your mama, child. Or wait! Help me."

I stood still right there and let the woman from the television look at me.

"How?" I asked her.

"Help me." The woman was smiling at me, grin drawn back to her ears.

"What should I do?" I really wanted to know.

"Whatever you can," she told me. "It'll come to you."

"Solemn!"

Mama was behind me.

Bev was gentle due to the situation, just trying to get in and out with no drama.

"Who you talking to down here all by yourself?" she asked. Solemn pointed to the window, wanted to say more to the woman from the television. But Viola Weathers snapped back away from her, into the men again. Bev glanced into the room, saw the private meeting. She grabbed Solemn's arm.

"But, but . . ." Solemn said.

"No buts . . . Now ain't the time for you to be actin' strange."

"But . . . it's the woman from television."

Beverly looked in. Shole was. Up until that point, Pearletta Hassle was only a thing to feel guilty about. Guilt was always mystery enough. But now the situation of her missing morphed into true fact. Bev didn't want to be nosy, but she couldn't help it.

"She's my child . . . you get to work!" the woman from the television howled.

And the white man nodded back to her, in order and in check. Respecting even. Viola Weathers was not the least bit daunted to stand strong in the face of a white while in the throes of some pain. He was intimidated by her. Solemn could tell. And Solemn had never seen a thing like it in her life. Now, she would do everything in her power, for the famous black lady from television and that poor woman down the way.

In a matter of minutes of more waiting, jail enough, Solemn saw the brown officer come out from behind the back and wave to them. She wanted to see the woman from the television again. Solemn was so giddy to think of it she tapped her hands at the chair's hard arms. But Viola Weathers did not appear behind him. The station had a back door.

Redvine arose to shake Bolden's hand: "Sir," her daddy called the brown officer.

When Bev arose and Solemn got ready to do so too, the men motioned them to sit down. Solemn had imagined she was here to solve something. How could she solve anything if she sat down? Her daddy and the cop went to the counter to chat, as perfunctory as bartender to alcoholic they seemed. They were the same complexion, same color, and nearly the same height except for the officer threw his shoulders back while Redvine's hung a bit. They met eye to eye, nose to nose, chuckle to chuckle.

Back in the car, the letdowns droned on when Earl turned off Nelly's song for the station of all his old songs Solemn was sick of. She hadn't even bought a thing to eat.

"Well, what we have to come all the way here for?" Bev asked Redvine.

"I handled it," Redvine said.

"I thought we was gonna get to talk?" Solemn asked. No one heard her.

"Well, bring Solemn all the way down here, in light of what's going on . . . we coulda stayed home." Bev was disappointed. Bad enough she had to leave her classes.

"I just explained the Longwoods were good peoples," Bolden said, and he turned up an old song he knew Bev liked a lot. "The man knew what I meant."

As quickly as it blossomed, the friendship with the Longwoods unraveled like knitting with its lead string tugged. Solemn's sheer fortune to have wobbled with the Longwood girl marked a mixed blessing; this type of fortune crossed the boundaries of decency to celebrate. In absence of congratulations for her luck and help, Solemn had the pall of a Barabbas. Nobody ever knew the Longwoods' daughter to run off before . . .

The Longwoods' fig and peach trees commenced blooming, shielding the family until Desiree came out—in a red sundress—straight to the Imperial. Solemn watched them all drive out the gate. The future she imagined—of growing up with a girl to be measured with, each new bit of breast or grown-out hairstyle, if their prom dresses would have matched, if they would have gone to the same schools, if they would have married brothers—sank. Desiree was supposed to stay part of Solemn's story, with no escape. Now one was phantom of accusation for the other. Solemn's association with the plagues of sorrow set down on Bledsoe clung to her name and back. She sensed them all talking about her. Like that poor woman, that poor baby. Now she was that "strange" gal.

Other than "Tell your mama I said 'Hi,'" the last time Solemn talked to Stephanie Longwood was almost the last day Stephanie Longwood talked to her daughter Desiree. And Bev, too. They switched from friends to second thoughts. Grudges are unbecoming. If the mothers had ever ventured to talk in depth again, both would agree they both agreed to the extra bingo game. To exonerate the survivor. To keep it civil. To be fair.

She wouldn't force her daughter. No. Solemn was getting to be *that age*—when the funny ways and moods and pimples showed up. Boys. For a girl who should have been smelling herself long time ago (by the new standards), Solemn was doing good. Bev also had to keep in mind Landon was gone. Akila around, but not Solemn's age.

So, when Desi Longwood got front page of *The Star-Herald* (in a pink blouse and with her hair straightened), Bev didn't mind Solemn slumping over burnt toast. And now, their friends (no one ever officially broke it) were on Channel 48 with *Mississippi News Now:* to talk of "The Miracle," to praise God for good luck, to become local celebrities.

Alice Taylor had told Red it was coming on. Red told Bev. Bev told Solemn. None of them had ever known anybody who made it onto television, the joke of living under blue sky of the place most folks only heard of because of its Oprah Winfrey. The interview was live, so the Imperial was gone. It would drive in soon. Bev sat with chilled morning coffee, in her robe, Red out looking for work, Solemn slumped in bed.

"You have no memory of it?" the bouncy-bounce yellow-haired Barbie lady chirped.

"No," Solemn heard her friend's voice say. "I was just walking, all by myself, back to my family. Then, I woke up in the hospital. My mother was there with me."

Solemn knew Mrs. Longwood's voice: "We're so blessed somebody helped her."

Somebody? Somebody? Her part cut out, her role erased, her stardom stolen.

Somebody was mad.

Solemn moved her mind elsewhere. She invented enough alarms to skip out on school—"sick," "the cat's lost," "my time of the month," "cicadas kept me up all night"—to consult herself at the well on the matter the woman from the television expressed. The mission of a gone daughter kept her seated under the big top of soapboxes risen up that spring as vocally as the cicadas unbridled for the first time in thirteen years. Corkboard notices and barbershop speeches and flyers of Landon's vocabulary, all by people who still carpooled and hitchhiked to town and Main and Catherine and Washington streets in hopes of government job postings after all: *The Klan is the Taliban, Bush the Devil, I am hungry and I am homeless . . . can somebody please buy me some chicken?, Buy Black, Acupuncture and Reiki Specialist Got the Key, Black Boy Beat in Bledsoe.*

The cicadas, indicted for every flat hairdo or stubbed toe or sudden layoff or sparse milking or stumbling hen, were Solemn's cover to whisk away and reflect on the fading "Have You Seen Pearletta?" movement . . . going, going, gone. She wanted to see Pearletta again, tried to, in every black woman coming her way or going her own. She felt empowered to make her materialize. Yet Viola Weathers slipped off of the television the way her daughter seemed to slip off the face of the earth, with only a few flyers spotted around. The world had yet to invent a way to find a Pearletta Hassle, even if it wanted to.

Solemn had a mind to make an offering, to the well. She was a teenager now, too old for the Barbies. She wished everybody would stop wrapping them up for her. Didn't they know she knew the size of the box by now? Three months to the day after the Festival, Solemn marched past the steep and the Longwoods' with a whole satchel of them—naked they were. She even decided to sacrifice all the change she had; the grown folks always declined her offer to trade the matching bills for it. She trained herself not to look in the direction of the Longwoods. She could smell the peaches already. The well was replenished, somehow. She looked into the pit of it, but it was too far down inside and too gray outside for her to see her face. Solemn plopped the dolls down one by one. Seven in total. Then, she tossed the coins in with one dump. She breathed her wish on top of the melody the coins made, for her to solve a crime and help the woman on TV and to sit on television herself now to talk about how she did it. A savior, on top of a singer. Mighty fine. If the doll's miniature noses and toes pointed up to the top in time, then her wishes had been heard. She would think about it, all of it, from now, so the clues would arise. In time, somebody else caught up to her. Or she to them. No matter.

SIXTEEN

Akila flicked the *Herald-Star* newspaper cutout back and forth in her left hand, newly decorated with a tiny discount stone Landon produced two hundred fifty dollars for at Walmart. Akila mailed off three bills—now to Fort Campbell in Kentucky—sealed in an envelope with the ultimatum scribbled inside. Too mouthy and inexperienced to be deployed, Landon would be home again for a few days in summer. Her window of opportunity was tight. Akila tapped her feet at the cement driveway under her and Solemn at the small picnic stand, with a few covered park benches for Mississippi visitors and travelers. They were at the logged Holly Hill rest stop, milepost 154 down Natchez Trace Parkway, at least an hour from where she was supposed to be. This late morning, Akila was supposed to run around in her mother's borrowed car only to shop for a wedding dress—white lace, though the family preacher who agreed to officiate faintly warned cream silk was least offensive for her circumstance. Solemn negotiated a price for her assistance: a nifty five dollars for half a day or ten dollars for an entire. This would bring her moving fund to three hundred dollars, Solemn confided to Akila. "To where?" Akila asked, and then said, "Never mind."

Viola and Edward Weathers took out ads in the major local newspapers, to plead to the public for information concerning Pearletta's disappearance. A more thorough portrait of her to leave behind than a crazed husband, baby in a well, and cheap motels. As it came clearer Pearletta Hassle really was a good girl set up a little better than the rest, there was rejuvenated interest in answers. This repositioning struck Akila as funny: no acceptance of fate or bad luck. These people expected a better image than that. They were discontent to sit down.

Akila thought, perhaps she could have something to offer to the mystery and debate. She did not quite understand Landon's enemies. They were so vague and bland. Nothing new about whites. She was unsure how the drying or dried oil fields scattered up the Mississippi related to a war she was told her country was in, or even where Afghanistan and any of the other sand-dusty places were on a map of the world. But here she could understand the need for answers to a daughter's disappearance. Perhaps murder. She would not remain silent. She would open her mouth. She would declare total anonymity for any information she provided, though a reward would be nice. It could start them on their own house. Maybe even sweepstake a real honeymoon. She wanted all that but could not afford it; maybe her help could be a way closer to it all.

A few weeks after the Festival on Easter Sunday, a patient night librarian at Warsaw Community Public Library let Akila into the microfilm space on a Monday it stayed open until eight. Akila wasn't keen on computers and the Web. She would do it how she had done things in school. There, she searched for the last name "Singer" with "trailer park" in the local papers, public records, county phone books, and genealogy maps. A speck of hope skid across Vicksburg. There, a Richard Singer oversaw a real estate operation of local apartments and storefronts. His main office was in the town's square, according to the address and the maps. A sweating glass bottle of pop was paperweight for a map Akila had only learned to read the week before. Then, she picked up the newspaper to read aloud: "'Pearletta Hassle is the daughter of Viola and Edward Weathers of Jackson, Mississippi. She attended Oakwood Academy in Huntsville, Alabama, for her business degree. She is twenty-eight years old. She has an older brother, Edward, and his wife, Shelia. And her nephew, Edward the

Third. And a younger sister, Patricia, a freshman at Oakwood. Here is a family picture of them all together. If you have any information, you may call—"

"Can I see it?" Solemn asked Akila, thinking she alone had conjured the trip.

"No," Akila told her. "You don't need to look at this."

"When we going to look at dresses?" Solemn asked.

They both talked about the thing they really didn't want to talk about. To them this felt like best behavior when it fact it was just maturity. Akila's heart begged to know: *Your daddy know Pearletta Hassle?* She had flip-flopped how to put it to Solemn many times, Bev even. Any practice left her tongue belly-up. The Redvines were good to her. They never judged her. Maybe even respected her. The churches and public aid offices felt like salt in the wound, but the Redvine place put her in cool waters. Solemn wanted to know if Pearletta Hassle was one of the nasty ladies: money on the dresser, mad woman at the door, curly panties on the floor, necklace between the teeth. She wanted to know if their babies should die and nobody should look for either one of them. She wanted to know if Akila would ever throw Landon's baby down into wells.

"Soon," Akila answered. Having Solemn with her certainly helped in case she got lost. It could explain away any delays (*I took her to a restaurant and arcade . . .*) and calm suspicions from people who weren't used to seeing young black girls just driving around their avenues. She was fairly confident they were on the right track, going south down the Trace and west at some point to glide into Vicksburg, so she went with her instincts. Akila drove with no driver's license. In Bledsoe, no one cared.

Akila's nerves primarily tingled with wonder at what exactly she was going to find when she came to Vicksburg and why it mattered. She had not known Pearletta for more than twenty minutes and an afternoon. She never went back to the motel, her job. She pretended to be sick for a few days. She told her family to hang up on any employee who called for her. She saw, like everyone in Bledsoe did (*"Mmm-mmm-mmm . . . such a shame . . ."*), the bland announcement of a gal last seen in Home-Away-from-Home: black, female, drugs and drug paraphernalia found in the room, dishevel, outstanding tab. There was nothing printed about Pearletta herself: who she was and what she could have been.

There was an hour to go to Vicksburg, with Akila lost in thought and Solemn thoroughly asleep, content to be with her imaginations of an older sister, satisfied to see a stretch of life beyond her part of the world, eager to know what awaited them in a different place, totally unaware how she was being used as a cover for those who might ask questions back home and out there. And Akila enjoyed her company as well.

Solemn awoke to an Outkast song on the radio. Akila's abrupt careen off the Trace headed into Vicksburg. The greenery stood high along the road. Akila seemed focused and urgent. She pulled into the first gas station of Warren County, to fiddle with her map. She tuned out Solemn to see if the gas station had a lottery.

We should play it, Solemn thought. She grabbed up quarters from the car's console. The lottery was something she had heard everyone talk about, watch the TV news for, laugh about while they guarded liquor and ate birthday cake, make faint mumblings while on their knees at church. She knew the folklore of her home at Singer's began with Redvine's lucky hit at the lotto. He couldn't have bought the trailer otherwise. At the very least, maybe some winnings could be her chance to stick out on the road a little longer with Akila. The lottery line was far too long. On top of it, the automatic crane in the better toy machine was jammed. The little dime-slot red horse outside was out of order. Solemn came back to the car with three pink gumballs and a spider ring encased in a plastic cylinder, from the cheaper game machine inside.

"Well, we gotta make a little bit of a stop before we go shopping for dresses."

"Where we gotta go?"

Akila pulled off.

"Well, Solemn, you probably too young for anybody to talk to you about all this kind of stuff. But there was a woman I met. Had a lot of problems and issues and just, well, stuff going on. She's that girl everyone's been talking about, Pearletta Hassle . . ."

Solemn rolled the gumballs round her tongue and thought about Pearletta Hassle, hurt bad—her mama said. And, yes, she had helped. She never told. She watched cows in pasture appear to flurry by, but she was really the one moving. Then, she pictured Desiree: retreated into something unfamiliar and unfriendly. Leaving her alone and absent of reflection and affection, once again dependent upon her mental enterprise alone, left to imagine discarnate beings waving at her in the clouds and sky.

". . . and, well, there are just people in this world who sometimes do bad things. Or, even if they didn't do a bad thing, they have their hands in the bad thing. And they don't have to pay for it. Or worse, no one even knows they did it. But, sometimes, you can do something about things. You can stand up, or at least you can do your part. Like now."

Akila pointed a finger past Solemn, onto the far-up road at Solemn's left. Two girls sat up ahead: one balanced on side of a square gray suitcase and the other leaned atop a lumpy gray potato sack. No more than fifteen, sixteen, for sure, they could not have been. One black. One white. Solemn cringed, just getting around to enjoy the breeze along her cheek and unsure if she was capable of an apposite demeanor for new folks. At sight of a slowed-down vehicle, the hitcher girls leaped and pulled their belongings up. Akila parked and stared. Yes, female they were, yellow and brown and pigtailed and pimple faced. A number of vehicles whooshed past and rocked the little car a bit. One girl quickly squeezed in behind the passenger side; Solemn's door was unlocked. The other appeared at Akila's window and reached her long arm for the door handle, to find it locked. Akila lifted the knob for her.

They looked a bit younger than Akila and a bit older than Solemn, like right in between, perfectly. They brought smells of dank denim and cigarette smoke with them. They explained how far they had come ("so far"), what led to their circumstance of sitting on side a lazy road ("families left us"), what led to the opportunity to jump in here ("I can offer you a pack of cigarettes for gas money," before "We don't smoke"). One girl sat atop her suitcase. The other held her potato sack between her legs, behind Solemn, pushing into the back of her seat. Their sandwiches seemed pulled from a magician's hat, so quickly they appeared. Tuna, sweet relish, mayonnaise, onions, pungent, sloppy. The hitchers—Shana and Law Anne—offered Akila and Solemn torn-off portions. They asked for water. There was none. Akila did not ask the girls where they wanted to go but other things: "You ever jumped out a window?" "You know how to choke a chicken?" "Can you drill a hole in concrete?" "Can you run five miles without stopping?" "Je, wewe ni bikira?" "No," Shana and Law Anne answered. "Too bad," Akila said. They drove on. Solemn thought they went further than they needed to.

The radio music was interfered with. Verdant plains around the car gave way to a chalky mist and slight drizzle, to bring gray kelpies face-to-face with the windshield like a drive-in movie screen tumbled down. The front bumper marked straight to a line of vultures and buzzards and cygnets crossing red sand road, who did not fly when the earth trembled with the approach of the Mustang, but they lay down under it in time. Solemn looked back to make sure. The birds arose into a line of naked and bald black girls and women holding hands and waving the car to please come back, as the earth trembled far behind them, but there was no hint to know what would come next. They carried secrets out loud and not silent in their mouths. They called at her to join them, but Solemn was going to stay where she was and knew she belonged. And there was just no room for all of them, so the car moved on down a road with no signs now, only what looked like coffins in a long-standing droke. Shana and Law Anne poked Solemn in back of her head. Akila drove on, laughing, snapping her fingers, so happy on her trip from Bledsoe. A gray unicorn ran alongside the car with its horn spilling its coins and dollars, from the energy of its frantic pace as well as the wind rocking the car now. The unicorn stayed until it flew into four-hundred-foot trees grown in seconds. Akila turned the radio down, to keep on talking to Shana and Law Anne—about their boyfriends and sugar daddies and old men and the bad guys. The unicorn told Solemn to tear the lottery ticket between her teeth to swallow its pieces down. The pastures along the road, once a highway, now turned a red carpet of veins, held the carcasses of cows with leaking udders and draining mouths and vulnerable eyes. Shana and Law Anne talked on and on and on, about the men whose faces they slashed and the women whose breasts they cut off and the town in middle of a desert where it was time for Akila to take them to right now—with no choice.

Shana or Law Anne pulled out a pistol to aim at their driver's head, while Solemn ate chocolate cake and spaghetti they slammed into her face. Then Solemn awoke to an Outkast song on the radio. Akila's abrupt career off of Natchez Trace Parkway headed into Vicksburg. The greenery along the road was high. Akila seemed focused and urgent. Solemn clenched a sticky pink gumball in her hand and saw a plastic black spider on her pinky finger. Desiree was not there to give the word-for-word and bit-by-bit account to. The sky was fine and dandy, and there was no one in the backseat of the car.

On guard now, and again, Solemn protested leaving the car.

"I need to stay in," she told Akila. But she didn't know if she would doze off and drift again into visions; they had multiplied since Easter Sunday.

"Nope," Akilah said. "Too hot. Mr. and Mrs. Redvine ain't gonna have my head if you die of heatstroke. Come on here, girl."

Solemn stared into the jewelry shop they passed. Beside were a mom-and-pop record store, Dollar General, a tobacco shop, and a tax accounting service, closed until winter. Akila led the way beyond the parking lot and inside the air-conditioned office. Bells jingled as they walked in. No one sat at the desk behind a countered partition in the small office. A few chairs sat in a waiting area with a magazine rack, water cooler, and coffee table decked out with vased azaleas and a shiny tissue-paper holder.

"What we doing here?" Solemn asked. She read *Singer's,* where she lived and what it told her to be.

"Just sit down," Akila told her. "Get a book."

Solemn picked up a *Smithsonian.* Akila looked around. Right next to a tusk crucifix was a moose head, its snout right above her and its lifelike eyes directed to the clock behind the desk, keeping time and revenge fantasy at once. Framed certificates of ownership, compliance, and professional membership ran along the wall. So did news clippings: *Singer Real Estate Distinguished Community Service . . . Singer Real Estate Breaks New Ground in Abandoned Area . . . Singer Real Estate Donates $100,000 to Establish Local Vicksburg Development Projects . . . Singer Real Estate Renovates and Opens Trailer Park in Bledsoe.* The family helmed the wall of their office—a larger portrait of a bald man, swan-necked woman, two sons. Twins, it appeared. Then, underneath this twelve-by-twenty-four cherry frame was the less formal narrative of their lives: sweet little boys in Boy Scout uniforms with checkered socks, beach-day faces turned away from the camera and onto an ocean most of their tenants had never seen, school pictures with bright bow ties pressed, commemorations of the boys' race-car and thoroughbred mountings. As Akila was about to look closer at the faces for some recollection of anyone she had seen before, the secretary finally acknowledged her: "Kin I help you?"

"Oh yes," Akila said. She had something rehearsed to say but forgot it.

"I'm just looking to apply to an apartment," she said instead.

"Applications at edge of the counter. Clipboards right next to 'em. Pencils in the jar. I make a copy of your ID when you done." The secretary snapped a button on one of the telephones on her desk, stacked to the top with papers, manila folders, receipts, calculators, carbon copies, and *Enquirers.*

"Hold on, Shelly. I gotta gal here." The woman snapped another button on her big brown phone. She looked at Solemn: "All kids extra. You can bring they birth certificates back." Then, "If you on public aid, we need your social worker's direct phone number."

She snapped a button on the phone again and started to talk.

Akila took a seat and looked over the paperwork. A form for the employer or public aid. A sheet to list where and what of check stubs. Explanation of rules and regulations. Brochure for Singer's Real Estate. She slipped the pamphlet in her pocket and pretended to write, with mighty and tender hopes, a need to act rather than just exist.

"We trying to get an apartment?" Solemn asked Akila. "We moving?!"

"Yeah, we are," Akila said, and she jammed her elbow into Solemn's skinny ribs.

The woman behind the counter looked up for a second. *Well,* she concluded, *that's for the social worker to handle. Not my job . . .*

"So, Barbara and Phillip got back together yet? Last part I saw, she was stuck on the yacht with the kidnappers. Phillip got in a motorcycle accident on the way . . . ?"

The doors swooshed open to the hot air. A man walked in. He wore tight beige pants and a wrinkled pink shirt and a Stetson. Akila noticed a name tag: *Bruce Singer.* The woman behind the counter catapulted from her seat. "Yes, we will return your call." She snapped a button on the telephone and slammed it down.

"How you doing today?" the man shouted in Akila's direction.

"Very well, sir," Akila answered back, her eyes pressed upon what she registered as part of what she sought. Solemn shut the magazine.

"Mr. Singer," the woman behind the counter said, "Alderman Hansley called. And so did Missus Turner 'bout the plumbing lines over her border on the Maple Street property, and the caterers for the lunch on Friday. Oh, and your ma."

"Thank you," Mr. Singer said, his eyes over the slips of pink phone notes. He was oblivious to Akila's stares. If this was any relation, he'd cleaned himself up since the last time he took a picture with some black gal. And he had gotten rounder. But, the face was the same. As was the thick red mound of hair Akila saw sprouting from the nape of his hat. Couldn't tell if there was gray or not. He was rounder than she remembered, but it was the summer now. Something about festivals, picnics, barbecues, and heat made people eat. But the green eyes, cat eyes, looked the same.

Hmmppphh . . . Akila thought, as the man went past her to enter the back offices.

"Are you . . . you Bruce, or Richard, Singer?"

The man stopped. Boy, really. Baby face, despite the business attire.

"I heard about your real estate company. Best in town, huh?" Akila asked.

"That's what we hear. But it's not my company. My father owns it. I'm just a worker as far as he's concerned. Bruce." He extended his hand.

"Nothing wrong with a little work for your father," Akila said. She fingered the pocket of her sundress. "Well, I came here to look for an apartment . . . my friend recommended me. She rented from you-all," Akila said.

Solemn had never seen any of them have too much conversation with a white man outside the doctor's office, hospital, school, and police station. Never in real life.

"Oh, really? Well, we let to a lot of people . . ." Mr. Singer started.

"Pearletta Hassle. You seen her around?" Akila asked him.

"Mmmmm . . . doesn't ring a bell," the man answered.

"Oh, why would it?" Akila turned and pretended to write. "She had her baby thrown down a well in the trailer park y'all own."

The man blushed. He rubbed his nose with his thumb stuck out from a crunched fist. "Well, I'm so sorry to hear that."

He looked at Akila, and Solemn, and then back at Akila.

"If you'll pardon me. Good luck on your application. I hope to see you in the family."

"Here," Akila said. "If you wanna know more or see if you remember."

The man took the crumpled "Have You Seen Pearletta?" flyer, with its bled ink.

"Oh-oh-," he stammered. "Well, thank you. Appreciate it."

"No problem," Akila told him.

"Did you remember you have a two o'clock with your pa to go over what to do about all the delinquencies?" the woman behind the counter shouted to Bruce Singer's back. Then, he broke eyes with Akila. In his eyes, she looked ashen and pitiful and hopeless and exactly what his family told him needed their consideration and mercy. The ones they were to help. He started to the back door of the small office. Akila watched him slam the door shut. She heard it click. A fever crescendoed onto her forehead. She threw the clipboard and papers at the counter. The woman called out, "Hey, I'm gonna need your ID or I can't process this . . ." Akila ignored the woman and grabbed Solemn, so they could finally talk about the thing they both, in fact, wanted to talk about: "Now we can go look for a dress."

SEVENTEEN

Guests would forget the preacher's sermon quicker than the bride's slightly dingy dress, or her purple-and-peach morning glory bouquet that made up for it, or the groom's gleaming Stacy Adams, or the baby ring bearer's screeching hesitation and flop-out, or Alice Taylor's overdone solo, or three modest lemon-and-butter-cream sheet cakes Bev was relieved the half oven could manipulate.

Orchestration of the day included Redvine's ten car trips to transport metal folding chairs and tables from basements of a church alliance in Kosciusko back to Singer's, at the foot of the steep, near the pond. There were pleas to Bev's great-aunt for a patch of her garden, blackmail to card-party friends and bar mates for donated dishes and silverware. BYOB was emphasized, unheard. But there was no way Akila's mother bought into the potluck twist Bev suggested. Instead, she contributed to the otherwise: three days of cooking and freezing and uncanning and tinfoiling until both mothers nearly nodded off in the pews soon as they sat down.

For Landon and Akila's one o'clock wedding, Solemn unfastened her cornrows the morning of to display a tough, crinkly crown throughout the day. She arose earlier than her parents, to be ready before she was rushed. She pinched a bit of her daddy's Old Spice deodorant, aware of herself now and taking no chances. She wanted to wear a baby-doll dress she bought at Dillard's with Desiree. Now it had already grown pilly, tight around her upper arms and frivolous to her behind. She was left with a hand in her mama's closet for permission to wear a yellow dress imprinted with raised vines and cherry blossoms. She had no shoes to match. She stuffed three crunched sheets of toilet paper into the toes of her mama's cork wedges and also borrowed a golden cross. She matched.

Solemn had an unusual lack of possessiveness to her brother, fed by the fact he was already gone anyway. She had a companion lack of fascination with his new bride. Akila would stay on in Bledsoe as she had been, until Landon completed another year. Then, lest he go off into the smoky places a half-arm's length away on the maps, he'd make up his mind if he would like to be stationed near home. The transition was none at all. Only a statement. It spoke to Solemn in confliction—of what Akila sighed she should not do and what Bev was occasionally driven to scream she wished she never had done. The effect of the day on Solemn was uneventful. Her interests were not peaked toward the direction of boys and men. Nor was it peaked toward a longing for her own day when she might be so carefully spoken to and of. Solemn most resented the absence of attention a part in the party would have given her: a solo, to share she wanted to sing, a distinguishable maid-of-honor or bridesmaid dress, so she was not a thief in the morning, and a verse in the Bible to read, so she was not sweating into anger from the front pew while Akila's cousin read his part from Numbers, to mispronounce the word that was her name.

Battle of the Cross Baptist Church left it to three ceiling fans and a straight-back piano to clutch its worshipers' attentions. A scarce wedding was somewhat different. It wasn't obligatory, or damning if skipped. People would not mind waiting. There had been no RSVPs sent back or spoken. Waste of paper and tongue. Bev made the date. Akila spread the word. The show went on. Bev filled her twelve pews with the congregation, her few living aunts, some of her high school friends, close cousins, a few Magnolia Bible College classmates, a remaining grandmother. Landon's friends—dressed in black—stood up in the back. Akila's side was only half-filled. They claimed they had not known in time. What her family lacked in concern and care the abandoned and hungry made up for in cheer. Strangers waited as well, wondering of the food after . . .

"Dearly Beloved, we are gathered here today to unite this man and this woman in holy matrimony, so that thy days may be long and thy lives may be fruitful upon this good earth. For God says, 'What I have joined, let no man put asunder.' And this union will make whole and holy the institution of family, created and mandated by God, so that the natural proclivities toward one another and inclinations we are born with can be directed aright. And for their parents, who have grown and sown these lives under cover of God's thunder and word, to be secured and comforted in the continuation of their names as servants of the Lord. Am I right, congregation?

"And today, for us all who have come to congratulate this blessed couple and partake as witnesses, we are reminded of the power of the Lord our God to give and to take away, to join and to divide, to create and to destroy, to cure and to plague, to comfort and to strike, to bless and to condemn. For we are merely shadows walking the Earth with the spirit of the Lord within us to light us into whole beings. Only that spirit can turn your light on, nothing else. Not money. Not love. Not a big ole house or fancy car. We are of no consequence and no reason. We are of no point and no result.

"Now, lest I take attention from this handsome couple before me, Landon and Miss Akila, I would be remiss not to take occasion today to remind ye sinners that the right hand of fellowship is always extended here at Battle of the Cross. Our door is always open. We receive you how you come. Don't be shamed to say you have sinned. Join the club. Or carry on in denial and secret and arrogance that you are so faultless. The hand of God reaches down, to grab hold of you and determine your destiny down a path to the scorching fires of hell or an invitation to the Pearly Gates of heaven. You decide.

"You decide when a pack of cigarettes shows its ugly face, to breathe the Devil's breath into the miraculous temple the Lord your God has blessed you with. You decide when the temptation to guzzle the nectar of inebriation calls out to you past the liquor store. You decide when you claim somebody or something you can't name forced you into bars yonder 'round. You decide when you are intoxicated by the whiff of a married woman's perfume or a single man's cologne and your loins get the best of you. Am I right, congregation? Don't get quiet now. Everybody was laughing and singing a minute ago. Now, you quiet. When you give up what you want, God gives you what you need.

"Party's over. No more fun. Too much work: to have a holy revival, a daily Sabbath, a period of fasting, a solemn assembly, a resurrection. But, we have a choice. We can fall down, like David and Job and Moses and Samson, but we can get up in a new day. We can fast the vices away. We can purify lying tongues and covetous eyes. We can run off the Devil and the commotion he brings with him. This very community we stand in today has reeked of God's displeasure. We have witnessed the fires, the floods, the murders, the storms, the tornadoes, the burglaries, the crashes, the wars, the shootings, the stabbings, the vagrancy, the molesting, the rapes, the abused children. In the bottoms of wells, in the rooms of motels, in the middle of fields on Easter. Signs are everywhere. They are provided for you. Don't say you weren't warned. Don't claim you didn't know.

"Now, so I can get back to this dear couple standing here, who have made the right decision to sanctify themselves before the Lord, thrown themselves down to the mercy of God to say they have sinned but demonstrated their repentance, I ask again: Who shall walk with the Lord God and ensure new generations fight this battle of evil on earth? How long will you stay bedazzled by earthly concerns? How long will you ignore the Holy Spirit and allow your dirty minds to dictate your course? How long will you submit to materialism and sexism and agnosticism and every other ism you can't control? When will you next find out your hands and your minds have gotten you into turmoil you can't just tiptoe away from? Be quiet. Don't tell nobody. Forget. Whisper. When? Will it be today? Will it be tomorrow? Will it be next week? Will it be next month? When?"

Over an hour later, no new baptisms were scheduled. However, Akila and Landon had somehow pranced out of the church doors to showers of rice and applause. Among the last they passed to hug was Solemn—curious as how to stand before them now, joined as one. Landon, boisterous as ever in uniform, pulled her off her feet. Akila tore Solemn into her arms until she, finally, smiled wide enough to make a promise.

Bev stood still and unemotional in her peach Le Suit—notating the invited who didn't show: that phony white woman, Ruby; the Longwoods, her father's negligent people, Redvine's fat-ass and gossiping sisters. To stay off that, she preoccupied herself with the particulars: if the few volunteers she scared up put the tables out by now, and the borrowed burners on low, and the thistle on back of the chairs, and the stagger grass on top of the tables to poison the flies. Redvine took well wishes from the driver's side of the Malibu, aluminum cans trailing the back of it. Landon would drive it tonight, off to the Days Inn in Kosciusko. The lodge had a pool and restaurants close by. Landon returned to Kentucky via Greyhound Tuesday morning, the first bus in the a.m.

Back at Singer's, more than the number who could fit into the church for the wedding appeared at its after party. They had only been told "The pond." Nobody would have expected pork and grilled chicken not to draw a mixed crowd. Hence the months of saving and special invitation to the butcher. The pewter pail serving as a wishing well ran just as dry as the one no one ever used anymore, though some relatives of the couple mentioned it more than once. Hall Carter offered to it, as did Alice Taylor.

Otherwise, guests loaded off unopened Christmas gifts and room clutter. Some made effort to get their kids out of shorts into school clothes, to at least look like they had prepared. Even more scoured their coolers and fridges for a dish to offer. There were impromptu salads, leftover potpourris, half-full barbecue sauce jugs, extra pop, pans of hopping John, potatoes mashed in a hurry. The beer and cakes went without saying. There was reminder to the smaller children, with chocolate-stained mouths and frosted fingers, to not reach for the bride. What had begun as an early morning, tossed and turned with all that was forgotten, became a tonight to divvy out what burst into too much.

Just from the grins on both their faces and careful passings of their son it was clear Akila and Landon loved each other. Whether they would sustain it was the bet. But for their day they walked in perfect step from table to table and flourished the manners family singed into their behinds. Akila had sewn herself a jacket for the evening. She also bargained a petticoat under her empire-style white gown and three-foot train, launched off on-site to the delight of her audience. Landon and his fellows, cognizant of their last and only resort to enlist in the military, sidelined the original purpose of their meeting to help the children light red, white, and blue sparklers from the Fourth of July.

Solemn aimed for the edges of it all, nervous from the commentary she heard from relatives she only saw from time to time: "She gon' be taller than all us pretty soon," and "My goodness, she talk so proper now," and "Bet them boys all over her," and "Oil of Olay clear that acne right on up," and "Where's my sugar?" Some plays of new music moved her to dance. But a few overeager cousins, more citified, ran her back to a bench. Bev told her to go ask who needed help with slicing more cake or shooing flies. But the helpers all liked overwork, for ownership and praise. And the fly poison held up.

When the sun set the atmosphere around them to steel gray, Solemn looked toward the Longwoods' trailer. But, even up close, she wouldn't have been able to tell if their lights were on. Did Stephanie peek out in itching to join them, her old friends? Had the Longwoods heard the announcements and fled to a prior engagement or family getaway, just to be polite? The boat and truck were there. The Imperial was not.

When the sky darkened so the citronella candles served a dual purpose and the un–newly married couples started to tsk in their mates' directions, Solemn longed for a dance with Landon or her daddy. Just one dance apiece. Under the moonlight. With everyone watching. With silence and regard. But Landon was always hunched up under Akila. Or she was giggling on his lap. Or they were at yet another table to outline all their plans excluding the evening's. The new mothers-in-law kept hold of Landon Junior. Redvine stayed involved in earth-shattering conversation with men who passed beers and improvised collective moneymaking schemes. Inside jokes. Men stuff. Unburied secrets. And Solemn caught sight of her father, in the odd mixture of lights and perfume and music. His profile cut out from the rest of the world like dark paper set on white. He waved at her and it hurt. He ballooned into more and larger than he was, stepping up with knees tall as rooftops and arms wide as . . . *no.* It was not real. She knew that now.

Solemn's ill-fitting wedges slipped and she almost tripped farther down the steep, past the party point, heading to the well now. For no reason, Solemn went. Behind her, the trees developed an anatomy akin to ideas and visions the preacher's sermon had created. She did not look back at them as she walked away, on her own. For much of the year, it hadn't been inspiring or worth it to make the trip. She had checked back often, but the little noses and feet of the dolls never pointed back up. But now Solemn needed confirmation what had been there at the well had actually been there and indeed it all had once included herself. Still, no one had thought to cover it. The flies and smaller depended on it for peace. A few conscientious residents might walk by it with a lawn mower, just so no one could say they had not. No one, until maybe today, had given any thought to redeem it as a centerpiece or landmark. It had been before, and always. It was why it had been built. Now, it sat before Solemn slumped down to a once-known lullaby.

"Solemn, Solemn!"

When Solemn turned to her name, Akila was there with her smile and wide eyes in the night. The dress Solemn had her hand in selecting stood out halfway up the steep with a stretch of bodies, joy, humor, and satisfaction behind it. Akila waved out to her, as if she had not seen her in such a long time or Solemn was onboard a boat for a voyage no one else had ever thought of. Her new sister waved wildly and earnestly, triumphant in a search through her guests and from her husband's side at last. "Come on . . . hurry, hurry up!" Akila shouted down to Solemn. "I'm 'bout to throw my bouquet!"

2

THE
FUTURE

EIGHTEEN

A wispy echo of tight little baby feet with smooth, soft soles, a few mistakings of spines in the pantry for a tiny thigh, a few months of hungering for more than day labor, wonder of what (if anything) his dutiful daughter remembered—all distracted his focus.

Redvine was the only man in the house now, a thought he hadn't fussed with since the two years before he married Bev. He missed his son. Then after Solemn happened to hold the hand of a girl gone down at the Festival (now less attended for it), he had less strength to compete for a daily spot at the electronics plant or a weekend odd job around Bledsoe. It was taking too much gas to get to Kosciusko just for nothing but a look. While he couldn't necessarily complain too much—*my kids good, never gave me too much trouble, wife rarely scrap, I ain't been perfect, they love me*—Redvine had to admit: he was slowing down. He could still be playing off high roller, had the future not been so guerilla. Now the Malibu and trailer and fine wedding were leftovers cooled. The duffel bag he once carried out the door to work held the stuff they piled to send to Landon: his mama's cookies and notes, DVDs, CDs, boxer shorts. Change.

The utility and just plain living bills piled. Work did not.

Mostly because Akila had gone on to take the baby, and there was no one to look after Solemn, and tuition money went extinct did Beverly permanently lose her classes at the Bible college. She settled for shelving books in the library. Lots of free books, more than welcome. The trailer had no room for them. Sometimes in twos or threes they hogged up books for the Oprah club, on account of it being on the TV and in the stores and something big in the world. Gave her something to read besides Landon's notes. She even thought about asking a few other high-attendance ladies to potluck with her after church, for a ladies' book club, like Stephanie thought of and they tried to plan. Bev figured the books were too hard. Nothing like the Bible, or a few of Landon's teachers gave like *Sounder* and *Roll of Thunder, Hear My Cry*. She saved those books. In January *One Hundred Years of Solitude* by a Spanish man and a white woman's *The Heart is a Lonely Hunter* in April. She heard a book in Russian was coming up. She wanted Ann Rule next and thought to write a letter to the Harpo station in Chicago. But she was too scared of her English. Bev knew Stephanie would read the books in a heartbeat. Forasmuch as it appeared Solemn and Desi were the twosome to note, she was the grown woman who most missed her friend. So much more marvelous she had felt.

The boredom expanded. Unfaith took root.

Landon stayed on in the service, stationed at Camp Shelby in Hattiesburg with Akila now, a daughter to add to his son. Though none of his notes and letters would admit (since, really, "Uncle Sam just a stepping-stone"), he wished for deployment. But with the steadiness and comfort and tax breaks, he was able to Western Union cash to Bledsoe. Fully adult. He set up a credit union account for Solemn, monthly deposits, inaccessible to her until she turned eighteen. Just fifty dollars a month, six hundred dollars a year, pamphlets about compounded interest in the holiday cards.

He hadn't killed anyone yet. Mysteriously, he began to believe America. Change.

Dandy snoozed all night, well as day. Unsynced.

More and more often, with the well water unattended and abandoned, brown boys frolicked in the Singer's pond, underpants wet against their drawers and the lines of their bodies drawing Solemn to wonder more. They laughed and shouted and splashed, foofaraw and kidding akin to what Solemn wanted. But she had no girls. Akila was gone now. Married. Desi slipped on to bigger public school, under straw boat hats to mark the present her parents gave her after she had her miracle. Famous now. Stephanie and Theo pulled the white-and-blue dory alongside their wide trailer; its anchor rested in Bermuda grass along with the pitchforks and garden tools. By end of a school year, with no festival to get her through the last leg of the effort, Solemn saw a deck of other gals switch between the peach and fig trees. Desi's father lifted and pulled the boat to back of a pickup. Then, Stephanie rode all the other girls behind in the Imperial, headed for the river most likely. When the Longwoods returned at night, they went past Solemn without stopping for even a wave. She thought to tear that boat apart plank by plank, down to the aluminum bottom and hull. Mr. Longwood was outside within the week after she imagined such, started on a dog-eared cedar plank fence to go around the yard, as if they had watched behind her back for her dreams. Solemn resented them even further.

She lived in antonym now. Letters and numbers remained squiggly and squirmy. She had lived with it all so long she lost capacity to become alarmed by it, and accustomed to it, like baby weight or adult teeth. Yet it still rendered her world different and difficult from the power to expect. More than relief and lifted weight was emptiness and buoyancy. It gave way to a restlessness and prickling stress to shake things up a bit. It zoned her into the television waiting for Viola Weathers to appear, to acknowledge she had tried to help and done her part for Pearletta. And she had—all around Singer's and outings into town she looked for her, waited for her, took the face on the flyers to good mental note and genuine care. Yet and still, the barefoot woman never showed up.

Don't know what possessed me to fill the science class turtle's pool with hot water the day of my special turn to tend to it, so the whole class gathered round it thinkin he was dancin for them. He was really just dyin.

"That one there, she grab more than one tray and don't even eat the food," the lunch ladies finally tattle-told on me. "Just waste . . ."

"Dear Mr. and Mrs. Redvine, Freshmen is working on mythology now. All students expected to choose a Greek or Roman god to create a diorama for final exam. They gosta turn in a paper. Not all families contributed to the school supply fund this year. I believe yours may have not. But a rainbow necklace of paper clips stole from my desk is not exactly what I had in mind as a acceptable project to turn in. I may have to flunk Solemn and she need four English credits to graduate," the English teacher wrote.

"That girl slammed the door shut on her locker partner's hand . . . this child gotta go to the health department for stitches. Ain't no way I can do this here," the school nurse told the principal when he wrote my last note.

Now, that one was an accident.

"Mr. and Mrs. Redvine, Solemn's . . . um . . . outbursts, have been re-ported and documented for quite awhile now . . . I mean, I have her records here . . ."

"How you have her records?" Bev asked the principal. "I don't even have her records. I tried to get them. 'Cause my friend Ruby said she knew somebody could get her in Piney Woods, just like that. Solemn's *that* smart. She's just had a rough year."

"Oh, Piney Woods is a fine school. You can't beat it, Mrs. Redvine," the principal said. "I'm quite sure Solemn has the smarts for such a stellar boarding school. She's very brilliant, actually. Her test scores among the highest in the school. So I'm sure she has the capabili-ties. I'm just not sure she got the demeanor."

"Solemn is no problem whatsoever at home, sir," Redvine inter-rupted. "All these messages from teachers, notes home, suspensions, meetings. Saying she start yelling in class, picks on other students, talks back to nobody. I don't understand it all . . ."

"She come home and do her homework," Beverly chimed in. "She sit all through church without disturbing nobody. It just seem like you people have all these little problems with her no one else got. I don't know. It don't make sense to me."

Solemn reclined in the corner without hearing any of it. She stared at a colony of ladybugs traveling up the room's office window, col-lecting themselves in the left-hand corner where the principal's chair leaned. They clamored atop one another and took off to less crowded places, only for a few to notice and hobble behind. The principal leaned back even farther and his elbow threatened the colony in the crook of his window. A loner settled on the point of his jacket at the elbow. Solemn watched it.

"I ain't sure what Solemn's like at home, but I know here at Miller's she can be a bit unpredictable, to say the least . . ."

He was just doing his job. There were more in his care beside Solemn. She was a disruption and a disturbance to the rest.

"I'm afraid she's no longer welcome. She's exhausted her suspensions. I'm sorry. The regular KHS may take her. And there are some GED homeschooling options . . . believe an alternative program in Jackson for students like her—"

"She's being . . . kicked out?" Redvine asked, a brow upturned. "I know there was a problem with her turning in her work and seeing the chalkboard. Solemn needs glasses. We're working on that." Solemn stared out of the window. Bev cried in her hands.

"Mr. and Mrs. Redvine," the principal said, "the staff asked me to meet with your family last semester about Solemn. Some wanted her gone then. I didn't. I wanted to see what happened this semester, give her a chance. But with so many teachers and students complaining she interrupts, has outbursts, doesn't do her part, curses, late to class, bathroom passes for the whole period, tardy, well. I just can't hope no more."

The round man scratched his fingers at his scalp. Every tiny orange dot of insect cascaded to the floor and back to the windowpane with the others. As he and her parents worked all that out, Solemn was gone on to the vending machines, with a taste for potato chips, for her last skip through the hallways as a formal student ever in life.

Come spring of 2004, with what she had already collected, her unicorn jewelry music box was too overloaded to stay secret. She had nearly seven hundred dollars balled up in socks under her bed. She talked to herself. Forget petty concerns hovered around success in spelling bees and multiplication table recitations, much less grand and opportunistic than her thoughts to leave Bledsoe behind. Like Landon. Nashville, Hollywood, New York, Chicago . . . on televisions and stages, just a slice of her voice heard.

NINETEEN

DIGICATE:
Join the wave of the future.
Be your own boss! Set your own hours!
Train others! Own a Business!
Revolutionary company merging new
technologies with proven educational systems.
6 Figure Income.

The future.

The future.

Cicadas had gone. Future was coming.

Waves and waves of it, coming soon, like the summer blockbusters, mercenary. Redvine could do more than mutter a "Fuck you" to the factories that wouldn't hire him 'cause, at forty-five, he was too risky. At least that's how they broke it to him at the electronics plant, an imposition since the main high school was about to graduate nearly twenty athletes (without scholarships) in June. Enlistments stalled; most weren't that brave to waltz coolly into Iraq after the black hole of Afghanistan took more than it sent back. The lines for humid day labor rivaled the circus camped out to audition for *American Idol*. It was too hot in those joints anyway. And dangerous. One time, the tip of his ring finger had almost skidded underneath a rubber belt on his pick line for the day. For all that hazard, he couldn't even afford to have a phone line installed at home.

Within three weeks of being dismissed to watch commercials in between Bev's shows and Solemn's pouts, when nobody was looking at him, at the pizza joint in town, Redvine zoned in past the ink-drained *Have You Seen Pearletta?* poster next to it and pulled the green tack out of the DigiCate sign, stuck on side of the building along with the other sun-washed papers for housekeeping and yard work and social services.

They were down to cold food and showers only, due to little money for propane. His plate of pickles and lunch meat half-eaten, canceled out by butterflies in his stomach, Redvine put on a tie, a blue button-down shirt with a collar, and his good shoes.

"You gotta interview?" Bev asked him, sunken into the *Oprah* re-run she missed that morning, due to picking up extra hours at the library. Open and close now.

"New company coming to town," he told her.

"I ain't heard about it. Where?"

"Yonder," Redvine said. "Out past the new development."

"Good luck, sweetheart."

Outside, Solemn dried off the Malibu she hosed down at Redvine's request. He thought it should have been shinier. Then he remembered: he had had to cut back on wax.

"Where my five dollars?" Solemn asked when he walked past.

"Give it to you when I get back!" Redvine shouted, jangling his keys. "I ain't got no change."

He needed the five dollars for gas to get to the Days Inn, for the informational session he was heading to. He'd make it up to Solemn, soon as he got to six figures.

A DigiCate banner in the lobby directed Redvine on where to go without having to see the front desk clerk. A younger suited white man eyed him as he tapped at the hotel switchboard. Redvine thought about letting the man know where he was going, but the instinct to do so sparked him back to why he had come to the info session in the first place. Insubordinate, he kept on. At the conference room, he met a black man and a Latina at the door. Their welcomes strong, their eyes wide, their handshakes firm. They appeared more upbeat than beat up. He knew he was in the right place.

"Just print your name and phone number and e-mail address," the Latina told him.

"E-mail?" Redvine said. "Oh, well, I gotta mailbox."

"Yes, just put it right on down for us."

The black man, stout and fired up, stepped in.

"No problem if you don't have an e-mail address. Phone number good for now."

"Okay."

Redvine jotted down Alice Taylor's digits.

"Okay, Mr. Earl Redvine." The Latina beamed: Maggie, according to her name tag. She markered his name on a peel-off badge to stick on his shirt.

"We'll be getting started here in just a bit," said Walter, the black man. "In the meantime, get settled and feel free to help yourself to some refreshments. Thanks for coming out."

After the table with the sign-up sheet was a round table in the corner holding a display of what looked to Redvine like Etch A Sketches. Bright and glowing thick rectangles with fat books beside them, and stacks of the same flyer he'd seen at the pizza joint. Near that table was a smaller one with canteens for water and coffee. There was a bit of a swarm. He didn't know the ladies and one man who stood around the table—all black, in jeans and sandals. So, he spotted three rows of chairs in front of a projector and sat down. No sooner he took a seat, another woman was in front of him—daring red suit.

"And how are you today, sir?" she squeaked through perfect teeth.

"I'm good . . . and yourself?" Redvine said.

"Great! Happy ya joining the team!" Her sticker said Heather.

Team went good with work. Made it go by quicker. Redvine thought this was fun.

The woman carried a black binder under her arms and a few pens in her jacket pocket. Redvine had a pen but . . . *damn* . . . nothing to write on. Of course, he should have thought of this. There were the flyers, at the table. So, with the bundle moved on now, he walked back to grab a few flyers. He poured himself coffee, kept it black. As he looked back up to the front of the room where a screen was, he noticed he was possibly overdressed. No one else in the seats wore a suit. One man, near the back, cradled a plate of doughnuts. One lady had on scrubs and a bonnet. A couple had two children—one in a stroller and a taller one gobbling chips from a bag set down in her mama's bag. A little more than a dozen people, and he was the only one in dress clothes besides those signing everybody up and walking around smiling.

I'm gonna get this job, he thought. He took a seat in the front row.

Two white men—boys really—came from a door connected to the conference room partitions. They didn't just walk. They danced. They didn't just talk. They belted. As much as they clapped between their words, Redvine wondered if it was a concert.

"Ladies and gentlemen, I wanna thank you folks for coming out here today on this hot and sweaty Saturday afternoon," one boy said.

"And hey, this is not about us. It's about you!" the other boy chimed.

"So just feel free to stop us if you have any questions."

"Don't be shy!"

"Now, I'm gonna be pretty straightforward. But I gotta warn you. He's the one you gotta watch out for the garboil with."

"I gotta question," said the lady wearing the bonnet.

"Fire away!"

"What's garboil?"

Redvine somehow gleaned that apparently (as "Connor" and "Jason" talked in either unison or circles), DigiCate was a recipe or marriage or coagulation (or something like that) of two critical concepts the world depends on: Digitals and Education. DigiCate was a combination laptop-encyclopedia-library. Better than the whole World Wide Web. 'Cause, they said, with the Web you can get anything you want—could be mindless entertainment, celebrity worship, even pornography . . .

". . . No discipline and restriction, far too all-purpose not to be dangerous. A time suck and counterproductive peril. Do you really want all that at your child's fingertips? God only knows what the World Wide Web will bring. A virus. No, a computer can't make you sick. Well, of course, if one person is sick and another doesn't wash their hands after they use the same keyboard . . . I understand certified nurse's assistants know all about spreading germs . . . But if a virus comes from one computer to another, or one Web site from another, it can crash everything. Then where are you when your child needs to finish a report for school or you need to know something for work? . . .

. . . "But no, DigiCate is strictly a walking digital encyclopedia. About a third of the cost of entire set of hardback books the competitors and traditional publishers want to sell you: *Britannica, Funk and Wagnall's*, a bunch of off-brands you don't even have to know about. Look, this is the future. Nobody's gonna be buying those anymore. We contain the whirlwind of the Internet and the familiarity of the tried-and-true encyclopedia into one place: at your fingertips, on our handy portable device. DigiCate Incorporated works our butts off to compile, update, and expand every single day from our offices in Silicon Valley. No, ma'am, Death Valley is the desert.

"This is not about death . . . This is about life! Living how you want to live! Making a difference in the world! Living on your own terms! Joining our sales force! You don't have to know about selling nothing, ma'am. We train. Walter back there—stand on up, Walter (looking good, man)—is the field coordinator and trainer for this entire region. 'Cause we want everybody included in this. Everybody taps the bigger cities. They forget about the margins. Well, who better needs a digital device of this nature than people who may not have access to the World Wide Web the way the rest of the world does by now? You're gonna be on the cutting edge. You'll be on the front lines. Well, sorry, pardon me. I mean no offense. Trust me, I have utmost respect for our servicemen. No harm intended. My cousin served in Kuwait . . . tore my aunt apart. So, yeah, my bad. But you'll be like pioneers. Well, er, we aren't talking about killing the Indians. Okay. You'll be at the head of the class, at the top, how 'bout that? Right, "Walter—head of the class!"

"This too confusing," someone grumbled.

"They talk longer than the preacher . . ." Redvine heard. "And them doughnuts ain't do nothing for me. I'm starvin'."

"I don't know 'bout all this," another person said. "Can't I just fill out my application and go? I think *Fresh Prince* bout to come on in lwhile."

"We get sick pay?" another asked.

"Is they gonna get to the point? All this talking just sickenin' me . . ."

. . . So, now, 'Maggie's' passing out some pens and papers for y'all. And our folders. Those are yours to keep, special gifts inside. Pens, notepads, refrigerator magnets. Definitely pass out our pamphlets to your friends. But we just want you to follow long best you can because our payment structure is unparalleled. Trust me, unparalleled. Well, how much you get paid depends on how far you want to go . . .

. . . Now, with our initial kit you get started with ten DigiCates, one just for you to get familiar with the product. It's totally free, complimentary. Now, the basic DigiCate retails for a thousand bucks, but . . . wait! We do have an installment plan. We've thought about all this a lot, trust me. We have. We want this to be affordable to all families and income brackets, so we've taken all economic budgets into account. Some of our installment plans start just as low as two hundred dollars, if they want to wait on the DigiCate until they can get down at least fifty percent of that. Yes ma'am, just like layaway. And, the DigiCate includes the warranty and five years of discounted update DVDs. So that means every few months we release an update DVD with brand new information and entries, because we're keep our customers on the cutting edge. But all this is explained in the materials. You got enough, 'Maggie'? Okay, great!

. . . So, the goal for you would be to offer the DigiCate to customers for a lump sum you get fifty percent commission on. You get twelve hundred dollars from a customer, you keep six hundred dollars. Because we can offer you each DigiCate for six hundred dollars. So, we give it to our partners—that's you!—for half off retail price. So, you sell two DigiCates in one week, that's twelve hundred dollars in your pocket for the week. Yeah, sounds good, right? Now we're talking, huh? Yup . . .

". . . You get yourself a good block of schools or maybe even some of these parent clubs, who gonna buy bulk orders. You could be done for the month. Or you get a patch of a village talking about it, buying them up. Sounds good right? And we're gonna start you off past Copper Tier to Bronze—so you can get your free DigiCate, exclusive to the Bronze level. And when you start to rise up to different levels—I come all the way up to the Diamond Tier, past Silver and Gold—then DigiCate will give you a discounted trip to our company retreat. It's in Orlando, Florida, this year. Next year, guess where's it's gonna be . . . Cancun! You know . . . in Mexico?

Redvine thought, *This ain't a job like I was thinking. six figures means one hundred thousand dollars. Least. But six hundred dollars a week fine for me. That's real good. Florida's nice . . . I can do this.*

When 'Connor' and 'Jason' took questions, Redvine turned to see few left to ask any. Most had taken the folders and left. The table of refreshments was over with. The man with doughnuts in his lap remained, asleep. So did the look-alike couple with look-alike kids, crying now. The woman with the scrubs and bonnet talked to 'Maggie,' about her grandson: day-care costs. She was thinking about taking in foster kids, Redvine heard her say. While 'Connor' dismantled the projector and screen, Redvine shuffled the papers in his lap into the DigiCate folder they gave him and he approached Jason.

"What'd you think, sir?" 'Jason' asked him. Redvine noticed his many freckles.

"Sound all right, just fine," Redvine said. 'Connor' waved "Howdy" to him.

"You meet Walter?" 'Jason' asked, motioning behind to the back of the room. The look-alike couple cornered 'Walter'. They wanted directions to the nearest bus stop.

"Yes, sir. He helped me in," Redvine told 'Jason'.

"Well, this was our last presentation here for now. We getting on to Mobile. But Walter'd come to your house. You live round here?"

"Yes. Well, no."

"Kosciusko?"

"Little bit further out. Take me 'bout twenty minutes to drive in if I'm lucky."

"Not too far. Trust me, you get deep in this business, digging up your territory, you gonna be driving for days. I mean, we've sold tens of thousands of these things."

"Oh really?"

"Really," 'Connor' echoed, as he set the instruments into a nifty leather box. Every part fit in just right. "Big ole clunky home computers a thing of the past, man. Laptops still got a chance, though. In the future, people gonna wanna be on the go. But I gotta tell you, the World Wide Web hit its prime few years ago."

"I thought everybody had the World Wide Web now. I keep hearin' 'bout it . . ."

"Oh, they do all right," 'Jason' said. "But so do the advertisers and marketers and corporations turning it worse than television. I mean, come on, least on your favorite shows, you know when to take a break for commercials, right?"

"True." Redvine chuckled. "Except for the Super Bowl. I like those a lot."

"Exactly," 'Connor' continued. "You have a choice. That's all gone online."

"World Wide Web is one long big commercial, trust me." Jason laughed.

"So," Connor went on (Redvine wondered if they were brothers sawed apart at a past point), "DigiCate is gonna give people an electronic device with encyclopediac information pretty stock and set, like a book you pull off the shelf. But it's free and clear of drama. A booklike search engine. It's portable, electronic, easy to read, fun, and sound-enhanced. It makes you feel like you're online when you're not. And you can even set it up to separate information and save entries into special folders you control."

"We got the edges of America up and running on board with

this," 'Jason' said. "New York is on it hard. California too. Chicago's coming along. Seattle's our biggest territory. Heather there's my wife. She shot through Seattle like a racehorse."

"It's kind of the innards of America we lacking now," 'Connor' said. "Trust me, Mister Earl, a year with this and, seriously, you could be just like Walter. He's on salary."

On salary. *On* salary. This meant guaranteed, sick or on vacation or no matter what. It was all so promising.

'Jason' and 'Connor' took Redvine back to 'Walter.' They shook hands again, to make plans. 'Heather' and 'Maggie' smiled back at him, Cheshire cat grins, while they swept up crumbs left near missing doughnuts and spilt coffee dots. 'Walter' confirmed Redvine's number. He paused. But luckily all the men had business cards with near-matching information. Redvine was going to stop at Alice Taylor's house straightaway to use the phone, let her know to expect an important call for him. He wasn't worried about the money to get started. He would find it, from somewhere.

Redvine strutted out of the Days Inn lobby and took note it had been okay, after all, to pay for Landon's honeymoon there. The front desk manager even smiled at him on the way out, so a first impression was reversed. He couldn't wait to get home to tell Bev. Or, maybe he would keep it close to his vest for a while, wait until he sold a thing or two for her to jump up and down for. They didn't even say anything about the background check that kept him from other work—that little obstruction-of-justice thing back in the day, really just mouthing off to white cops. He wondered if his sisters would lend him some dough, snap out of superstition he was so bad for not visiting his parents more while they went down. He couldn't say he blamed them. He had been a standard baby of the family, incapable of babying anyone else. But he cried the most. Didn't that count? How long could they hold it all over his head? It was bygone, just like his part of the little life insurance he was actually happy they used up for the funerals and the debt. He would have made a business with it, had they not been so ornery and handed him some. One monkey, even two, don't stop no show. He'd get money somewhere else. He had more on his mind than mending fences with a family he might have to put a fence up to once he made six figures.

Beggars they'd become. He didn't have time or mind to think of the naysayers and critics.

And also because, well, anyway . . . the Malibu was out of gas.

On the favored lift to a bowl of gas at the nearest gas station and back to the Malibu, Alice Taylor let Redvine in on boys she knew in Jackson. They were into "that stuff," but hey, they *had* kept her trailer out of foreclosure and got one of her son's trucks out of repossession and calmed Rent-A-Center bounty hunters for her. They wouldn't pass up a little interest for a short-term loan. Redvine could go ahead and give her number out, for good cause. She'd take his calls, plus make a few others of her own for him.

With instant coffee and sweet potato pie waiting, 'Walter' drove a leased burgundy Lexus out to Singer's to break everything down better than Solemn could manage, once she and Bev pushed through all the papers. The women cleared away the random seasonings, bills, junk mail, Solemn's homework, and all the unfinished paperwork for the Tudor home bid. It was actually a very good and workable table.

'Walter's' pen was gold, real. Redvine could tell. He ran his fingers along the *DigiCate Classic Volume* for six hundred dollars to him and twelve hundred dollars to his clients, an authenticity certificate, and a frame. But, 'Walter' said, the catalog was vast. For the reluctant customers, there was the bonus of a *DigiCate Standard Desk Dictionary* and *Geography Catalog*. Only a few hundred. Said they sold those most often.

Bev glowed up to serve the men more throughout it all, but she was concerned. "You think we can afford all this?" she asked, furrowed and peckish, a last smile to 'Walter' before he pulled out their plot.

"It's for the future," Solemn heard Redvine say.

The future sounded greedy.

Alice Taylor had driven Redvine up to meet boys in Jackson already. He could do the interest, the deadline, and the terms. Explained it off to Bev as a bank loan. 'Walter' would bring by DigiCates, personally, for Redvine to start. He was ready. The future had to come along now. It was the past that was too unaffordable.

TWENTY

The Weathers' wood-paned, wall-length mural to Pearletta—their "challenging" one—performed its function and made its case: she hasn't always been this way. The wall testified she selected light-pink Mother's Day cards with flower vases on the front. She went to prom, boy 'cross the avenue. Content in braces. Wondrous onstage. Gentle with a violin. At home in velvet. Enamoring even in chunky heels. She was pretty but not photogenic, a miscommunication that may have twisted if not sealed her fate. Her face on news bits or five thousand flyers printed on bank paper, driven throughout 39090 and surrounding bayous, provoked people to glance once. Just once, because she was dark.

Viola Weathers used to pride herself on toughing with no AC and now she kept it cold. Too cold. But no one had heart to say. She preferred to serve only green dinner mints with mint green tea, as much for everyone's nerves as to match the color of her housepaint newly refreshed. "He did it just for me," she smiled, after church, on Saturday she believed was best. She said she read somewhere that green communicated "life." Without base and lashes and rouge, she looked sane. Upon a second Easter past the last one anybody could say they saw Pearletta, Viola ascended herself from rumor slayer and battle-axe to the one who would have rolled the stone to find

Jesus' tomb empty. Apropos. Seamless comparison. A good dream at night.

The Magnolia State and its timber-hushed lands were nowhere near as fussy as their mystique led on. The terrain was friendly, amidst cypress swamps with no tides and packets of thicket in black holes on any map, and exceptional woods. It made up for the haunting antebellum homes and quite courageous Confederate flag posters. Short of randomly digging holes in the ground through it or tracing every single hole in the wall where no one blanketed anonymity for too long, Justin Bolden was at a loss of answers to truly condole himself, let alone the Weathers. As with very few before. And all, no matter their age, were children. Pearletta's mother called him. So he answered. It went this way sometimes, he was learning: blasts from the past, unlikely friendships, a constellation of names, sedimentation to knights in closed position for life. Thank God he had stayed near his parents, his daughter. How many more could there have been, here and there, farther away, and up or down, to the cities? Even now, as he knocked on forty's door, the brain picking and names and all of it clicked his clock into worry about dementia, enough to speed it up. Now, he stood in a stranger's living room in a circle of prayer before talk.

When she had called him this time it was really for the company and no news. For, two years later of little sleep and strident crying spells and emergency room doctors coming up with little but heartbreak, Viola Weathers sat down. They were going to move. Like most victims would, if only they could. Mr. Bolden must come to say good-bye.

"Pearly played the violin in school for me. I started viola when I was five. I was named to go to conservatory, but, well, I met Father. No regrets. Pearly liked to read on the porch. It's why Father put in that swing. She brought the baby up here a few times. Oh, the baby just loved that swing. Thank God she left that nigger home. Heathen, he was. And, you know, kids won't come round you when they're on the crooked and broad. But anyway. That sofa chair you sitting in there? I caught her playing with herself in it one night, watching this late mess on cable. TV's gonna be the death of us. I keep it off. Now, that picture there we took on break to the north, Kansas City. Father's people there. Say they got miles of new white houses on long drives. Black folks in 'em, too. And, still warm. Snow even, but warm. Oh, Pearly liked that cup. She liked the little blue lattice on the edges, gold on the rim. Pearly loved anything at all complicated. The handle ain't as round as it seems though. Nope. Little more creative. Little ridges on the inside if you wanna scratch your finger or readjust without setting down the cup. Nice shape. Like Pearly's . . . So, Mr. Bolden, you want some fried green tomatoes and pot liquor?"

"Well, um. Sure."

"Come with me."

She walked Bolden to the kitchen in back through two halls of what she called her "manor," sliding her fingers along the lid of an upright piano and straightening shoulder-brushed wooden picture frames. Pearletta would show again one day, like a cat shot off in heat rushed back to have the litter. Itinerant—so all the more capable of exhaustion, hunger, and destitution. They'd take her back any way she came. They would leave a forwarding address with the neighbors and one of the new young tellers still at the bank Mr. Weathers left. He couldn't add or subtract well since Pearletta's disappearance. Viola never mentioned her other boy and girl, just holes in a doughnut they were now. The stricken siblings had first escorted Bolden through Pearletta's third-floor back bedroom, since Viola couldn't make it up the stairs in her non-public condition. A shame, the bedroom was. Department store perfume and makeup hoarded in such telling piles as to adjourn the concept of brand. A has-been's overstuffed and tantrum-battered closet. School projects and notebooks and college textbooks crying for help from sunken shelves. The dresser top was greasy; the mirror was smudged and flecked with nail polish. Shame. He could tell it cost good money. Like with any girl, the off-tune music boxes and tangles of common jewelry remained, stuffed animals in astonished poses in the corners. Magazine covers taped to the walls. Posters; Pearletta once adored Britney Spears and U2. Condoms and a league of the one shoe missing spread under her bulky queen bed. Yet the sheets stayed stretched, unde-

famable, and white. Pearletta had always known it was there, perhaps, for little to nothing to do, to just climb on in it at time to use
her key again there.

Viola had allowed him and him alone—"the black fella"—trust to
pinpoint defamations. Him and only him. Just tell her, first, what
fault he found. Now, Viola said, room was cleaned 'cause she had a
little grandson who grew to like it, for the view of the backyard
swing set and sound of the bird feeders, woodpeckers and mourning
doves drawn. Bolden could see the room's windows, heavy white
drapes starched and panes down, when he stood in the former root-
vegetable garden now entombed by disdain.

"All things change, as you know," Viola explained. She was thin-
ner. Her lessened dreadlocks swung back inside, for her to cook and
serve her husband first, drowsy in his La-Z-Boy. Then, she would get
the good policeman's plate ready. Out back in the gazebo, Bolden
slipped back the mosquito net and made himself comfortable in a
wrought-iron chair at a matching table teetered out of balance. A
monarch let itself in.

Out of the sun, away from the station and his precinct grounds
and with perspective to go along with the Buick, Bolden noticed different things from time to time. *There is a breeze. Shade is the noblest
mercy. The sky ain't always blue. Leaves ain't all the same. Ants are quite the
characters.* Day or night, the wildlife camouflage among it all, to guard
the living from the reproach of dead silence. He saw a squirrel round
off for what may, even lower critters cut through grass and silt loam.
The swing set and slide were scratched and scraped from good use.
Pearletta had to be dead. So long as a door to a home like the Weathers' was open and a four-poster bed overlooked a swing set stayed
set, even the most committed junkie would have sulked home by now.
Mr. Weathers' fishing poles drooped and his bait pails tipped against
a wood chalet shed, the door cracked with the ins-and-outs of inven-
torying life, prepping to relocate a lifetime. Its witty, sand-dusted
mementos stacked atop shelves and tables and racks Bolden wanted
to get to know. With Viola scatterbrained inside, and Bolden too
polite to rush her, he went alone.

A crow faceup and wings spread lay at the edge of it. Probably warm. Bolden nudged it with side of his Doc Marten behind sprouts of maidenhair at side of the shed. Besides tougher signs of the industry a banker was not known for but relished nonetheless—a leaf blower, a push lawn mower, axes and saws—the shed stored the run-off of a family clearly once intact and going places. An ivory crib and rocking horse, practice basketball hoops, three matching ten-speeds, a ruffled and collapsed above-ground pool, an old Easy Bake Oven set, golf clubs, and marked boxes of clothes meant for dona-tion. A construction of antique hard drives, computer screens, scan-ners, typewriters, and even a floor-model Xerox machine sat covered by painter's plastic. Atop a carpenter's table were paint pans and cans. The mint-green color Viola pointed out seemed to be the only color used from the many there, all mild. If only he had met Pearletta here and not there. If only there had been no Singer's Trailer Park awaiting her . . . or if Pearletta had waited here, longer, in colors of life and with sound of bird feeders, on porch swings.

Viola tapped Bolden on his neck and he shivered.

"Didn't mean to scare you," Viola said. "I gotta start on this shed soon."

"No," Bolden told her. "A nice one. I'm curious 'bout the size. It hold so much."

"We had it custom-built," Viola told him. "Expected more grand-kids . . . Pearly wanted to hog this on up, too."

"Oh?"

"That girl wanted it all. Before we could crack champagne on the side or cut a ribbon to it she already thought it was hers. It was gonna be her little art studio."

"I ain't know Pearletta was an artist."

"She wasn't. Could've been though. It was just excuse to run on off from us and do things in secret and keep folks guessing, like now, I guess."

"Oh, well, okay."

"She was impatient with painting. So we bought her the stuff to start that pottery bit, 'fore she went off to Oakwood. Actually used it all, too. Still, when she showed up from time to time these last few years. 'Bout a year after all the mess in that there park."

"Yes, Singer's," Bolden said. "There's good people there, despite . . ."

"Keep dreaming," Viola said. "The pottery appealed to her nature a bit more than the painting, you know. It was dirtier. Tough to handle. Business, we told her. We was paying. Black child in Mississippi ain't got no business thinking 'bout majoring in no art. Or black child in all America for that matter. But you've done mighty well for yourself, Mr. Bolden. You wanna see some of the stuff she made? It really is pretty."

Bolden followed Viola to a spacious dugout behind the toys. He saw an electric potter's wheel and stone slab table, unopened bins of clay, and sealed tins of glaze.

"This little pug mill last thing we bought Pearly," Viola said. "Cost a fortunte nearly. When she lost the baby. Divorced that dopehead we told her not to marry. Cost us another fortune to untangle that braid. But the pug mill was my gift. To cheer her up."

Bolden looked at the stacks and stacks of clay circles and glazed vases belonged to Pearletta. He moved near them. Viola skipped past him to resituate the dozens of sturdy works, as she really had only been doing in the shed at times she intended to start purging it. There was music behind the labor; depending on the shape and the glaze, a different sound came when any of it touched. Some pieces had broken, in clumsiness and poor judgment more so than incoherence or rage. However, since she had an audience, Viola was much more careful and systematic about her fiddling. This-away and that-away some needed to be, looked better as, matched colors better, sized up closer . . . the touching of it all and the sounds. Even the dirt it uncovered added to the melody.

"Looka here," Viola said. From a bowl of knicknacks she pulled a small teal work: a long, thin tube with a hole at one of the ends, a round bowl at the other. The inside of the bowl was fragrant, charred. "Pearletta loved her incense. Too much smoke for me."

"It's a nice color," Bolden told her. "May I see it?"

Viola passed the bowl to him and went on back to her task upon a stack of Pearletta's intaglios devoted to nature, rivers, and suns and hilltops with trees. She would keep them, for Pearletta's traveling mural. Had never thought of these, though Father would have to drill in hooks in addition to all else had to be done to get ready. Bolden sniffed the bowl. He smelled the remains of more than a few sessions of weed smoking. That part of what it was used for, probably more, was still apparent in the odor. Bolden noticed the pipe's bowl was not perfectly round. It was indented in the middle, into a heart. And his fingertips sank into imperfections at the side. Or no. Marked, a teeny engraving added after the fact, given how little depth the etching held. With his back to the door where the sun shot through to give Viola even more light, to see she had mixed in a magneta ashtray with the intended purple plate set and this wasn't the way, Bolden made out the message on the side: *Redvine . . . xo, xo . . .*

It would take him just a few days to recall, out the names and faces creaking up what he used to think was a pretty sharp mind, where he knew the name from. And why.

He wondered just how much more Pearletta sprinkled around for them all, unforgotten, unloaded consciousness, snuck in and quickly tucked out of view. Always running. And, as he watched a woman move about her modest shed in back of what she called her "manor" and walked through as the lord of, he resisted the bite of judgment at the before that could have dismayed this after. There had to have been money to get Pearletta Weathers some help before it came down to Pearletta Hassle. It could have been done quietly. Faraway. Maybe they had tried. For the victims he always had to suspend judgment. He put the weed bowl in his pant pocket, a defamation but at least one with a name on it. Maybe a clue or help down the road, if Pearletta was still walking them.

"We was supposed to eat something, right?" Viola asked him, rearranging still.

Bolden let her know she was right, and so they ate.

TWENTY-ONE

Seventy miles down the Trace was a strong, persistent Pearletta flyer, wading in a clogged late-spring drain. And Solemn had chalk between her fingers. In a race with others' apathy and better things to do, Solemn marked up Singer's gate: just Pearletta's name, that's all. Gypsum and limestone attracted her to side of the bank if Bev went, or official buildings like the post office when Bev sent back off to Landon, or park benches and other neat creations of the Arbor Society. Solemn marked the sidewalks in front of the town boutique, jeweler, and a hair shop. Turned so Solemn's face kept blowback from chalk, swirled in the hurry and commitment to spreading Pearletta Hassle's name. One day she sighted a *Have You Seen Pearletta?* sign. Later that night in Singer's, she heard a carry-on between a man and his "bitch" . . . who would go missing just like Pearletta. Solemn believed this was because of her, making it all up on her own.

Parents watched her hunt and inspect coincidence. Bev, tolerable. Redvine, alert.

The GED forms and papers and folders and Scantron sheets arrived each month from the State, to pile at the kitchen table. Now there was the new computer thingy she explored beyond "Be careful." Most nights, the DigiCate screen glowed in the dark in her bedroom or on the couch, its battery cord so hot Solemn kept a little fan by it. Too bad Desi wasn't there to mess it up with her. The Longwoods would have bought one. She knew it. But, oh well, television had turned them funny acting. They even left the fruit dangling like Eden, so comfortable folks got they just showed up in daytime with bags and pails . . .

Solemn, you burnin a candle . . . 'bout to burn this house down? Mama asked.

Those things do kinda smell like sumthin burnin . . . , Daddy noticed.

What I really wanted to know wasn't in books or the DigiCate anyway. I mostly found what I already knew: Oprah was in there but not Kosciusko. Mississippi was. Underground Railroad, too. President Bush, Iraq, and Twin Towers. New York City and Jennifer Lopez, Mariah Carey and hip hop, but not Outkast. I needed to write the DigiCate people, tell 'em to include Pearletta Hassle too. Then I punched M on the machine. I kept goin down these clunky, worrisome, and even fuzzy lists, down to "Magic: a form of creation outside of natural circumstances and normal human consequences."

But it all seem so natural to me. Now the consequences another matter. I just kept on readin, 'bout the rabbits in hats, black wands, sorcery, cauldrons, potions, spells, and cults. But I knew all this already, too. It was basic. Maybe necromancy was the one thing new. I was just tryin to figure myself out. I ain't see myself as powerful as all that. If so, I would've carried away on a broom to all the places I wondered about but the Malibu ain't have gas to get to. Past Houdini and doves, I read 'bout special powers to disappear, fly, control, move, shake, strike people dead and raise them, too, see the future and make it, too. This was nothin worse than movies at Halloween time. On and on, deeper into it, till my appetite lost and my supper cold on the stove and my folks gone to the store without me and Dandy's water bowl run dry, it was the future I was most interested in. I kept on clicking through DigiCate, wantin to know how the future talked.

"White Magic" and "Superstition" sounded good, helpful even—the type of stuff me and Mama sometimes say "This a lie," to on the talk shows, when a serious person play like they can hypnotize a stranger or tell an audience member they mother not really dead. And they was gods who gave the rain and crinkled women who sold dirty teas to make everything better.

Workin under covers in my bedroom, with Dandy twistin round the cat-nip at foot of the bed, I tapped on the Good Witch of the North and the Wicked Witch of the West. Dorothy's story I knew. It was most fun I had had since Desi.

Why you keep clickin your feet like that, Solemn? I paid my folks no mind. I just opened another groove of excitement: "Salem Witches." Hah.

"Several young girls became afflicted in fits and convulsions throughout Salem, Massachusetts, disturbing their homes and interrupting the sermons. Not too long after pinpointing several women in the parish and throughout Salem who told people tales of horoscopes, fortune, and alternative spiritual beliefs, the citizens began to inflict a series of harsh interrogation and punish-ments among the collected women they deemed evil spirits. The women were not represented by formal counsel, nor did many of them receive appropriate and fully conducted trials. Twenty people, mostly women, were executed."

When the screen went black, I realized I forgot to charge the battery long enough. It went off right in the middle of the several pages about it. Only 'bout an hour I had without the charge, even on a brand-new one I snuck out its box. When I went to fuss with it Mama said "I don't think we sup-posed to mess with those, Solemn." But I kept on. I ain't understand why she wasn't happy I was least at home. With these maniacs 'round Singer's. And really, 'sides the Longwoods, ain't neither one of us had no real friends. Them church folks was too funny. I smelled the liquor on they breath. And where was Pearletta at? She just slip off like time? Least Solemn wasn't gonna slip away inside the DigiCate. Or let some boy slip inside me. No matter what you do some folks ain't never gone be satisfied. I knew one thing. If I was really a witch we'd all be rich up in here. What's the point of making crazy stuff if you can do anything at all? I'd make money.

"Sometimes, you gotta wonder if there are witches for real," I told my mother. "That's what I think. Gotsta be. Specially according to this. Twenty witches got killed in America, long time ago."

"Out all the things you could be reading and thinking about with that thing," Bev told her, "you gotta wander off into something scary."

"This what I'm interested in," I said, and went back to my screen.

Little girls started it. Nine and eleven, I read, my fingers runnin across words. Close to me and Desi a few years ago, sound like. And, like I also had just a few years ago, right 'round time I first had blood between my legs and my face in the mirror started to look incorrect to my own eyes and I met The Man at the Well and I put my lips on Desiree's and we all blasphemed Easter with the Festival, I recognized myself in them girls: sweaty, fitting, in contempt of grown folks around them, overprotected, chased in the woods, and shook back to attention lest the preacher get mad.

Seem a high price to pay for misbehavior. And no matter what side of misbehavin I'm on—the one interruptin or the one called "strange" for touchin those interrupted—I think I saw to make sure nobody never paid any more attention to me for nothin out the ordinary beyond that already said and done. If I really was a witch, and that's what all this tellin me, I wasn't tellin nobody. And if I wasn't, well . . . either way, I was stuck.

Meanwhile, future came into hurry and worry and commitment to spread the DigiCates. The boxes took over whatever floor space there had been in Bev and Redvine's bedroom. His family laughed him off. At least they were good practice. The DigiCate was not assembled into one piece as it had been at the Days Inn and when 'Walter' brought the show-off one to the trailer. It had a wide screen with a long neck to attach to a broad keyboard, covers to put on here and there, and several CDs to download depending on the desired subjects. So, Redvine knew he had bought one just to keep assembled for folks to see it wasn't hard. He gave up on making extra off a sample.

"Why you starting with the church I don't know," Bev told him. "If the collection plate empty when it's your turn, what you think that mean?"

Very day Redvine brought a few DigiCates to church, the preacher tired out the flock, finger licking and flipping pages faster while he rolled through Revelation: lashed out at electronics for 666 stamped on their foreheads and injected into the arms, with robots reading the numbers for a special Devil club. Solemn made sure she read along and looked interested, and smiled at the new visitors. After this, the tried-and-true members turned their noses down to the wristwatches they checked all through Redvine's pitch. Besides, they had just sprinkled the collection plate with their lasts. When Redvine set a DigiCate on top of a few trucks or the bench in the churchyard, not even Solemn's enthusiasm could wiggle attention. Once, his batteries died mid-sentence.

Singer's was no use. Many trailers didn't have a phone yet.

"TV just fine for me," the few people Redvine brought it up to said.

Security was too tight at Montfort Jones, and other places. Redvine spent many days halted, tongue-twisting: "I don't have an appointment." But this was 'cause of the phone. If he could only get one, he could make appointments in advance.

Redvine used some of what Landon sent him to slip a grand into Alice Taylor's hands for send-off to the boys in Jackson, as he promised her he would in a month.

No use with the electrical plant boys and men. It wasn't that there wasn't work. More electronics than ever. But Redvine heard it was all ordered on the computer now—not in the stores like the electronics plants shipped it all off to. The boys knew. But the older men weren't buying it. So they stood and they stood and they stood and they stood in lines for less pick lines to pick from, culminated.

School was out, nothing but the government-working teenagers chiseling gum off school desks and scrubbing chalkboards and waxing floors and repainting letters on the buildings. Any parents or kids or teachers left behind in summer school were not looking to stay ahead of the curve, hence there would be none. The few he talked to just didn't know what he was talking about.

But there was a dazzling import from a college in the Catskills, as she explained, with spirit. Redvine met her when he was looking around a junior high school at tip of the county, where the import was for the next two years via a special program to teach in underserved areas. She was an olive one, sprite linen jacket, and caked red lipstick run past her lip line. She saw Redvine wandering the hallways, equally as inappropriately dressed for the weather. But the jacket helped him fit in better than just a good shirt all by itself. Outside Singer's and Bledsoe and the black part of town, Redvine was still sultry. He had courage. Down a hallway neglecting to mention it was still broad daylight, the brand-new teacher led him into her old classroom and proceeded to pitch herself.

"I didn't want to just live off my parents' money all my life," she told him. Two brown boys wrung out mops in the back of her class-room. One shoved textbooks back into a steel cabinet newly Lysoled. "Antoine, make sure all the books in the whole cabinet are in order by the numbers on the spines, sweetheart, so we can keep up with them when we let them out."

Antoine started all over.

"They almost sent me to the border of Texas. I speak Spanish. But I wanted to be here. People love this place, because of Oprah Winfrey. Who wants to go to Texas? I mean, after all, the Bush dynasty? Works for my parents, I guess. How do you vote, sir?"

"I don't. What you teaching?"

"Geography."

Luck.

"May I show you our specially priced *Geography Catalog*?" he asked her.

"Wow . . . that sounds wonderful."

While he got settled with it, the teacher went back to pull the industrial fan closer to them, as well as to fill two Dixie cups at the water fountain in the hall. By now, she had kicked off her heels and slid around in her stockings. When she came back, Redvine clicked through the buttons and keyboard and screens, surprising himself with each maneuver. Before long, the boys stood in the back of the classroom cracking jokes. Redvine and the teacher kicked their legs back and forth underneath the round table while they played with the DigiCate. Under "Countries of the World," Redvine started with Afghanistan to impulse the teacher into a way to teach about the war. Then he skipped up to Zaire, which he'd never heard of, but the teacher was most excited. She could teach them aaaaaaaaalll about their people. Starved for reprimand, the brown boys came to the front of the room to be with Redvine and the teacher.

"What do y'all think of this?" the teacher asked her charges for the next week.

"What is it?" said one of the brown boys. He drank a grape pop and had replaced his red bandana on his head into a skeptical arrangement.

"It's a digital encyclopedia, almost like a computer with its own World Wide Web," Redvine told them.

"We ain't got that Internet round here," Antoine said.

"We are working on it, Antoine," the teacher told him. "This seem like something you-all would see as essential to reinforce what you're learning?"

"I thought it was a Xbox," the brown boy said.

"No, son," Redvine told him. "No games here. Learn something though, help with your schoolwork. It's portable, too. Seem like something y'all like?"

"Long as I ain't gotta read the whole book," the other brown boy said.

The teacher was pleased and explained to Redvine she had a special budget aside from the other teachers, endowment from her program. Once she filled out the forms . . .

"How long that's gonna take?" Redvine asked. He thought back to what 'Walter' told him to tell everybody: "I only have a few left, ma'am."

"Oh, well, in that case," the teacher said. She would be the first one she knew to have one of these and certainly able to talk about it in the next staff meeting as well as the teacher program's upcoming powwow to get set for the year of changing lives. Had she not been so prudent from the "community relations" trainings she would have written Redvine a check on the spot. He didn't look bad. Not at all. Few of them did. But she was hesitant to give out her home address, just meeting him brand-new and being in a small-town apartment alone. She asked him for time to get a money order. In just a few days, Redvine walked a one-thousand-dollar and a two-hundred-dollar money order into the post office of Koscuisko. The one clerk sent him out to come back later in the day. At top of the doors opening, he would have taken all her change. So he knew this was the way. He wanted to stay a man who took all the change.

With just five more sales (three in full, no layaway wait)—to a farmer outside Kosciusko, the two bank tellers in town who knew him well enough to cash his checks without a balance on hand, one retired secretary working the Farmers Market at Catherine Street, and Hall Carter in credit to their income tax refund later—DigiCate afforded the Redvines a real Bell South line straight into the trailer. Finally. DigiCate afforded more and better food in the Redvine refrigerator.

Redvine dumped the Everclear and Bacardi 151 diluted with water for bottles of industry wine and brand-name six-packs in the fridge. Once Solemn's new optician and even her old principal came along in atonement, DigiCate afforded Bev the showy perfume bottles she had once collected. Redvine went to a black family-owned office store on Veterans Memorial Parkway, going-out-of-business sign in the door. Fine-cut business cards the owner's son made him, dirt cheap.

But it took nearly a month for all this to come true.

When the Malibu sailed past the electronics plant early in the mornings, it only pretended to have somewhere more to go than just not there. Same for the usual spots the men collected to wash down cars, set stone, break up concrete, forage junk parts. Anybody racing past it all gotta have a little something-something, they thought. When Redvine celebrated without bragging, he wound up footing one more round or dropping more people off without nary an offer for gas money or trouble. He made offers, sure. To come by for a demonstration or give him a few bucks for a catalog was too much for most. One night, Redvine looked out the windows while he got drunk on what was left of some of the wedding whiskey. He saw Singer's, Bledsoe, the well, friends who no longer spoke. Everything and all in between was like a beer can turned up with only the tail end of a craving left. He had never figured himself for a traveling salesman, but if he was going to be like 'Walter' and buy himself a gold pen something had to change. Fast.

"In the Delta," 'Walter' said when he called back. "Ain't nobody covered it yet."

"Kinda far to drive," Redvine said.

"Naw, just a little bit west and north," 'Walter' said. "You get there, it's yours."

So the next little black thing come into the house was a cell phone. Bev thought it was a remote control, so fat it was. Boost Mobile—just a little contract for Redvine to sign at one of 'Walter's' friend's shops in town. It was essential if he was going on the road; so 'Walter' said. Went good with the phone at home now, if he was gonna be out on the road away from Bev and Solemn. It took just two days of Solemn staring at Singer's gate, no Landon to talk to and Bev prone to the television now, to ask, "Can I go this time?"

By end of June, a right foot dirty from the heel to the big toe hung out of the Malibu. The car sailed on the Trace and through Sunflower County into scorching Bolivar County. The foot twirled sometimes right on the edge of the passenger side window, at fall of the door and window ledge, in the sunlight or moonlight or wind. No matter the weather or the road, there was the dangly foot, even if a sprinkle. There was no way Solemn was going to know men were out and she was at home. No. Not anymore.

In event of a storm or tornado warning, the Malibu stayed in Singer's. If the prognosis was clear for more than a night, the Malibu parked outside a Motel 6 if there was disappointment and a Howard Johnson's if there was one of the three sales. Solemn let the blowback of Southern road caress her unpolished toenails. She could press buttons on its small keyboard to enlarge the screen as much as she needed to, like the big-print *Reader's Digest* books. She had no reason to squint. Redvine paid her ten dollars a day, come hell or high water, rain or shine, no matter what, to drive with him.

When a curious or baby face let in from time to time, he approached any living or great room he was invited into: *Could the DigiCate fit here? Or here?* He loved self-assemble desks, bare tops of fireplaces, cubicles in a china cabinet where broken photos or passed-along china used to be, old frame houses with shelving built into the banisters and stairs, breakfronts with wide expanses and bare roofs . . . *Gas cheap . . . Two dollars a gallon if I time the trip right . . .* The investment of traveling seemed the best path so long as he didn't hit the brakes much or speed out the gas, stayed in the passing lanes.

No more groveling for a quick break. Now Redvine had an opportunity: to ride ride ride against the sunset and the dawn with the radio blasting. His cigarette break was just the ashtray in his car. No more begging to go out for a smoke ("Boss"), unable to savor it for thinking about who taking his place on the pick line. On the road,

Redvine snapped his fingers and forgot how small his bedroom was or how quiet the rare sex had to be.

That part of it all was joyful.

But he wasn't selling anything.

An optimist, he kept the remaining five DigiCates on hand at all times, bound in heavy cardboard boxes like slaves, packed and stacked tight with ornate box tops to keep them contained. The sales demonstrator had Solemn's fingerprints all over it, but Redvine let it go.

Even Solemn learned the type of customer who just might buy; ones who actually took the material into their hands were worth coming back for. If more than five and no more than ten minutes passed of Daddy talking without one touch from a startled housewife or cold husband, let alone perky children, Solemn whined she was hungry. So they left. No more wasted time. On to the next. From amoebas to Buddhism to the Chicago World's Fair to Freud to the Kentucky Derby races to xenophobia, Solemn tapped through the DigiCate screens in excitement and inertia during her car rides with her daddy. All too often, she interrupted playlists and disk jockey banter to ask questions:

"Hey Daddy, did you know ornithomimosaurs were a dinosaur look like ostriches look today?" "Daddy, you know Sacajawea led the men Thomas Jefferson sent when she was big and pregnant?" "Daddy, you know the Hellenistic period had a queen named Cleopatra Grandma talked 'bout all the time before she died, and she committed suicide?" "Daddy, you know Beethoven was deaf?" "Daddy, you know . . . ?"

Redvine didn't know any of it. He didn't care. Which made him wonder why the hell he was asking others to. And to pay one thousand dollars for it on top. Something for everybody, he guessed. Was the house gonna be bigger than the promises, for all this? To all of Solemn's questions, and proposed answers, Redvine just gave a head nod. He kept his eyes on the long and promising road, sandy and saffron, searching for winners who'd make him feel like one in kind. But most who would actually let him through the door were like the following.

TWENTY-TWO

Those Watsons lived among about eight hundred other people at the edge of Merigold, Mississippi, along the eastern hem of Arkansas, in a shotgun house with a built-on porch, on a nook replete with working water pumps. Three bedrooms wound around a curved hallway with a bathroom tucked all the way in the back. A window inside this would not shut. A brown curtain hung over it instead. Bubble flies buzzed in. On top of the floor-model television, the entire of the family's hardback book collection rested: the *Origin of Species,* mostly Jackie Collins and Danielle Steel and V. C. Andrews books, *The Godfather,* a Bible. The window fans were decent and young enough to still talk over.

"A day laborer with a construction company," he said.

"A laundress," she said. Still, in 2004. Mrs. Watson had five lines strung out back between sweet gum trees. She had three steel and pewter washboards inside, two more tubs in the backyard. As soon as she finished pinning up the latest batch, she came inside to sit with her husband and the salesman who showed up wearing a sport coat in ninety-degree weather. Solemn frisked in the front yard, kicking rocks. The son watched her.

"The gentleman's selling encyclopedia computers," Mr. Watson kept repeating to his wife. She heard him the first time. "Ain't that something?"

For a salesman to come calling meant there was something noticeable about him. Had to have been something attracted the guy to his house. And his daughter was smart, he told the talkative salesman. She placed in the regional finals of an NAACP spelling bee and won the county oration award run by a Baptist church league.

Mrs. Watson cocked her head and leaned against the wall, wanted to half-whisper and half-shout, *We don't need no encyclopedias . . . kids got them computers in school now.* But her husband looked to be enjoying himself. The stranger seemed nice.

"Supper?" she asked him.

"I'd love to," he said.

The young girl with him—"Solemn . . . *S-o-l-e-m-n*"—asked for two plates. The men decided to shake on it, half now and the rest later.

"No cash in the house" resulted in Redvine's acceptance of a check. He had taken them before, albeit never from a day laborer and laundress with no vehicle. Redvine hung behind for Mr. Watson's ceremonial assemblage of the DigiCate, its many cumbersome cords on a shelf he had his wife remove her family picture from.

"Man, you could drill two more two-by-fours in the wall below this shelf, to almost make for a real desk to set it on," Redvine theorized. "Make it easier to work on that way. Watch the cords though. Can run hot. I gotta come back to this area soon for another prospect. Or, you know what, send me a mail order before the end of the month. Lemme give you my business card. I got my own account and phone number. And definitely, if you so inclined, pass 'em out to your friends to call me. Earl. Earl Redvine."

Redvine first left the Watsons' home with a stomach full of Coors, great northern beans, rice, and neck bones—plus a five-hundred-dollar check in his hands in exchange for the supper and conversation. He and Solemn checked into a Howard Johnson's just because.

Less than a month later, Redvine pulled the Malibu to edge of the dirt road where there would have been a curb elsewhere. Here were only thinned patches of yellow grass. A bunch of kids played on top a pile of deflated tires. A Saint Bernard chased after the ones rolled down the road. Across the street, a few women sat in lawn chairs in a front lawn missing the lawn part. A few men in sleeveless shirts and jeans crouched down on the corner. They shot dice. Not too far off the road, the son met him.

"My daddy ain't here," the son said.

"Well, hello," Redvine said. "I'm Earl Redvine, from DigiCate—"

"I know who you are," the boy said.

"Well, yes, I remember you too. How DigiCate working out for you?"

"Fine . . . Mama!"

The son ran around to the back of the house. The women across the way peered at Redvine. Redvine caught the laughter at his back, in his honor. He turned around to see the group waving at him. He waved back and his wedding ring caught a sunray. One woman said, "Aw . . . shoot!" She got up from the lawn chair and twisted while she slapped hands with the women. "I'll take him anyway, darlings . . ." She laughed.

Solemn heated up in the car. She came out to meet her daddy at the porch. Mrs. Watson came from the back of the house, clutching her wet gray-and-pink-checkered dress. She did not have the same grin on her face they had met her with. Pinched face instead. Her boy stood in the doorway, thumbing the screen.

"Nice to see you," she told the salesman. "You too." She smiled at his daughter.

"You as well, Missus Watson," Redvine said. "Your husband 'round?"

"Oh no. He's on a job."

"Is it somewhere near here?" Redvine asked. "I really need to talk to him."

"Well, yes. I 'magine he's working the area. They don't send him too far. Sumthin' I kin help you with?"

Both Watson names had been on the bank check, or contract in this case. But Mr. Watson wrote the check and so it was with him whom Redvine should discuss it.

"Well, no, I really should talk to your husband 'bout our deal," Redvine said.

"Oh," Mrs. Watson said, with her hands on her hips. Solemn shuffled.

"I understand," Mrs. Watson finally said. Then, "I kin give you a new check."

"Well," Redvine said, "it'd be better if I had the cash. So, you know, I could cover what I lost. 'Cause, you know, I get my commissions on the sales, but technically I bought your DigiCate myself. You understand what I'm saying."

"Oh, I understand. Hold on." Mrs. Watson began to walk back to the house. Then she motioned back. "Please, sit on the porch and get out that sun."

They heard Mrs. Watson's voice between her son's, what sounded like shuffling inside drawers. Ten minutes later, the women across the way started to laugh good-byes and hug away. The kids and Saint Bernard moved down the block somewhat, aroused by a cart of ice cream and shaved ice. The crowd of men on the corner scattered. Ten more minutes later, Solemn had lain back in the hard secondhand kitchen chair recycled to patio furniture. She dozed off. Five minutes after this, Redvine rapped on the door.

"Well, you'll have to forgive my manners," the wife said. "Sorry. I just been in here lookin' all round. You know . . . all them little places you forget about."

"I understand."

The teenage boy appeared behind his mother. In his arms, he held what was left of the DigiCate. The three cords to run it and charge it were a mess. Copper wires poked out. A few dents on the chrome top, which 'Walter' had claimed was hard as granite.

"This all I could find," she said. Mrs. Watson opened her right fist, full of bills and coins. "It's the middle of the week, so I ain't been paid for my washin' yet. That come on the weekend. You know, when everybody come to pick up what they left with me. I'm kinda behind this week. But by the end . . . Can you come back then?"

"It's such a drive," Redvine explained. Solemn saw behind them that one of the women who had been in the yard across the street appeared.

"Seen you come out the back and just had to come over to see if the washing was done," the lady said. Then she looked over at Redvine. "How you? I'm Valerie."

"Earl. Earl Redvine."

"Yeah, Valerie," Mrs. Watson said. "I'm fixing to do yours next. Should be done by the time the sun rise tomorrow. I been back out there all day . . ."

"Take your time . . . I wanna look at some of them records Troy selling off. Shame he gotta give 'em up. I know how long he been collecting them. We all know how it is."

"Oh, and yes . . ." Mrs. Watson fumbled the cash around. Finally, she grabbed at a twenty-dollar bill and crunched the rest in her right hand.

"I forgot I owe you this, for the groceries for Estrella's spelling bee picnic and all." She held it out to the woman on her porch.

"Girl, you betta put that money up," Valerie said.

"Valerie—"

"Now don't you go insult my intelligence. I ain't been thinking about them groceries. Shit, I probably ate and drunk up half of 'em myself. What you cook today?"

"Some squash, greens and fatback, red potatoes, a pecan crumble. I'm boilin' a chicken. Waitin' for it to float. But Valerie, lemme give you this money while I got it."

"Gimme a plate instead. Money ain't never been my friend. Soon as you give it back to me somebody gonna take it back from both us. I been thinkin' more about getting some clean draws back in my house." She glared at Redvine.

"Clean draws are important," Redvine said.

"I bet they is, for a man like you, clean as a whistle and— Well, I'm gon' leave that alone. Talk to you later, girl. Just come by when you done. Wrap me up a plate." Before Valerie got halfway out the yard, she was waving, "Hey there now!" to a passing sedan with the wheels falling off. She whisked into the street to catch the halted driver.

"You know," Redvine second-thought, "don't worry about it. We give away promotional copies all the time, for prizes and stuff."

"But we never entered a contest. Please, I insist," Mrs. Watson said.

"So do I," Redvine told her. "Have a good day. Enjoy the machine. If you want more, just call DigiCate or mail in an order form."

"We will," Mrs. Watson said. "I promise you."

"Fair enough." Redvine grinned. He turned and slapped Solemn on her shoulder to go. The man and his daughter walked across the yard back to the Malibu. The man pulled off in such an expert and stylish fashion the tires did not even roll out any dust from the dirt road they had mistakenly traveled onto.

'Walter' was in Orlando now. Or maybe Mobile or Dayton, as Redvine found him once while he hunted down advice on how to sell Digi-Cates back to DigiCate. He was actually trying to break through 'Walter's' cell phone on a Monday night, in the week he took off to rethink things, when Alice Taylor drove up into the yard, with two of the chipped-toothed and pockmarked boys from Jackson in the passenger seat and back, hard-core and maybe horns under their caps or 666 tattooed on their wrists, and their Ruger pistols pocketed only because Solemn was out front in the yard with lightning bugs at her knees, letting the mosquitoes tear at her while she twirled Dandy up with string.

The future was here.

TWENTY-THREE

The landscape stayed too long plain and uneventful, relieved here and there by the triangular roof of the only houses at the road for miles on the Mississippi Blues Trail, then finally Route 61 headed back to Attala's parts and Bledsoe and Singer's and bed. Once, a ghost town riveted the way. A sprinkling of trailers in the distance provoked Solemn to wonder how many girls inside could be like her. She was not alone. She had to imagine. Redvine was untalkative. His thoughts were scattered. No knots or knocked loose teeth or broken bones—yet. He wouldn't stay that way for long, he knew. He needed a big sale. Big. Not one. An entire lodge or block or ladies' club, maybe. He decided this time, Delta and back, would be it. As Solemn fingerprinted what could have been discount sales if left clean, Redvine noticed the statement of a silo it took minutes to look forward to but a second to pass. *I'm going west or east?* he thought.

Then, half mile later, electric and cable cords in taunt crisscrosses. *Seem like we already been this way,* Solemn felt.

Finally, a courteous pickup truck leaning half its body into the grass of rock road as Redvine did the same with the Malibu, so they both could pass. He barely knew where he was. He was just driving along. Then, in front of him, more than a few dissimilar houses crowded along a road, bearing owners' insignias on the mailboxes and kick-stood bikes in the yards. Where there were kempt mailboxes, there was income. Where there were bikes, there were children. Where there were mailboxes and bikes and children, there was the future to ride into. He stopped regretting Bolivar County, Mississippi.

"Finally." Redvine sighed.

He reached into the glove compartment through the textures of their life stuffed inside: silky handkerchiefs Bev took to church, wrinkly carbons of contracts filled out but unsigned, scratchy foil around melted chocolate Solemn hoarded, a tough hemp sack ensuring his car registration and driver's license copy remained producible. Smooth and silky was the brochure for the Tudor homes. He flecked his collar and slapped his eyelids alert. On a weekday, there would be women behind any open curtains. Depending on their enthusiasm, he might have to find the nearest diner or coffee shop to rest until their husbands came home. He would bring Solemn inside, with him, to show his daughter.

He could have chosen the pebble-laden path leading up to the one-story white shingle house, basic and plain like a letter envelope, hedged by crape myrtles. There was another one like it across the street, a little longer and accented by a tin roof topped along a skinny driveway, wisteria fringed. He saw pickup trucks, spare tires, and carriage-size dome trailers in one yard. And though the region wasn't a fan of brick, these first two houses shrunk into shame next to several bi-level red- and yellow-brick ones. Those ones had balconies dart out from a few upper rooms. Solemn recognized the start of something in the jerky steering. Redvine patted the brakes to survey a house or yard, predict the occupants' occupations, guess at the character types. He knew what to look for: A little shed signaled collectors of impulses more than needs. A barn. If a barn was full, some profit off livestock maybe. If it was vacant, unnecessary, then there was an inheritance. He listened to a distant coach house when it said renters or relatives capable of leisure came around seasonally. The combination of all three was unusual, but he spotted this sum inside an enclave of winding road fit for just one car at a time. So, not much traffic or movement. What traffic there was, was predictable and never rushed. The house was weather-beaten into a hav-ocked conveyance. Its yard was chock-full of a few dull and shiny vehicles, entrance set apart by ornate black posts. It was just the rapacious display he feared, for the groveling required. But altogether, it was the better hope.

"We gonna stop here," he told Solemn.

Solemn was absorbed in a listing of presidents seemed just up-dated to "Bush," on "Cleveland, Grover," now, since she had seen the *Cleveland County* sign awhile back, saying it was home to him. Redvine swerved around to reach his briefcase in the backseat. He set it in his lap. He chugged the last of the tepid coffee in his thermos. He reached into his shirt pocket for ammunition against poor breath or weak voice—a Halls. Solemn got the radio to hurdle over the usual country and western into 103.9, urban contemporary. Redvine pointed to the stack of properties kitty-corner to the Malibu.

"I'll be here," he said to her. "Stay in the car. Or come to that door."

Solemn looked across to an entrance with three frosted floral panels and a gold emblem door knocker. In a place where there was scarcely a need for anyone but the postman to see a number to know the address, she took the door as her reference. Redvine exited the Malibu and opened the back door. He gathered the display models Solemn had already run through. It was a toll on his recently aching shoulders, even when he alternated sides, if he remembered.

A few songs later I noticed I ain't seen my daddy. He ain't motioned me inside to meet nobody who care to meet me. He ain't come back to the car. He wasn't kept standin out on the porch. He was inside the house still. There. A porch light shined in the afternoon. The sprinklers went haywire. It was hot. I wanted to walk in the water.

This pebble path massaged my feet. I felt 'em, but rocks couldn't cut me. I carried my flip-flops in my hand. A barefoot woman I was. I could smell the berry pie, felt the fresh-watered grass, heard somebody laughin, saw the paper on the porch. It was next to roses. I knew rosebushes was nearly im-possible here, Mama said. Maybe, since somebody live here succeeded, Daddy found a customer who was tough-talkin him. Them ones always held him up. They didn't ever buy shit though. I pressed my ear to the door. I ain't hear nothin. I rang the bell. Some pretty chimes. I stood there for what seem like a long time, had my ear against this frosted door. I ain't hear nothin. Finally I grabbed hold of the warm sweaty knob to let myself in.

This first room was more than what I had imagined could be there. The wooden floor was dark and light and medium planks. A shiny black cat—no, telephone it was—sat at the door. It had its whole own table with a cushioned chair pushed into it, like the kids table at Thanksgiving. A Bell South phone book was in a cubby under the table. What I first heard like this cluckin at me, like from a teacher or old woman's tongue, turned out to be a grandfather clock. I ain't never seen one of those. I eased forward on the floor like it was a frozen lake, first 'cause I had no idea if it might creak and next to scoot out in secret if I needed to. Past the foyer was a parlor with huge patterned couches. A table large as my bed rested in the middle. Another table was a chess game with pieces laid out underneath on a glass step, teacups rested on top. I sized it all up: this leather photo album with a clear openin on the cover, for the yellow picture of a couple drowned in a wedding gown fit for two brides, a book of Mississippi swamps, paper called The Bolivar Commercial *and* Time *and* Life *magazines just like my mama keep.*

"Daddy?"

I wondered if it was a furniture set outside. Mmmmmmmmmmmm . . . lemonade or iced tea and biscuit cookies come with that. In the next part, a piano sat black in a corner. A parrot cage. The birds was green and blue, part pink and yellow in some spots. Not even one wing flap to let nobody know they was here. Painted pictures of off-yellow and cream faces decorated the walls—dark wood framed, faces jut out, lookin like they had some complex messages. Boys and girls mostly. A few women. One man. The back door shined. I thought it was a light tunnel in back of the house. Yeah, I got a little mad, walkin through the cut slant in the kitchen, with every one of the dozens of porcelain cups and hundred stacked glass plates and handy teapots and tiny cauldrons and glass carafes stored behind small glass doorways. Who the fuck get to live in a dollhouse?

———

Redvine had walked up to the house same as Solemn. No one answered. He rang the bell, a couple times. He never would have otherwise, but he tried the knob. It was loose. He stepped in. Maybe this
was the type of place where there were servants, a maid or an assistant. Someone to answer the door. So he had walked in and stood,
half-expecting anybody who was home would sense a stranger in
midst. And that stranger, a black man, would be something to shout
out against. But he was a salesman. He had a daughter and even a
business card with him. And he would claim he had come to look for
her. He—*didn't know why*—grabbed a pair of *R*-monogrammed cream
ladies' gloves dangled on a coatrack hook; tiny and dainty they were.
He had always taken pride in being a small man, and the women
had always loved his small hands. The women had loved more about
him, too. He could have been even less faithful than he had ever been.

Earl Redvine had no idea how he would explain himself were he
caught walking up crouching and moaning stairs, just to check. Instinct guided him to that as well. But again, no one. Just more of
the same. The room doors upstairs all open. Beds made. Rugs pulled.
Closets closed. The neckties and necklaces dangled from the corner
of a mirror in one room. An inkhorn alone on the hallway secretary. A bathroom punctuated the middle of the mouthful of a hallway Redvine walked down. A clawfoot tub centered the room. The
bathroom sparkled. Not a speck of soap or toothpaste on the oblong
vanity mirror. A linen shower curtain hung from a few rungs, without a wrinkle in it. A stack of magazines rested on a small table near
the bronze tissue paper holder. A vase, dried nettle and sage.

Redvine called, "Hello?" All he saw was all he did not have and
maybe never would—the hole in the doughnut. There was a final con-
solation in it. Being his age. He had a son in the military. He had a
daughter-in-law. He had grandchildren. He had a daughter, unruly
but not without hope of being broken into respectable conformity.
He had a beautiful wife who remained faithful in her ways with him
and optimistic about all he attempted. He had indiscretions undis-
covered and covered up, by another man and a well no longer used,
fittingly. And the roof over his head had no payments under it. It
was his. He owned it. He had accomplished much.

But he cried.

He cried for secrets he put on his daughter and a missing woman he did not really know. He cried his son and daughter never fell down steps the minute they learned to walk. Actually, they never had steps to fall down. He cried his son was married at a one-room church and his daughter could not marry in a cathedral. He cried someone was allowed to have bi-level and tri-level homes with barns and coach houses and lawns and pet dogs whose coats shone as if they had been waxed. He cried he never went to college or the military or anywhere else would get him beyond a few states around Mississippi. He cried, so much so he did not even see his daughter appear on the top floor of the house.

She caught him in the master bedroom. She had thought about it. A lot.

She giggled some when she spoke: "You know, we could just take they stuff."

Redvine snapped out of it, came back. He focused on Solemn, so much taller and like her mama she had gotten, without him being able to pay bills, let alone attention.

"Yeah," he kind of told her and himself. "I guess we can."

Redvine stuffed rings and necklaces and broaches in his pocket. He moved frantically. But Solemn, who made him do it, did not. "Go back and empty those things out the boxes and bring 'em here . . . now!" he shouted. "Should be four or five boxes."

Solemn's footsteps down the stairs and across the wooden floor sounded hollow. She heard the parrots chirping. But no, it was not a father or a mother or a son or a neighbor come through the back door to catch her and her father inside of this home, rummaging. Solemn shot out of the door. Once in sunlight, she looked across the yards. Folks were inside, locked and holed up. Perhaps eating lunch. In all the time she had ridden with her father, they had never come upon a house with the doors unlocked.

Solemn opened the door of the driver side to remove the key from the ignition. She went to the back of the Malibu and slid the key into the trunk's keyhole. The click sounded louder than ever. But there was still no one around. No cars on the road. No neighbors in the yards. It was quiet and peaceful. She lifted the lids off the tops of the DigiCate boxes and tossed the heavy machines into the trunk. She perspired under her arms and between her legs. Sweat dripped down from everywhere, it seemed. She resolved to go inside the house and use some of the soap she had seen in the bathroom: *French Milled* engraved atop it. She wiped her face as the sweat tickled it, so to not wet pretty soap. She took a last sweep of the avenue before she stacked four boxes into one another. Then she walked back to the house and let herself in like she really lived there.

By this time, Redvine was downstairs with a neat pile of jewelry at the door. The pile was a gleaming high tangle of wristwatches, stopwatches, necklaces, lockets, rings, bracelets, cameos, and cuff links amidst a shiny miscellany.

"Throw all that in there," Redvine told Solemn. Then, he grabbed a box and hustled to the back of the house. Solemn grabbed a few handfuls from the pile. She heard a crash. She caught Redvine smashing the doors from an imposing cabinet of ammunition and guns. He used a fireplace poker. Like somebody Solemn had never seen, Redvine tore into the cabinet and threw stuff in a box. He looked up only to tell Solemn he needed a new box. She followed him into the kitchen. *A man there in back of the kitchen, broad bellied and white, stern. Ready to lock our hands in little round chains. Hah. He only a stretched-out apron hung down from a nail, his coat strings tied behind.*

And so it went. Father and daughter tore through a house in Cleveland, Mississippi, on a quiet afternoon when the *Richards Family* (as engravings on the jewelry introduced them) had decided to take advantage of the nice day to go to the Ellis Theater for a show. An impromptu trip, bluegrass music along the way, the usual seats. Everyone knew them. "Ain't no crime round *here*." Traveling salesmen came and went; Girl Scouts showed up with cookies; neighbors received neighbors' packages to set on doorsteps.

From the house, Solemn and Redvine collected jewelry and artillery and silver and china. They ransacked a breakfront and desk drawers. They snatched down unopened bottles of aged whiskey and bourbon and scotch. They piled up silk scarves and wrapped kitchen crystal inside them. They found loose fifty- and hundred-dollar bills and Susan B. Anthony dollars and Indian buffalo nickels. There was a coin collection. He uncovered a set of gold pens—*To Thomas Richards, for 30 years of dedicated service to Bolivar County.* He threw them in, jinxed and mad he had ever thought he could be a good enough salesman to buy some of his own. He found a laundry bag in a dumbwaiter behind the kitchen. He dumped out the rank linen and towels to find a few empty pillowcases. Heavy cotton. There was little way to walk outside with two vintage phonographs, one small television and one boom box he found without some potential notice or injury to their finer parts. He spared them. He gave the pillowcases to Solemn to carry out. He watched her carry them across the lawn, straining and losing her balance. If her plans were intercepted, she had already imagined a role: she would be the babysitter, or the cleaning girl, or the help who helped the seniors keep their prescriptions up to date. Her daddy stayed hidden inside. She was the one who did the transporting. And with each new box placed in the back of the car seats there was new excitement and reward. Daddy must have sensed her nature. Some excitement was what Solemn craved. Some adventure and risk taking. And, the last time she walked into the house to see what Daddy had found, she found him sitting alone in the kitchen: relaxed and content. He sweated. He smiled at her. The Richardses had a coffeepot. The hemp bag of coffee near it had a Spanish name. It was nothing he had ever heard of. Redvine brewed himself a cup.

"Bring me my thermos," he told his daughter.

He sat at a cedar kitchen table with a gleaming varnish he wished someone would hire him to put into place. He knew how to varnish. His father taught him the apt pressure to give so the glimmer wouldn't pucker and split later. It made everything look better than it was and anything that was not better look pretty damned good.

Solemn bought him his thermos. Redvine filled it with the coffee he made in a pot in the Richards kitchen. Solemn left to the car. "Redvine" to others, "Red" to his wife, "Earl" to himself. He'd leave it there in the house. Because so many other men looked up to him for sticking by his children. Because he always made the honest, however harder, living. Because Bev's neck really was long and pearls rewound her face. Because nobody really know shit really anyway so it's okay for everybody not to know it all about him. Because Solemn really belonged in a new paid school, some place can handle her intellect. Money talks, louder than any voice . . . On top of the tables, cascaded over steps to a brand-new house, piled in the bank, under the bed, under the floor, in the clothes on his back, everywhere . . . money would be.

The last time he lifted his thermos to drink in the house, a seam along the middle of the index finger of his ladies' glove stretched to a rip and then a full tear. Redvine rinsed his porcelain coffee cup when he finished. He poured the remaining coffee from the pot into his thermos. It was the last thing he took out of the house. A long drive home, back to Singer's Trailer Park in Bledsoe, was silent save for Solemn's songs on the radio.

TWENTY-FOUR

Bev worried and wondered why Red hadn't called. She didn't want to bug him, concentrated on her spaghetti instead. With a little extra money, she had driven herself to the Farmers Market on Catherine Street especially for tomatoes. Solemn came in and scooped a mound of it all into a bowl, chewing a loaf of garlic bread. Bev woke up.

"Where your daddy?"

"I don't know," Solemn said.

Bev elbowed up from the couch. "You don't know?"

"He outside."

Bev sighed. Straight answers had become as impossible with Solemn as straight hair. She looked outside and saw Redvine outside smoking.

"Come on in . . . I'm warming up spaghetti," she told him.

Redvine put out his cigarette and came in. Bev had picked up a box of Franzia at the gas station for dinner. She poured him some. Unsettled and a bit rickety, so she spilled a little on the floor, wiped it up. He hushed into the new phones a lot. And Alice Taylor had never come by before with strange friends for him to drive away with unless he came back sweaty drunk. For the most part, Solemn went out with him. But not all the time. He would be gone for a night.

Never before had Bev thought of Redvine and another woman. Never at all. But Stephanie seemed to know better, maybe. Was she stupid?

"How'd it go?" she asked him.

"Good," he told her. "Some folks want me coming back next week."

"Okay," Bev said.

Redvine hid his collection in the unused space of manufactured storage units under the trailer. Once he took care of the utilities and six months' plot rent and food for summer, he consulted his relatives and folks like Alice Taylor—apologetic—on what was coming up. Or he just stopped by for no reason now, with a trunk of gifts to sell. Birthdays, graduations, weddings, anniversaries, christenings, baptisms, anybody he heard was tumbling into love . . . The DigiCates baned, Redvine could give the people what they really wanted now. Through the month, he parceled out much of the space's contents to far-apart pawnshops, secondhand stores, and resale shops in Memphis and Jackson. He only took a little at a time. The terse clerks had seen it all. No questions were asked. Redvine shredded the claim receipts he received more than twenty-thousand dollars cash for, when much of it was said and done. On his way back to Bledsoe, he threw the scraps of paper in miscellaneous gas station and pit-stop trash cans. Alice Taylor got hers, hurried it up between hands rolling weed or money all day. Days on the road ended. Just like that.

"If that 'Walter' or them DigiCate folks call here, hang up," Redvine told them. When Bev fussed about impoliteness, Redvine ended it: "Treat 'em like salesmen."

Abruptly Redvine gave Solemn glasses one day with little explanation but a pat on her back. The clear-framed jewels helped Solemn renew her relationship with grass, distinguishing between points and blades to comprise the whole she had once only seen as a green blob. The patterns in fabric—corduroy, crocheted, burlap—came to life higher than touch alone. Even the sky held definition to marvel at. Solemn realized the proper dimensions and proportions of the scar in her right knee, not nearly as pronounced as she had thought.

Smaller. She still used the leftover DigiCate—to yank font size down smaller and smaller until she couldn't see it anymore, going deeper and deeper each time.

"You shouldn't sit up in the house all by yourself," Redvine tried to explain once. He was more often now thinking about the boys he could one day come home to find in the house with her, behind the thin accordion doors, naked and twisting and involved in the unspeakable. But Solemn was immune to it all, having heard the sounds in the middle of the night and behind the doors of Desiree's trailer and from the car Landon had sometimes parked near the trailer with a girl inside.

"I'm good," Solemn answered.

Now she smacked gum when she talked to him. She wouldn't watch a show with them together. She looked outside the window all the time and wound up gone for hours, to the well or around Singer's or throughout the makeshift roads she walked alone on now, barefoot.

"Why y'all let me stay out of school?" Solemn suddenly asked, breaking into his mind. As he thought about it, she answered for him: "I wouldn't have let me do that."

"I thought it's what you wanted," Redvine said.

"Well, it wasn't."

"I did everything I could to get you in the Kosciusko high school, but you didn't have the credits." She sucked her teeth. He went on. "Minute I asked you to come on the road with me, you said, 'Fine.' Now, you treating me like I didn't care or something?"

"You only care about Landon. It's always been like that."

"Where you get something like this from?"

"He's your boy. Mama told me you didn't want me at all. You wanted a boy. I was supposed to be named Solomon. I got this old cutoff name instead."

"Now Solemn, your mama's lying. I never said anything like that. You always been my adorable little girl."

"You wouldn't have let Landon leave school. That's all I was saying."

———

On Solemn's birthday, the Redvines sat at their kitchen table before fifteen unlit candles on a chocolate sheet cake. The TV was off. And the radio was on Solemn's favorite station. A prime rib smoked on a platter in front of them, devoured before anyone bothered to touch their scalloped potatoes, green beans, and biscuits. They planned to visit the movie theater after dinner. They voted between *The Village* and *The Notebook*. Even though she was outnumbered, Solemn won. They settled on *The Village*. It had been nearly two years since they had caught a show all together. Solemn had on a brand-new pair of jeans and sky-blue glitter flats. And finally, her glasses: clear rimmed, large, personal follow-up appointments with an optician.

Earlier that week, Redvine presented his wife with a choker string of pearls. Fake, but good enough for sale in a jewelry store alone, not the simple section at Walmart. He ran down the laid-off Greyhound driver who now lugged a suitcase of Avon across Singer's. From her, he bought Night Magic and Emeraude for Bev. He told her to be sure to stop by with each new catalog. Delightful surprises. The occasion was none.

"Business is good," he told Bev.

"You like your steak, Solemn?" Redvine asked.

"Yes, Daddy," Solemn responded, lips greasy.

"Lemme show you how to hold your knife and fork, little girl," Bev said. She put her hands around her daughter's and the fork and pressed Solemn's middle finger down the spine of the fork. "This the proper way to do it."

"I don't like it that way," Solemn said. Bev all but took over her plate and started to cut the meat. Solemn slammed her fork down on her plate. She snatched her hands away. She balled her right fist and stuck it into her cheek.

"Solemn, what's gotten into you?" Bev wondered.

"Nothing," Solemn said. She turned away and crossed her arms.

"Apologize to your mother, Solemn, right now," Redvine added.

"For what? I didn't do anything."

"I don't like how you talked to her."

"You can't tell me what to do."

"Lord . . ." Bev pushed back from the table.

"Oh, I can't?" Redvine peered. Solemn jumped up from the table. Her parents stood with her. She pounded Redvine in his chest with her fists and kicked at his knees. He stood defenseless against Solemn. She was furious. He bent down to steady himself.

"Solemn!" Bev shouted.

"You can't tell me what to do! You're nothing! You're nothing!"

Bev gripped Solemn and turned her around so fast the girl almost tripped. She shook her. Redvine came between them. Solemn ran to the door and out into the yard. With no shoes on and tiny rocks prickling her feet, Bev ran after her.

"Get in here, right now!"

"No!" Solemn shouted back.

"Lord . . . you gonna have the neighbors callin' the law on us . . ."

She was about to sprint to Solemn and drag her inside by her back ponytail, if she had to. Redvine grabbed his wife's shoulder.

"Just let her go," Redvine said.

"I just don't understand . . . Here we are having this nice supper for her birthday . . . ready to go to the show."

"Just let it go. She'll come back."

"But we ain't even gave her all her presents."

"Bev, look, trust me on this. We gonna go on to the show by ourselves and leave her by herself tonight. You wanted to see *The Notebook* anyway."

"No." Bev pushed him loose. She didn't care who thought she was a witch for it.

She wasn't about to watch Solemn march on, that damned well. Had started that mess back up again. Was she gonna jump? Just normal growing pains. Hormones and loneliness. Aftershocks. Maybe even a boy. Landon gone. Redvine strange. Bev was just tired of it. Not sick yet. Just tired. The ungratefulness and self-absorption of them all. By God they were going to be normal for just one night, even if it killed them.

Redvine had no choice but to follow his wife and daughter on down there; stomping up dust Bev was. She didn't care who saw. *Let 'em talk. They gone talk about me anyway* . . . Her younger child bent over rim of the well whose waters had gone rank. Her husband stormed behind her, unable to keep up. Tripping even, to fall without his wife there to catch him. By the time he grabbed his wife's hands, slapping at Solemn leaned back onto the mouth of her little well, the guts of a secret spilled over.

"He talks to that poor, poor woman and threw her baby down the well!" Solemn yelled at her mother, feeling better each yell. "Pearletta. He talks to her while you're gone and he's why *that baby* died. He talks to her and drive her and he told me not to tell!"

"Solemn, what're you talking about?" Bev cried, her face smashed by her two hands, head twisting from side to side, a set point at confusion, looking back and forth between them both, wondering what all this had to do with cutting a steak right.

"Solemn, now that's enough," Redvine said. He came between them.

"It's never enough!" Solemn shouted.

"That woman is gone, Solemn," Bev said. "Nobody even knows where she is!"

Stephanie, Theo, and Desiree Longwood were along with the rest who watched from indeterminable places thin trailer blinds allowed. Stephanie crossed her arms. Vindicated, in some ways, at her decision to part. Her husband wondered, feeling the least he could for the good word was stop good people from making fools of themselves. Stephanie was not happy to see the girl twist and turn ahead of her parents now turned against themselves, grabbing and catching and holding and unholding until Solemn seemed their last concern while they shouted about something. The last thing she liked to see was anybody out of their mind. The girl stormed in direction of their trees. And Desiree smiled, ready to unlatch the door and pick it up again, color life once more. But the Longwoods turned off all the lights and the TV, and they locked their door.

Solemn knew better than to knock there. She had no other friends. Crows guarded the edge of her well. They always were so a part of things, but so black as to soak up the light and oversimplify their existence, unlike a clear wind. Maybe she could leap inside the Longwood dory and hide for a night. Eventually, she'd have to go home. The trailer, not money emboweled in a music box or secrets locked in her mind or even somebody else to talk to, was the most concrete thing she had. She had to go back.

'Cross the way, near the woody frazzle she and Desiree once enjoyed for the mystery and privacy, she saw a woman strung between the hickory trees in a mint-green hammock of fabric, feet and hands hung over the bough. Girl was young, not quite like her but not too far above. She was 'sleep. Maybe she didn't see the ruckus. Solemn didn't remember her being anywhere near when she marched along the way first time. She was life passed by. And she was wearing the glasses, slid down her greasy and pimply nose. Had she known a gal was near, she would not have acted like that. How did she miss her?

"How much more I miss?" she said aloud. "Who I'm gonna tell?"

And to the ones being so nosy it looked like she was talking to herself, surefire sign all was lost. Funny-farm time, just a matter of time, knew it all the time.

To the center of her earth, Solemn forced herself to move. She didn't dread punishment. She knew she had won, for now. The victory was bittersweet; along with the gut spilling was the illusion cracked: on the night of the lightning bugs and a fall and a hunt for that woman and a craving to see or hear That Baby, for maybe it was part of her, Solemn knew plain as day why The Man at the Well never went away from her no matter how far she tried to run. Redvine was not only near it all that night, but he was there. All Solemn could say to herself (nothing to nobody else, for days) was, *Why?*

TWENTY-FIVE

A promotion to detective augmented him above the trenches, at least directly. He could arrive when and if it was all cleaned up. His salary jumped. But it was no better.

Justin Bolden, married and "Detective" now, sat in Café on the Square, near the window. He had a black folder. A mug shot. A rap sheet. A few newspaper clippings an obit reporter scared up for him. The rest public record. An unsettling connection of the man whose name was spoken to the very trailer park he had narrowly escaped.

A waitress refilled the coffee on "Y'all ready to order?"

"The usual," Nichols said.

"Two apple pies," Bolden said. "One to go." For his wife.

His boss turned to him: "Boy, you expect me to do what? Now, I can't believe."

"I'm just saying," Bolden continued. "Well, I know these people. Good family."

Nichols' retirement party was already scheduled at the local Elks lodge—three months in advance. He had already pulled out the few cases of Old Crow bourbon from when he graduated from the police academy. And he had met with pension officials about his disbursements. Anything coming on top of his now was a nuisance, not a case.

Bolden, as well, was above being a desk boy who answered a department calling from South Sharpe Avenue in Cleveland. He was not one to pull into Singer's Trailer Park with a warrant for Earl Redvine's arrest, his pistol cocked and bullhorn alarming dreamers, who woke up to look between slits in blinds. He knew the women: Solemn and Bev hurled out of bed with hands up. He knew the man: Redvine jiggling off his wedding ring before he came out the door—while registered guns and other shit he bartered belonged to a magistrate in Cleveland. And the magistrate had complained. Very loudly.

"I don't know what yas talking about," Bev and Solemn heard Redvine say. Cops pushed his head down into a patrol car. He looked at the women, square in the face, with a smile. "This nothing," he said, before the cops locked the door.

Solemn stood on the porch, looked back and forth inside and out, at her mother talking to the police and her father not crying about anything now. With flashlights and billy clubs, the three officers stomped in and out of the trailer with demands to Bev:

"Look heah, unlock every compartment and cubby, even the underneath . . ."

Earl's duffel bag, once carriage of tools and food for a day, had about twelve thousand dollars cash in it.

"I . . . I don't know." Bev shook her hands and said, "I didn't know."

They drove Redvine away.

They had a phone now. When Earl called her, he told her all about it.

"I just found a bunch of stuff, trunk of my car," the blithesome man offered, tired and chill. He had his own pack: Kools. He asked for water though. "My girl, my daughter. She ain't say nothin' to me about picking up no stuff. She come along with me sometimes. Keep me company. I just park and canvas, door-to-door. That's what I do. I'm a salesman. Call my boss. I got his card at home. I think I got the number memorized though. Walter's his name. He our regional manager. I work for a brand-new company. DigiCate. Wave of the future it is. I ain't never know one of my customers was a judge. My girl, Solemn, she unpredictable. Like to wander, she do. Always have.

Just get into stuff. Like money, too. I gotta pay her for everythang: wash the car, iron my pants, feed the cat. Now I found out why all that money was missing out the purse I keep from sales. Solemn like this. She strange. Now, I axed her. Several times I did. I wanted to know where that stuff come from. She told me she saw some folks sellin' stuff in a backyard, gave 'em the money she took from me just so they could unload a bunch of it. I shouldn't have believed her. My main concern was her takin' the money from me. She apologized. But time it take me to trace back to all the houses I walk up to? And I thought about it. What if I go back to people who say the stuff theirs just so they can say it? That wouldn't get it back where it belong. Look, my trailer small. We barely got room for our feet half the time. My wife and I . . . well. We gettin' a house soon. And my son, he in the military. He a soldier. He gotta wife and they like to bring the babies to visit. So, yeah, we gettin' a house soon. I'm not just gonna go sellin' off folks' stuff like that. I got in a little trouble back in the day. I was young, a hothead. I just went before a judge and that was it. I been law-abidin' all my life. She ain't mean no harm. She a good girl, gettin' her GED. Now, I did call up to them police stations in the area, see if anybody was missin' stuff. I did."

"Bell South don't show you calling no police precincts recently, Mr. Redvine. We got your phone records."

"They got those?"

"They do."

Nor did any of the Richardses' nearby neighbors' memories record a black fella showing up with machines to sell on a hot day in July. And the few Richards neighbors who were consulted didn't remember a yard sale that day, either. Or that whole summer.

"This Redvine fella got arrested when he was sixteen," Nichols reminded Bolden. "Caught up in a rattle against some officers out in Bledsoe. Slap on the wrist, then."

"He was a boy," Bolden said. "We all had them moments."

"I didn't."

Bolden let that pass.

"Look, he got a son in the Army. You remember? We met 'em in the motel where that Hassle gal went missing."

"So what?" Nichols shouted. "I meet a lot of people, Justin. I can't go taking their words for it, just 'cause we interrupted some motel weekend? And we don't know if she went missing from there. That's just last time anybody seen her with ID. Kid thrown down a well and husband a druggie nut. Hell, I'd gone on and disappear, too."

"Well, it all makes sense. None of Earl Redvine's fingerprints were found in the Richards home. We ain't took the girl's yet."

"And we won't. You talking about a child, goddamn it. A *child*. What she gonna get for it? He needs to do time just for lacking common sense to know better. How the hell can a father sell shit he had to have known his gal stole?"

"Money," Bolden answered. "I mean, I been out to the place a few times. Nichols, it ain't much." He was off that day and night. He would have handled things differently.

"Look," Nichols interrupted, "if you wanna go 'round playing Robin Hood to your people, go right ahead. Couldn't blame you. Might even be part of your job."

Bolden tipped the glossy folder to the side. He threw a rap sheet across to Bolden. The name at top was Brett Singer.

"His father owns Singer's Trailer Park and a little bit in between, to explain what he would have been doing there. This gal Akila Redvine was there last time anybody saw Pearletta Hassle. She worked there back in 2001, 2002. I verified that with the owner."

"Yeah, but she never rented a room at the motel. At least not rightfully," Nichols said. "So she's either a liar or a thief or both."

"She's not lying about having been in the motel same time as Pearletta. We met her there." The piles of cocaine grains Bolden managed to sneak finger licks of had been enough to smear Pearletta. The strands of long, red white-folk hair left in the showers were considered the biggest accident—that one of *them* might actually run around with such a druggie whore who neglected her own child. Didn't matter where the niggers came from. They were all druggies, crooks, whores, shufflers, looters. It didn't matter what Viola and Edward Weathers said or how many times they showed up in Kosciusko with demands for an investigation. It didn't matter how Viola used her husband's fraternity to coax two black reporters into printing up her daughter's story in Memphis and Jackson papers. Case on that black trailer-park gal—and her baby and crazy husband, too— was closed.

"I requested prints. I'm running them again."

"That's your call," Nichols said.

"New suspects and information."

"You expect me to crack open some black gals' cases as trade-off for letting a Negro rob a judge's estate?" Nichols asked Bolden. "Good hardworking folks go out to the movies, and come back to see their house been wrecked? This ain't right."

"I'm sure the Richards can afford to replace everything they lost."

The waitress came over to throw a plate of chicken gizzards, gravy, biscuits, and two apple pie slices in front of the men. She left plastic containers along with the tab, then whistled off. Bolden sank into the booth and car-watched the parking lot.

When faced with the younger Redvines earlier that week, he had—again—remembered Landon's face, the contempt in his eyes for the "POPOs." Bolden was used to it from black men, but with a much higher octave behind them in Landon's case. The Redvines were humble and didn't seem to like mess. And he chalked up Redvine's name on Pearletta's paraphernalia as the type of crush any decent woman should have, with a man beating her ass in a trailer park and such better options scattered all around, not too far away. In every instant, the Redvines were brief and accommodating. This one was no different, with sincerity of the trade-off Akila Redvine offered for her father-in-law evident in the fact it lacked any threat behind it. If anything, what struck him was the timidity with which the wife spoke: "I shoulda said something earlier, 'bout that woman hanging out with those people own the land . . . I didn't wanna go getting good people in trouble for nothing. The Redvines been good to me. I ain't wanna bring them no glare."

Bolden had the weight of confusion on his head. He pulled out the named pot bowl from one carton of evidence a dark black girl of any class was allowed. Then, before anybody knew he turned up that day, he flicked through the paper matter. To a photograph of Pearlatta with a man whose face came up quick to match what Akila said.

The entirety of Singer's Real Estate Holdings, Inc., included a few private cabins at Hawks Lake Lodge outside Vicksburg. Behind that poor woman Pearletta Hassle, there was a Kimberley Williams—found in a deep ditch near Hawks Lake Lodge. It took Bolden a few days after he met the Redvines to get Warren County support services to return his call. When an evidence technician met Bolden in the property room, he saw for himself the plastic bag of combed red Caucasian pubic hairs from Kimberley's vaginal area. But, couldn't nobody find the semen collection though.

He went on, staying behind and pushing off sleep, to flick through the missing persons database at headquarters—scanned police and coroner's reports—for women with dark faces and caring families and stories dense enough not to be flat-out lies.

Another one caught his eye: At the start of the year, a Shahari Montgomery washed up where the Mississippi River Watershed drained into the Gulf of Mexico, a tattle of treeless marsh. She was faceup amidst marsh roses and bleach-white fairy candles, washed of melanin. Her toxicology report found meth. Her sister and grandmother reported her missing for three months, last known to be obsessed with a new boyfriend. White. The boy never came in the house. Honked from the curb and brought her back late. A half-incorrect license-plate number the grandmother recalled finally scrambled into the Department of Motor Vehicles registry as that of a blue Jeep— belonging to a Richard Singer of Vicksburg. This was noted, Bolden saw. "I ain't seen the Jeep in months," transcripts quoted. "Brett run it in the ground. That's how he is with stuff." Then, this new spring, a Brett Singer was stopped for driving under the influence on the Trace. The arresting officer reported a young black woman with him— passed out sleep in the backseat. When stirred due to the commotion, she explained she carried no identification. Her name was not taken. His was. They called his daddy once more: no mug shot, no fingerprinting, "keeping this hush." Brett's brother—twin—picked him up the next morning. In return favor, Brett was finishing up one hundred hours' community service: helping his daddy and brother fix up the low-income housing the family owned.

Most recently, at one of Warren County's Fourth of July celebrations, a Brett Singer denied any part of a melee set off faulty Class B fireworks that did not detonate properly—caused burns and busted eardrums to a few in the nearby crowd, all for a stunt. Prankster he was. Another slap on the wrist.

"Even if this . . . this theory you done concocted had weight to it," Nichols said, "it's hardly enough to say we don't have to punish the Redvines for being crooks."

"Forensics still got the hairs collected from Pearletta's bathtub and Kimberley Williams' rape kit. Shahari Montgomery's DNA might be in that Jeep, if this kid ain't wrecked it by now. Now, if there are matches . . ."

"So what? We show up in Vicksburg tearing hair out of Richard Singer's son's head? Driving off with his fleet without telling nobody why?"

"No," Bolden said. "We subpoena DNA samples. We get a warrant on the Jeep."

"On what grounds? Some black gal who cheated her way into a seedy motel room, fornicating, having a made-up conversation in a motel room with a poor woman?"

"It wasn't a made-up conversation. She knew Pearletta Hassle was on dope."

"We told her fella we thought heroin was involved, Justin!" Nichols yelled. "We told everybody we talked about it with. That woman is a junkie stacked in one of the crack houses where they done sold off their IDs to kids who wanna buy liquor. Just to get a quick rock. Tryin' to forget she left behind the good life she could have had for a druggie nut in a trailer. We can't go scapegoating a boy like that until—*if*—she turn up."

"What if she doesn't?" Bolden pleaded. "We don't even check? We just do nothing for families out here probably having nightmares as we speak?"

"I ain't trying to get them Weathers amped up again."

"We don't have to tell 'em who we bring in for questioning."

"We need a reason to collect samples, fingerprints. In this case, a good one."

"So we just go with what we know about Earl Redvine, for taking some . . . some *things*? We ignore what we don't know elsewhere, for lives of these girls? Like we done so many times before? Like we did when we found Pearletta's baby out there in that well? Just an acre from where we found a family who stole some guns they ain't used."

"Do your damned job, boy," Nichols said. Then he was out the door.

For him to sit back awhile was the only defiance Justin Bolden had to give. He knew it. But he could pretend. He had a daughter to worry about, and a wife, and a mortgage now. He wouldn't have much of an inheritance beyond his parents' house declining on cinder blocks. He had needed the promotion just as much for money as for prestige. He saw where the resources were funneled, who or what took longer attention spans. The fact anyone believed what they stood by in this case shocked his system.

He just walked into people's unprettiness and problems and desperations as a disciplinarian, like a principal packing heat or that faraway uncle who knew how to get a man killed. If he had it his way, he would have tripped a white man like Brett Singer in the middle of the night and drug him down to an unmapped part of Texas to dig a hole in the desert sand. Instead, he paid the tab his boss left him with.

"Now you know what all to say?"

The confirmation was made as if the practiced speech was as innocuous as slicing off a lizard's tail. Presumably, Solemn would grow back, however crooked or bent. And Solemn knew what to say about it all, to think not of the lies but of getting out of Bledsoe, closer to the cities and the TV and the stars and all of it. Her home was too sullied now, leaden and bleak. She had no fear Redvine would harm her, but he was suspect. And anyone who had a problem or concern or imperfect life either disappeared or got treated like a witch. Maybe it was the trees, the dark, the roads, the well, the fields.

Landon needed to return to Hattiesburg, for his assignment, if not the children. Akila refused. "In case the cops need me." Bev Redvine had already called to be directed to Detective Bolden, a name she remembered well from jagged times around the season when Pearletta Hassle lost that baby and Stephanie almost lost hers. Now, it was her own. She knew nothing. She never heard Redvine mention anything about stealing nothing. He would have surely told her. They had that kind of marriage.

Had Akila known all this was coming out of Singer's, she would have told Landon to kiss her ass and go home. But that fork in the road was too far back now. She was stuck on its prongs. She helped tidy up Solemn's hair and snap-button, coverall-jean dress. It was one of the new things. Solemn gave in against flip-flops or sandals. She had on white bobby socks folded down and jammed into blue buckled shoes. Her arms and legs were baby oiled. At raised hemline, her knee scar was still prominent. And what she had to say about it all was what she always thought anyway: "I wanna go."

Landon and Akila showed up to help piece it all together—with the proper English and thought processes born of traveling, a more integrated life, dodging overt prejudice, juggling the covert kind. Tense nights in the trailer lingered until the morning, with promises of financial support should Redvine get locked up. Insistence none of this was going to happen. DigiCate terminated Redvine's contract, once 'Walter' told the big boys what he heard. The mobile home was owned. Bev could always pick up more hours on the shelves at the Bible college. They could sell the Malibu. Or she and Solemn could pack up and get the hell out of Singer's. The Longwoods had. Husband and wife chopped down peach and fig trees at cracks of dawn a few mornings before they silently left. The squirrels, raccoons, crows, and possums raced to the splattered tale of fruit left long before anyone at Singer's showed up with their barrels and plans to sell what they ferreted. Maybe, no matter if they got out of this here or not, it was time for the Redvines to go. Good fishing and low prices in Tennessee, Bev heard. Maybe. But for now . . .

Beverly, Akila, and Solemn Redvine sat waiting for Mr. Bolden.

"Please, in here." He extended his hand toward the room behind him. They all filed in and scooted back chairs. Solemn sat in the one Akila set out for her.

"Would anybody like water or coffee, soda pop, chips?"

"No. We ate already," Bev Redvine said. "We just had a very nice pizza dinner up the street at Solemn's favorite place."

"Yeah, I love that spot, too," Bolden said. "Wife hates it, 'cause she's had to pick me up a few wider belts. But what can you do? Solemn, how are you today?"

She had certainly grown. So had he. She mumbled something.

"Thanks for coming in," he finally said. "And a family attorney...?"

"We gonna get one," Bev told him. "My son helping us out."

"Sure," Bolden said. "So, Mrs. Redvine, as Solemn's legal guardian, since she is a minor, you know everything here is taped and possibly watched?"

"I do."

"And Miss Akila is not necessarily a guardian, but..."

"I'm here to witness."

"Yes," Bolden said. "Witness. So that's fine. Normally, we only allow those in question and perhaps their legal guardians in here. But seeing as though Solemn is a minor, we can go ahead and make an exception."

"Thank you," Bev said.

Bolden circled his mouth to talk. Akila asked, "Have you found out any more about Pearletta Hassle and the Singer folks?"

"Mrs. Redvine, I personally want to thank you for coming forward," Bolden had rehearsed. "The information you provided opened doors nobody had explored. And, that's priceless. I informed my superiors of what was discovered and tried to take it all into consideration for the case here. The investigation is ongoing at this time. I'll be sure to update you on the proceedings, if you wanna keep in touch about 'em."

"Certainly I wanna know what happens," Akila told him.

"I'm sure it means a lot to you, if you would go through all your trouble to track down the owner of your in-laws' home and accuse his son of that kind of involvement."

"We own our home," Bev stated.

"Not your home per se," Bolden stated, "but the property in general. The park. There is a connection there. Which would somewhat explain what this man was doing in Bledsoe to begin with . . ."

"Owners don't come 'round that much," Bev said. "Truth be told, my family and I didn't know that woman much more than you asking us to help her move."

"Well, it may have been a good thing, rest assured. As I said, all this is ongoing. But, as you know, Earl Redvine—your husband—was taken into custody for home invasion and possession of stolen property in correlation to an estate robbery in Cleveland, where he says he took Solemn."

"Yes," Bev said. "Solemn loved to go out on the road with Red, and he loved to take her. I figured it was good for her to get out and see something new, you know?"

"Sure," Bolden said. "And, as you found out, I've been assigned to the case to get to the bottom of things. Now, if you don't mind, I'll ask Solemn some questions."

"Go 'head," Bev said.

"So, Solemn, you understand I'm an officer of the law?" he asked the young lady he couldn't help but still see as roadkill, stretched out on her back on an off-the way road.

"You remember we met before," he continued. "A few times. You were a little—"

"I remember you." Solemn rolled her eyes.

Bolden proceeded. "Now, Solemn, you also understand you're going to be answering questions as part of a criminal investigation? That means the things we discuss involve crimes."

"I understand."

"Okay. Now, just answer and tell the truth. And your mother and sister are here to support you. And you can also ask me questions, if you like. Just stop me and let me know if you don't understand anything I've said, okay?"

"Fine." Solemn's eyes settled to the front desk outside the window.

"Okay, how old are you, Solemn?" He positioned his pen and the paperwork.

"I just turned fifteen."

"And what is your occupation . . . or no, excuse me. Where you go to school?"

"I don't."

"Solemn's homeschooled," Bev offered.

"Oh, okay. Clever way to keep up with her, huh?"

"Something like that." Bev sighed.

"And, back in July, you and your father visited Bolivar County in his car, in order to sell some computer equipment . . . Digital . . . er . . . ?"

"Well, he sell 'em. I just come along."

"Yes. Your father works as a traveling salesman, and you travel with him?"

"Yes." Her eyes followed a fly buzzing throughout the office.

"Okay, now . . . Solemn, you payin' attention?"

"Solemn, listen to the man," Bev said.

"And do you go inside every single house with him or stay in the car, or what?"

"Mostly, I just stay in the car," Solemn recalled. "He doesn't really go into too many houses 'cause people don't let him in like that. It's a lot of white people."

"I see. And are these white people at home when he comes into their houses?"

"Yeah."

"Say 'yes,' Solemn," Bev said.

"Yes, they open the doors."

"All the time?"

"Yes."

"What about in Cleveland? Your father ever go into a house nobody let him into?"

"I don't know. If he did, I didn't see it."

"So, you aren't saying 'No.' You're just saying you ain't see?"

"I think she's saying 'No,' Detective," Bev said.

"Well, I have to make sure with her."

"I never saw Daddy go into anybody's house when the owners wasn't there and steal a bunch of stuff he sold later," Solemn said.

"Got it," Bolden said. "When you went into these houses with your father, did you ever touch anything?"

"I guess I did," Solemn recalled, her eyes up top of it all. "But my mama told me never to use anybody else's toilet. It's impolite."

"Did your mother ever tell you not to take anybody's things?" Bolden peered.

"Yeah, she has. 'Thou shalt not steal.'"

"Now your daddy said you went to a yard sale, while he was knocking on doors?"

"Not really," Solemn said, and she clucked her tongue to the roof of her mouth. She stared at the front desk again, with all the official busyness and computer monitors and even a woman police officer. She wondered how long it took her to get that job.

"Can you explain what 'not really' means?"

"Well, there was a lot of stuff in a house and I took it."

"Just like that?" Bolden quizzed, with his face turned to Bev's.

"Yup."

"What did you take?" Bolden said, picking up a pen and starting to write now.

"A lot of stuff . . . rings, diamonds, nice radios, some guns."

"You took guns outta a house in Cleveland?"

"Yep."

"What kind of guns were they, Solemn?"

"The kind that shoot."

"Were they small, big, short, long . . . did they look like this?" Bolden inched up and unholstered the the .22-caliber he hitched to the back of his slacks.

"Some of 'em," said Solemn, still.

"And you weren't scared to touch 'em? You ain't think a gun would go off?"

"Not if you don't pull on it."

"Touch that one."

"Mr. Bolden, I don't want her doing that," Bev interrupted.

"I'll touch it." Solemn's fingers glided to the warm black object on the table. She circled thoughts of what to do. She imagined, for a moment passed slow, effects of a blistering and sudden blast on the people's heads before her. The Man at the Well appeared in a chair. That Baby wiggled on the floor in the corner of the room. The woman from the television smashed Bolden's head on the table, and a line opened up on his forehead. That poor woman jitterbugged in a corner. They swished back to figment.

"Where were the guns you found?"

"Uh . . . in this big tall thing, this cabinet. It had locks on it, so I broke it with this long thing I found in the living room."

"The fireplace poker?"

"What's that?"

"What color was the house?"

"White."

"Somebody let you in?"

"The door was unlocked. I was in the car all by myself. My daddy was down the street somewhere. So I went in."

"And . . . you just started taking stuff out? Stealing, a crime, for no reason?"

"I wasn't stealing anything. I just wanted to see some of the stuff. It was fancy."

"Did your father tell you to do it?"

"Earl would never have done that," Bev interrupted.

"Mrs. Redvine, *please*. I'm asking your daughter."

Akila spoke: "I need to go to the ladies' room." She rushed out to go sit in the car.

"My daddy didn't tell me to do anything. He wasn't there. I just did it."

"So you just walked around a bunch of houses in a place you never been, tried the knobs, found one that was unlocked, and decided to let yourself in?" No more notes.

"No. I didn't try any other houses. Just that one."

"The white one in Cleveland?"

"Well, I don't know where we was when I went in the house."

"Why that one?"

"I don't know. It just looked like the door was unlocked."

"How you tell if a door unlocked just by looking at it from the street?"

"I just had a feeling."

"I don't believe you, Solemn."

"I'm sorry I did it," Solemn recalled she was to say. "I didn't think anybody would get mad about it. It looked like these people had a lot of stuff as it was, so they wouldn't miss anything. My daddy didn't sell any DigiCates for a long time and I was just helping. But the people in the house looked rich. I didn't think they'd care."

"But, Solemn, you had to have known some people wouldn't like it if they came back home and found out a total stranger had been in their home, going through their private things, touching their stuff, taking whatever they wanted. I mean, these people are very impor-tant. They're not happy. They want someone to pay for this. And much as I'd love to help you, you go before a judge and you're gonna be sent to a detention center. Now, we can try to get the time reduced . . . but that'd be up to a judge."

"Well, I didn't think about all that. I just thought about the stuff."

"Okay, Solemn," Bolden groaned. And for once, he wished it weren't his vacation around the corner. "Okay. If that's what you say, I have no choice but to believe you. But you do know you're going to have your picture and fingerprints taken and all that? And if it all matches up, if some neighbors remember your face or if your fingerprints match ones found in the house . . . well. Solemn, this is really serious."

"But I'm only a minor."

"Yes," Bolden said, with his eyes square into Bev's, "you sure are that."

3

THE
NORTH

TWENTY-SIX

What appeared to the black people of Bledsoe to be a mount of gods where fates were handed down was nothing more than halls of secretaries, three-line phones, typewriters, computer databases, and bathroom meetings across a few precincts and a courthouse. What appeared to be sensational for them was customary for forces above them. What caused hysteria and alcoholism among the poor was a string of checked boxes and eye contact among the rich. It was all a syndicate.

Had Solemn not been coincidentally known to a token black officer turned detective, in one of the few noteworthy zip codes of Mississippi, she would have gone to Lincoln Training Center: to be detained for petty mistakes, tied down for illegal whippings, doused for defiance, tripped for oversleeping, starved for attention and dinner, then breakfast and lunch, passed in state education exams just for knowing how to write her name—no more. Solemn would have slept in barracks reeked of vomit and abandonment, unmanaged. She would have had patches of hair twisted loose by the bullies among them who confused domination with a chance. She would have been at the mercy of hard stone floors. She would have spoken to her visitors at slim tables in sweltering rooms. She would have found weed, cigarettes, and crack. If she had not found them, they would have found her. She would have been forced onto imprecise meds arresting her mind, changing it from what she could relate to.

However, there came an arrangement. The police weren't stupid. That was not the test. The question was: "Do we care?" And they did not. At the northwesternmost edge of Mississippi, on 1-55 North, just a baby's breath from Memphis, was a group home for girl truants and wards of the state: the Fanny O. Barnes Home, named for a rich white reverend's wife who sent a few of her black help's girls to private schools, paid so long as their mothers put up with mean and spiteful bosses like Fanny was before she died.

First in a tiny office of the Attala courthouse outside a courtroom, Bev and Solemn signed a lot of papers nobody bothered to read out loud.

Then Akila took Solemn for cheeseburgers and fries at the Tracys' diner.

Next Bev met Earl at the jail to bring him home, few words between them but the same story.

Finally, Akila snatched Solemn out of the trailer before they got back. Landon covered for her. Solemn made sure to grab one thing. The jewelry and music box with its black threaded sides now unraveled, the unicorn missed a foot. She was warned. No girl in Fanny O. Barnes could have money anywhere but on the books—no trades. But still. She needed it.

"Solemn, we gotta go now!" Akila shouted from somewhere in the dizzy, blurred, and pin-striped world Solemn could not hold in her mind for too much longer. "We can't start off breaking the rules . . ." she echoed on.

When Solemn unrolled and opened the socks where her money went once the jewelry and music box became unnecessary and immature, nothing was inside them. Not one dollar at all. All that time. All that work. All those years. Nothing. Solemn recalled her hands through a house in Cleveland, thought about bigger hands and what they do.

At the Days Inn where they once honeymooned, Akila and Landon packed Solemn two suitcases and a hatbox full of four pastel General Dollar sundresses on summer clearance, a pair of tennis shoes, jeans, an alarm clock, deodorant, feminine products, toilet paper, lotion, and baby powder—like she was off to college. Had it not been for the state sheriff who trailed them in a dead giveaway, she could have been.

Next morning Landon's new Buick LeSabre drove up the snaking driveway to the group home shrouded in a clearing razed for its purpose. Solemn perceived a mansion—first she had ever seen in real life, up closer than at the edges of interstate roads. It had columns, a fountain, a flagpole, pillars at the seams, balance, depth. Vines braided into the outside. Along its side appeared to be a flower garden, through an arch: periwinkles, marigold, and sunflower patches she could tell. Not a squad car parked in sight. No guards stood at the door. And, she was to live here? It was a punishment, to them. To Solemn, it was a dream come true. Solemn knew a thing or two about maps from the rides with her daddy. Memphis was in reach. Nashville was attainable to her. Chicago much closer.

Mittimus in hand, the sheriff confirmed his transport inside then snuck back out to his car. To nap. Landon, Akila, and Solemn sat in the corner of a lobby with nothing but a custodian and his whistling. There was no greeting. The custodian saw so many come and go. He did not trust a one of them. They were all nice in the beginning, sure. Next thing you know, he would clean up shit dumped purposefully outside the toilet, a reflex of abuse they were used to. They tripped him when he passed. At some point, a woman with glasses on a chain came to hand them some forms, placed in such stern order on a clipboard there was no way to disorder them. There was no invitation to observe what went on behind two curtained French doors leading to the back.

"Who do we put as her legal guardians?" Akila asked, the pen in her mouth.

"Daddy and Mama," Landon said. "This ridiculous. Somebody should be out here going through this with us. Wait here. I need to find somebody who runs this place."

"You think I should put us down? We bringing her here . . ."

"Do what I said."

Akila understood her husband. Their nerves were brittle. A new house, new job, new babies . . . now this. Landon thought his parents were smarter than this. Now the Redvines were exactly what everyone thought niggers were: caught up in the criminal justice system, statistics, undesirables, broken, ridiculous.

According to the scribbled sign on the office's glass window drawn shut, the front receptionist was now on a bathroom break, which was either diarrhea or a lie. After a five-minute wait, Landon had enough. He toured the hallways to search for staff, a few of them involved in interrupting disruptions or explaining schoolwork to hard little faces. He wore his corporal's uniform on purpose. He planned to throw it in the cleaners soon as he left Fanny O. Barnes. Already, it felt sooty and dirty just being in there. But for now, it served a purpose: to walk his little sister through this menacing dump and let anybody who saw her know she had a brother who had access to the guns. It was working so far. Few staff members who did glance in his direction, though they did not help, stood at some attention and wondered at who he was and what he was doing there.

The war finally show up in Mississippi?

The facility's hallways were a maze its staggering exterior had only hinted at. Landon ended up right back at the receptionist desk. She still wasn't back. He saw no bathrooms, or water fountains, or bells on the wall. The muggy home sent his blood boiling and shut down any patience he acquired in a brief appointment to reconnaissance. He headed toward sounds of pots, pans, and running water. He smelled what turned out to be breaded chicken, green beans, and mashed potatoes from a kitchen far back. Above long and steaming trays was an older black woman alone, with a snaggletoothed young white boy. The woman taste-tested her gravy. Her subordinate mopped the floor.

"Excuse me!" Landon yelled. Only the cook looked up. She motioned him over. He stared at her upper right chest and saw a copper tag pinned, the name Ruth Golden. She put hands on her hips and peered at his face: "Yessuh?"

"Miss Golden," Landon said, "I'm bringing my sister here for her first day, and no one's here to help us in or see her on her way properly. Where do I go?"

Ruth Golden set the ladle on side of her brown gravy pan.

"Come on with me, baby," she said.

Landon returned to Akila and Solemn with Dr. Pamela Givens.

Dr. Givens' office was a former unmarked closet near the emergency back door where they hid the trash. She wore tweed in Mississippi and Tennessee near fall. A chain fastened her spectacles, too. She was directed to the only child in the room. She knew the story. But she never knew shit. She just went by what she was told.

"Well, sorry we don't have personal greeters around here. Come on back."

The walking tour was down two hallways passed by two hall-size rooms of faces, lethargy, and tension. They kept on down the hallways to her office. She pointed out relevant rooms. But all the while, her head split to another direction of inside talk:

These folks ain't got a clue. They done had it with this child and think I'm gonna work a miracle. And I ain't. If she's a hooker, forget it. She's hooked. If she's a pimp, she's done. If she's a gal with no daddy, forget it. She's feral. If she's a girl with no mama, I'm lost. That's in its own little category I'm still trying to figure out myself . . .

"We have three floors," the orientation began. "Main floor for everybody. Better behaved get the top. Lesser in middle. All the doors alarmed. All the windows alarmed, too. This is not a jail, so we don't keep bars. But it's a special code to get the windows open, 'cause this ain't no hotel, either. We don't pay for air-conditioning here. But we understand the conditions. This is Mississippi, or Tennessee, depending on which way you looking. Windows only open a few inches. If they want a fan, they gotta check one out with Miss Bernadine at the front, and check it back in."

The orientation continued long enough to get back to her office one could easily pass, a display of Margaret Burroughs prints and African sculpture and books.

"Please, sit down." She motioned to them and sat herself down in a grand armchair. "Four days a week I'm here and one day on the weekend. We keep at least eight people in here all the time: secretary at front, three people in the kitchen, some volunteers, formal staff. Janitor ain't part of it."

Landon took one of two extra seats. Solemn took the other. Akila stood. Other than her art, Dr. Givens' office was uninviting. It was cramped, with file cabinets and bulletin boards with pinned letters and photos of the graduates who reached back with pictures, invitations and programs for their babies, weddings and graduations. Dr. Givens' certificates from her past degrees and accomplishments set in prominent frames behind her desk: Spelman for psychology, Emory MBA, Tennessee State Ph.D. in education. Most who came into her office did not know what the letters meant or where the schools were. The window faced a once hopeful but makeshift vegetable garden, intended to be a group-home project. Instead, it withered to playtime.

"What's done to get them an education?" was the first thing Landon asked.

"The best we can," Dr. Givens answered. "For the most part, they carry on pretty independent till it's time to eat. Individual lockers. Shower and dress time always supervised. It's only one bathroom stay open after hours, on the first floor, by the front desk. Need a key. Nobody go outside without permission and watch, usually when we have enough volunteers. I been here thirteen years. Ain't never had one girl drop out on my watch. Now, we have had two jump out the windows. First a white gal. Died. Accident. Some muddy haints got to working her mind down. She couldn't keep up."

She pulled out Solemn's files.

"The other one, little black gal, we knew she was trying to. But this was before we got the alarms and the stops on the windows. Matter fact, it's why we got 'em."

Her orientation was rusty. Usually, the charges arrived alone or in a patrol car, the only talk being, "Sign here."

"So, Solemn Redvine: breaking and entering, estate robbery, possession of stolen property . . ." Dr. Givens went on. "Well, young lady, you shole got some sticky fingers."

"Solemn's been a good girl all her life," Akila said. "This whole situation just a misunderstanding. Even Solemn don't seem to know what happened."

Dr. Givens stared at Solemn with her glasses slid to the edge of her nose.

"That true? You don't know a thing about how you got here?"

"No," Solemn told her. "I forgot all about it by now. It's been a long time."

Dr. Givens thought this young girl was unaware of what a long time really was. According to her papers, Solemn Redvine was supposed to serve two, three years at Fanny O. Barnes (two if she was perfect), from Mississippi State's Department of Corrections' assessments, from Singer's homes origin, from Bledsoe stock. And, according to some other notes and letters and signs and calls and vague mentions she could recall, Solemn Redvine was to spend it as if she was a child who truly had others waiting for her. Or the type of child who could leave with a future or a vengeance. So, the meeting was short. It was formal, a courtesy really. It was much more than most received. Since, well, this girl, Solemn Redvine—with her Singer's address and Detective Justin Bolden's notes and private turned corporal in the Army brother, and two thousand dollars Akila left in her top desk drawer before Dr. Givens put it inside the neat inside pocket of her faux brown leather purse—did.

Sat in Sunday best, Solemn watched Akila and Landon walk out of Dr. Givens' door. She was about to lift herself up to start walking out right along with them. But Landon put his arms on one shoulder. He said some words she did not quite catch. Akila did the same. Solemn looked between the two. Dr. Givens stood behind her brother and sister-in-law. She took off her glasses to twirl them around her finger. She seemed totally different than she was at first. She spoke chatty-like now. She grinned. Landon and Akila lingered their eyes upon her near the door. Then, they turned to go suddenly and quickly in an about-face, away from her. The woman led them out. They did not look back.

Solemn wondered where they were going and how long they would be. Maybe they were hungry. They had passed a roadside diner named Rosie's and a Shell gas station with a hamburger, taco, and hot dog counter inside. Maybe they needed to eat. Before they returned to finish the tour. This woman needed to show them the ways there and back. Okay. Solemn reclined back into her seat and put her head

back. She gave very first notice to the room's drop-ceiling chande-
lier. It was the room's original, from 1966. It was wide, dark, dusty,
intricate, and overwhelming. It bore down like a spider to deracinate
her more than she already was, to graze its tentacles onto Solemn,
then yank her up into the life of its web. And to fight the fear of the
vision's returns and the malaise of secrets when her heart beat or
not, Solemn knew she now had nowhere to go but to love. She just
didn't know the way.

Fanny O. Barnes kept fifty disgorged and ragamuffin girls. Their of-
fenses ranged from infant sexual assault to petty larceny to hooking
to car theft to abandonment. To keep them in check were three day
people, two custodians, a food services quartet (only the elder cook,
Miss Ruth, exempt from taunts or ridicule), one secretary until 5:30
(Miss Bernadine), one freelance social-working nurse and nutrition-
ist weekly, volunteer community college interns to fill in, and at least
two regular people at night to look out for whichever one was sleeping
at the time. No security guards. The entire staff split that job. Any
workers were supposed to be certified in CPR and basic self-defense.
It depended. Most of the dorm parts were stationed on the lower
second floor for faster accessibility. The more volatile girls stuffed
in a twenty-bed open-space dormitory. Petty offenders and better
ones got third-floor quarter rooms and a few double rooms at the
corners, doled out for good behavior or two thousand dollars tucked
in top drawers.

Wilena. Lisa. Mona. Carrie Mae. Terina. Erika. Shante.

The Day Staff's degrees entitled them rights to look over kids who
had a variety of issues their case notes never fully revealed. It took
time to recognize which girls would attempt to have sex with the
grown-men staff and which ones would attempt to fight the grown-
women staff. No amount of psychology or sociology coursework could
fully prepare them for the tsunami of venom poured from the wounds
of not knowing a father, or knowing disdain by a mother, or being
an ensured check to a foster parent, or losing a battle with siblings
for a home. Still, they put B.A. or M.A. behind their official names

on every incident report, release form, work order, and nutrition request. It mattered to them.

Unlike the day people, the Night Staff were day laborers; they got no benefits but hourly pay, punishment for wrong turns or no degrees. So, they blamed the girls for every issue and disaster of their lives. God forbid they started sneezing or glimpsed a gray hair or stuffed themselves into constipation. It was all somehow related to "them girls," all them girls' fault. Some of them even occupied the position of near temps: they only got the call from Fanny's at the top of the night, if somebody called off or there was a disaster. They arrived and punished any problem, nightmare, or desire incompatible with the plans to sleep. That was pretty much anything.

Regina. Cora. Julie. Lolly. Margaret. Tyesha. Jamie. Marisa.

The moment Landon and Akila evaporated through the French doors of Fanny O. Barnes, a woman entered to take over Solemn now. She held her hands out to the newest girl, but the long red fingernails looked daggerish and pernicious.

"Hi . . . Solemn?" The woman looked at Dr. Givens.

"Yup, that's it," Dr. Givens said. "Miss Solemn Redvine, from Bledsoe. Married parents. Brother in the Army. How the hell she wind up here, I *do not* know." Dr. Givens rattled around in her desk for her cigarette case. There was nothing in the one she found.

"Oh my . . ." Dr. Givens said. "Jane, I'm gonna run out for a while. Or maybe you can run to the gas station for me. When your break?"

"I just got here, Miss Givens," Jane said.

"What you mean you just got here? This late?"

"I got here soon as I could, once Miss Bernadine called me. Tamia called off."

"Again?"

"I don't know . . ."

"You got any squares?"

"Naw, I don't. But I saw that one, uh . . . can't thank of that boy name now."

"Which one?"

"You know, in the kitchen . . . got that lisp."

"Oh, him. I can't thank of his name, either. Ain't here enough for me to know it."

"Well, he here today. I saw him smoking out back when I parked. I can go—"

"No, no. Let him *work*. Don't disturb him, 'cause he just take that as excuse to sit down and never get up again. You know what, I'm just gonna run out. I gotta play my numbers today anyway. Take this young lady up to her room. We got a nice corner one open for her, right?"

Jane frowned. "Well, we was just gonna leave that one child up there by herself. You know, 'cause of . . ."

"Oh yeah, I know." Dr. Givens rose up from her seat and smoothed down her skirt. "Well, she can't get privileges to hog up a whole room for acting the way she do."

"I think it was supposed to be a privilege for everybody else. It's some beds free in the dormitory."

"Jane, I ain't letting a bed in a good corner room go to waste no more. I got more girls coming and they're cutting my budget again."

Jane shook her head and she sighed.

"Miss Solemn, I'll be seeing you later. Jane, anybody ask where I'm at tell 'em I went to a meeting. Oh, and Miss Solemn, here's your orientation book."

Dr. Givens fussed around on her desk and grabbed a thin stack of stapled papers. When she rushed into Solemn, Solemn smelled fruity perfume under the gleaming gold chain around her neck. Dr. Givens smiled at her. She set the papers in Solemn's lap, with the words "RULES" and "PROCEDURES" printed big on front.

"Leave your things," Dr. Givens said. "Inspection. You'll get them back."

The only original item Solemn came in that now remained from her old world abruptly cut off was a golden cross Landon placed around her neck.

Solemn followed Jane. Up the stairs and down a hall with no pictures on the walls, Solemn bypassed the dorm other new girls were thrown to. It was empty, with racks of barely made beds spread out less than a few feet apart. Solemn went straight to a corner of the upper floor. Jane knocked once. She knocked again. Finally, she barged in on *Majority Simmons*—as a crayoned sign on the door announced. The room's occupant was naked and extended across a narrow bed, on top of a Strawberry Shortcake comforter. A sketchbook blotted out her face. Her arm shook back and forth. She did not bother to stop scribbling or move the sketchbook when she spoke.

"Okay, I don't know who in my room right now, but I ain't answer and tell nobody they could come in." She was a white girl.

Jane answered, "No closed doors, Majority. You know that."

The sketchbook whirled across the room. The spine's edge hit Solemn in the cheek.

"I didn't close the fucking door! The wind shut the door!" the girl shouted. "It's hot in this son of a bitch. You bringing bitches in my room while I'm naked?"

The girl's lips were dark, claylike. She shook her head, tried to catch up to where she was, remembered how why.

"What're you doing naked Majority? It's five o'clock."

"So? Heatstroke ain't got no schedule. It's hot. Shit."

"If you was so hot you could've gone to the study room with air-conditioning."

"That bitch told me I couldn't go to the study room no more 'cause she said I wasn't studying."

"What bitch?"

"I don't know her name. The new one. Don't know what the fuck she doin'."

"What were you doing, Majority?"

"I was drawing. Y'all said I could draw down there when I finished my lessons. I been finished with that easy shit. I learned all that shit—algebra, Constitution, all of it—in third grade. Y'all slow down here. So don't blame me 'cause I get done early and I got talent. That's why I'm in here burning the fuck up."

"Put some clothes on, Majority."

"Get out my room and I will."

"Do it now."

"I ain't 'bout to turn around and bend down and walk around with you standing there looking at my ass. Shit. You probably homo. And I ain't never seen her before."

"This is your new roommate, Solemn Redvine, from—"

"I ain't ask for no fuckin' roommate! Only reason I agreed to stay up here in this hot-ass room 'cause Miss Bernadine told me the room-mate was leaving. All y'all do up in here is lie. It's too fuckin' hot in here for two bitches . . ."

"Majority, you keep this up and you won't have no room. You will get a violation and be carried back to Lincoln so fast you'll think you got on your first plane ride."

"So!" the girl howled.

She plopped a pillow over her chest down to her private parts, shook her head.

"It's too much damn confusion around here . . . One person say go to the study room. Next person say go. One person say I ain't got no roommate. Now here she come."

A radio the size of a deck of cards rested on the desk at the top of the room between the two beds. The antenna was stretched to its limit, with foil on the ends.

"Majority, you have my word. Now, I don't know who told you you couldn't—"

"It was that new bitch. That fat-ass one. It was her."

"Yeah, Holly. Well, she don't know everybody yet. I'll talk to her myself."

"I told her I could draw in there and everybody else said that was fine."

"And you right, Majority. I'm sorry 'bout that. I'll talk to her. I promise."

The girl had a cuss for every piece of clothing she put on, down to both socks, which did not match. Her feet crunched papers of her drawings and the lead from her pencils added to the stains already worked into the soles of her feet. She stormed out.

A white boy, personally, brought Solemn her meal to her room: baked chicken, mashed potatoes dripped with gravy, green beans. Solemn shook salt and pepper at the plate on the tray, mixed in butter, and devoured the meal as the one familiar thing about where she was. According to the "RULES" and "PROCEDURES," she could choose to visit the locker room shower stalls either at night or in the day. She decided she would never go in. Would she be doomed to just slipping on the floor, or her head banged into a bathroom mirror, or her face drowned in a toilet? She pretended to sleep after this.

In middle of the low evening, the girl she had to sleep next to now showed back up—huffed, puffed, and hostile even after she closed her eyes. In middle of this first night, Solemn slept not one wink. But she saw Majority looked on her bed like a pile of rags wet with oil or water. White girls weren't something she had experience in. For all she knew, her blue-vein roommate was a real witch if there ever was one.

TWENTY-SEVEN

Solemn stepped with bare feet onto the cool floor. The girl in her room had maybe dressed to eat or gone away. Even made her bed, so it looked more like one Solemn had seen during a hospital visit or two: waiting too patiently not to be up to something. There was a shuffling in the hallway, not as boisterous and chaotic as one heard before the bells rang back in school. Still in her nightgown, she met a processional walking down the hall, in a loud manner she knew would have never been tolerated at any of her schools.

"Where's this to?" Solemn asked the line streaming as evenly and silently as a runny nose. The girls—mostly brown and black, just a few thin-skinned and pale whites—appeared to be professionals, worker bees, on their way to something useful.

But they were only on to breakfast or the shower rooms, one of the girls explained. A few grown-ups stood along the wall, expecting charges just to know. None noticed the new face. Solemn got in the breakfast line. She looked for Jane.

Solemn was toughened up, sure. But everything from a clipboard to an open door to a good night's sleep appeared to be like pulling teeth here. She mustered courage to ask a girl, a somewhat friendly face, about Jane, "You know that one?"

The girl hunched her shoulders and muttered; "Uh-inuh."

Another girl intervened. "Which one that? 'Cause we don't be knowin' they names. Ain't no point for you to know 'em, girl. They all be gone quick. We just call 'em all by a number. You new?"

Solemn nodded. The girl went on to explain . . .

Tomorrow, Jane could be Worker 1. Holly could be 2. 3 could be Vincent or Tyrone. Depended on who was there. Jane was not in sight, but another one was, to lead Solemn where she belonged amidst the brash, showy, and either too loud or terribly quiet girls she stayed mixed with. After lunch—sandwiches and fruit cocktail with plastic-wrapped utensils, like real school—Solemn learned her job that day would be pulling up weeds, by herself, in the garden decorating the grounds for visitors.

A male staff member hung close and talked on his cell phone. No one asked if she had two whole parents, or kids, or a middle name. Her favorite songs and singers did not matter, she guessed. So, she concentrated on the dirt. She kneeled in the garden with its fuller bloom hibernating for now, as cooler air was coming, and she kneaded the earth round and round in her hands like a stress ball. The earthworms and dottier bugs rolled in and out the ground plus around the leaves. Grass stains covered the caps and scar upon her knees, from so many trips and falls in Bledsoe; harvested daydreams it all was now. Yet she had her peace. For this trip closer to the cities and aboveground of rejections in Bledsoe and an adventure taken much earlier than those who just went off to war or college, Solemn was grateful. Between the stems to sprout petunias and pink ladies and daisies come spring, Solemn inched close to a fat fairy's wand left behind—slim leaf, soft cottony puffs, bent in direction of where the sun most shone upon it. A unicorn's root, Solemn had heard it called. With her back to them all and her behind in the air and her hair let down over her face, she mourned the girl who once stuffed bills and coins in a jewelry box with a unicorn's chipped horn on top.

In getting the hang of it all, Solemn saw the staff's assignments were so relentless she started to mark the weeks on the backside of her introductory manual. Ninety-nine, by her count. It was actually 102.

There was always a mess to be mopped, a sill to be dusted, a pest to hunt, a pitcher to set out back in the sun with tea bags and molasses—but the girls could not venture a sip. It was never complete. Classes were nonexistent. She and the others studied from a set curriculum handed down in a copied spiraled notebook, with final tests in back: to cover basic math, reading, grammar, and industry.

Charlotte. Danielle. Kioko. Unity. Jo Anne. Kelly. Juwana.

Solemn melted into what turned out to be another whisk of disappointment carried over from the biggest thing in a trailer home being her imagination: Majority's rugged and gruff ways of being. They included just not speaking to Solemn or sharing with her, or helping her along, or doing any more than waking up with silent treatment to go to sleep with a snore. The only time Solemn had a reason to think she would not have to be focused on something else besides herself was when it was time to eat. The cafeteria was designed like a rich man's dining room, with soft, comfortable cushions in the high-backed chairs but little to no light. The plates were all the same size and carried the same portions. Dietary restrictions weren't kept up with. It wasn't the food. Solemn and her new friends were served quickly and in the same order all day by a Miss Ruth and whoever else on the schedule had decided to join her that day.

Although not as repellant as the average show-off or know-it-all, Majority had to jump up to tell her own audience, "Oprah come from my block y'all!"

One or two girls thought they knew better, but Majority wouldn't concede.

"The studio where that audience at right outside my window in Chi," she insisted. "What you talkin' about? Oprah from Chicago . . . mark my word, nigga . . ."

Solemn could have helped her, let her know she knew the truth. But she figured it would invite more scorn and wrath and contempt than she could handle as it was.

After a spell, Solemn shrank her new mansion down to its more appropriate designation: she was in an orphanage, like Annie or Oliver. The staff used the children to take care of the home, the grounds, the cellar, the attic. Some of the three dozen other girls were branded with coiled skin from atrocious burns they had all but forgotten the moments of, missed teeth from accidents and fights. Over half of them all were illiterate.

Sharika, Liza, Alfina, Merriweather, so on and so forth.

There was one phone in the office every girl had to sign up to use. Solemn had not signed up yet. They had to have so many "points" to get their packages and letters. Solemn was only one of a few who ever received any. She left them unopened in the office, afraid of what Majority might do to the olive branches Bev sent: a Mariah Carey record, Maya Angelou memoirs, a copy of the *Sounder* book with the DVD movie too. Dr. Givens turned a blind eye and strutted through occasionally with inspectors and contracts, clusters of suited whites who stood with hands behind their backs. "The State," they were. They smiled bizarrely at any who had the nerve to look them straight in the eyes.

The minute Solemn sat down, the secretary or a volunteer or a Day Worker or a Night Worker told her to get up and start to work on something else.

The tops of pill bottles stuck. The cough syrup coagulated. The roaches flew. The mirrors cracked. The second Solemn closed her eyes she thought she heard Day Worker 1, or Day Worker 2, or Day Worker 3, or Miss Bernadine.

Soon, a few girls got in a chokey kinda fight at supper. They knocked Solemn over by accident. A tender circle skidded onto her elbow.

Sooner, man Worker 2 or whatever motioned Solemn to the broom closet.

She went to see what he wanted.

His privates poked out of unzipped pants. She ran.

The workers listed her next tasks from inside her dreams. On the day of her turn, she awoke and saw the day's tub of dishwater prepared in advance. When it was not her turn, the baking soda and steel wool set by the feet of the two bathtubs scared her off from washing nonetheless. A sore throat made no difference. A fever had no point. A tantrum was moot. Cramps were worthless. The only surefire way out of the rotation of labor in the home was to study. All the time, and hard.

Solemn was bossed by voice, gesture, and sign into a far-fetched thirst for Bledsoe.

"On Sunday, if yas want to, sign up for chapel. Make sure you got a clean skirt. Only if you ain't go no points . . . Quit that running. Where my pen go? Y'all done . . ."

Chapel was disappointing in what it promised. So, Solemn never signed up again. When the Fanny girls shot out from the van, the free ones moved closer to their parents. But these boys and girls worked, too: they held the door open, passed out programs, swept chapel steps, pushed cars out of potholes, corrected sloppy-hanging choir robes, added tissue to the bathroom. Their heels were not too high. Their hair was just enough. Everything but the music was quiet. And some of them traveled around walking and humming or driving to some more of them later on, with baskets of turkeys and sweet potato pies in backseats. And it actually looked fun now, from where Solemn sat.

Solemn watched them as she rode back to Fanny's in her van with the others, past the used-car lots and cattle farms and roadside junkyards and convicts digging in wild grass. If there was something to watch on TV—a pivotal game, a pertinent news story, the lottery numbers—there was peace back at the home. But, the next morning, they were all once again moving around in the ocean of work whose waters never receded. Solemn relinquished the power dolls, hallucinations, savings, prayer, and comparing to whites once held. She had no corners of her own, no alone place to touch herself thinking about anyone, girl or boy, who excited her. She blocked it out entirely. Her options at Fannys unsupervised visit to the bathroom or early-morning sneak to the garden (where she one time saw soon flowers smashed to death by a pair of thrusting bodies who scooted atop it) touching herself with Majority in the room—were limited.

Majority's sketchings were her lifeline at Fanny's, a running theme. She begged Scotch tape from Miss Bernadine to paper the walls of their room, some consideration to respect the family photos Solemn would not admit turning to. Majority concentrated on the visions she once took for granted from the sixteenth floor of her project building, which bordered Chicago's most essential and lengthy interstate. She included the Ferris wheel of Navy Pier and the impressive domes of the Museum Campus. Within tens of thousands of painstaking pencil points were creations of hundreds of skyscrapers across the downtown addresses Majority herself had rarely traversed, only saw on the news—where people went to real jobs, got to talk to news crews, and shopped off bootleg.

On an unexpected night, prompted by nothing, Majority's invitation to Solemn was an itching and competitive question: "What you do?"

Solemn had pretended to sleep.

"Huh? Oh, you're talking to me now?"

"Hey, I ain't know you. I'm from Chicago. In Chi, you don't talk to strangers."

Solemn was not ready to open up.

"Where you from?"

"Bledsoe," Solemn said quietly. She was near sixteen. Three years to go. Or nearly two, now, until she was eighteen. *Three years,* she thought, as she spoke.

"Where's that?"

"It's downstate, past Jackson."

"Oh, you from here, too."

Solemn was only going to have a conversation with Majority so she could have some influence over their radio. She knew, from her own intake, it could not have been Majority's alone. She just did not want to risk trouble it seemed Majority was fond of.

"What you do to get sent up here?"

If Solemn remembered nothing from Mrs. Longwood's lectures, not knowing the meaning at the time due to the humor of the delivery, or Pearletta Hassle's vacation from Singer's Trailer Park with the cross of notoriety fixed into her name, or Landon's forever and a day uprising plans, which never came to pass, it was to never tell anybody too much of your future or past. They'd shit on the former and sadden the latter.

"That's my business," Solemn told her.

"Aw shit . . . I got you fam. Undercover. I gotta check everybody out."

"So do I."

"I mean, we gotta stay in this room with each other. And I ain't gay. So . . ."

"I'm not gay."

"Oh snap! I was wondering . . . 'cause, you know, I like a good dick. That's it."

Solemn fingered the cross around her neck, Bledsoe at her throat and appreciation to it lodged there, though she wasn't gonna speak it.

When it seemed warm and friendly and fun, she was nearly afraid to ask Majority what she had done to get sent all the way from Chicago to here. She asked anyway.

When she was nine, Majority found a full egg in a hen her mother told her to cut up and she wondered. When she was twelve, she found a crisp mouse slipped into the batter of the cornbread her grandmother told her to slice and she knew. She would be the first to admit she wasn't the smartest. But she was smart enough to know she wanted better things to do. Sex was not necessarily on her list of things to do, but it was a thing to do. Majority's aunts and grand-mothers grew tired of yanking her back from the Chicago streets outside the Horner Homes where they lived, as white women with relatively less offense or danger so a higher score of peace. They saw her sashay into their cinder-blocked units with fistfuls of money she could produce no check stub for. She was mixed. And that's how she liked it. She made more and got treated better that way.

"We ain't raise you like this girl!" some of them shouted. They had, in fact, raised her like this, since she was theirs and she was doing it.

"She gone come up pregnant," others groaned. They knew, because they had.

By thirteen, Majority promoted herself. If not for the fact she had an address and the keys to it, she would have been just like the others. She kept the batteries of the outside to herself. No, to them, her family, her elders, she would be all smiles and bravado on the subject of her alternate life: easy entrance to the single-bar nightclubs, Chrysler car rides, lace gloves, strappy stilettos, plum lipstick, shoplifted mink eyelashes, gleaming red nails and toes, professionals (in training) to spruce up her makeup and hair. She secretly devoured all the cod-liver oil and Sucrets in the cabinets at home after a night of hoarse screaming with other girls over the whereabouts of the money they were supposed to split evenly. Before she got into the elevator of her building, or walked up sixteen or nineteen or twenty-one flights (depending on which relative or latchkey kids she planned to use in alibi), she threw away the one shoe left behind on the nights she had lost the other in a sprint from uncertain outcomes: buzzing police lights, detectives in unmarked cars, drunk pimps wondering why the girls were all standing and talking but no one was screwing, or simply a bus that refused to show up because three buses were covering close corners all at once. She tore through boxes of Epsom salts at home to soak the calluses and corns so much walking and posturing gave her every week. She reserved the missioned ballet slippers some University of Chicago kid had paid some do-gooder student club money for, as the antidote to rest her feet at home.

She had not known her father too well, but few of them had. Rather than whimper into helplessness about it, the women wore their broken family tree like a badge of honor, not a reason to ho. So what an uncle high on heroin dropped four blind puppies her pit bull birthed from the sixteenth floor, because he thought they were rats, and he would have done the same thing to their mother, had she not gouged out his stomach between her jaws Majority had to release on her own? So what they had closed down her main junior high school to put her on the train to a neighborhood where she had not one cousin or friend tribaling her—but an instant group of foes? So what her Social Security number was foraged by relatives she barely knew, to turn on the lights, phone, cable, electric, and gas for those who had bad credit—so she would have to pay off theirs before she got her own? So what one of her mother's boyfriends liked to rub her legs and another one liked to boss her for the hell of it? So what they used the bathroom in the bathtub when the toilet backed up and it took a week for a janitor to come? So what? So what? So what?

Her people found no explanation for it but the music. Yup. All the radio and television's fault. Every movie on the TV had wild-haired women with bright red lipstick and shiny dresses. Every song on the radio was about getting to bed, or what was going to happen once they got there. All the girls wanted to look like a rapper's CD cover. They expected to glow in honey and plunge into water with magical powers to keep their hair straight after they came out. They wanted to look mixed. Well, Majority was really mixed—even better. So, the grown folks complained of all this, observed it, and took note—but none of them turned it off. Same for the new cables. Especially late at night, when the blush-washed shows came on in thirty-minute stints. Little story. Less lines. No memorable names. Just a mysterious man shown up to find a woman who had been waiting for him on a different soundstage, in a different outfit, with a different score.

By fifteen, and 2003, Majority's people were sick of her. She was an embarrassment. They consulted on a solution that would have made no sense if they were black or fifty years before: to turn back. She was to leave the city in the North and head to the Bible Belt relatives who never thought a Northern voyage was proven enough. She was to trade elevators for porch steps, buses and trains for walks, concrete for dust, skyline for horizon, cable for radio, fast food for gardens. She was to help out a great-aunt blinded by cataracts and the housemates who all cursed arthritis. She was to be bussed to a high school and make friends with girls. She was to reconnect with virginity and be watched.

Two uncles took off work from an Old Style brewery in Wisconsin to fetch them in Chicago. Majority's mother sat in the backseat with her for twelve hours. During them, she broke down the family tree in a notebook of names and photos Majority had ignored before. She secretly took note of the nearest road with many cars. Once they arrived in a plot of Magnolia, Mississippi, no map could assist them. She strained to hear something more than a little music on a porch where no one sat or a dog barked from its rope chain. She stared, aghast, at the young-people attire she saw, with no fashion or trend in the dress codes. She arrived at the powder-blue house of peeling paint and a top floor/attic with her nose in the air, but not at all high enough to negate the undercurrent of pee and pork no amount of Chinatown perfume could overshadow. A meal was ready.

Her great-aunt Suzette and the other ladies, Bonnie and Doris, were devastated caricatures of the pictures Majority had been shown. In her eyes, they looked and sounded like men, with the balding heads to prove it.

Majority's mother took up for her. "Chicago is just so dangerous now," she explained. "The niggers up North way different from the ones down here. They love the trouble. And we couldn't afford to live nowhere where the school didn't have fifty kids in the classrooms."

"It's fifty kids in the whole school 'round here," Suzette assured.

"And so many churches, you know," Majority's mother continued, "but with everybody working and tired and fighting the city, I have to tell you, we never went."

"Elder Bellamy come pick us up every Sunday at seven," Bonnie explained.

"And, you know, Majority trying to be a good girl and go on to college. I tell you. All the niggers 'round the corners and in our building . . . Oh yeah, it's nice and high and pretty just like you all see from the pictures, but . . . it's a lot to look out for in there."

"We tell 'em she ours and nobody touch her," Doris declared.

Majority's uncle and mother spent just one night twisted and discomforted on floor pallets. Majority got the couch that was hers from now on. In the morning, the adults awoke stiff and cranky but confident of what was best. Bonnie and Doris cursed arthritis to cook everyone breakfast. On the way out to the car, Majority saw her uncle press several bills into Suzette's hands, as she reached out with no insurance of the count. While Doris walked her mother and other uncle to the car, Majority saw Bonnie counting the bills. For her. Just like in Chicago.

"So finally, I threw my aunt's stanky ass on her kitchen floor. Then I pushed Bonnie round that house with a bread knife till she showed me where the money my people sent was. And I punched her before I left the house, while they friend was sleep."

"My mama would strangle me if I thought about talking back."

"My mama wasn't there. She was in Chicago, sending money to these bitches for my care and they wasn't doing nothing but drinking whiskey and chewing snuff with it."

"Where you go when you left the house?"

"Now see, that's when I should have your country ass with me. You used to all this . . . this . . . dark. I walked 'round like a damned nigga in the old times. I ain't have that massa on a horse with a whip. I member the North Star. That was it. Just 'cause I 'membered it didn't mean I could find it. And even if I had found it I didn't know where North would take me there. I just walked around with no bags and money in my bra till I heard or saw or felt or I don't know . . . something in them woods."

"What?" Solemn leaned her face straight on to Majority's. She had met her match.

"I don't know what it was. It was something. Can't call it. Wasn't gonna let it just tap me on the shoulder so I could find out. I know I turned my ass around."

"You went back there?"

"I didn't have no choice."

"Least you had sense enough to turn around. What happened back there?"

"Them old bitches grabbed me by the throat soon as one of 'em heard me coming up the porch. They beat my ass like a team. Just ganged up on me. Then they called the police. They kicked me out on the porch and left me there till the POPOS came."

Majority said she choke-held pit bulls and had sex. Three canes took her down?

"What?" Solemn moaned.

"They didn't even bother to call my people first. Just threw me out, kid. Called it robbery and assault. I beat them and take my family's money . . . it's assault and robbery. Some family beat me and keep my money . . . it's a whipping and 'Oh, we forgot.' I got here last Easter. Two years to go."

"Or less, for good behavior," Solemn reminded her.

"Who you think you talking to? Shit. I'm Majority. I don't know how to behave."

TWENTY-EIGHT

How? Just how?

How can you live with yourself, you old uneducated and unenlightened damned fool? You sitting here in your camper truck, trailer, manufactured home, whatever you call it. Your "property." Returning telephone calls. Grinning from ear to ear. Nodding.

"Oh, she doing fine."

She is?

Dusting picture frames. Washing dishes. Reorganizing closets. Hanging clothes on the line. Collecting stuff for Helping Hands. Praying for the less fortunate. Reading the daily lesson. Tassel bookmark in your Bible. Pearl comb in your head. Lotion on your behind. Gold studs in your ears. Man in your bed. Food in the fridge. Bills in the mail. Wash sorted and done. Put away. Supper fixed. Now what?

Man don't touch you no more. You don't touch him. Not sure who started it.

You say now, "Lord, I'd give my life . . ." For what? Your reputation? A man? A marriage? A lie? What's the truth? Do you know?

"If I could go back . . ."

You can't. Don't nobody care if you cry. Who's wiping her tears?

"At the time . . . ," you say. Well, the time done passed. And some more gonna pass, too. You gonna do it too. Hard.

You having a hard time picking the colors for the hatbox to send. White polka dots on baby blue from Claude Julian's, basic brown from Leonards's.

Don't matter. Not as much as you think it do. But go'n ahead. Make a fuss over it. Pretend. Keep the tissue paper smooth. That's right. Pat it down. Palms in center. Okay. Now fluff the ends. Check the wax paper 'round the brownies. Tighten the cheesecloth 'round the jerky. Take the bright orange discount tags off the panties and socks. Roll the nightgown so it don't wrinkle. You'll take the big books when you visit. Save postage. Put the top on. Won't fit. Rearrange it all. Pick the top up out of the corner. You didn't have to throw it over there.

He's avoiding you. He's ashamed. He's a liar. He's a cheat. He's a drunk, now.

Why didn't you just take her kicking and screaming and throw her in the well? Would have been more humane. And honest. You could have thrown her out in the storms. Waited for lightning to strike twice. Or traded places. Stephanie wouldn't have done Desiree like this. Felt sorry for folks, huh? Pitied the women. Thought you was a saint. Well, now it's you.

"She still got college . . ." No, she don't.

"I'm attending the Bible college."

So? Made you feel good to brag about yourself for a change.

I raised my kids good . . . , you thought, knowing and seeing and feeling shit wasn't right. It wasn't right. Just wasn't right. You know. You have options. You have yourself.

Breaking dishes now, huh? Know you can't afford it. You gotta make the odd-job money stretch. Further now. Man don't like to eat on paper plates, that's what you told the girls, right? Yeah, you did that. Taught 'em how to be perfect ladies. Perfect is the problem. Lady good enough. Church praying for you, her, y'all. Now what?

When police tore you out the bed with nothing on but a gown, you should have told the child to hide. Hide, child. Hide . . .

But no. You uncovered her. Exposed her, like a thief in the night at the break of day. And for what? For what? A man? A marriage? A lie?

You believed a man. A man. A goddamned man. Like a fool. And you didn't believe him. You believed a story, not him. Then you pinned a tale on your daughter. You talked her into it, you witch. That's right. Just go to bed. Get on in there. Cover up, knowing you already too hot. Nothing else to do so might as well sweat. Wake up in the morning. I'll be waiting. What? Oh. Yeah, know you can't sleep. You shouldn't.

That cop knew your black ass was lying. So did you, Miss Holy and Miss Perfect. Even got the mother of your grandchilds in on it. And for what? For what? Half the money went to paying folks off anyway. And what else? Some bills? Steak? The movies?

Now what you got? Daughter-in-law ain't speaking to you. Son ain't got time to bring the grandkids. Man at work, or broke. But never too broke after work to go drink?

He gonna come in once you talking to yourself in your sleep, out loud, finally. He'll be on the couch. Resentful. Ashamed. Daughter locked up. House empty. Go on. Get out of bed. One last thing. Always. First is easy. Last never let you go. Set the package by the door so you remember to send it in the morning. Keep on. Give yourself something to do. Anything. Oh, is there a baby crying? Yes.

TWENTY-NINE

Pearletta Hassle's file was closed. That woman from Bledsoe, at Singer's Trailer Park, somewhere near Kosciusko, was long gone from their midst and her case was closed. It was in a file cabinet betwixt stacks of tall, dusty steel in a cellar of the precinct, where only relatives in denial or maybe the scant ambitious criminal justice students put in a request to walk through. Complaints filed. Scenes mapped. Witnesses deposed.

Fires: arson for insurance and orneriness and jilted lovers' returns to peaceful sleep. Robberies: for drugs, alcohol, rent, Christmas, boredom. That kidnapping of a woman whose pimp offered her up to his superiors, for a balance unmet and unattempted after one ho fought him all the way to the altar. The missing boy who walked to the town square for a marriage license, last seen in argument with uncles who claimed he never paid for copper he mistook as a wedding present. The cat lady who found one of two dozen she fed, not run off for a winter return but instead staked on her gatepost with no neighbors talking. A few wives who showed up with slashes at their jaws and breastbones for some husband who was too drunk to stand up or sit down for questioning. The petty store owners who could not find the hirees they had given a chance, once the cash registers broke loose. The relatives of children smacked into oblivion by parents who had issues the relatives could no longer turn a blind eye to. The crossing guards at a few busy stops in town who noted the plate numbers of one too many cars that raced through their open palms. The dog fighters who had not known it was illegal so expected payment for bloody wins and shallow graves. The ladies sudsing scalps past midnight, who gave an entire week's take to masked boys come through the beauty parlor doors with knives over squeaky voices. The property owners tired of junky cars parked on inches of their religiously tended lawns. The drivers turned bikers or walkers who claimed the mechanic was shadier than the tree they had met him under. The babysitters turned upside down after the fathers of the children came home earlier than they had said at first. The dope dealers—multiplied and multiplying.

And, a baby found in the well of a trailer park people rarely complained about or from. A gal catatonic on the road after the baby's mother made the complaint, about a man wearing the same scarf the gal held. A couple out there claim the gal carried their daughter off to be witched and cursed by a stormy accident. The gal's sister-in-law spilling secrets about one of them whose people refused to leave a black woman's fate burlesqued. And now, despite how nice her parents seemed, the gal touching all this sent damn near to Tennessee for a theft her hands simply could not have carried the entirety of.

Case closed.

Bolden watched his own daughter go off to high school, with her friends coming by, her behind lifting and her breasts falling. Much as he couldn't bring himself to talk to any preacher or shrink about it, Solemn Redvine was one of the faces his black coffee miraged as he got ready for the days. One morning his wife reminded him his workload meant he hadn't satisfied her in well over a month, when she rubbed him out of sleep before his alarm buzzed. He was too shaken from dreaming of a running black girl like his daughter to get on top. There were a few instances where he thought the back of a customer's head at the desk was this same girl coming back to ask no questions and barely answer his. He found her dactyloscopy sheet misplaced—he never filed it away—in middle of a *Mississippian* he was just about to throw in the trash.

One Tuesday afternoon, his day off, with a belly full of his wife's Bob Evans sausage and lighter coffee and apple pie breakfast, Bolden showed up at the Redvines' door like a white man with no purpose but control.

It looked different in daylight. The trailer home was calmer now. The nest emptied, the better dishes chipped, the pillows flat, the cat old, the screen door locked. When she heard the patrol car pull up, Bev ceased scolding flies. She answered before Bolden knocked. By now, they seemed to be old friends. Maybe she could have watched him grow up, or he could have watched her grow old. No matter what they were and had been, there was a tendril of trust. And, since it was early afternoon and no one needed anything painted or hauled or fixed, her husband was home matter of fact.

What next? she thought.

Their phone was cut off. Even privilege to just talk in peace and comfort was gone in the backlash. The cordless beige thing had been a short and sweet luxury. Probably for the best it was gone. Its entourage came by too often, and they never dropped so much as a quarter or a pound cake for their use. Bev could have tried to pick up work here and there, watching kids or braiding hair or sitting seniors, in order to keep the telephone on. Now, telephone rings scared her. She hated surprises. Been too many. So, whatever shit hit the fan these days was messengered straight to the door or handed by the postman or heard on the street. But Bolden did not hesitate or waver, as if he was thinking about it, in getting out of the car. His head up and his walk easy. No bad news.

"Howdy," Bev said to him.

"Good day," Bolden said.

"Is it my daughter?" Bev checked in with Fanny O. Barnes every single week, sent off packages and cards, scheduled to give Solemn something to look forward to, like when she had hummed to her belly with Solemn inside. She would have heard.

"Or my son?" He sent her postcards picturing red sand or American flags from Kuwait.

"Oh no, ma'am," Bolden told her. "I was just in the area for a matter. Stolen car."

"Whose?"

"You wouldn't know him."

"We all know each other."

"How's your daughter, Mrs. Redvine?"

"She's adjusting."

"Fine," Bolden said. "Speaking of which, your husband home?"

"I'll go get him for you. Wait here. Oh, and nice of you to check in on us."

Redvine came to the door with a pillow pattern punched in his face, eyes swollen and crusty. His jeans were lopsided and he hadn't sucked a cough drop to freshen his breath. He never presented himself this way, but these days he was sketchy. So far as he knew, there were no warrants for him anymore, unless one counted talk of the town. The cop was solo and his lights were off. Redvine had meant to get the beer in the morning, but Bev threatened to call Landon if he tried. She was sick of it. Only now it wouldn't be proper of him to offer. The time they could have been friends had passed.

"Hey woman," he told Bev, "bring us some sweet tea. Real sweet."

"It ain't cold yet, Redvine," Bev said. "Give the ice time."

"How you doing, Detective?" Redvine asked.

"Can't complain," Bolden said.

"First time we met you was bringing my daughter home. Our hero. Now you got me wondering if I'm on probation."

Bolden was kind. On an early Tuesday afternoon, folks who worked night were sleep and those who worked day were gone. Those who didn't work at all were gone, too, looking for it. Singer's was a lot more chill these days. People didn't hang out in the yards like they used to. Many had left, gone on up north or farther down south where it was building up, too. The number of empty plots was more than it had been when the Redvines first arrived. White families came in, temporarily, during travel. There was no crowd to see this latest visit of policemen come down to his crook of the world.

Bolden laughed. Redvine came down the steps and fixed up his pants. In the past, he and men had leaned on the Malibu or sat in the lawn chairs Bev propped up. But he sold the chairs to a mother giving her daughter a graduation shindig. The Malibu was gone. Only ladies sat on blankets in the grass. Redvine started to walk to the skinny path in between trailers, away from his wife's ears. Bolden followed him. They walked along just thinking, past where the Long-woods' fig and peach trees were trying to grow back, into the direction of the well.

"Where you wanna begin?" Redvine finally asked.

"At how this should end," Bolden said.

"Well, you tell me."

"Your girl draw a lot of commotion to her, it seems. I was just wondering how alone in that she was. It's been on my mind."

"Solemn been dramatic since the day she was born," Redvine answered. "She made us think she was a boy until she was damn near born. She had my wife hollering so bad. That girl had the nerve to try to push out with her bottom."

"And then she grow up to wind up in the middle of the road by herself in the middle of the nights, and dropping out of school, running loose in festivals or parades until somebody get struck by lighting, breaking into homes her daddy sells the stuff off of. That's a bit more exciting life than most gals like her."

"And daddies like me. I ain't appreciated all the trouble either, sir."

At the well, Redvine leaned on it while Bolden stared down it. His escape from well waters—drinking it and otherwise—had only been by chance, he knew. The only thing put him on the other side of things the night the other King got beat—riding around with the guns to keep peace, rather than fighting to stay calm—was his own persistence to know he hated to want for anything, not a paycheck let alone a mere rich man's offer or odd reason for one. He was spared hunger for a woman to lose her child in a well, to need movers all of a sudden so he could get paid, the shameful competition of standing in line hoping more employees than usual called off so he could take his folks out to dinner. He was comfortable in who he was, with a decent promotion to leave him with a ceiling of authority—even if daily challenged, always disrespected, rarely believed. The Redvines had met their own standard—raised two kids who weren't close to threats or criminals. Bolden knew this much. He had to give them some credit for it.

"You know that woman who lost her baby out here. Pearletta?" Bolden said.

Redvine was too hungover and tired to lie today.

"She may have had affinity for you . . . Was it an equal one?"

"I been thinking about getting this back together." Redvine put his hands on the scratchy rope still reeled to the steel bucket of the well's crank.

"Sure you could do it," Bolden said.

"Nobody need it now. I got some welding experience. Lot of it, actually. Could make a rim. I'd have to bungee down, rake the bottom, siphon the top. We all got Hinckley now. Hall made a killing off us with that one. Wish I had thought of that one."

"I done thought about how a father like you think to raise a girl so strong and quick to get all that stuff up out that house in Cleveland, without him looking or seeing or even knowing where she was. Yet you seeing it was gone got you paid anyway. As a father, I'd like to get some tips on how to get a girl to that. I could shole use her."

Redvine knew too many cats whose pasts were just as checkered as their pants. He was not one of them. Had there been work, or at least better and more of it, he would be out and about at it now. He married a stoic woman who employed a semblance of God to keep the combustion out of his heart and his home. He hadn't been perfect. He was aware that if he done what his son did when he was his son's age he might have allowed whites to heckle him all the way to the Persian Gulf. Then he wouldn't be here to watch over his children now, best as he could. Solemn would have her whole life before her and he would make it up to her. He would buy her a real house, an attraction to a husband: maybe one who worked at a bank or doing taxes or roofing houses under the umbrella of a real company in Jackson. Landon had told him he'd help do so, but no. He would do it on his own.

"I really don't have nothing to say," Redvine told the cop.

"It's less what you have to say and more what I want you to know," Bolden told the man. "Solemn's been changed."

"So have we all," Redvine answered. "So have we all."

"Changes can always be corrected," Bolden said.

"They most certainly can," Redvine said. "Don't I know it? I knew Pearletta somewhat. I looked in on her from time to time."

"How so? For what?"

"Damn, I left my squares in the house. Do you smoke?"

"I don't. My daddy did. He still paying for 'em."

"I'm getting there. I gotta make that change one day, too." Redvine had dipped down to snuff. He dug into his pockets for the sandwich bag of it he kept now.

"You can make some changes right now."

"I am. Every day I make change. I never been in position to do too much for nobody but me and mine. But if I coulda, I woulda put Mrs. Hassle in a better situation. Folks keep quiet. It's the rules. But I can tell you ain't nothing out here no accident."

"Except Solemn doing time?"

"I'm not worried about my daughter, Detective. This will change. She got her whole life 'head of her and . . . This is sealed."

"It will be. Should be. Unless she does something else, any more trouble."

"She won't. I'll make sure of it."

"Really?"

Bolden put himself in Redvine's shoes. Redvine had a family, a fatherhood, a property of his own, a pride. At least he dug down deep for that. He was savvy enough to be congenial from the start, with a family who were the same, so made them worth a bit more effort. They were like the Weathers in that sense, only not as loud and proud and well off.

"You're lucky I'm a black man," was all Bolden could say.

"That makes one of us."

They went back, leaving thoughts of the women behind to speculate on the new houses put up on the old oil fields. The new development was already finished. It had actually been done ahead of time, rushed to accommodate the interest and asking prices. They talked like all the others around them talked about it: it should have been for them, but they would be okay anyway. The moving vans were seen all around. Some of the most stubborn had even already secured agreements to mow the new people's lawns, clean their gutters, trim their hedges, lay extra concrete, and carry grand furniture into just the right corner and view for homeowners who changed their minds often. The ice was cold now, the tea sweet. Probably overly so. And despite his questions unanswered and unasked, Bolden even let Redvine lean on his patrol car while they drank it.

THIRTY

Well, to me, freedom mean you got the right to speak your
mind, talk about whatever come into it, and that's it."

"And not be scared 'bout nothin'. Not even being in here."

"'Specially not being in here."

"I ain't scared of none of these motherfuckers."

"Shit, I ain't either. If I wasn't in here, they meet on my block,
man . . . damn . . ."

"Settle down, ladies," Dr. Givens cautioned.

"You said we could say what we wanted to say."

"That's true, Majority," Dr. Givens said. "But we have rules here.
I want you to be honest, but I expect you to conduct yourselves like
young ladies getting ready to meet young gentlemen."

"Ain't nobody ever called me no lady. Shit."

"What's gentlemen?"

Juice, pretzels, licorice, and sometimes freeze pops placated them
for their ninety minutes. Part sound-off, part counseling, part theat-
rics, part expression, all mandatory.

"Solemn," Dr. Givens started, "you have anything to add to our
discussion on freedom, and what it means to you?"

"No," Solemn muttered. She wiped her glasses with her shirt.

"What about how you plan to spend your time when you leave

Fanny O. Barnes? What are your plans? I know you have a family. Have you discussed them?"

Shit if I got plans I ain't gonna share 'em with y'all. Girls with burning coal for eyes and foul mouths. What if I had run away in Cleveland? That freedom?

"What was that, Solemn?"

"Nothing."

"Well, you have to have some answers, thoughts about life beyond here, Solemn."

"No."

"Man, would this girl come on and say sumthin'? I'm tired of sittin' in here . . ."

"If she don't wanna say nothin', why she gotta say sumthin'?"

"Uhhhh . . . I was not talkin' to you."

"Bitch I'm talkin' to you."

"Damn would all y'all shut the fuck up?"

"What's for supper?"

"They got Polish sausages tonight."

"Ooh, yeah."

"I did not tell nobody they was dismissed yet!" Dr. Givens shouted. Miss Ruth knocked on the door. Supper was ready. It was a notice second-bested only by the call for meds. Without a proper dismissal, the girls scrambled to their feet and out the door. Majority was first. Solemn was last. Dr. Givens caught her.

"Miss Redvine," she said, "please produce an essay on freedom by the next group. Or you'll have points. Leave it with Miss Bernadine. She'll make sure I get it."

Dr. Givens waited to hear what she always did from Solemn. That one word, crisp and untelling. She heard nothing. Solemn only yanked away from her, to supper.

A few hatboxes tipped off top of the file cabinets and it was pissing Miss Bernadine off. As they did with regularity, another package from Bledsoe arrived. Once Miss Bernadine checked them for contraband, as cold medicine and Tylenol were, they belonged to Solemn.

The hatboxes carried the scent of her home straight to Solemn's head. The scent had no name and no comparison. It had scenes of days spent fiddling with Barbie dolls, or at the FM dial for a stubborn response, or forks against stoneware plates, and even a distinct smell to the Bledsoe mist. And the cat, Dandy.

Majority enjoyed the heartfelt menagerie more than Solemn did. Majority's only interest was money in her commissary and its exact accounting for at all times. Both the same size, Majority tackled Solemn's new wardrobe just as Solemn suspected she might.

Redvine and Bev took the bus up from Bledsoe after two months. Alice Taylor gave Redvine and Bev a ride from Singer's to the Kosciusko bus depot around 8:00 a.m. She would be back later in the evening, around 11:00, to pick them up. This way, the couple did not have to spare for a hotel. They had depended on cabs to await them, but they were mistaken. Visiting hours began at three o'clock. Solemn sat in the outdoor Family Area of Fanny's, in the open with curled moonflowers at her feet. Her folks would not arrive until 4:16, after another rider was persuaded to ask about their lingering and then offer them a ride to Fanny O. Barnes, past multiple golf courses. The rider asked no questions about the person they were to visit. Or why. Miss Bernadine directed them to a local car service to arrive at 6:00 for the five-dollar ride back to the bus station.

Their daughter had gained thankful weight as well as an estimable inch. Bev took note for the next time she sleptwalk around Walmart, Goody's, or Super Ten, to size up her daughter's ever-changing size. Redvine stood with a collection of DVDs under his arms and a basket of pretty-smelling potpourri, candles, and soap. Solemn sat prepared with the unchallenging projects she was given along with the others: figures made with Popsicle sticks wound with yarn, fingerpaints, magazine cutout collages, self-portraits in pencil, unoriginal poetry. From their room's window facing the back, Majority watched. She had never once had any visitors arrive all the way from Chicago.

As if it were a festival, Bev had uncovered and ironed the gingham picnic cloths to wrap inside the thatched basket, where she placed baked butcher ham sandwiches, macaroni salad wrapped in a plastic bowl in melted ice, homemade chocolate chip cookies, and warm grape pops. Redvine smoked Kools and watched the ladies eat. Bev started their talk.

"You made any friends in here?"

"No."

"Not one?" She noticed her parting gift: her cross at Solemn's neck.

"I don't want to hang around these people," her daughter said.

"How's the school lessons?"

"Easy."

Redvine excused himself to walk among the flowers. Some years had passed, possibly a decade or more, since he brought home bouquets for his wife. He had relaxed at bringing home a paycheck, a guard, security, necessities, "things." And still, with his shortcomings and oversights and setbacks, he was loved. For now, he was saving for an attorney for Solemn. When he could afford to . . . which was not yet. But it would be soon. He came back and spoke his first words with Solemn since Akila yanked her from his house to bring her to report here. He was unrehearsed, low, gaunt.

"I really have missed you, Solemn."

She did not respond.

"And things are going to be better for us when you get out of here. It won't be long. You're gonna be living in a house, after this. And go to college."

"I don't want to go to college," Solemn told him. "I want to go to the city. Nashville. Chicago. Then, maybe I'll go to college there."

"City's a rough place, Solemn," Bev said. "And we don't know nobody there. I think you should think about coming back home. Life will be better."

"I'm gonna go to work," she told them, pushing her glasses up against her nose with her arms crossed. "And make a lot of money, so we won't ever have to steal and lie again." Here, she said what she wanted.

"I haven't been a perfect man," Redvine explained. "We all make mistakes. But I do love you. I'm sorry. I know you've been put through a lot."

Talk turned to mutual grounds of television, Dandy, the books. Solemn would report what she needed them to know. Bev spied on her limbs, saw no bruises or welts. She had every tooth still in her mouth. No plugs in her hair, unbraided, to Bev's chagrin.

"I really don't know if I'm ever gonna know what all happened in Bledsoe," she said. "No matter what it was in particular, it was a lot in general."

"Solemn, what happened in Bledsoe is we love you and we still do," one of them said, united front going home to be alone and probably enjoy it.

Fine. It didn't mean she didn't love them. However, in her eyes they diminished and cooled off, adjusted down to the regard of siblings. Their promises lost the potential of Christmas presents and surprise riddles to delight her, even the one that she would see them again—soon and much more often, now.

Solemn stared down into the washbowl, at the cloth in it, mostly playing in the water more than washing up, buying herself time by herself. The residue of gray suds formed chalky pictures in the bowl. The fizz and scum convoluted into people waving their hellos and good-byes, so many people. Solemn stared down. She broke up the shimmery portraits with her washrag, put it over her face and 'round her body. Then a new portrait came back the minute she soaped up the rag again. She had mind to throw the soap against the medicine cabinet. The mirror was removed to prevent fights with broken glass. Or she could wet it just enough to slick over the floor so the girl behind her could slip. But then she might lose points. She added those like coins, too.

She paid no mind to the line probably behind her. The rest of the girls really didn't care about the solo time they could earn in a private bathroom. The privilege was just a power trip and to practice manipulation over the staff, to make sure they still had the same charms they thought they did that got them there to begin with. But Solemn wondered when she was going to have her space. She hadn't grown up with it.

"One day," said the girl standing behind her, just the height of her neck.

I know I locked this door . . .

"You gotta be patient," said another girl, towered over her at least a head.

They were not so much startling as annoying. These faces were a distillation of women on dirt roads and little girls who sucked candy with her on Easters. These voices were a mockery of all her mama and Akila and teachers had spoken to her. Their postures were akin to Majority's when she stammered to be taken seriously or just taken, period. Their attitudes were just as cocky as the Weathers woman who swooped down on her in dreams.

"Work hard," they said.

"I do. I always have!" she yelled. To all of them, none in particular, but in an outburst that sent the deformities behind her to the exit she herself could not find.

Day Worker 1, 2, or 3 banged on the door. Banged and banged and banged.

"Miss Redvine, ya time up," a woman said. "What you doin' in there?"

What if she was sick? What if she was messy? What if she was sore? Even in Bledsoe, she had owned the toilet when she was on it. She had slept in a room with nothing but her cat to maybe sit up there, too. Here, she had nothing. What could she do?

Solemn stormed out of the bathroom to sink into the group room. Majority gaggled around in the corner with some of the Mississippi tomboys who talked too slow and roundabout to turn her on, though they tried. The unspoken rule was in real life and outside the secrets they shared at night, she stood off from Majority. Self-imposed solitary confinement teamed up with the good manners she had been taught to earn her a respect among peers and staff who noticed.

"Got somebody come see you," Dr. Givens appeared behind her to say.

"Who?" The woman just wouldn't let up on her, treated her special, and Solemn wasn't buying it until she knew how much it really cost.

"Well, come with me and see," Dr. Givens said.

"I'm not gonna come see somebody I don't know who," Solemn said.

"Miss Redvine, since you insist on being difficult—"

"I'm one of the best ones here," Solemn argued.

"Since I can't even dispute that, I'll just tell you then. It's Detective Justin Bolden from Kosciusko, where you from."

"My parents fine?"

"Come on here, gal . . ."

None of them knew when the State would come in to inspect, and it was best they all stayed on cordial toes for anything looked like it. Bernadine was off to the cafeteria to get him coffee when Solemn came up to the front. Bolden stood immediately. Already, in just the short time since he had seen her last, she almost met him nose to nose. She saw her distorted face in the silver of the badge overtaking his breast.

"Hi Solemn," he said.

"What I do now?"

Caught off guard, charmed even, Bolden smiled.

"He was up here in the area. He come to check on you," Dr. Givens told Solemn.

"I know I just popped up. I don't want to intrude," Bolden told her.

"No intrusion, Detective. My office okay? Any excuse I have to—"

"I noticed a garden on the grounds."

"Most of the flowers dead now. Won't bloom for another couple of months."

"Dr. Givens, it'll be just fine. No special accommodations required. I was in the area and decided to stop. I'll only be a minute."

"That okay with you, Solemn?" Dr. Givens asked.

"Do I gotta choice?" Solemn said.

"Hell no." Miss Bernadine had coffee for Bolden and a cold cola can for Solemn.

"Well, since he came all the way here, I guess," Solemn agreed. She had heard a little bit of it, the special favors the brown cop created for her. The rule of favors was one she planned to use to work both ways for herself, whenever she could.

In the garden, Solemn couldn't exactly be excited. She knew the brown cop had not come to take her home. They would have told her by now so she could get her stuff.

"I been looking over your case a lot Solemn," Bolden said.

"For what?"

"Just because. Well, because it's my job."

They came to a small path meant to mark the exit through the clearing the property sat upon, the way out and forward, or back. It was pink and gray and teal spread by state prisoners' uncompensated, sunburnt hands. On it, Solemn wondered how to kill someone. But she saw Bolden had no pistol at his hip the way he always had before. She couldn't take it and blow his brains out, as she imagined back in Bledsoe. Home. With her up thumb on one hand and a gun in the other, it would take just one slow driver to stop for her in order to get up to Nashville. Or back to Singer's, to click shut the door of her trailer and never come out again. To sleep all day and maybe die stuck to the couch like redone upholstery. To hump and shiver into a cat like Dandy. Maybe go live down in the well. A wild well woman she could be. Plenty of water, frogs, and spiders to munch.

"I take care of things in the immediate time but sometimes beyond it," he said. More and more he was putting days off on his parents and his child, like today.

"I never talked to a grown man by myself," Solemn warned him. "'Cept for my teachers. And the principal, I guess."

"I tell my own daughter to keep it that way," Bolden said.

"You seen my mama and daddy around town?"

"No."

"Oh. I thought they'd be the only ones come visit me here. Maybe my brother and his wife."

"Yes, Landon and Akila. I remember them."

"Why? That's your job, too?"

Her hostility made more sense than a warm welcome. His order of business had once been to make a change, yet he was part of a system where all he did was change what lies he accepted or told. Rarely was there justice or peace. Only the next day and maybe a moment of conversation where the truth was at least thought, if not said.

"Coming here ain't my job," he said. "But I could go see about your parents, if that's what you want."

"Okay. They comin' to see me soon."

"That's good to know. It seem like they like you around here," Bolden told her.

"How you figure that?"

"I have ways of reading people. That is my job."

"Oh. Well, I'm gonna think about being a police officer."

"Well"—Bolden laughed—"I think that would be good. You know, sometimes, the women don't want to talk to men. The whites don't want to talk to blacks. So, you could really make some sense to more people. I could see you in uniform."

"But I really want to be a singer, in the big city," Solemn admitted as they sat on the bench. "The police job just would be to make sure I stay on my feet and have a lot of money before I get big."

"That would be smart. Make my job your day job, happier one at night."

"Well, if I get on *Oprah* I'm gonna have to perform in the day. I'm gonna be flexible."

"You young enough to make it happen."

"But I should go to college, too."

"That's a way to make much more money than I do," Bolden said. "For the work I have to do. It's not a lot to make up for it."

"You ain't got to wait for nobody to call you to work, or tell you no."

"I see things I don't like. A lot of things."

"I do too. You have to learn to like them."

"I can't." Bolden smiled.

"That's not your job?"

"No ma'am. When and if I start liking any of the shit I see, it's time to quit."

Fanny's stuffy décor and air sat behind Solemn to remind her she was only having a free pass for a while. Best not to get too comfortable. While she drank her cola and Bolden slurped his coffee, she knew he had never thought she was a witch. The window of opportunity passed for him to even think of asking the girl to stand up to her father, go against him in any way. He didn't like it, but the Redvines were family. And a black girl in Mississippi would go back to that family for all her life, always a refuge from stiff minds and dead-end roads and gas station clerking and top-floor corner apartment dalliances for pay. She had a family, at least, and that always meant one last chance to start over from the bottom of any rock.

Solemn broke that one sin again. She took just a few pages of sketchbook paper to start jotting down the secrets she could have told the brown cop. Words were boring, though. Trite to write. She wondered if Bolden was married. Fancy-doodled his name down a few times, to think of him. Oh yes, he said he had a wife. Married. She'd never thought about it. But she thought and thought about dark girls on mattresses with no sheets. Big pretty beds and hair and stone jewelry even. She wasn't much of an artist, no. But there was the attempt on the pages stolen to record what was hidden, to always keep it so she could spotlight it all once more, when she needed it. And she fell asleep in the room this way. Not even Majority huffing like a dragon could pull her out of it.

And after breakfast, with Jamiqua and Henrietta and Concepción and Tina who couldn't read fighting over the channels and the gals braiding hair and the staff talking among themselves until they spotted an offense to correct, Solemn zombied in the group room. Channel 7 was always safest in turmoil. She curled on the uncomfortable couch with the pillows from the end, a shield to her gut, in wonder as to why the brown cop came all the way to see her. No questions. No guns. Just talk.

Majority came near.

"You got you some fine man coming up here for you, honey," the girl said, hazed about before Solemn, with her eyes barely open.

"I saw him. Who was he? Don't be shy."

"Nobody," Solemn told Majority.

Majority twisted her face until Solemn had no choice.

"He a police officer from where I come from."

"Yas look like y'all was tweaking."

"We were not."

"That's what you say . . . He was old, honey. Like your daddy or something."

The trumpets blared to announce the newscast. Majority didn't stop.

"Solemn like old men, y'all." She held crinkled brown paper in her hands. She had been in Solemn's stuff, snooped through the mindless jibberish to find the name: "Officer Bolden." In one of the three pairs of jeans she had and a flower shirt, too small, Majority waved the papers in front of Solemn. When Solemn reached, Majority ran.

It was just enough to get the rest started. A ruckus to concern the girls, with Day Staff off joking. A reason to get Dr. Givens out her office or off her smoke break. The snickering and laughing and chanting spread, until a dozen or more pointed at Solemn.

"Solemn like old men, y'all." A few of them said it, laughing at her with squiggly funhouse faces. "No wonder we can't get her," some of the boys said. "She probably oochie-coochie in the bathroom with the staff, y'all, ha-ha!!!"

Solemn balled herself up. Majority continued, jiggling Solemn's shoulders. Solemn ran to the TV, to stare at it and block them out. Over the noise she listened to the television, heard, watched, listened more, and heard again.

Of her very own Yockanookany River, just past Ethel, in her county: Attala. And the woman from the television back on now, seated on a couch in front of a cream wall this time. In "Jackson," it said. And the "victim" bound and gagged and here now and naked and unseen for two years, the woman was. Or had been.

Her barefoot and poor Pearletta. It was.

Then, Solemn knew, with the jerking and juking clowns taking the joke too far, and her guts blown away like chalk, there was really no such thing as magic after all.

It was nothing even to cry about. It was much more for her to scream about.

———

Then, Solemn was back home in Bledsoe, Bev keeping watch. Or maybe Red. Could have been Akila. Mrs. Longwood too. She spoke all their names at points.

Such thinking was normal. "Rest and time away from the rest of the hopeless is what she need," Miss Bernadine said. They already knew the rule about this one, to go easy on her, privilege and special and good home and all the rest they never heard. Dr. Givens was spare with the meds. Fanny O'Barnes was no psychiatric facility. Not at all. But sometimes, in sagacious caution and care, she made that call. It really wasn't too good at all for Solemn Redvine to fit it too right in her mind where she was and what surrounded her, or how she got there and why. Because she really didn't belong there.

"Hey, baby," Redvine said, duffel bag at his shoulder and good hair smelling like bergamot and The Man at the Well too afraid to come past him. "I never knew that woman. I ain't put no babies in no well. Your mind just playing tricks. Go to sleep."

Ativan on hand with Vicodin.

Orange juice with ice. Swallow swallow swallow.

THIRTY-ONE

There had to be a way to wash memory like silk: best done quick, under a cold tap, soft rub, hung high to let untampered air take control. Not a wrinkle or crease should make it through that way; good as new and almost never worn it can be. The ones who had met Pearletta Hassle with him—Nichols and Hanson—were gone. He called first, to the Attala County Coroner's Office, where he took over a bathroom so water from the cold faucet could wash him up first. For just a few minutes, some mouthfuls in his hands and splashes to his face. When he came out, in uniform and steadiness, he got right to it.

"Oh, Justin! How you?" the cupcake at the desk asked him. He wasn't sure why. Then she reminded him they had gone to high school together, a few years apart.

"Forgive me," Bolden said. "Right. Rita. Good seeing you."

"No apologies necessary." Past the jacket and makeup he knew the smile more than the face. He soon recalled she had been a friend of his daughter's mother, one of the faces around her in the lunch room. "Up in here, we don't expect too-right minds. Glad to see you still doing the police thing. What is you, a detective now?"

He could have filled out the form she passed with his mind wandering.

"Something like that," he told her, grabbing the pen affixed to the counter.

"Gotsta be better than chasing these fools. These drugs got so bad round here."

"It's working out," he told her. "Never saw you here before. How long . . . ?"

"I was in the incinerator," Rita said. "Ten years. You wouldn't have seen me."

"Oh," Bolden said. On the line by "Decedent," he wrote: "Pearletta Hassle."

"First opening on front came up, I went for it," Rita told him.

"So guess that means we'll be seeing each other more often, then?" he said, a smile added to the good note of the coincidence.

"Let's hope not too much more often," Rita told him. She worked her burgundy silk-wrapped nails across his authorization request. "So, Pearletta Hassle. Oh, right. Yes."

"Me and my partners was first on it."

"How's her family? That woman . . . her mother. I tell you. We remember."

"Haven't talked to them. Yet."

"So, looks like it's been less than twenty-four hours. Preliminary done, autopsy pending, sometime today. Maybe tomorrow. Either way, you should be fine to take a look."

She slipped back to a corkboard and grabbed a key few wanted.

"They should have masks and VapoRub down there. And you need scrubs?"

"No." He was smoking now. As he walked to the elevator to get to the basement, he snapped the filters off two menthol Newports and put them inside his nose.

Past the Mexican security guard, Pearletta rested in a room without instruments or windows. The thin and pale technician passed Bolden gloves, then stood by with his cell phone set to Solitaire. Bolden zipped the dark-gray body bag down a foot. He was pleased to see Viola Weathers would recognize Pearly's face. At least. Despite two front teeth knocked out, the records of the dental work her parents started to give her a better life were kindest to her at death. Shock's din was undramatic and someplace else. Hers wasn't the first undignified corpse he had seen. It was just the first he had known alive before. She wasn't shriveled or mummified, just cloaked in moist grave wax from whatever time in the river. It hadn't been that long, he could see. She was still formed, however loose. He zipped down farther past her breasts and the arms bent back with what looked like clothesline. Looked like she had broken her hand, probably set back at the scene but flailed now with the disturbance. He turned it back inside with the other grazed up her side. The darkest part of her was her forearms, her own doing, he was sure.

"Toxicology already back," the man said.

"And?" Bolden asked.

"Usual."

The bruising began on right side of her jaw and kept on around her neck, at tip of her shoulders, and around her areolas. Without any bullet holes or jagged entrance wounds defiling her upper body and torso, there was no need for him to zip down past her privates. It had been neat, clean, a strangle, a beating, an accident perhaps—the final result at least. He would have paid good money right then and there to know whom her fingernails told on, the pet names her vagina spoke, whose hair blended with her own.

Right around here she was, must have been. There was no way for any *Have You Seen Pearletta Hassle?* to work if she didn't look like herself anymore, where it probably went after a while. Had there been a relationship, a real one, that is, it would have been known before three years. Wasn't no way a rich white boy could have managed that this long. But even if the boy had only been the catalyst who helped skedaddle her off in vertiginous addiction, make her forget who and what she was, sent her off to others who took her sex and hunger before she was tossed off somewhere else, there was that part played. Couldn't discount it. "It's a shame," the technician felt obliged to say, as anyone bypassing the hospitals and hospice to come to them had to be. "Any suspects?"

"Don't know," Bolden said. "I'm gonna sit this one out. I just wanted to see her."

The great majority of the people at Singer's had always been kind, that common piece in the waned force that had attracted them there. Even if, at four in the morning, any one of the weary was awake to go for a cigarette or cry in the dark about one thing or another, they would have kept it secret they saw one of their own fucking with that well, not even asking nobody what they wanted or thought. Car lights off. Racket.

And since the plot rents rolled on in and the scandals rolled on out, nobody outside the gates came out there anymore anyway. Nobody who had better to do thought about them, anymore, a season of cicadas and hot mess passed. White folks showed up to marvel, camp for a night or a week, go on, and remark how friendly every single good Negro they met there was. Either way, murmured by next morning and hallelujahed into common knowledge across forty acres by end of the week, every last one of them was glad somebody finally sawed through the heavy hemp rope, unbolted the rusted crank, chipped off the rotted head, and put a thank-God perfectly fit steel rim over that goddamned outdated and wealth-smirking and witch-alluring well.

THIRTY-TWO

FREEDOM

Night Worker 2 be here on Thursdays. She like to smoke. Miss Bernadine complain she smell it in the office in the morning. So Night Worker 2 go outside to smoke now. I seen her from our window. Night Worker 2 tiny. Night Worker 2 scared of us. I seen it in her eyes. She be so nervous one of us get out the bed. Night Worker 2 go out the back kitchen door to take her smoke. Our room face the back. That's how I seen her. That's the only door back there under our window. I seen that, too. Night Worker 2 look out to the road and the garden when she smoke. Night Worker 2 don't look up when she smoke. Nobody look up when they smoke. They look out or down. Night Worker 2 be here Thursday. I seen the schedule in the office when I went to Miss Bernadine to count my damned money. Night Worker 2 gone go out to smoke on Thursday. Night Worker 2 gone have that big nigga working with her too that night. But he be sleep. Thursday night, Night Worker 2 gone get her ass beat when we hide in the freezer till we see her go out. That's freedom.

"Majority, ain't no way I'm gonna turn this mess in. I think Dr. Givens meant something else by freedom. But you can write real good, Majority. Real good."

Since the mockery incident, Majority had calmed. She would do better, she promised Solemn. And the Staff. She had. She had been especially nice to Solemn.

"You want my cookies, Sol?" "You hot, Sol?" "You cold, Sol?" "You want me to turn the fan off?" "I got the store pads, scented with wings. Take all the ones you need."

After the "emotional seizure," as Dr. Givens explained it to her, Solemn could stay in her room and avoid the others. Other than going to the bathroom, Solemn waited on her body to ask her for a bath. This went on for three days the first time and five days the next. This went on with her wearing robes and stumbling, pale as a melon abused to early picking and sale, through the hall until Majority or a Worker led her back.

The twist-off top stems of vine tomatoes slipped out a trash bag with a hole in it. The stems only have five prongs, but Solemn thought she saw a pile of spiders, and the other girls pointed at her, laughing when she cried.

She ran out the shower room with thunder and lightning heard. It was just water.

She looked out the window when she woke from a nap, no appetite but tray set down in a chair seat by her bed anyway, and thought The Man at the Well knocked.

Rather than wonder how she hadn't left this and all of it in Bledsoe, Solemn figured on who might have the real scoop: Miss Bernadine. She knew it all.

"You s'posed to be up here, Miss Redvine?" Miss Bernadine asked Solemn, while she recounted the books and fanned her light-yellow blouse back and forth.

"I'm goin' back," Solemn said, uninterested in dinner: fried chicken, again.

"I know you is. Shit. And you need to put something on your feet, Solemn. That's why you sick now—"

"I was looking for the paper," Solemn said. "I wanna see about the woman they found in Ethel."

"Oh yeah. I heard 'bout that. Lord have mercy . . . shame."

"I knew her."

"Oh, everybody knew that woman. Surprised her mama didn't go beat up on *Oprah* trying to talk about that girl. Got sick of them folks . . . Said she was on drugs hard."

"She wasn't on drugs when I knew her," Solemn said.

The first rule Miss Bernadine told anybody clocking in for the first time was: "If they say number one, know it's number two. If they offer a favor, look for a cross. If they give a compliment, give 'em a write-up." But she remembered Solemn a little more deeply from her brother and her manner: Bledsoe, in Attala County for sure.

"How you know that woman, Solemn?"

"She used to live where I lived back in Bledsoe," Solemn said. "In a trailer park."

Miss Bernadine asked, "Well, good God, girl, was she your neighbor?"

Solemn told it to Miss Bernadine.

"She was my daddy's ho for a minute," Solemn said. "She had his baby too."

"You know what, gal," Miss Bernadine said, jotting the words she would have about it with Dr. Givens around on the back of her mind, "now *that* I can believe."

When she got home, Miss Bernadine double-backed through the Jackson *Clarion-Ledgers* she had piled up in the doghouse after she read them to find the obituary and the report. It was one of the more interesting stories from her career at Fanny's, unloaded from her mind onto her sympathizers at the card games and bingo get-togethers and "How you doing?" sudden knocks. Wasn't a person in Mississippi, it seemed, who didn't hear Viola Weathers' mouth. Miss Bernadine actually liked them better when she knew the real truths: Every single one, not one of them not, had a story. And that story was almost always somebody else's passed down and unadmitted. She came to the group room the next day to bring Solemn what she could find, not too much about a black druggie whose family had left the Delta: she come from Jackson, was a college student, lost a baby few years back, wasn't too much seen since then, and any information about her or what was done could be directed to the same folks who hadn't cared too much before.

To wait in the freezer room was certainly an option, though it was padlocked from the outside. How to get in and how to get out were the challenges. Majority had her ideas. Solemn did not trust or believe. One mistake and what had been her perfection up until that point would condemn her for more time than she had come in with—and most certainly somewhere much less accommodating. Solemn turned to a clear page of paper to start listing what she remembered of fractions and the electoral college, for her GED.

"First-aid kits upstairs and in the office and in the back of the cafeteria. Keys to the freezer in the kitchen. Cafeteria door lock from the inside and outside. My guess is she gotta leave it open with the door stopper we use at dismissal. Now, if we just have a reason to need that kit, and get carried into the kitchen or something, then me or you could grab the keys to the freezer, let ourselves in there later on and out soon as we can see that bitch go out the back door."

"What would we have to do to need the kit?"

"I don't know . . . something. Fall down the steps, knock out a tooth, shit . . ."

"Then, we have to go to the hospital, with a patrol . . ."

"Well, shit. I can't think of everything." Majority scratched her privates under her purple lace panties. She pulled at her wet hair.

"I don't think this worth it. I really don't need no more trouble."

"I don't, either. But I can't stay here no more. I'm sick of this shit. Cleaning and slaving and getting bossed around and missing out. It's a whole world out there . . ."

"This ain't so bad."

"You must not know what good is."

"I do."

"It wouldn't be so bad. What you think they gonna do? Call the FBI? We ain't that important, Solemn. We really, really ain't."

"Where would we go?"

"Chicago . . . it would be easy. We look young, Solemn. People would help us."

"I don't know . . ."

"You know what. Just cut me. Get mad and slash me or something."

"Then, *I'm* gonna get in trouble."

"Won't matter. You'll be gone soon after."

"And what about you, your face?"

"Not my face, bitch. My chest or something I can cover. Well, wait a minute. I don't know. I got some pretty titties. Can't mess them up. Okay, my arm."

"What I'm gonna cut you with?"

"I don't know. Shit. I'll find something in here. I'll snatch a switch off the trees and sharpen it with a pencil sharpener."

"We can't sharpen the pencils, Majority. We can't drink from glass bottles. The mirrors sealed off. The scissors blunt. The hangers is plastic."

"Wait a minute . . . I know. One of them damn steel wools. I get one of those out the kitchen. My cousin taught me how to unwind it, then wind it back up sharp and tight."

"You gone get tetanus from that."

"They gave us them shots. Damn, Solemn! Would you stop worrying? Think positive. Have some heart. Don't you worry about the details. Leave 'em to me. But, when it's time to go, now, you gotta be ready to go. Don't think. Just go."

The introduction of escape was one of the few things Solemn could think about now that it was all over for her inside, like a better secret now. Thursday came and went, with the matter dropped. And the next Thursday as well. And the Thursday after that. Many many many more Thursdays until it was Christmastime. So many of them never got anything as it was. Solemn, however, was expectant. She had made her requests for cassette tapes and DVDs, from home. They hadn't come yet. Solemn was sure they would. She didn't know the situation. A cheerful season didn't stop the groups from hypnosis by television, causing it to need more guarding from staff than the youth themselves did. Occasionally, there was a consensus dictated by the tomboy or ones who couldn't read too good: *Bounty Hunter,* NASCAR, the NBA, any morsel of a rapper rapping.

The others became amusing, less vicious than Solemn initially perceived. No doubt, many of them remembered the brother and sister-in-law who had brought her in. They drew her up in their minds as haughty, and not worth the effort. Solemn always did what the staff said, as she had always done, down to what had led her to them. But she wasn't much of a writer and failed to deliver the "Freedom" essay on time.

"Well, prolly too much to ask anybody to concentrate in here to write a single word but 'hell,'" Dr. Givens told Solemn. She had a book holding a brown man's face on the front, black background, ripped cover at a corner, water stained along the edges of the pages. "But here. Man from Natchez wrote this. You might like it, Miss Redvine."

Solemn opened the book—*Native Son.* And she began to read it, searching for Mississippi within it. But the book and the man it was about were both in Chicago. She planned to take her time with it. Chicago sounded rough but good. Solemn couldn't put it down. Sex in the movie theater, rapes and same thing as Mississippi: white people to work for, to have a good job. With the book, the television appeared a tyrant now, an antiseptic, even when it wasn't switched on to anything good. Other girls sat it out, too, in a safe concavity on couches near the bookshelves, along with her. They smiled and took note of other titles around them, in the power but politeness of all the little words.

Day Worker Jane interrupted Solemn once, at the very end of the so long and shocking book, before the part called "Trial," after the killer thug Bigger was caught. Solemn was moody at the speeches with no points to her, so she let herself be led to the kitchen. Long before lunch, aromas of cinnamon and vanilla and nutmeg were a decongestant to her predicament, enough to almost send Solemn to tears. It smelled like Christmas. Well, it was.

She helped punch out snowmen and gingerbread men and Christmas trees from stencils in cookie dough. For once, Miss Ruth was smiling and she was not even sweating under a bonnet. She stood in front of the fan with her hands out, feathering her white blouse upon herself and making jokes with the young kids who had shown up that day to work. They were supposed to make many hundreds of cookies, kept in the freezer to use throughout the long season and have something to offer any visitors who made the season a point. And they sweated inside the kitchen, Miss Ruth keeping watch over the children and her utensils and her freezer and her meat and her pots and her warmers and her thermometers and her sheet pans. Hers. She smiled at Solemn, too much. She walked over to the child, one she saw often, who never spoke too much or caused a ruckus or blamed her when and if a few bugs wandered to the food.

"Howdy," Miss Ruth said to the brown child, punching out the figures quickly.

"Hello, ma'am," Solemn said to the woman. Unlike the rest of them, who were complicit with hostility, Miss Ruth was a stability there Solemn knew. The stability sat down beside Solemn, to admire about four dozen figures Solemn had prepared for Fanny's girls, set the trays Solemn put them on to the side, and continue on with her together. The stability set down charming tubes of red and green sugar sprinkles to add to the creations. The stability passed them to Solemn, knowing the child would know what to do. Then, the stability guided her on just how to soak the stainless-steel stencils in warm water to keep the remnant dough off the edges, so the characters would come forth when the dough cooked warm, sweet, delightful to them.

"Where you comin' from, darling?" the stability asked Solemn.

"I'm from here," Solemn told her. "Mississippi."

"Me too," the stability said. She grabbed a hunk of the sticky sugar dough and had several figures cut out in a minute or two. Expert and sharp. Just for them.

"Been here all my life," she told Solemn, as her workers mopped the floor, shined the pots, washed the plates, and scraped away the burnt spills from the burners. "I like it."

And they worked well that way just so, for an hour or more, with adequate results.

The discrepancy of her background resonated to pity and trust, as Miss Bernadine asked Solemn to come to the front office with her to help sort the mail, since "your hands too damned pretty to get messed up with Comet." Once Solemn finished stuffing papers inside different slots and slicing open envelopes relatives sent, she saw Akila's name.

Dear Solemn,

I hope you get my letter and the money I sent you too. I know it's not much. But I ain't working. Your brother's back again. Solemn, he done changed. We'll go check on your folks. Junior just turned 3 and he's talking now more than ever. I wish you could see him. Eva is 2. I missed you at her party. Your parents came. Rented a car and everything. I was proud of them for it.

With his experience over there, Landon finally getting to work in surveillance for the Army. He like that. We may be moving to Virginia. I might hate that. It means I wouldn't be able to see my family. At least not easy. We'll get back there, I'm sure. I really like sitting at home, reading books, doing crossword puzzles, watching game shows. He wants me out organizing and bowling with the other Army wives. It's a lot of other black women here. So, that's good. I never had a job besides the motel. I been thinking it's time for one. But he won't be having it. He want me home with the kids. I guess I'll obey.

I wonder how you doing in there. I hope the other kids aren't too much of a negative influence. I don't know if you remember when we went to Vicksburg few years ago. Together. I lied to you. I told you we was going to look at apartments. Well, I really was looking into something I found out about. You remember the woman you helped move, gone missing from Singer's. I heard things from her that I thought mattered. I tried to use it to help you, and the situation. Ain't seem to matter much. I guess what matters is we tried. She seemed like she could have been you or me or better than me. Like she had a future. She been found Solemn, dead. None of what happened to you make sense to me. Only what you can do after it make any sense now. I would enjoy for you to come live with us when you get out of Fanny O. Barnes. Maybe you could enlist in the Army too. It pays for your college, far away if you want. I would like having you around. You're good company always.

Love, Akila

Solemn folded and unfolded the letter, her first—as her mama preferred brief and blunt cards to say the words for her. Finally, she pasted it on their wall. Majority had had her eyes on the bare space, prepared with many ideas to archive her own gallery of tomorrows. For in Chicago the money and phone calls and pictures of all who were growing up and going on without her seemed to be the extent of it. And a good one at that. Solemn had been granted permission to use the bathtub without a staff member to watch outside the door, since they were short. She returned blushed and moist, to find Majority in a brood that had not been present since her first few months there. She did not probe. Instead, she sat down to braid her hair, or at least learn how to.

"Parents coming up dropping you off gifts, brother in the army, sister ain't got to work. I read the letter she sent." *Damn.* Majority just refused to be forgotten or ignored.

"Why that make me important?" Solemn sighed.

"I bet you come from a big house," Majority told her.

A big house? A big house? Hmmm . . . away from Bledsoe, around the even lesser fortunate or perhaps the more. She was a blank slate. She could be who she wanted to be.

"I may not know nothing about the projects or *Good Times* or *Cooley High,* or all that, but I been through some shit too, Majority," Solemn challenged, measuring up.

"Whatever. Bitches in big houses with daddies and big brothers don't know shit."

"Bet you police never shined up your house in the middle of the night when you was 'sleep and told you to come out or else."

"Huh! Please. They don't even shine the lights where I'm from."

"Bet you never seen somebody kill somebody else."

"Please . . . I seen it damn near every day."

"Bet you nobody ever tried to kill you after you saw it."

"Bet you folks tried to kill me before I saw shit."

"Bet you never talked to swole-up baby ghosts roll in the grass long after they got dropped in the same well you had to drink from and man ghosts from the trees with no face who chased you 'cause you saw it and girl ghosts with burned-out heads and eyes 'cause you held her hand when lightning struck and the stabbed-up girls could have been your sister come along sit on your pillow right there."

"Bitch, you got me."

In regard for Majority's feelings, Solemn removed Akila's letter from the wall. The detritus of hope for a normal life would later be packed into a pillowcase as an essential matter, a survivalist tool for the day when her worse judgment got the better of her. Majority filled the space Solemn left on the wall, with a portrait of her roommate, in a bed of clouds supported by the hoods of trees she had never bothered to sketch before.

THIRTY-THREE

Fog spoke to Fanny O. Barnes on that particular Thursday on to its night.

"It's our cover," Majority giggled.

"It's a bad sign," Solemn prevised.

Miss Bernadine would not have considered missing work due to a little fog. Dr. Givens did. All the other workers only braved the day because the next was payday; they would have a hard time explaining where their illnesses had run off to in just twenty-four hours. Near the weekends proved to be the best chance of overtime in the kitchen, when primarily younger kids who kept it going had already begun to party. Miss Ruth saw the mist as a reason to call off for the day and night. There was choir practice; it carried on even in the rare event of hail. But it was more fulfilling for her to work than to sing.

The fog crept in that morning, to stretch her Rottweiler's run through her generations-grown nursery of Bradford pear trees. She called and whistled and shouted in the misty dawn. The full-grown puppy finally forced Miss Ruth to trudge, nimble as ever, through the damp back lawn. Then she caught his shadow against the chopping block her husband used to make good use of. The fog was no match for her familiarity with her off-the-way ranch home. She even avoided the ditch before the main backyard started, tugging on her Rottweiler's neck; he had busted out the door without his choke chain. Then, he slipped away from her again, eager to play. She caught him. He struggled. He disappeared. She caught him again. He loosened. She mystified him with another wrangle. This went on for ten minutes at least. Of course, she would be present in the kitchen. She always was. Due to the dog, Ruth Golden wondered if she should even go in on time or at all that day. She settled upon reputation: reliable, come hell or high water. Her uniform was pressed night before, as usual. In fact, she had built up several over the years. Her life, caretaking before widowed, now creating menus for Fanny's, where the souls appreciated her much more than they showed. She knew this for sure.

For the last week, those two girls Solemn and Majority both asked for extras at supper: more saltines, an extra roll, another apple (or two), seconds at a sandwich. Miss Ruth did not see: they slipped stuff in their pockets or bras or backsides. They finished chores early. They communicated in group. Majority cleaned up her mouth. Solemn said, "Yes." If the Staff cared, someone would have noted the changes. The communal equation simply shifted to a bit more peace, easy time, and energy to tackle the others.

Those two girls' last supper at Fanny's would be spaghetti, meatballs, garlic bread, an iceberg lettuce salad, and a chocolate pudding. It ended around 7:00 p.m.

The first break in plans came. Night Worker 2 switched places with Night Worker 1. Majority lingered. Solemn was chicken.

They watched the high school kids who worked cafeteria at night leave their elder supervisor, Miss Ruth, pulling hot trays from the burners all by herself.

Night Worker 1, the big Negro they called him, was there to corral them out of the cafeteria and into the study or game room. There was little to no time. Solemn was stuck in her seat with her hands in her pockets and Majority before her. She had conceived their plans as play. No. She was going to Virginia with Akila. In about fifty weeks. Or was it sixty?

"Come on, hurry it on up," bellowed Night Worker 1.

"My stomach hurt," Majority said. "And I'm sick of Sol. Dawg, I gotta see this bitch every single day."

"Majority, not tonight. Come on."

Night Worker 1 turned his attention to a few girls whose tempest in a corner seemed more urgent and pressing. There were just never enough eyes, hands, feet.

"Go ahead," Majority said to Solemn, sitting across from her.

In Solemn's pocket was a steel wool pad fashioned into some sort of short rod. Majority had done her best. Solemn didn't think it was sharp enough to break skin. They practiced on the slit in her knee Solemn already had. Sure enough, it bled—quickly, as Majority assured her it would. Majority wore a crew-neck T-shirt and had marked the spot of the offense with a piece of Scotch tape.

"We didn't practice," she whispered to Majority.

"We didn't what . . . ?" Night Worker 2 had diffused the situation and handed out his threats. He returned to the two girls left.

"Let's go, Miss Redvine and Miss Simmons. Now!"

"I just told you I'm tired of seeing this bitch and you don't even care . . ."

"You ain't got to go home, but you got to get the hell out of here," he sang.

"No," Solemn said. "Why I wanna go with somebody who don't wanna go with me? Maybe we should . . ."

"You know what," Night Worker 1 said, emboldened by his heft and breadth in a way few staff could muster, "why don't you both go on in that kitchen, get to work? It's been a long time since y'all done the cafeteria rotation. I know."

"Work!?"

"You heard what I said. Got thirty minutes. Miss Ruth need some help. They left her there all by herself. And y'all bet not give her no problems. I ain't playing."

And he walked out to leave them. Just like that.

The pair stood in the kitchen, banging through pots and pans. Miss Ruth offered them soft baby-blue bonnets and sticky yellow gloves for their hands. Knives were locked up in a drawer. The bright steel freezer, source of the meats and milk and frozen goods, looked much smaller than Solemn had remembered it. Miss Ruth's white work coat hung on the first exposed nail Solemn had ever noticed at Fanny's.

Miss Ruth stood buried in a waist-high tub of pots and pans. She broke down the potato and flour churn. She was a worker bee, foundry wife, barren mother to all the children who got dropped off with her precisely because she had the room. *They too hard on these kids anyway,* the stability thought. And these girls were not the worst offenders. They had shown no real violent streaks, only foul mouths. As a matter of fact, in the staff meeting that month Solemn was discussed as two of the few rehabilitative epitomes.

Solemn watched the clock. Miss Ruth would be finished soon. But the kitchen aide held back. Canned tomato sauce stained mercilessly. Tonight was unusual—and longer. And, Miss Ruth retained the perfectionism that earned her the job. One girl was experienced in battle. The other had only had them by surprise. And Solemn now thought of Virginia and a uniform and maybe a dorm room next. A real one. She needed boredom. It helped her imagine. Here there was none. The rage and hostility against her parents who orchestrated her fate boiled to the surface. She could be a dutiful daughter, relied upon and obedient. Or she could "show them."

How will they feel, and what will they dream, if I am gone? What do I do now, if nobody's watching?

Plop plop plop ploppity plop plop goes the little baby down the well . . . plop.

Where the keys?

Ordinarily, Majority told her, somebody had to check the freezer temperature before they left the kitchen at night. Perhaps Miss Ruth had the keys in her pocket. Or in the kitchen office. She was mystified of the next steps. Majority chatted with Miss Ruth. She looked to say something to Solemn one moment and whisper curses the next. Solemn could not discern. The snaggletoothed white boy who usually mopped came in the room.

"I'm gone Miss Ruth," he stuttered.

"Gone?" Miss Ruth turned.

"Yes'm. I'm gone."

"Thank ya. See ya tomorrow."

"All right now."

Miss Ruth started to ask the girls to go check if he got all dangerous puddles off the floor or made sure to turn every pot over on its head so dank pools of water wouldn't sit overnight to poison her tastes for the next day. Least he had come in, more than most of them on a day when news trucks came to show the people there was truth to the fog.

Solemn went back to the crook of the kitchen where the pots and pans stayed. She ran water in the stained industrial-steel sink and put the stopper in bottom as scalding-hot water tumbled down. She played in the water.

"I shole appreciate you girls' help," Miss Ruth told Majority.

"We help more often, they let us do something different," Majority answered. Solemn stood, limp. She would wash everything all over again, with the pots and pants dripping soap in a huge tub to be ready for oatmeal and grits and farina in the morning.

"Whew," Miss Ruth sighed. "Lemme just sit down a minute."

Miss Ruth sat in a chair underneath the eight-by-ten framed portraits of Clinton and Bushes and King and Kennedys and Fanny O. Barnes herself. She splayed her legs, wiped off her sweaty coal-colored face with a towel, before she fanned herself with it.

Any old-timer could have told those two girls Fanny's only landed where it did due to depletion of acres of surrounding timber fields, now naked and blank, infested with untamed nutsedge and sticker weeds and cattails and tree stumps before a cypress swamp, ignored and undiscussed, so as to not detract from the glamour of golf courses the county was most famous for. Five hundred yards from the back door, with the forgotten kitchen lights still on and the doorstop stuck in the cafeteria doors as if it were open for the morning, Majority and Solemn came upon the first leg of the elder timber fields, in another direction from the south from which they had first come. Solemn ran through without stopping, misinterpreting the leftover stumps for headstones and fossils. She took a jackrabbit for Dandy, back in

Bledsoe and Singer's she was. Now. Then. For a minute. Maybe more. Majority hollered the entire way—begged Solemn to slow down for her, let her keep tail, understand her citified fear, stop the guesswork.

"Don't leave me. Wait! I can't see!"

Solemn jutted her face forward and cut the spring night, stuck her nose out like a plane's, dependent upon gravity and lift at once. Whether she flew straight, left, right, or back, she was unsure. The fog canceled out the light. Once, two miles out, Majority caught her from behind. She reached for her roommate's collar, to force Solemn into a paired sprint. She clutched the clasp of her cross necklace instead. It snapped off, but not before it cinched Solemn in her bottom lip and cut her up there.

Why my feet fit these shoes? Why this bra hold my breasts? Why I got jewelry? Why I see so clear now without my glasses? Did I ever need them? Is . . .

On the floor in the kitchen of Fanny O. Barnes, Miss Ruth did not know how to succumb. Strangled by her work coat strings, she knew how to breathe. But not how to not. First Solemn had not watched. She listened. Choked. Swallowed the smell and taste of it. Once the fascination passed there was shame in herself for being there. She thought herself back to the trailer park bedroom, hopes to hear her mama flush the toilet in middle of the night, or feel the cat-pat paws at her tender breasts, or see her daddy come in later than he should have to fill the living room with calm of a man. She withered into a wish for a walk to the well to scare herself for the hell of it and then go right on back home to watch a movie. She sank down to a craving for the hard seat and cramped writing top of a school desk, where she had always paid attention even when it appeared she did not.

Majority surprised herself even. It was as silent as either one of them could have hoped for. Night Worker 2 forgot them. No formal count until time for meds. Maybe Night Worker 1 would look for them. The hope wasn't high. The highest danger of discovery for their absence was another charge who questioned where they were. Put them out. But Solemn was not that popular to be missed. The majority were relieved when Majority was gone. How long did they have to get away? Two hours? Three?

How long I been running? Solemn thought she had sixty-seven weeks to go. It was sixty-four.

She saw a second of two of it: bleached white orthopedic shoes, kicking. Then, the shoes scooted along against pots and pans clanging. And Majority danced around the kitchen, back and forth, side to side, pulling and pushing; a jiggly aura she made. No weapons. No kicks. No punches. No fists. No stomps. Two white apron strings were enough. Then, from Miss Ruth, Solemn sensed a last breath unshackled to hurl itself through a tunnel of life disregarded without it. In the inside where everything is bigger and louder but feels like it isn't even there—better than a queasy ride at a carnival, more wild than she imagined Disney World, easier than a stage—an energy rumbled in Solemn.

She recovered at least one part of the secret: to give Majority a fight, to twist and writhe with an unfortunate soul squat and inert in unawareness, a cynocephalus and rogue. The hooks and hangers on the ceiling stilled to form watch over the moment, just another. In the glimmer of long, flat stainless-steel counters was the glare of a sweat river washed up from the floor onto their backs. With the girls fighting now, Miss Ruth took aim at her own throat, to release the little strings. But she kept her eyes on those two girls.

Those two girls . . ., was mostly all she thought.

Solemn heard "No!"—more before it and after it. She stopped and backed off. Majority's nose was smashed red. Then, Solemn saw her for who she really was. The girl tore down a set of keys from the hook and tussled with the wooden door's fancy knob. Then, she ran through the torn screen door to the open back door. Solemn looked at Miss Ruth thrash and extended between her steel cauldrons.

. . . breathe aye aye oh awa iwa owwa ow ahhhh ohhhhhh breathe. . . .

Once outside, those two girls hesitated and turned in a circle of disorientation. Solemn stood in the garden, assaulted by gaze of moonflowers. They charged into the flowers. The stems with thorns made it through the tough pants the girls wore, lashed out, and scratched both their legs up the minute they stepped into the garden outside the door, no amount of fabric capable of blocking the jabs. Solemn saw herself walk through the back door to join others in the game room and stay mute. Now, acres and then miles away from the possibility, she simply shouted it as she ran. No choice now.

"You crazy! Stay away from me. Stay away!"

"I'm crazy? You crazy? You a liar! You didn't do nothing."

"You ain't said nothing about that, Majority. You lied about that."

"Yeah, but who running now bitch? Who out now bitch? You! 'cause of me."

"We didn't have that long. We didn't have that long. Now. Now . . ."

But arguing cost breath. So they stopped. Majority was already so wicked ahead she tore the grass from under her feet to wipe her nose. Chi fights taught her that. No blood on the clothes. Just ain't sexy, let alone the attention it bring.

They had left stockpiles of food in their rooms. There had been no recent rain, so no puddles or water to anticipate. It felt hot like noon. The extra clothes, pictures, and unicorn jewelry box Solemn stuffed into a pillowcase were left behind as well. Majority's sketching would be soon ripped off the wall. All that was supposed to follow them into the freezer, and then out the door, into their new lives, or old lives back at home. With nothing but the clothes on their backs and shoes on their feet and a gold cross around Solemn's neck, they had run out the back kitchen door. With no destination or plan, only something they imagined as freedom now turned nowhere to go and a need for new names. Had it all been different, so different, how they ran, they could have competed as athletes—in track, to scholarships, gold medals, money. Now they just swallowed heaves of fog and breath for their homes with no maps, no star, fables or lessons, no ground, no anchor, no compass. Solemn ran so long, so aimlessly, so hard, she collapsed. Every blue moon seemed to pass as she coughed her way up again. Majority caught up. She collapsed, too, half on Solemn's back. She looked up for her elusive North Star, as she had done when she came to Mississippi already wanting to go home. All black. Nothing. The timber fields were behind now, at least. Had to be a road not too long now.

We ain't stoppin'.

Majority gulped her breath. She began to drag Solemn by the feet, passed out from exhaustion and shock. She needed her. Solemn understood the night, already led them this far. So she pulled her, to rest but not to stop. Solemn might be pulling her next. But she sputtered awake, hacking and kicking. Awoke to a chalky expanse and connected to nothing but a new stranger hanging on to her by the feet. No one but her. Not her mama. Not even a lightning bug or a cricket or a mosquito. A jackrabbit shot close.

"Get up!" the stranger shouted. "Get up, now! Come on . . . there's a road."

So, they started again. Walking this time. Solemn did not recognize nowhere. But she walked feeling somewhere would eventually show up. Majority latched two fingers to the back of Solemn's jeans. Solemn sped up, renewed and no longer so smothered by her wishes. She tolerated this girl child behind her, whom she had slept near and even once felt a creamy excitement for.

She walked. They would be caught. They could be murderers. Or she would be something to do with it, just like with her daddy. Or she would be blamed entirely. And she was to blame. She walked this way, now. It was just supposed to be a plan. No action. None of it, none of it, not a moment of her, had been planned. Except maybe her sight of that long white ark stopped ahead on the road. Solemn squinted so her eyes could draw back on a curtain of fog. She read: *ANTIOCH'S.*

Two girls appeared at an edge of I-55 North soon as one of the first of Hank Williams's gospel songs began on the radio. A retrospective series. A remnant, along with the shotgun, of training with men alone. The driver was a woman, widow peaked.

Given the fog, she inched along tonight. To Indiana, today and tonight. When she saw those girls, she had been ready to stop—anyway. Had to toss cud. The figures crept, one behind the other, with the one in front having a slight limp and her thumb stuck up. It was pitch-black. If not for her dome headlights and her assurances of the vehicle, well . . .

She squinted. The hitchers were young. One black. She had only seen white hitchers in all the times she decided to not stop. Blacks knew better. On 55 North this evening, there was no rough traffic or even many travelers. She caught baby faces in her windshield. She passed them. Then, "Shit." Up ahead on the road, she pulled over.

Her heart told her to make no time. But two young girls out in the middle of the night? Not one. *Two?* How terrible. They'd be picked up by lecherous men; one was a risk, but two were too good to pass up. The shotgun was in back of the trailer. Should she unlock the hatch to get it? Was she pessimistic? It wasn't so late. Only a little before 10:00 p.m. And she had packed extra tuna sandwiches and took desserts from the last buffet.

While she thought about it, the two girls walked up and decided for her.

Solemn passed a stream of drooped eyes and lapping tongues extended behind the rig's cabin. The cattle filled the night with wails and groans and the scent of earth turned over. The cows shook the trailer with their patient stomping. They pressed their faces against the tin gateposts. Their snouts dripped with liquid they shook away in streams.

"Howdy!" the truck lady yelled from her driver's side let half-down. And she was black, too. "What y'all doing out here like this?"

"Lost," Majority told the truck lady. "We not from 'round here."

She ran around the front to the side of the truck. Solemn stood back, waiting to be asked. The truck lady looked friendly but skeptical. She had only rolled down the window, not yet opened the door.

"Where you from?"

"Chicago."

"Well, what yas doing all way down here?"

"Family reunion. We came all way down here for it. Family left us."

"God. What kinda family you got?"

"They all had to get back to work. We just wanted to stay longer. We was staying down at the motel . . ."

"Which motel?"

"That one, the one, the one, uh . . . up there."

"Oh yes. Uh . . . the Eight Ball?"

"Yes ma'am, that's it. We ran out of money before my mama and daddy could wire us some more. They wouldn't let us stay."

"Well, that's no good.

"Hello," the truck lady said to the dark girl stood back against the tableau of fog, stirred gravel, exhaust smoke, collection of mosquitoes.

Solemn shifted her feet, and waved. She wanted to ask how far to Bledsoe, which she should have known from the maps. Daddy. Akila. Landon. They showed them to her.

Majority continued to spin a tale, conditioned and pathological and degenerate.

"I can give you gas money, if we make it to a Western Union. Then, we can just get us a new hotel and catch the bus from there."

"I'm gonna be in Indiana 'fore dawn," she said. "Chicago right next door."

It was as much an invitation as Majority needed to jump in. Solemn stood back, weak at her knees, doubtful if she could hoist herself up on the running board to slide in.

"Oh my God, thank you," Majority told her. "Thank you so much. I just can't believe, can't believe you would give us a ride. We been walking so long."

Majority slithered to the middle. She reached out her hand to help Solemn up.

The gift of the handshake was the sense it gave for the first time since the truth of it, so Solemn felt inside her body where she was, for real now: not in Bledsoe anymore.

And it had been damned near a year but just never registered. She made it. Out.

The lady roared her truck back into gear on 1-55 North. The giant trees of Solemn's South extended soon into mythology, their branches and leaves outstretched toward her, her vision blurred and senses askew, and her lovely trees and their branches were waving, beckoning, wanting her to talk back, to bid proper good-bye. For the next two hundred miles to Nashville, according to signpost, Solemn would not turn 'round to remember them or to forget them, either, for recollection of a time a woman did and she turned to salt. Solemn had a different taste in her sixteen-year-old mouth: freshness and sweetness of life.

I'm like the cicada...I come back... Then, *How come I was so ungrateful?*

A man whose name she did not know sang out from the radio, about sweet baby Jesus and a house of gold.